PROBLEMS in THE ORIGINS and DEVELOPMENT of the ENGLISH LANGUAGE

Sixth Edition

John Algeo   EMERITUS, UNIVERSITY OF GEORGIA

Carmen Acevedo Butcher   SHORTER COLLEGE

 WADSWORTH
CENGAGE Learning™

Australia • Brazil • Japan • Korea • Mexico • Singapore • Spain • United Kingdom • United States

For product information and technology assistance, contact us at
Cengage Learning Customer & Sales Support,
1-800-354-9706

For permission to use material from this text or product, submit all requests online at
www.cengage.com/permissions
Further permissions questions can be emailed to
permissionrequest@cengage.com

ISBN-13: 978-1-4282-3147-4
ISBN-10: 1-4282-3147-1

Wadsworth
20 Channel Center Street
Boston, MA 02210
USA

Cengage Learning products are represented in Canada by Nelson Education, Ltd.

For your course and learning solutions, visit
www.cengage.com

Purchase any of our products at your local college store or at our preferred online store
www.ichapters.com

Printed in Canada
1 2 3 4 5 6 7 13 12 11 10 09

PREFACE

This book is intended as a supplement for courses in the history of the English language. Though it has been specifically designed to accompany *The Origins and Development of the English Language,* sixth edition, it can also be used with other textbooks to illustrate how English has evolved from its prehistoric beginnings. The sixth edition, like the earlier ones, assumes that one can best gain a good knowledge of any language in its historical development by working with samples of the language in its various historical stages. The treatment is conservative. Students are introduced to the history of English without being asked to master at the same time a new view of grammar. The instructor is consequently free to reinterpret the data in whatever theoretical framework he or she likes.

The problems included are of various types. Some ask the student to demonstrate knowledge of specific facts to be derived from the textbook or a similar source. Others provide supplementary data for the student to analyze and draw conclusions from. Still others are open-ended problems, notably the illustrative passages at the end of several chapters, which can be used in a variety of ways to demonstrate the structure of English at various periods in its history. Some of the exercises are intended for class discussion; others are designed to be worked out independently, with the answers to be written in a format that permits easy checking.

The manual contains so much material that selectivity in its use is necessary. Some of the problems, such as 1.17, on the history and plan of the *Oxford English Dictionary,* might be assigned to individual students for oral reports. Others, such as 1.19, on the process of dictionary making, can be the basis for extensive research assignments. Still other exercises, such as 1.18, on using the *OED,* are large enough for the questions to be divided among the students in a class so that no undue strain will be placed on limited library facilities.

Experience suggests that the chapters can profitably be taken up in more than one order. The most obvious order, that of passing from first to last, can be varied by following the three introductory chapters with the last three chapters on the lexicon, and then returning to the central chapters; the advantage of this arrangement is that drill on the sounds of Modern English can be continued during the study of the lexicon to lay a firmer basis for the consideration of historical sound changes that begins with Chapter 4.

The changes in this edition are mainly the correction of errors in the fifth edition and such other changes as were needed to bring the sixth edition of *Problems* into conformity with the sixth edition of *Origins and Development of the English Language.* Some old material that proved less useful has been omitted, and a few new exercises and relevant websites have been added to meet new needs.

The materials used here have been derived from many sources, often with some simplification of the data for the sake of the student but without distorting the authenticity of the samples. Specific acknowledgments are omitted in most cases, but thanks are due to the legion of academic giants whose pioneering work has made this, like all pedagogical works, possible.

The debts acknowledged in earlier editions are still owing, along with those mentioned in the preface to the sixth edition of *Origins and Development of the English Language*. The first author's wife, Adele S. Algeo, was involved at every stage of the preparation of the original work and most of its subsequent editions; she is in this, as in many other ways, his other self. The second author's colleagues and students at Shorter College have provided the community in which scholarly work flourishes, and she thanks her husband, Sean Butcher, for his constant, invaluable support.

John Algeo and Carmen Acevedo Butcher

CONTENTS

1 LANGUAGE AND THE ENGLISH LANGUAGE
AN INTRODUCTION

1.1 FOR REVIEW AND DISCUSSION

1. Below are some terms used in Chapter 1 of *Origins and Development of the English Language,* 6th ed., where they are defined either explicitly or by the context in which they occur. You should be familiar with all of them. Consult a recent dictionary for any whose meaning is not clear to you.

speech	analytic language	paralanguage
ASL (American Sign Language)	concord (agreement)	conventional
language	word order	arbitrary
system	function word	echoic word
duality of patterning	prosodic signal	onomatopoeia
sound system (phonology)	sign	syntagmatic change
lexis (vocabulary)	morpheme	paradigmatic (associative)
grammatical system	free morpheme	change
(morphosyntax)	bound morpheme	social change
collocation	allomorph	Old English
part of speech	base morpheme	Middle English
noun	compound	Modern English
verb	idiom	diachronic
adjective	oral-aural	synchronic
adverb	homophone	dialect
affix	homograph	idiolect
prefix	homonym	register
suffix	transliteration	acceptability
inflectional suffix	translation	Whorf hypothesis
inflection	orthography (writing system)	open system
synthetic language	kinesics	displacement

2. How old is language? What evidence can be advanced to suggest an answer to that question?
3. What theories have been suggested to explain how language first began? What are the weaknesses of these theories?
4. What are the characteristics of human language that distinguish it from animal communication?
5. What are the major differences between speech and writing as expressions of language?
6. What means, other than speech or writing, do human beings use in communicating with one another?
7. What is meant by the statement that language is a *system*? What levels or varieties of system does language have?
8. What devices does language use to indicate grammatical relationships?
9. The distinguished philologist Otto Jespersen invented an artificial language called Novial. Of Jespersen's project, G. B. Shaw said, "Everybody can learn Novial, there is very little grammar in it; but one must be English to understand how one can get along splendidly without grammar." What did Shaw probably mean by the word *grammar*?
10. Which of the following provide the best characterization of "good English": *pure, correct, aesthetic, commonly used, prestigious, literary, appropriate*?
11. What is the function of a dictionary?
12. What effect does the arbitrary and conventional nature of language have on its historical development?
13. Make a summary list of misconceptions and popular errors about language.

14. Suggest some arguments both for and against the idea that thought is unexpressed language.

15. The history of the English language is customarily divided into three periods: Old English, Middle English, and Modern English. Look up those terms in several dictionaries to find the dates assigned to the periods. Can you suggest an explanation for the discrepancies which you are likely to find?

1.2 HUMAN LANGUAGE AND ANIMAL COMMUNICATION

In each of the pairs below, one statement is typical of human language while the other is more characteristic of animal communication. Mark them HL and AC respectively.

1. _____ The system produces an unlimited number of novel utterances.

_____ There is a closed repertory of distinctive utterances.

2. _____ The topic of communication is present in the immediate environment of the utterance.

_____ The utterance may be displaced in time or space from the events with which it deals.

3. _____ Meanings are represented by combinations of individually meaningless sounds.

_____ Each meaning is represented by an individual sound in a one-to-one relation.

4. _____ The system is acquired by learning.

_____ The system is transmitted through genetic inheritance.

5. _____ The connection between the signal and its meaning is usually arbitrary and conventional.

_____ The connection between the signal and its meaning is often iconic and natural.

6. _____ The signals of the communication vary continuously and analogically represent continuous meanings, like the length of a bar on a bar graph or the loudness of a cry.

_____ The signals of the communication are discrete and represent discrete, clearly separate meanings, like the difference between the numbers 1, 2, 3. . . .

1.3 WRITING AND SPEECH

1. Speech has certain resources for conveying meaning that writing can represent imperfectly at best. Say this sentence aloud in a way that will convey each of the meanings indicated below: _He's a very enthusiastic person._

I am simply giving you the fact.
I like him; his enthusiasm is to his credit.
I dislike him; enthusiasm is depressing.
I am hesitant or reluctant to describe him.
I mean him, not her.
I am asking you, not telling you.
Is that what you said? I can hardly believe it.
The degree of his enthusiasm is quite remarkable.
Enthusiasm is the only good thing about him, and it isn't much; I could say more, but I won't.

Describe as precisely as you can how the various meanings are signaled. Can any of these meanings be shown in writing by punctuation or typographical devices?

2. Can these pairs be distinguished in speech? If so, how?

blue blood (aristocrat)	blue blood (cyanotic condition)
red eye (cheap whiskey)	red eye (bloodshot eye)
hot line (direct telephone line to Moscow)	hot line (heated cord)
New Year (January 1)	new year (fresh year)
long shot (a kind of bet)	long shot (shot-putting at a far distance)
short order (quickly cooked food)	short order (brief command)
big head (conceit)	big head (large skull)

a man's store (store selling men's clothing)   a man's store (store owned by a man)
a fishing pole (rod for fishing)   a fishing Pole (Polish fisherman)
a bull's-eye (center of a target)   a bull's eye (eye of a bull)

3. Can these pairs be distinguished in speech? If so, how does the distinction differ from that of the pairs in the preceding list?

New Jersey (the state)   new jersey (blouse purchased recently)
old maid (spinster)   old maid (serving-woman of advanced years)
little woman (wife)   little woman (small female)
Long Island (the place)   long island (any elongated island)
good and hot (very hot)   good and hot (hot and good)

4. Each of these sentences is ambiguous in writing. Say each sentence in two different ways to make the potential meanings clear. Describe the means you use to make the spoken sentences unambiguous.

Old men and women should be the first to abandon ship.
The doorman asked her quietly to telephone the police.
She gave him an order to leave.
They went by the old highway.
He painted the picture in the hall.

5. Are these sentences usually distinguished in speech? Can they be distinguished?

He came to.
He came too.

He found a pear.
He found a pair.

The straight way is best.
The strait way is best.

The mathematics department is teaching plane geometry.
The mathematics department is teaching plain geometry.

The directions read, "Leave address with Miss Jones."
The directions read, "Leave a dress with Miss Jones."

1.4 WRITING IS NOT LANGUAGE

All four of the following passages, as well as this paragraph, are representations of the same language, although they may look somewhat dissimilar. They are merely alternate ways of recording English which are useful for different purposes. You should be able to read them in spite of the unfamiliar symbols and combinations.

ᵻhis is printed in an augmented rœman alfabet, ᵻhe purpos ov whiᵬh is not, as miet bee suppœsd, too reform our spelliŋ, but too improov ᵻhe lerniŋ ov reediŋ. it is intended ᵻhat when ᵻhe beginner has aᵬheevd ᵻhe iniʃhal suksess ov flꝏensy in ᵻhis speʃhally ɛɛsy form, his fuetuer progress ʃhꝏd bee konfiend too reediŋ in ᵻhe present alfabets and spelliᵹs ov ᵻhem œnly.

ðis iz printəd in ə fənetik ælfəbet, ðə pərpəs əv wič iz nat, æz mayt biy səpowzd, tə rəform awr speliŋ ɔr tuw impruwv ðə lərniŋ əv riydiŋ, bət tə rikord ðə prənənsiyeyšən əv iŋgliš æz ækyərətliy æz pasəbəl. ðis ælfəbet iz yuwzd bay meniy liŋgwists in ðə yuwnaytəd steyts fər raytiŋ ðə sawndz əv madərn iŋgliš.

ᵺis iz printəd in ə fənetik alfəbet, ᵺhə pûrpəs əv wich iz not, az mīt bē səpōzd, tə rəfôrm our speling ôr tōō improōv ᵺhə lûrning əv rēding, bət tə rikôrd ᵺhə prənunsēāshən əv wûrdz in dikshənârēz. this âlfəbet, yōōzd in thə standərd kolij dikshənârē, iz tipikəl əv such sistəmz.

This is printed in a reformd speling kauld Angglik, the purpos of which is to maek the orthografi of our langgwij moer regueler and eezier to lurn, and dhus to impruuv the lieklihood that Ingglish mae be adopted as an internashonl augzilyeri langgwij. This alfabet, aultho wiedli noetist at wun tiem, is not much uezd nou.

3

1. Which of the four writing systems looks most like the conventional spelling of English, and which least?

   _____

2. What special difficulties are presented by each system? _____

   _____

   _____

   _____

3. In 1961, when the Augmented Roman Alphabet was first noticed by the American press, *Time* magazine said of it, "If successful, it may revolutionize English." What misconception is implicit in that statement?

   _____

   _____

4. Another writing system for English is the Shaw Alphabet, chosen as the best design for a totally new alphabet in a contest established by G. B. Shaw's will. With the aid of the reading key below, transcribe the following sentence into normal orthography:

THE SHAW ALPHABET READING KEY

The letters are classified as Tall, Deep, Short, and Compound.
Beneath each letter is its full name: its *sound* is shown in **bold** type.

Tall: peep · tot · kick · fee · thigh · so · sure · church · yea · hung

Deep: bib · dead · gag · vow · they · zoo · measure · judge · woe · ha-ha

Short: loll · mime · if · egg · ash · ado · on · wool · out · ah

roar · nun · eat · age · ice · up · oak · ooze · oil · awe

Compound: are · or · air · err · array · ear · Ian · yew

The four most frequent words are represented by single letters: **the** ρ, **of** ſ, **and** �, **to** 1.
Proper names may be distinguished by a preceding 'Namer' dot: e.g., ꞓ�ｏſ, Rome.
Punctuation and numerals are unchanged.

4

5. English can be represented by many other writing systems, some of them—such as Gregg shorthand—very different in appearance from our conventional orthography. What other such systems can you mention?

Do any of them stand for normal spelling rather than for language directly? _____

_____

_____

_____

1.5   THE SOUND SYSTEM: CONSONANT SEQUENCES

The sound system of Modern English permits certain combinations of sounds and precludes others. Here is a list of the regular sequences of consonants that can begin a word. The sequences are given both in their most common spelling and in phonetic symbols within square brackets. The phonetic symbols will be explained in Chapter 2; they are given here so that you may refer to them later. For each sequence, write a word that begins with that combination of sounds. If you have difficulty thinking of a word, use a dictionary.

pr-	[pr] _____		*cl-*	[kl] _____	
tr-	[tr] _____		*bl-*	[bl] _____	
cr-	[kr] _____		*gl-*	[gl] _____	
br-	[br] _____		*fl-*	[fl] _____	
dr-	[dr] _____		*sl-*	[sl] _____	
gr-	[gr] _____		*sp-*	[sp] _____	
fr-	[fr] _____		*st-*	[st] _____	
thr-	[θr] _____		*sk-*	[sk] _____	
shr-	[šr] or [sr] _____		*sph-*	[sf] _____	
tw-	[tw] _____		*sm-*	[sm] _____	
qu-	[kw] _____		*sn-*	[sn] _____	
dw-	[dw] _____		*spr-*	[spr] _____	
gw- or *gu-*	[gw] _____		*spl-*	[spl] _____	
thw-	[θw] _____		*str-*	[str] _____	
sw-	[sw] _____		*scr-*	[skr] _____	
wh-	[hw] or [w] _____		*squ-*	[skw] _____	
pl-	[pl] _____		*scl-*	[skl] _____	

The foregoing list of initial consonant sequences could have been extended with other combinations:

1. The initial sounds of words like *pew, cue, bugle, gules, few, view, mew, hew, spume, skew, smew,* and for some speakers *tune, dew, new, student, thew, suit, zeugma, lewd,* include a consonant or consonant-like sound that is not recorded in the spelling. What is this sound?_____

_____

2. Some combinations are rare or recent in English, such as the [pw] sound used in some pronunciations of *puissant* or the [bw] sound of *bwana.* Four quite recent consonant sequences begin with the initial sound of *ship.* Can you supply words to illustrate them?

schl- [šl] _____   *schm-* [šm] _____
schw- [šw] _____   *schn-* [šn] _____

3. Dictionaries often record sequences that are seldom heard because they violate the system of English. What dictionary pronunciations do you find for the initial consonants of *phthisis, svelte,* and *tmesis?*

_____

_____

4. There are a number of foreign names like *Mrumlinski, Pforzheim,* and *Pskov* that English speakers sometimes make an effort to pronounce "properly." Can you think of any other foreign words or names that contain initial consonant sequences not permitted by the habits of English? _____

_____

The consonant sequences that begin English words are not merely a random selection of sounds combined in any order. They follow a precise system which we will not detail but which you should be able to describe after you have studied Chapter 2.

A quite different and more complex system prevails among the consonant sequences that end English words. In final position, English permits such combinations as [mpst] as in *glimpsed,* [mpts] as in *exempts,* [lkts] as in *mulcts,* and even [mpfst] as in the admittedly contrived "Methinks thou *humphst* too much."

1.6 THE GRAMMATICAL SYSTEM: PLURAL SUFFIXES

The common plural ending of nouns, written *-s* or *-es,* is pronounced in three ways. Thus *duck* adds an *s*-sound; *dog,* a *z*-sound; and *horse,* a vowel plus the *z*-sound. This kind of systematic variation in the pronunciation of a meaningful form is called morphophonemic alternation.

Write each of these nouns in the appropriate column, according to the *pronunciation* of its plural ending: ace, almanac, bag, book, burlesque, church, cough, cup, dish, dress, fall, graph, hat, house, hunch, judge, lad, lash, lathe, maze, moor, myth, oaf, pillow, room, tax, thing, train, wisp.

s-SOUND	*z*-SOUND	VOWEL + *z*-SOUND

1.7 THE GRAMMATICAL SYSTEM: TWO CLASSES OF NOUNS

Nouns are used in various patterns:

Consider these words:

A. He likes _____.
B. The _____ is good.
C. He wants a(n) _____.
D. _____(e)s are good.

ambition	chicken	fun	light
amiss	courage	home	loathe
ask	cup	house	news
bank	desk	illumine	noise
cash	dessert	lamp	seldom

1. Which of the words will fit into none of the patterns and thus are not nouns?

_____

2. Which of the words will fit into patterns A and B, but not into C and D?

_____

Such words are called *uncountable nouns* or *mass-nouns.*

3. Which of the words will fit into patterns B, C, and D, but not into A? _____

Such words are called *countable nouns* or *unit-nouns.*

4. Which of the words will fit into all four of the patterns? _____

Such words function as both mass- and unit-nouns, often with some change of meaning.
Give five different examples for each of the three noun subclasses:

MASS-NOUNS	UNIT-NOUNS	MASS- AND UNIT-NOUNS

1.8 THE GRAMMATICAL SYSTEM: TWO FUNCTION WORDS

Although native speakers of a language manage its complex system with ease, they often have difficulty describing the system which they habitually and unconsciously use. Function words, described on page 4 of *Origins and Development*, are especially complex in their use. For example, what is the difference in use between the function words *some* and *any*?

1. Observe the use of unstressed *some* and *any* in the sentences below. The starred sentences are ungrammatical as long as *some* and *any* are pronounced without stress.

I know some examples.   *I know any examples.
The class needs some liveliness.   *The class needs any liveliness.
*I don't know some examples.   I don't know any examples.
*The class doesn't need some liveliness. The class doesn't need any liveliness.
Do you know some examples?   Do you know any examples?
Does the class need some liveliness?   Does the class need any liveliness?
Don't you know some examples?   Don't you know any examples?
Doesn't the class need some liveliness?   Doesn't the class need any liveliness?

Describe the systematic difference you observe in the use of *some* and *any*.

_____

_____

2. The use of *some* and *any* is more complex than the sentences above would suggest. Consider these sentences:

The book has some exámples.
The book has sóme examples.   The book doesn't have sóme examples.

What is the difference in use and meaning between unstressed and stressed *some*? Which *some*, stressed or unstressed, can be omitted without changing the meaning of the sentence?

_____

_____

_____

3. Now consider these sentences, in which a relative clause follows the noun:

The book has some examples you want. _____
The book doesn't have some examples you want. _____
The book has any examples you want. _____
The book doesn't have any examples you want. _____

In the blank after each sentence, indicate the appropriate meaning:

A. 'all examples'   C. 'some but probably not all examples'
B. 'no examples'   D. 'not all but probably some examples'

1.9 THE GRAMMATICAL SYSTEM: DEVICES TO INDICATE RELATIONSHIP

The following constructions, which are written in bad newspaper-headline style, are ambiguous. Rephrase each headline in at least two different ways to make the potential meanings clear. You may need to change the word order, change words, add function words, or alter the inflections.

Heavyweight Fights Tonight _____

_____

Bank Rates High _____

_____

Presidents Elect to Appear _____

_____

Closed Truck Stops _____

_____

Whiskey Still Illegal _____

_____

State Wins over Opponent _____

_____

New Student Assembly Held _____

_____

Army Cashiers Failure _____

_____

1.10 THE GRAMMATICAL SYSTEM: RELATED SENTENCES

1. The matrix below contains sentences that are generally similar in meaning though quite different in syntax:

	ACTIVE		PASSIVE	
	Affirmative	*Negative*	*Affirmative*	*Negative*
Statement	Adam has seen Eve.	Adam hasn't seen Eve.	Eve has been seen by Adam.	Eve hasn't been seen by Adam.
Yes/No question	Has Adam seen Eve?	Hasn't Adam seen Eve?	Has Eve been seen by Adam?	Hasn't Eve been seen by Adam?
Wh- questions	Who has seen Eve?	Who hasn't seen Eve?	Who has Eve been seen by?	Who hasn't Eve been seen by?
	Who has Adam seen?	Who hasn't Adam seen?	Who has been seen by Adam?	Who hasn't been seen by Adam?

Complete the following similar matrix:

	ACTIVE		PASSIVE	
	Affirmative	*Negative*	*Affirmative*	*Negative*
Statement	Socrates is drinking hemlock.			
Yes/No question		Isn't Socrates drinking hemlock?		
Wh- questions			Who is hemlock being drunk by?	
				What isn't being drunk by Socrates?

2. There are yet other transformations a sentence can undergo. Supply the appropriate form of *Socrates is drinking hemlock* to match the sentences on the left.

Adam has seen Eve. Socrates is drinking hemlock.
It is Adam who has seen Eve. _____
It is Eve that Adam has seen. _____
Adam is the one who has seen Eve. _____
Eve is who Adam has seen. _____
Seen Eve is what Adam has done. _____

3. Write the appropriate negative for each affirmative sentence on the left.

He can play the *Minute Waltz*. He can't play the *Minute Waltz*.
The rain will stop. _____
He is growing a beard. _____
The movie has started. _____
That movie has an X rating. _____
The sun came up this morning. _____

4. Write the appropriate passive for each active sentence on the left. If there is no correct passive write "none."

Eve ate the apple. The apple was eaten by Eve.
Xanthippe was emptying the pot. _____
The wrestler weighs 250 pounds. _____
Mr. Holmes will look after the problem. _____
Dr. Watson will look before Mr. Holmes. _____
The coach made the athlete practice. _____

5. Make a question out of each sentence on the left by using the appropriate question word for the italicized items and making any necessary changes in wording and order.

Ishmael was the sole survivor. Who was the sole survivor?
Ishmael was his name. _____
Captain Ahab was looking for *a white whale*. _____
He nailed a gold coin *to the mast*. _____
The crew wants to *return to port*. _____
The voyage will be done *very* soon. _____

1.11 MORPHEMES

Divide the following words into morphemes by writing them with slashes at the morpheme boundaries. For example: *hat/s, pre/view, power/house*.

boomerangs _____

deforest _____

freedom _____

growth _____

indoors _____

likelihood _____

normal _____

pineapple _____

playwright _____

reflexive _____

somersaulted _____

songwriter _____

sovereignty _____

spelunking _____

unthankfully _____

1.12 FOR DIFFERENT LANGUAGES, DIFFERENT SYSTEMS

Language systems differ from one another in many ways. Here are four sets of equivalent expressions from different languages. The second column is Melanesian Pidgin, spoken in New Guinea, the third is Latin, and the fourth is Esperanto, an artificial language invented in the nineteenth century.

ENGLISH	PIDGIN	LATIN	ESPERANTO
a good man	gudfela man	vir bonus	bona viro
a good woman	gudfela meri	femina bona	bona virino
a big house	bigfela haus	casa magna	granda domo
a little book	smolfela buk	liber parvus	malgranda libro
a man's wife	meri bilong man	virī uxor	edzino de viro
a woman's house	haus bilong meri	feminae casa	domo de virino
a wall of a house	wol bilong haus	casae paries	muro de domo
I look.	Mi luk.	Videō.	Mi rigardas.
He looks.	Em i-luk.	Videt.	Li rigardas.
She looks.	Em i-luk.	Videt.	Ŝi rigardas.
I see a man.	Mi lukim man.	Virum videō.	Mi rigardas viron.
He sees a woman.	Em i-lukim meri.	Feminam videt.	Li rigardas virinon.
She reads a book.	Em i-ridim buk.	Librum legit.	Ŝi legas libron.
I see him.	Mi lukim.	Eum videō.	Mi rigardas lin.
He sees her.	Em i-lukim.	Eam videt.	Li rigardas ŝin.
She reads it.	Em i-ridim.	Eum legit.	Ŝi legas ĝin.
You look.	Yu luk.	Vidēs.	Vi rigardas.
You looked.	Yu luk.	Vīdistī.	Vi rigardis.
They (are) read(ing) a book.	Em i-ridim buk.	Librum legunt.	Ili legas libron.
They (have) read a book.	Em i-ridim buk.	Librum lēgērunt.	Ili legis libron.
This man is big.	Disfela man i-bigfela.	Magnus hīc vir.	Tiu-ĉi viro estas granda.
This woman is good.	Disfela meri i-gudfela.	Bona haec femina.	Tiu-ĉi virino estas bona.
He is a man.	Em i-man.	Vir est.	Li estas viro.
It is a book.	Em i-buk.	Liber est.	Ĝi estas libro.
It rains.	I-ren.	Pluit.	Pluvas.

Each of the following statements describes the grammatical system of one or more of the four languages. If we were considering a larger body of material, some of the statements would need qualification, but for this exercise you should suppose that the expressions given above represent the complete corpus of each language. Circle the names of the languages to which each statement applies.

1. Nouns must be modified by an article, a pronoun, or a possessive noun.   Eng.   Pid.   Lat.   Esp.

2. Nouns, as a part of speech, can always be identified by their endings.   Eng.   Pid.   Lat.   Esp.

3. Adjectives, as a part of speech, can always be identified by their endings.   Eng.   Pid.   Lat.   Esp.

4. Adjectives have endings that change according to the nouns they modify.   Eng.   Pid.   Lat.   Esp.

5. Adjectives usually follow the nouns they modify.   Eng.   Pid.   Lat.   Esp.

6. "Possession" is sometimes shown by a function word.   Eng.   Pid.   Lat.   Esp.

7. "Possession" is sometimes shown by inflection.   Eng.   Pid.   Lat.   Esp.

8. The pronoun of the third person has different forms for different genders.   Eng.   Pid.   Lat.   Esp.

9. Nouns change their form when they are the object of a verb.   Eng.   Pid.   Lat.   Esp.

10. Pronouns change their form when they are the object of a verb.   Eng.   Pid.   Lat.   Esp.

11. Verbs have a special ending when there is a direct object expressed or implied.   Eng.   Pid.   Lat.   Esp.

12. Verbs change their form to agree with certain subjects.   Eng.   Pid.   Lat.   Esp.

13. Verbs change their form to show the time of the action.   Eng.   Pid.   Lat.   Esp.

14. Grammatical meaning is shown by changes of vowel pronunciation within a word as well as by endings.   Eng.   Pid.   Lat.   Esp.

15. A linking verb is required in all sentences of the type "X is Y."   Eng.   Pid.   Lat.   Esp.

16. Verb inflections can be added to nouns and adjectives.   Eng.   Pid.   Lat.   Esp.

17. Every sentence must have a subject.   Eng.   Pid.   Lat.   Esp.

18. The usual word order of sentences is subject–verb–object.   Eng.   Pid.   Lat.   Esp.

Translate these expressions into each of the other three languages:

ENGLISH	PIDGIN	LATIN	ESPERANTO
a big man	_____	_____	_____
_____	smolfela meri	_____	_____
_____	_____	paries magnus	_____
_____	_____	_____	bona libro de viro
She is a woman.	_____	_____	_____
_____	Disfela haus i-smolfela.	_____	_____
_____	_____	Eum legunt.	_____
_____	_____	_____	Vi rigardis libron.

1.13 LANGUAGE SYSTEMS ARE CONVENTIONS

Even echoic words are conventional. On the left are a number of words designating various noises and on the right are the sources of those noises. Match the two columns. The correct answers are printed below, but try your ear before you look at the key.

_____	guau	1. a Spanish dog
_____	glouglou	2. an Irish dog
_____	kuckeliku	3. a Serbo-Croatian dog
_____	plof	4. a Hebrew cat
_____	bim-bam	5. an Italian sheep
_____	amh-amh	6. a Swedish horse
_____	bats	7. a Hungarian pig
_____	gakgak	8. a French turkey
_____	tsiltsul	9. a Swedish cock
_____	bè	10. a Turkish duck
_____	yimyum	11. an English nightingale
_____	av-av	12. a Dutch door slamming
_____	gnägg	13. a Russian door slamming
_____	jug jug tereu	14. a German bell ringing
_____	röff-röff	15. a Hebrew bell ringing

Here are three translations of the paternoster corresponding to the three major periods in the history of our language: Old English (or Anglo-Saxon), Middle English, and early Modern English. The first was made about the year 1000, the second is from the Wyclif Bible of 1380, and the third is from the King James Bible of 1611.

OLD ENGLISH: Fæder ūre, þū þe eart on heofonum, sī þīn nama gehālgod. Tōbecume þin rīce. Gewurðe

þīn willa on eorðan swā swā on heofonum. Ūrne gedæghwāmlican hlāf syle ūs tō dæg. And forgyf ūs ūre

gyltas, swā swā wē forgyfað ūrum gyltendum. And ne gelæd þū ūs on costnunge, ac ālȳs ūs of yfele.

Sōðlice.

MIDDLE ENGLISH: Oure fadir that art in heuenes halowid be thi name, thi kyngdom come to, be thi wille don in erthe as in heuene, yeue to us this day oure breed ouir other substaunce, & foryeue to us oure dettis, as we foryeuen to oure dettouris, & lede us not in to temptacion: but delyuer us from yuel, amen.

EARLY MODERN ENGLISH: Our father which art in heauen, hallowed be thy Name. Thy kingdome come. Thy will be done, in earth, as it is in heauen. Giue vs this day our dayly bread. And forgiue vs our debts, as we forgiue our debters. And leade vs not into temptation, but deliuer vs from euill: For thine is the kingdome, and the power, and the glory, for euer, Amen.

1. Try to make a word-for-word translation of the Old English by comparing it with the later versions. Write your translation in the blank spaces under the Old English words.

2. Some Old English words that may look completely unfamiliar have survived in Modern English in fixed expressions or with changed meanings. Finding the answers to these questions in a dictionary may help you to translate the Old English paternoster:

   What is a 'bishop*ric*'? (cf. *rīce*) _____

   What is the meaning of *worth* in 'woe *worth* the day'? (cf. *gewurðe*) _____

   What are the Old English words from which came Modern English *so* and *as*? (cf. *swā swā*) _____

   _____

   What is the Old English source word for Modern English *loaf*? _____

   What is the meaning of *sooth* in *soothsayer* or *forsooth*? (cf. *sōðlice*) _____

3. What three letters of the Old English writing system have been lost from our alphabet?

   _____

4. At first sight, the letters *v* and *u* seem to be used haphazardly in the King James translation, but there is a system in their use. Which is used at the beginning of a word? _____ Which is used medially? _____

5. What different forms does Old English have for the word *our*? _____

   Can you suggest why Old English has more than one form for this word? _____

   _____

   _____

6. List three phrases from the Wyclif translation in which the use of prepositions differs from that in the

   King James version. _____

7. List three phrases from the Wyclif translation in which the word order differs from that in the Old

   English version. _____

   _____

8. In general, does the Middle English version appear to be more similar to the Old English translation or to the King James translation? Give several reasons to support your answer. _____

_____

_____

9. The King James version of the paternoster may be familiar, but in many ways its language is archaic. Rewrite the prayer in normal, contemporary English. Notice the kinds of change you must make to avoid an ecclesiastical flavor.

10. What reasons might an Elizabethan have for thinking the language of your version to be "corrupt"? What reasons might an Anglo-Saxon of the year 1000 have for thinking the language of the King James version "corrupt"? Why would they both be wrong?

_____

_____

1.15 THE QUESTION OF USAGE

Which of the following expressions are considered good usage today? Which would you yourself say differently?

_____ 1. "These kind of knaves, I know." (Shakespeare, *King Lear*)

_____ 2. "I want to take this opportunity of thanking you on behalf of the Duchess of Windsor and I." (Edward, Duke of Windsor, in a radio speech, January 1965)

_____ 3. "and this she did . . . with a certain melancholy, as if life were all over for her and she was only shouting a few last messages to the fading shore." (J. B. Priestley, *The Good Companions*)

_____ 4. "I shall return." (General Douglas MacArthur on leaving Corregidor, March 1942)

_____ 5. "I only asked the question from habit." (B. Jowett, *The Dialogues of Plato*)

_____ 6. "The great point of honor on these occasions was for each man to strictly limit himself to half a pint of liquor." (Thomas Hardy, *The Mayor of Casterbridge*)

_____ 7. "No data is as yet available on how far this increase continues." (*New York Times,* August 10, 1958)

_____ 8. "Those assemblies were not wise like the English parliament was." (J. C. Morison, *Macaulay*)

_____ 9. "Here there does seem to be, if not certainties, at least a few probabilities." (H. G. Wells, *Mankind in the Making*)

_____ 10. "Whom do men say that I the Son of man am?" (Matthew 10:13)

1.16 USAGE AND THE DICTIONARY

1. Below are a number of usage labels employed in some dictionaries. Which of them appear in the entries of the desk dictionary you use, and what does your dictionary say in its prefatory material about the meaning of those terms?

archaic	dialect	informal	nonstandard	offensive	slang
argot	disparaging	jargon	obscene	poetic	standard
British	formal	literary	obsolescent	rare	substandard
colloquial	humorous	localism	obsolete	regional	vulgar

_____

_____

_____

_____

2. The following expressions evoke varying reactions among English speakers. First decide whether you regard each as acceptable or not; then look up each in three or four dictionaries and note the usage labels or comments that are given for it.

ain't (as in "ain't I") _____

anxious (in the sense 'eager') _____

_____

but what ("no doubt but what . . .") _____

_____

contact (as a verb, as in "I will contact you.") _____

_____

disinterested (in the sense 'not interested') _____

_____

finalize _____

irregardless _____

nauseous (in the sense 'nauseated') _____

_____

they (with singular antecedent) _____

thusly _____

1.17   THE OXFORD ENGLISH DICTIONARY: HISTORY AND PLAN

One of the most useful tools for studying the history of the English language is the *Oxford English Dictionary (OED)*, originally named *A New English Dictionary on Historical Principles (NED)*. It is the best dictionary of its kind for any language in the world. Abridged versions of this work have been made, but students should become familiar with the complete *OED*, in one of its forms: print, CD-ROM, or online. Examine the dictionary in one of those forms and read the prefatory material in the print form or consult the Web page http://dictionary.oed.com/, and click on its tabs and links that will take you to a more up-to-date account. Note especially the following points:

1. The *OED* is based on a large collection of citations. How were the quotations originally gathered and by whom? How are they gathered today?
2. From what kinds of material and from what historical periods have the quotations been taken?
3. How many quotations were gathered for the first edition of the *OED*, and how many quotations were actually used as illustrative citations in the dictionary?
4. What "new principles of lexicography" were followed by the first editors of the *OED*?
5. Who was responsible for the initial preparation of the dictionary materials, and in what year was the work begun?
6. Who were the chief editors of the first edition, the four-volume supplement, and the electronic version?
7. What difficulties did the first editors encounter as they prepared the material for publication?
8. In what year was the first fascicle of the dictionary published? In what year was the first edition completed? In what years was the four-volume supplement begun and completed? In what year was the second edition published?

Write a short report on the *OED*, considering questions like those above and explaining why the *OED* is uniquely valuable among dictionaries. For what purposes is it most useful? What limitations does it have? That is, for what kind of information or for what uses might you prefer another dictionary? For more background on the history of the *OED*, consult these books: K. M. Elisabeth Murray, *Caught in the Web of Words: James A. H. Murray and the "Oxford English Dictionary"* (2001); Simon Winchester, *The Professor and the Madman: A Tale of Murder, Insanity, and the Making of the "Oxford English Dictionary"* (2005), and Simon Winchester, *The Meaning of Everything: The Story of the Oxford English Dictionary* (2004).

1.18   USING THE OXFORD ENGLISH DICTIONARY

The questions about each of these words can be answered from the information in the *Oxford English Dictionary*. In addition to its printed version, the *OED* is available electronically on a CD-ROM and online. The electronic versions are significantly easier to use than the printed one. The online version is especially notable for being kept up-to-date with frequent revisions.

1. algebra   From what language is this word ultimately derived? _____

What nonmathematical meaning has the word had? _____

According to Burton in his *Anatomy of Melancholy,* who invented algebra?

_____

Was he right? _____

2. anatomy   What was the earliest spelling of this word in English? _____

What misunderstanding created the word *atomy*? _____

_____

In what century did the word come into common use, as opposed to the century of first occurrence?

_____

3. anesthetic   Under what "main form" is this word entered in the *OED*? _____

In what century was the word first used? _____

Who is credited with proposing the term? _____

4. ask *v.*   In what centuries was the spelling *axe* used? _____

From what dialect did the spelling *ask* enter Standard English? _____

What prepositions other than *of* have been used in the expression "ask (something) *of* a person"?

_____

5. belfry   In what century did the *l* first appear in the spelling of *belfry*? _____

In what century did the word acquire the meaning "bell tower"? _____

Name another word in which an *r* has been replaced by an *l*. _____

6. cheap   The adjective *cheap* results from the shortening of what phrase? _____

_____

What was the meaning of *cheap* in that phrase? _____

Are cognates (related forms) of this word common in other Germanic languages?

_____

7. child *sb.*   Are cognates (related forms) of this word common in other Germanic languages?

_____

The word has had five varieties of plural. Identify them by citing one spelling for each.

_____

What does the word mean in Byron's poem *Childe Harold*? _____

8. collate   What other English verb is derived from the same Latin source as *collate*?

_____

What is the oldest English meaning of this word? _____

What technical meaning does the word have in bookbinding? _____

_____

9. crocodile   What is the oldest spelling of this word in English? _____

In what century was the modern spelling introduced, and what was the motive for its introduction?

_____

Who was the first English author to refer to a crocodile's weeping? _____

_____

10. dip   Are *dip* and *deep* cognate (historically related) forms? _____

Was *dip* first a noun or a verb? _____

What does the noun mean in thieves' slang? _____

11. diploma   What two plural forms has the word had in English? _____

_____

What is the literal sense of the Greek word from which *diploma* ultimately derives?

_____

What meaning of *diploma* connects it with *diplomat*? _____

_____

12. error   In what century was the spelling *errour* generally replaced by the current form?

_____

What sense does the word have in Tennyson's "The damsel's headlong error thro' the wood"? _____

_____

How did the word acquire that sense? _____

13. ether   What was the earliest sense of this word in English? _____

When was the word first used to name the anesthetic substance? _____

Which English spelling is earlier: *aether* or *ether*? _____

14. father   In what century did the spelling with *th* become common? _____

What medial consonant did the word have in earlier times? _____

In what other words has a similar change taken place? _____

_____

15. fiber   What is the main entry form of this word in the *OED*? _____

What is the earliest English meaning of the word? _____

How do the quotations of 1598 and 1601 suggest that the earliest meaning is modeled on Latin usage?

_____

16. glamour *Glamour* is an altered form of what common English word? _____

What is the oldest sense of *glamour*? _____

Who is responsible for popularizing the word in standard literary English?

_____

17. gossip This word was originally a compound of what two words? _____

_____

What was the earliest meaning of the word? _____

In what century was the word first used in the meaning "idle talk"? _____

18. humour *sb.* Which pronunciation is older: the one with or the one without the *h*-sound?

_____

What did Shakespeare mean by the word in this phrase from *Julius Caesar*: "the humours / Of the danke Morning"? _____

In what century did the meaning "amusement, jocularity" become common? _____

_____

19. inn *sb.* Is the word related to the modern preposition-adverb *in*? _____

James Howell wrote, "Queen Mary gave this House to Nicholas Heth, Archbishop of York, and his successors for ever, to be their Inne." Are we to suppose that the archbishop ran a public house? If not, what? _____

What are the Inns of Court? _____

20. jail *sb.* Briefly explain why this word has two spellings in contemporary use.

_____

Give the date of a quotation which suggests that the word formerly had two pronunciations. _____

_____

Examine the quotations cited for the first definition. Which spelling is more common in official records? _____

21. knave *sb.* With what contemporary German word is *knave* cognate? _____

What is the earliest recorded meaning of *knave*? _____

As a name for a playing card, which word is older, *knave* or *jack*? _____

22. leech *sb.*[1] What semantic connection is there between this word and the homophonous *leech, sb.*[2]?

_____

Can you offer any explanation for the lack of figurative uses of the word after the sixteenth century?

_____

Why was the *leech-finger* so called? _____

23. legend What is the etymological sense of the word, that is, the meaning it had in the language from which it is ultimately derived? _____

What is its earliest recorded meaning in English? _____

In what century does the sense "unauthentic or non-historical story" appear? _____

24. **Mrs**. What is the origin of the title? _____

In what century did the abbreviation become common? _____

Mrs. Bracegirdle was a popular actress on the Restoration stage. Why would it be wrong to assume that a Mr. Bracegirdle was her husband? _____

_____

25. **nostril** This word was originally a compound of what two words? _____

_____

In what century was the *r* first metathesized (reversed in order) with the vowel?

_____

Judging from all the quotations, which spelling has been more usual: that with *th* (*þ*) or that with *t*?

_____

26. **off** What is the origin of this word? _____

In what century did *off* become the only standard spelling of the word? _____

_____

Explain how *off* has come to function sometimes as a verb. _____

_____

27. **pandemonium** What is the earliest meaning of the word? _____

Who coined the word? _____

In what year is the sense "uproar," as opposed to "place of uproar," first recorded? _____

28. **plow** What is the main entry form of this word in the *OED*? _____

What is the difference between the two spellings in current English use? _____

_____

What is the earliest recorded meaning of the word in English? _____

29. **prestige** What is the earliest meaning of the word in English? _____

Although there are quotations from 1870 and 1881 illustrating the word in its earliest meaning, how do they suggest that the meaning was already obsolete? _____

_____

What evidence is there in the quotations that the meaning "influence or reputation" was derived from French? _____

30. **protocol** What is the etymological sense of *protocol* (its meaning in the ultimate source language from which the word is derived)? _____

What is the earliest sense of the word in English? _____

If the editors of the *OED* were rewriting the fifth definition today, what changes might they make? Specifically, which two qualifications might they omit? _____

_____

31. quiz In what century did the word first appear in English? _____

What was its earliest meaning? _____

When and where did the meaning "short test" develop? _____

_____

32. rooster What is the source of the word? _____

How is its use limited geographically? _____

In what century was it first used? _____

33. salmagundi From what language was the word derived? _____

Which two occasional spellings of the word show the influence of folk etymology (see *Origins and Development*, pp. 241)? _____

Cite a quotation which clearly shows the connotations of the word when it is used figuratively.

_____

34. shift *sb.* What is the origin of the noun? _____

How did the word acquire the meaning "garment"? _____

_____

What meanings not listed in the *OED* has the word acquired in contemporary English?

_____

35. snob What is known about the origin of the word? _____

_____

What was its earliest meaning? _____

Who do the quotations suggest popularized the word in its current sense?

_____

36. sphinx What plurals does the word have? _____

In what century was the spelling *spynx* used? _____

Was the English word first applied to the Greek or the Egyptian creature?

_____

37. story *sb.*[2] What is the apparent origin of this word? _____

_____

According to the *OED*, what distinction is usually made in England between the first story and the first floor? _____

_____

Which meaning of *story* is reflected in *clerestory*? _____

38. swing *v.*[1] Which past tense form is older: I *swung* or I *swang*? _____

During what centuries was the past participle *swinged* used? _____

A fifteenth-century recipe says, "Recipe [take] brede gratyd, & eggis; & swyng tham togydere." What is the cook supposed to do? _____

39. thimble Describe the origin of this word. _____

_____

Name another word which has developed an excrescent *b*. _____

Give the earliest quotation you can find that implies that thimbles were made of metal.

_____

40. tomato   What is the oldest English form of the word? _____

How is the spelling *tomato* explained? _____

What earlier English name did the tomato have? _____

41. uncouth   What is the earliest English sense of the word? _____

In what century is the modern sense "uncomely, awkward" first recorded?

_____

Explain the meaning and origin of *unco* in Burns's poem "Address to the Unco Guid."

_____

_____

42. victual *sb*.   In what century does the *c* first appear in standard English, as contrasted with Scottish,

spellings of the word? _____

What is the origin of the *c*? _____

Examine all the quotations dated after 1800. Describe any change you detect in the use of the word

during the nineteenth century. _____

_____

43. wretch *sb*.   What is the meaning of the Modern German cognate of this word? _____

_____

What is the earliest meaning of the word in English? _____

Judging from the spellings of this word, by what century had final *a* sounds changed in pronunciation?

_____

44. Yankee   What origin of this word do the editors of the *OED* think most plausible? _____

_____

Why do they prefer it to the other possibilities they list? _____

_____

The word apparently originated as a derisive term. How early does it seem to have acquired a neutral

connotation in some uses?   _____

45. zest   If a recipe calls for a teaspoon of grated zest, what ought the cook to use?

_____

Does the seventeenth-century quotation suggest that the word was in common English use at that

time? Explain your answer. _____

_____

How early was the word used metaphorically? _____

1.19 THE PROCESS OF DICTIONARY MAKING, OR EVERYONE A LEXICOGRAPHER

The English vocabulary changes constantly. No dictionary can keep up with it. So if you have a sharp eye, you can find new words not yet in most dictionaries.

Choose any of the recent English words listed below or some similar term that you may have noticed, and investigate its meaning by a technique like that of the *OED*.

1. Look for examples of the word in books, magazines, and newspapers. The library catalog, the *Readers' Guide to Periodical Literature,* the *New York Times Index,* or similar indexes will help you locate relevant material. Using a Web search engine like Google can be very productive. LexisNexis is an extensive corpus of recent texts that can be searched online. Look especially for quotations whose context helps to define the word or that indicate when the word came into use in English.

2. For each use of the word that you find, prepare an index card giving the information described in the "Historical Introduction" to the *OED*.

3. When you have collected enough useful quotations, frame a definition for the word and illustrate it with the quotations. Your definition should be based on all the quotations that you have collected. If the quotations justify it, you may need to recognize more than one sense for the word. List the "main form" of the word and write the definition and quotations in the style of the *OED* (you need not write further identification or form history).

SOME RECENT ENGLISH WORDS

biodiesel	ginormous	pimp (a vehicle)
blamestorm	google (*vb.*)	pornographication
crunk	gorno	post-kinetic environment
cyberspace	hypermile	ringtone
drama queen	I-reporter	string theory
emo	lifestream	supersize
Facebook	lolcat	wiki
forever stamp	muggle	woot

1.20 MONITORING THE LANGUAGE FOR NEW WORDS

New words are constantly entering the English language. Some we borrow from foreign languages; others we make up out of the resources of our own language through a variety of processes that are taken up in Chapter 11. A department called "Among the New Words" appears in most issues of the journal *American Speech*; it records and documents new words not yet in general dictionaries.

1. Read several installments of "Among the New Words" in *American Speech* and write a short description of the kinds of new words that are reported in those installments and the sort of evidence cited for the existence of the words.

2. Read several issues of a newspaper, a news magazine like *Time* or *Newsweek,* or a special-interest magazine like *Popular Mechanics,* and note all the instances of words that seem new to you.

   a. For each such word, prepare an index card giving the information described in the "Historical Introduction" to the *OED*.
   b. Look up the words you have collected in a recent dictionary to see whether it records them.
   c. Write an installment like "Among the New Words" reporting and documenting the new words or new meanings that you did not find in that recent dictionary. In your introduction include the bibliographical information for that dictionary.

3. Changes that occur in a language (in its pronunciation, grammar, or vocabulary) are its *internal linguistic history*; changes that occur in society (that is, in the lives of speakers of a language) and have an effect on the language are *external linguistic history.* Considering the kinds of new words you read about in *American Speech* and the kinds you found when you monitored some newspapers or magazines yourself, be prepared to discuss how external linguistic history affects the vocabulary.

2 THE SOUNDS OF CURRENT ENGLISH

2.1 FOR REVIEW AND DISCUSSION

1. Define the following terms:

phonetic alphabet	vowel	intrusive schwa
consonant	high, mid, low	homorganic
place of articulation	front, central, back	metathesis
manner of articulation	rounded, unrounded (spread)	substratum theory
voice	schwa	superstratum theory
stop (plosive, explosive)	diphthong	phonological space
bilabial	tense, lax	ease of articulation
alveolar	vowel length	tempo
palatovelar	monophthong	folk etymology
palatal	off-glide	spelling pronunciation
velar	glide	hypercorrection
fricative (spirant)	primary, secondary stress	overgeneralization
labiodental	acute, grave accent	distinctive sound
interdental	unstressed syllable	contrastive pair
alveolopalatal	assimilation	phoneme
sibilant	palatalization	allophone
glottal	dissimilation	aspiration
affricate	elision, elided	complementary distribution
nasal	aphesis	free variation
liquid	apheresis	nondistinctive sound
lateral	apocope	glottal stop
retroflex	syncope	unreleased
RP (received pronunciation)	intrusion	virgule (slash)
linking *r*	svarabhakti	broad transcription
intrusive *r*	epenthesis (epenthetic)	square bracket
semivowel	anaptyxis (anaptyctic)	narrow transcription

2. Identify the organs of speech.
3. Describe the place and manner of articulation of the English consonants.
4. Describe the articulatory positions of the English vowels.
5. What are some important kinds of sound change? Give an example of each.
6. The discussion of the phoneme in *Origins and Development* includes seven characteristics which might be summarized as follows. Look up the word *phoneme* in several recent dictionaries. How many of the characteristics are included in the dictionary definitions?
    (1) A phoneme is a class of sounds used in speech.
    (2) The sounds of which a phoneme consists are phonetically similar to one another.
    (3) The sounds of which a phoneme consists alternate with one another in complementary distribution or in free variation.
    (4) The difference between two phonemes is contrastive (that is, phonemes serve to distinguish utterances from one another).
    (5) The difference between two sounds belonging to the same phoneme is not contrastive (that is, allophones do not serve to distinguish utterances).

(6) The speakers of a language commonly regard the sounds that make up a single phoneme as the "same sound."

(7) Two sounds that belong to the same phoneme in one language may belong to different phonemes in another language.

7. The difference between vowels in the English words *sit* and *seat* is not phonemic in Spanish. On the other hand, the difference between [t] sounds in English *tone* and *stone* is phonemic in Chinese, Classical Greek, and Sanskrit. If you are sufficiently familiar with some foreign tongue, cite some similar variations between the phonemic systems of that language and of English.

8. A Korean general who wanted Westerners to pronounce his name not [pæk] but rather [pɑk] changed its Romanized spelling from *Pak* to *Park*. What dialect of English had he probably learned? For most Americans what spelling would most adequately represent the pronunciation General Park wanted?

9. What is the meaning of each of these symbols as used in transcribing sounds?

$$[\ ] \qquad \qquad / \ /$$

2.2 WRITING PHONETIC SYMBOLS

Phonetic symbols should always be in printed, never in cursive, form. Do not try to join them together like the letters of the longhand alphabet. Write [bot], not [*bot*].

Phonetic notation does not use uppercase and lowercase letters like those of our conventional spelling. All phonetic symbols are lowercase. *Jones* is transcribed phonetically as [ǰonz].

Always enclose phonetic symbols within square brackets. The brackets indicate that the symbol stands for a sound. When you refer to a symbol as a written letter of the alphabet or as part of a normal spelling, it should be underlined or italicized. Thus, *boat* represents a spelling; [bot] represents a pronunciation. Use one opening bracket ([) at the beginning of a phonetic transcription and one closing bracket (]) at the end; do not set off each word or each symbol with a separate set of brackets.

Notice the wedge over [š ž č ǰ]. Always write it as part of these symbols. Distinguish it from the circumflex mark which may be used over vowels, as in *rôle*.

Distinguish clearly between these pairs of letters:

[n] and [ŋ]   [d] and [ð]   [i] and [ɪ]   [u] and [ʊ]   [e] and [ɛ]

Write [æ] with one continuous stroke of the pen:

Write [ə] with the loop at the bottom:

Here is a list of most of the phonetic symbols you will have occasion to use. Each symbol is given in both printed and handwritten form. Practice writing the symbols distinctly and legibly.

b	b	____	w	w	____	ɛ	ɛ	____
d	d	____	z	z	____	i	i	____
f	f	____	g	g	____	ɪ	ɪ	____
h	h	____	ŋ	ŋ	____	o	o	____
k	k	____	š	š	____	ɔ	ɔ	____
l	l	____	ž	ž	____	u	u	____
m	m	____	č	č	____	ʊ	ʊ	____
n	n	____	ǰ	ǰ	____	ə	ə	____
p	p	____	θ	θ	____	aɪ	aɪ	____
r	r	____	ð	ð	____	au	au	____
s	s	____	ɑ	ɑ	____	ɔɪ	ɔɪ	____
t	t	____	æ	æ	____	y	y	____
v	v	____	e	e	____			

23

2.3 TRANSCRIPTION FOR READING PRACTICE

Since English varies somewhat from one dialect to another, no transcription can represent the speech of all readers. The pronunciation indicated by this transcription may differ from yours in various ways.

Read the words aloud. Write each word in conventional spelling. Some of the pronunciations correspond to more than one spelling.

• pæt _____	rɪč _____	træpt _____
• pɑt _____	rɪǰ _____	θwɔrt _____
• pɛt _____	bæg _____	kyʊr _____
• pet _____	tɔɪd _____	šaʊr _____
• pɪt _____	hyuǰ _____	straɪk _____
• pit _____	ðɪs _____	bɑks _____
• pʊt _____	ðɪz _____	blɑks _____
• pət _____	θɪm _____	krɔld _____
• pərt _____	sən _____	glænst _____
• paʊt _____	ləv _____	skrəbd _____
rɑt _____	ɛr _____	sɛnts _____
rɔt _____	hɛr _____	sɛndz _____
rot _____	ɪr _____	šərts _____
rut _____	wər _____	čərč _____
raɪt _____	wɛr _____	ǰəŋk _____

2.4 MORE READING PRACTICE

Here are some sentences in phonetic notation. To assist you, the punctuation and word division of conventional writing have been used. Stress has not been indicated.

Read these sentences aloud using the pronunciation represented by the symbols. Notice any instances in which your own pronunciation differs from the one transcribed here. Unstressed vowels may very likely differ. Also notice that the pronunciation a word has in isolation may change considerably when the word is spoken normally in a sentence.

H. L. Mencken, who penned the following aphorisms, was a Baltimore reporter and social critic. He is best known today as the author of a popular work on English in America called *The American Language*, which is still readable and useful. These remarks show his sardonic side.

[æfərɪzəmz frəm eč ɛl mɛŋkən

wɛn ə mæn læfs æt ɪz trəbəlz, hi luzəz ə gʊd mɛni frɛnz. ðe nɛvər fərgɪv ðə lɔs əv ðɛr prərɔgətɪv.

frɛnšɪp ɪz ə kɑmən bəlif ɪn ðə sem fæləsiz, maʊntəbæŋks æn hɑbgɑblənz.

kɑnčənts ɪz ði ɪnər vɔɪs wɪč wɔrnz əs ðæt səmwən me bi lʊkɪŋ.

ivəl ɪz ðæt wɪč wən bəlivz əv əðərz. ɪts ə sɪn tə bəliv ivəl əv əðərz, bət ɪts sɛldəm ə məstek.

æn aɪdiələst ɪz wən hu, ɔn notəsɪŋ ðæt ə roz smɛlz bɛtər ðæn ə kæbɪǰ, kəŋkludz ðæt ɪt wɪl ɔlso mek bɛtər sup.

suəsaɪd ɪz ə bəletəd ækwiɛsənts ɪn ði əpɪnyən əv wənz waɪfs rɛlətɪvz.

tɛmptešən ɪz ən ɪrəzɪstəbəl fors æt wərk ɔn ə muvəbəl bɑdi.

bəfor ə mæn spiks, ɪts ɔlwiz sef tu əsum ðæt hiz ə ful. æftər i spiks, ɪts sɛldəm nɛsəsɛri tu əsum ɪt.

wɛn wɪmɪn kɪs, ɪt ɔlwiz rəmaɪnz wən əv praɪzfaɪtərz šekɪŋ hænz.

ɪf wɪmɪn bəlivd ɪn ðɛr həzbənz, ðe wʊd bi ə gʊd dil hæpiər. æn ɔlso ə gʊd dil mor fulɪš.

ə bæčlər ɪz wən hu wɔnts ə waɪf, bət ɪz glæd i hæzənt gɑt ər.

dəmakrəsi ɪz ðə θiri ðæt ðə kɑmən pipəl no wɑt ðe wɔnt, æn dəzərv tə gɛt ɪt gʊd ən hɑrd.

pyʊrətənɪzəm ɪz ðə hɔntɪŋ fɪr ðæt səmwən, səmwɛr, me bi hæpi.

ə pæstər ɪz wən ɪmplɔɪd baɪ ðə wɪkəd tə pruv tə ðɛm baɪ hɪz ɪgzæmpəl ðæt vərču dəzənt pe.

ə kætəkɪzəm. kwɛščən—ɪf yu faɪn so məč ðæt ɪz ɔnwərði əv rɛvrənts ɪn ðə yunaɪtəd stets, ðɛn waɪ du yu lɪv hɪr? ænsər—waɪ du mɛn go tə zuz?

ɛpətæf. ɪf, æftər aɪ dəpart ðɪs vel, yu ɛvər rəmɛmbər mi æn hæv θɔt tə pliz maɪ gost, fərgɪv səm sɪnər æn wɪŋk yər aɪ æt səm homli gərl.]

CONTRASTIVE SETS

(handwritten note in margin: Any 5 vowels, Any 5 consonants)

A contrastive set is a group of words which differ from one another by a single sound. Thus *hat–bat–rat* are a contrastive set which differ only in their initial consonants; *hat–had–ham* are another set which differ in their final consonants; and *hat–hot–hit* are a set which differ in their vowels. A contrastive set like *causing–caulking–coughing–calling* differ only in their medial consonants. Notice that it is a difference in sound, not in spelling, that we are concerned with. Furthermore, notice that *shawl–tall* are a contrastive pair because they differ only in their initial sounds, [š]–[t], but that *shawl–stall* are not a contrastive pair because they have more than a minimum difference, [š]–[st].

On this and the next pages are a number of contrastive sets which show variation in (1) the vowel, (2) the initial consonant, and (3) the final consonant. Make each set as complete as you can by adding words which show a minimum contrast in sound. For example, on the page devoted to initial consonants, the next word in the third column might be *dough* or *doe*.

VOWELS

[i]	leak	feel	lead			beat	peel	meat	keyed	bead
[ɪ]	lick	fill	LID	miss	kit	BIT	PILL	MIT		
[e]	lake	fail	LAID		KATE	BATE	PALE	MATE		
[ɛ]		fell	LED			BET	PELL	MET		
[æ]	lack		LAD		CAT	BAT	PAL	MAT		
[u]	Luke	fool	LUDE		COOT	BOOT	Pool	MOOT		
[ʊ]	look	full					PULL			
[o]		foal	LOAD		COAL	BOAT	POLE	MOAT		
[ɔ]		fall					PALL			
[ɑ]	lock					BOUGHT	PAUL?			
[ə]	luck				CUT	BUT		MUTT		
[ər]	lurk	furl			CURT	BERT	PEARL			
[aɪ]	like	file	LIED		KITE	BIGHT	PILE	MIGHT		
[aʊ]		foul	LOUD			BOUT				
[ɔɪ]		foil	LLOYD							

INITIAL CONSONANTS

[p]	pie	pooh	Poe	pay	peas	pore	pain	pill	pail	peer	pair
[b]	by	boo	beau	bay	BEES	BORE	BAINE				
[t]	tie	two	toe		TEASE	TORE					
[d]	die	do	DOE	DAY		DOOR	DANE				
[k]	Chi	coo			KEYS	CORE	CANE				
[g]	guy	goo	GO	GAY		GORE	GAIN				
[č]		chew				CHORE	CHAIN				
[ǰ]		Jew	JOE	JAY	GEEZE		GAIN				
[f]	fie		FOE		FEES	FIRE	FEIGN				
[v]	vie				VEB		VANE				
[θ]	thigh										
[ð]	thy		THOUGH	THEY	THESE						
[s]	sigh	sue	SO	SAY	SEIZE	SOAR	SANE				
[z]	Xi	zoo									
[š]	shy	shoe	SHOW		SHES	SHORE					
[m]	my	moo	MOW	MAY		MORE	MAIN				
[n]	nigh	new	NO	NAY	KNEES	MORE					
[l]	lie	lieu	LOW	LAY		LORE	LANE				
[r]	rye	rue	ROW	RAY			RAIN				
[w]	wye	woo	WHOA	WAY	WEEZE	WORE	WAVE				
[y]		you	YO	YEAH		YORE					
[h]	high	who	HOE	HEY	HES	WHORE					

25

	reap	lip	ape	ripe	cap	roup	sip	babe	rap	Bab	lope
[p]	reap	~~liB~~ lip	ape	ripe	cap	roup	sip	babe	rap		lope
[b]		liB	Abe		cab	rube					Bab
[t]	~~Meet~~	lit	ATE	write	CAT	ROOT / MOOT	SIT / KNIT	BAIT / MATE	RAT	BAT	
[d]	read	lid	mD	RIDE	CAD	RUDE		BADE	RAD	BAD	LOAD
[k]	reek	LICK	ACHE				SICK	BAKE	RACK	BACK	
[g]	~~league~~	~~pig~~						BEG	RAG	BAG	
[č]	reach	Leach			CATCH					BATCH	
[ǰ]		age			CAGE			~~Beige~~		BADGE	
[f]	reef	f			GULF	ROOF					LOAF
[v]	reeve	LIVE			CALVE		SIV				LOAVE
[θ]	wreath	~~teet~~		WRITHE		FRONT			RATH	BATH	
[ð]	wreathe	~~th~~	~~bathe~~	WRITHE				BATHE			LOATHE
[s]	Rhys	MISS	AGE	RICE			SIS	BASE		BASS	
[z]		LIZ		RISE		RUSE / ROSE			RAZ		
[š]					CASH	LUSHE			RASH	BASH	ba
[ž]								BEIGE			
[m]	ream	LIMB	AIM	RIME	CAM	ROOM				SAM	
[n]	SEEN			RHINE	CAN	RUNE	SIN	BANE	RAN	BAN	LOAN
[ŋ]	RUNG						o	BANG	RING	Ba	
[l]	reel		ALE	RILE		RULE	SIL	BALE	RAIL		
[r]	a		a					BAYER			LORE

2.6 THE SPEECH ORGANS

This diagram, a conventionalized cross section of the head, identifies some of the important organs used in producing speech.

Identify each of the following organs by its number from the diagram above.

_____ alveolar ridge	_____ nasal cavity	_____ dorsum or back of tongue
_____ epiglottis	_____ oral cavity	_____ trachea
_____ esophagus	_____ pharynx	_____ uvula
_____ hard palate	_____ teeth	_____ velum (soft palate)
_____ larynx	_____ apex or tip of tongue	_____ vocal cords (glottis)
_____ lips	_____ blade or front of tongue	

2.7 A CLASSIFICATION OF ENGLISH CONSONANTS

Complete the following chart by writing the phonetic symbols in the appropriate boxes so as to show the place and manner of articulation for each sound. For simplicity's sake, the stops and affricates are combined in this chart although because the latter are part stop, part fricative they are often treated separately. A dash in a box means that no English consonant phoneme has that place and manner of articulation. Such sounds, however, do occur in other languages (for example, the Spanish voiced bilabial fricative in *haber*) and even in English, as allophonic variants (for example, the common labiodental nasal in *emphatic*). You need not be concerned with such seemingly exotic sounds for a description of English phonemes, but you should be aware that they exist.

Consonants [b, d, f, g, h, k, l, m, n, p, r, s, t, v, w, y, z, ŋ, š, ž, č, ǰ, θ, ð]

			PLACE OF ARTICULATION							
			labial		*dental*			*palatovelar*		*glottal*
			bilabial	labio-dental	inter-dental	alveolar	alveolo-palatal	palatal	velar	
MANNER OF ARTICULATION	*stops and affricates*	voiced		___	___					___
		voiceless		___	___					___
	fricatives	voiced	___					___		___
		voiceless	___					___		___
	nasals			___		___				___
	liquids	lateral	___			___		___	___	___
		retroflex				___				
	semivowels		___	___	___	___	___		___	___

2.8 THE ARTICULATORY DESCRIPTION OF CONSONANTS

Write the phonetic symbol for the sound that is described:

voiceless bilabial stop _____   voiced alveolar fricative _____

voiced labiodental fricative _____   alveolar nasal _____

voiced velar stop _____   lateral _____

voiceless affricate _____   (bilabial) velar semivowel _____

voiced interdental fricative _____   voiceless alveolopalatal fricative _____

glottal fricative _____   bilabial nasal _____

Give a phonetic description, like those above, for each of these sounds:

[t] _____   [b] _____

[s] _____   [ž] _____

[ŋ] _____   [y] _____

[ǰ] _____   [f] _____

[θ] _____   [k] _____

[g] _____   [r] _____

2.9 TRANSCRIPTION: INITIAL CONSONANTS

Write the phonetic symbol for the *initial* consonant sound.

bone _____	circus _____	pneumonia _____	sugar _____
take _____	zero _____	psychology _____	Czech _____
cold _____	charade _____	ptomaine _____	khan _____
gizzard _____	gendarme _____	chaos _____	whole _____
choice _____	mount _____	knot _____	mnemonic _____
giant _____	gnash _____	ghetto _____	thought _____
phase _____	llama _____	cello _____	though _____
valley _____	wring _____	sword _____	ouija _____
thin _____	one _____	czar _____	rhythm _____
then _____	unit _____	xenophobia _____	science _____

2.10 TRANSCRIPTION: FINAL CONSONANTS

Write the phonetic symbol for the *final* consonant sound.

ebb _____	breathe _____	hiccough _____	paradigm _____
ripe _____	rice _____	receipt _____	talk _____
odd _____	rise _____	lamb _____	myrrh _____
lack _____	tongue _____	debt _____	half _____
watch _____	sing _____	indict _____	foreign _____
hedge _____	sign _____	opaque _____	cortège _____
leave _____	off _____	rogue _____	mustache _____
bath _____	of _____	cough _____	coalesce _____
bathe _____	night _____	days _____	allege _____
breath _____	fall _____	solemn _____	ache _____

2.11 TRANSCRIPTION: MEDIAL CONSONANTS

Write the phonetic symbol for the *medial* consonant sound or cluster.

medal _____	reason _____	feature _____	pizza _____
metal _____	recent _____	gradual _____	exist _____
pudding _____	fishing _____	nature _____	taxi _____
putting _____	vision _____	patient _____	regime _____
ether _____	leisure _____	pleasure _____	finger _____
either _____	pleaser _____	pledger _____	ringer _____
other _____	Caesar _____	cupboard _____	anger _____
author _____	seizure _____	subpoena _____	hanger _____
faces _____	fuchsia _____	soften _____	sinking _____
phases _____	future _____	Stephen _____	singing _____

2.12 A CLASSIFICATION OF ENGLISH VOWELS

Complete the following charts by writing the phonetic symbols in the appropriate boxes to show the place of articulation for each vowel. For the distinction between tense and lax and between rounded and spread vowels, see exercise 2.26.

Vowels [ɑ, æ, e, ɛ, i, ɪ, o, ɔ, u, ʊ, ə]

			FRONTNESS OF TONGUE		
			front	*central*	*back*
HEIGHT OF TONGUE	*high*	tense		—	
		lax		—	
	mid	tense		—	
		lax			
	low	spread		—	

Diphthongs [aɪ, aʊ, ɔɪ]

A diphthong is a combination of two vowels pronounced in a single syllable. The tongue moves from the position for the first vowel to that for the second vowel. The arrows in this diagram indicate the direction of movement. Write the phonetic symbol for each diphthong at the beginning of the appropriate arrow. The vowel [a] is low central.

	front	*central*	*back*
high			
mid			☐
low		☐ ☐	

(2.13) **THE ARTICULATORY DESCRIPTION OF VOWELS**

Write the phonetic symbol for the sound described:

high front tense vowel __i__   high back lax vowel __ʊ__
mid back tense vowel __u__   mid central lax vowel __ə__
low back vowel __ɑ__   low central to high back diphthong __aʊ__
mid front lax vowel __ɛ__   mid back to high front diphthong __ɔɪ__

Give a phonetic description, like those above, for each of these sounds:

[u] __Laa HIGH BACK TENSE Vowel__ [ɔ] __LOW BACK Lax__
[ɪ] __Bɪt HIGH FRONT Lax__ [æ] __Low Cent. to MID Frund DiP.__
[e] __MID FRONT TENSE__ [aɪ] __Low cent. to HIGH FRONT DiP.__

2.14 TRANSCRIPTION: VOWELS AND CONSONANTS

Transcribe the following words in their entirety, thus: *hat* [hæt].

dip _____   hug _____   buck _____
deep _____   hung _____   glows _____

shell	_____	wife	_____	voice	_____
shake	_____	slouch	_____	sedge	_____
fool	_____	moist	_____	cow	_____
wool	_____	hue	_____	soy	_____
soap	_____	teach	_____	tall	_____
saw	_____	path	_____	chuck	_____
job	_____	youth	_____	prize	_____
pad	_____	pull	_____	they	_____

2.15 TRANSCRIPTION: HOMOGRAPHIC SPELLINGS

Transcribe the following words.

(handwritten: Apr 10)

lose	[luz]	plaid	_____	blade	_____
loose	lus	laid	_____	bade	_____
plough	plau	said	_____	façade	_____
though	~~ðau~~ ðo	done	_____	sweat	_____
move	muv	tone	_____	treat	_____
wove	wov	touch	_____	great	_____
dove	dəv	couch	_____	gaunt	_____
tomb	tum	blood	_____	kraut	_____
comb	kom	good	_____	thyme	_____
bomb	bam	mood	_____	theme	_____

2.16 TRANSCRIPTION: SILENT LETTERS

Transcribe the following words.

through	_____	hour	_____	indict	_____
wrong	_____	lamb	_____	answer	_____
psalm	_____	gnaw	_____	solder	_____
hymn	_____	folk	_____	plumber	_____
build	_____	phlegm	_____	rhythm	_____
calf	_____	reign	_____	renege	_____
two	_____	corps	_____	salmon	_____
who	_____	queue	_____	subpoena	_____
sigh	_____	kiln	_____	cologne	_____
know	_____	gauge	_____	croquet	_____

2.17 TRANSCRIPTION: SUFFIXES

Transcribe the following words.

clapped	_____	paved	_____	heated	_____
squelched	_____	breathed	_____	crowded	_____
talked	_____	housed	_____	bomb	_____
laughed	_____	rouged	_____	bombard	_____
frothed	_____	combed	_____	sign	_____
glimpsed	_____	moaned	_____	signal	_____
wished	_____	hanged	_____	strong	_____
rubbed	_____	filled	_____	stronger	_____
bulged	_____	shirred	_____	test	_____
begged	_____	rowed	_____	tests	_____

30

2.18 TRANSCRIPTION: VOWELS BEFORE [r]

Transcribe the following words.

leer	_____	lure	_____	story	_____
lyric	_____	lurid	_____	sorry	_____
mare	_____	poor	_____	starry	_____
there	_____	pore	_____	hire	_____
Mary	_____	four	_____	higher	_____
merry	_____	for	_____	flour	_____
marry	_____	far	_____	flower	_____
fur	_____	borne	_____	pure	_____
furry	_____	born	_____	fewer	_____
hurry	_____	barn	_____	fury	_____

2.19 TRANSCRIPTION: VARIANT PRONUNCIATIONS

Transcribe the following words.

suite	_____	shred	_____	luxury	_____
greasy	_____	schnitzel	_____	tournament	_____
syrup	_____	wash	_____	thither	_____
bouquet	_____	roof	_____	chicanery	_____
brooch	_____	orange	_____	garage	_____
dais	_____	hog	_____	homage	_____
creek	_____	egg	_____	vehicle	_____
catch	_____	aunt	_____	spinach	_____
with	_____	million	_____	junta	_____
onion	_____	height	_____	strength	_____

2.20 TRANSCRIPTION: HOMOPHONES AND NEAR HOMOPHONES

Transcribe the following words.

candid	_____	maw	_____	shut	_____
candied	_____	ma	_____	shirt	_____
taut	_____	can 'able'	_____	do	_____
tot	_____	can (n.)	_____	due	_____
yon	_____	have	_____	hole	_____
yawn	_____	halve	_____	whole	_____
bomb	_____	tarred	_____	ladder	_____
balm	_____	tired	_____	latter	_____
witch	_____	wife's	_____	click	_____
which	_____	wives	_____	clique	_____

2.21 PRIMARY STRESS

Indicate the primary stress in each of these words by writing an accent mark over the vowel symbol (or over the first symbol of a digraph) thus: *sófa*, *abóut*.

abyss	ketchup	gluttonous	consecutively
almond	massage	heresy	debauchery
basket	message	improvement	executive
beguile	abolish	industry	fashionable

decent	accredit	platinum	immediate
descent	collector	successor	nominative
engaged	detective	alternative	obtainable
figure	division	annually	parenthesis
harangue	element	caressingly	sensuousness
impose	fallacious	circumference	servility

2.22 PRIMARY AND SECONDARY STRESS

Indicate the primary and secondary stresses with accent marks: ´ for primary, ` for secondary. Write the marks over the vowel symbol of the stressed syllable.

backlash	almighty	adversary	assimilation
cartoon	attitude	aftereffect	attitudinize
concourse	incorrect	confidential	depository
foresee	iota	halfheartedly	philosophical
good-by	panhandle	necessitate	expeditionary

2.23 TRANSCRIPTION WITH PRIMARY STRESS

Transcribe these words phonetically and indicate primary stress on the transcription; for example, [əbáʊt].

seldom	_____	visit	_____	except	_____
image	_____	command	_____	produce (v.)	_____
adjust	_____	comic	_____	above	_____
oppose	_____	stomach	_____	pleasure	_____
martyr	_____	accept	_____	genial	_____

2.24 TRANSCRIPTION WITH PRIMARY AND SECONDARY STRESS

Transcribe these words phonetically; mark both primary and secondary stress.

local	_____	oblige	_____	analog	_____
locate	_____	obligate	_____	analogical	_____
location	_____	obligation	_____	consolidate	_____
locative	_____	obligatory	_____	consolidation	_____
absolve	_____	apply	_____	migrate	_____
absolution	_____	application	_____	migration	_____
propose	_____	applicable	_____	migratory	_____
proposition	_____	applicability	_____	intellect	_____
actual	_____	operating	_____	intellectual	_____
actuality	_____	operation	_____	intelligent	_____

2.25 THE PRODUCTION OF SPEECH SOUNDS

The diagrams in this exercise represent in conventionalized form the positions of the speech organs for certain English sounds. Notice the position of the velum, the lips, the tongue, and the vocal cords (a straight line indicates voicelessness, a jagged line indicates vibration and voice). For vowels, a grid has been added to help in estimating the tongue's position; for diphthongs, the tongue's final position is indicated by a dotted line.

[p]

[b]

[m]

[k]

[s]

[š]

[i] or [ɪ]

[u] or [ʊ]

[aɪ]

What sound is indicated by each of these diagrams?

[   ]   [   ]   [   ]

[   ]   [   ]   [   ]

[   ]   [   ]   [   ]

Complete these diagrams by adding the velum, lips, tongue, and vocal cords to indicate the sounds called for.

[g]   [d]   [ŋ]

[z]   [ð]   [v]

[e]   [ɑ]   [aʊ]

Sounds can be looked at in different ways. On the one hand, we can think of them as individual segments that follow one another in the chain of speech like beads on a string; this is the view implied by normal phonetic transcription, which is the most useful way of recording sounds for practical purposes. On the other hand, we can think of each sound, not as an indivisible unit, but rather as a bundle of "features." Each feature is the consequence of an articulatory movement of the speech organs, has characteristic acoustical properties that can be recorded by instruments designed for the purpose, and produces its own special effect on the ear of a listener. All the world's languages draw from the relatively small number of these phonetic features to create the many diverse phonological systems of human speech. The features are the real elements of phonology—the atomic building blocks from which a sound system is constructed.

Below are listed the features that are of importance for English. Each feature listed here has a binary value—that is, it is either present (indicated by a plus mark: +) or absent (indicated by a minus mark: −); none can occur in part or by degrees.

1. **Sonorant** sounds are produced in such a way that spontaneous vibration of the vocal cords is possible; they are, consequently, normally voiced and only exceptionally voiceless. Nonsonorants, also called obstruents, are produced with the air passage so constricted that voicing requires a special effort; they typically occur both with and without voice.

   + sonorant: vowels, semivowels, nasals, liquids
   − sonorant (obstruent): stops, affricates, fricatives

2. **Consonantal** sounds are produced with a radical obstruction along the midline of the vocal tract.

   + consonantal: stops, affricates, fricatives except [h], nasals, liquids
   − consonantal: vowels, semivowels, [h]

3. **Syllabic** sounds occur at the peak of a syllable, with just as many syllabics as there are syllables in each word uttered. Nonsyllabics cluster around syllabics on the margins of syllables. Nasals and liquids can be either syllabics or nonsyllabics, depending on their use in an utterance.

   + syllabic: vowels, syllabic nasals, syllabic liquids
   − syllabic: stops, affricates, fricatives, semivowels, nonsyllabic nasals, nonsyllabic liquids

4. **Continuant** sounds are produced by an air flow that is not completely interrupted at any time during the production of the sound. Noncontinuants, also called stops, completely block the air flow at some point in their articulation.

   + continuant: fricatives, nasals, liquids, semivowels, vowels
   − continuant (stop): stops, affricates

5. **Nasal** sounds are produced with the velum lowered, so that air escapes through the nose.

   + nasal: nasals
   − nasal: stops, affricates, fricatives, liquids, semivowels, vowels

6. **Lateral** sounds are produced by directing the air flow out of the mouth through a side channel, normally around one or both sides of the tongue.

   + lateral: [l]
   − lateral: all other sounds

7. **Anterior** sounds are those made with an obstruction in the front part of the mouth, from the alveolar ridge forward, and with no obstruction from the palatal region back.

   + anterior: labials, interdentals, alveolars
   − anterior: alveolopalatals, retroflexes, palatovelars, semivowels, vowels

8. **Coronal** sounds are those made with the blade or front of the tongue raised from a neutral position.

   + coronal: interdentals, alveolars, alveolopalatals
   − coronal: labials, palatovelars, semivowels, vowels

9. **Sibilant** sounds are produced by forcing the air through a narrow opening produced by a groove in the midline of the tongue; they have a characteristic "hissing" effect.

   + sibilant: [s, z, š, ž, č, ǰ]
   − sibilant: all other sounds

10. **Voiced** sounds are produced with vibration of the vocal cords.
      + voiced: [b, d, ǰ, g, v, ð, z, ž], nasals, liquids, semivowels, vowels
      − voiced (voiceless): [p, t, č, k, f, θ, s, š, h]

11. **Back** sounds are produced with the body of the tongue retracted from a neutral position. In English this feature applies only to vowels and semivowels.
      + back: [u, ʊ, o, ɔ, ɑ, ə, w]
      − back (front): [i, ɪ, e, ɛ, æ, y]

12. **Rounded** sounds are produced with the lip opening narrowed by "rounding" the lips, that is, by protruding the lips and pressing their side edges together. In English the feature is characteristic mainly of vowels and semivowels.
      + rounded: [u, ʊ, o, ɔ, w]
      − rounded (spread): [i, ɪ, e, ɛ, æ, ə, ɑ, y]

13. **High** sounds are made with the body of the tongue raised above a neutral position. In English this feature applies only to vowels.
      + high: [i, ɪ, u, ʊ]
      − high: [e, ɛ, æ, o, ɔ, ɑ, ə]

14. **Low** sounds are made with the body of the tongue lowered below a neutral position. In English this feature applies only to vowels. The mid vowels are nonhigh and nonlow.
      + low: [æ, ɑ]
      − low: [i, ɪ, e, ɛ, u, ʊ, o, ɔ, ə]

15. **Tense** sounds are produced with tense muscles of the tongue and with relatively more effort; they are held longer and give an effect of greater forcefulness. The feature is relevant mainly to vowels, although in the most common forms of American English it does not apply to the low vowels.
      + tense: [i, e, u, o]
      − tense (lax): [ɪ, ɛ, ʊ, ə]

Complete the chart on the next page by writing a plus or minus, as appropriate, in each box. The "plus over minus" entered in five boxes indicates that the syllabic feature can be either present or absent for those sounds. The completed chart will show the value of each feature for every phonemic segment of English.

Identify the phonetic feature, plus or minus, that defines each of the following sets:

1. [l] **+ LATERAL**
2. [m, n, ŋ] **+ NASAL**
3. [θ, ð, t, d, s, z, n, l, r, č, ǰ, š, ž] **+ CONSONANTAL + CORONAL**
4. [p, t, č, k, f, θ, s, š, h] **− SONORANT** − SONORANT
5. [u, ʊ, o, ɔ, w] **+ ROUNDED**
6. [e, ɛ, æ, o, ɔ, ɑ, ə] **− HIGH**
7. [i, e, u, o] **+ TENSE**
8. [p, t, č, k, b, d, ǰ, g, f, v, θ, ð, s, z, š, ž, h] **− SONORANT**
9. [i, ɪ, e, ɛ, æ, u, ʊ, o, ɔ, ɑ, ə, y, w, h] **− CONSONANTAL**
10. [p, t, č, k, b, d, ǰ, g] **− CONTINUANT**
11. [p, b, m, f, v, θ, ð, t, d, s, z, n, l] **+ ANTERIOR**
12. [s, z, š, ž, č, ǰ] **+ SIBILANT**
13. [i, ɪ, e, ɛ, æ, y] **− BACK**
14. [æ, ɑ] **+ LOW**
15. [i, ɪ, e, ɛ, æ, u, ʊ, o, ɔ, ɑ, ə, m̩, n̩, ŋ̩, l̩, r̩] **+ VOICED, + SYLLABIC**
    (The dots under a consonant indicate that it can be a syllable.)

Each of the following sets can be uniquely defined by specifying two features. What are they?

16. [f, v, θ, ð, s, z, š, ž, h] **CONSONANTAL +** and **CONTINUANT +**
17. [h] _____ and _____
18. [i, ɪ, e, ɛ, æ, u, ʊ, o, ɔ, ɑ, ə] _____ and _____
19. [i, ɪ] _____ and _____
20. [p, b, f, v, m] _____ and _____

37

THE PHONETIC FEATURES OF ENGLISH

	p	b	t	d	k	g	č	ǰ	f	v	θ	ð	s	z	š	ž	h	m	n	ŋ	l	r	w	y	æ	e	a	iː	i	ɛ	ɔ	ʊ	u	c
sonorant																																		
consonantal																																		
syllabic																		±	±	±	±	±												
continuant																																		
nasal																																		
lateral																																		
anterior																																		
coronal																																		
sibilant																																		
voiced																																		
back																																		
rounded																																		
high																																		
low																																		
tense																																		

not applicable

In addition to the kind of phoneme we have been dealing with, which is a class of phonetic events, there is another, called the systematic phoneme, which accounts for phonetically diverse sounds in related words. For example, in *mean/meant, clean/cleanlier, please/pleasure, repeat/repetitive, weal/wealth,* and *seam/ semp-stress,* the first word in each pair has the stressed vowel [i], whereas the second has [ɛ]. The alternation of [i] in a root with [ɛ] when certain suffixes are added is too widespread and too regular to be fortuitous. One way to account for it is to say that there is an underlying vowel, a systematic phoneme, that we might symbolize as [ē] although it is more accurately described as a cluster of features like those in the preceding exercise. Under certain circumstances that can be stated by general rules this systematic phoneme is realized as [i], and under other circumstances as [ɛ]. One of the interesting aspects of this way of accounting for the alternation of sounds in present-day English is that it mirrors, at least approximately, the historical changes English sounds have gone through. Not only is our present sound system the result of past changes, but it still carries within it the evidence of its history.

In each of the following groups of words, the italicized spellings stand for phonetic segments that correspond to one systematic phoneme. Write the phonetic symbols for those segments. In later chapters we will investigate the historical changes that produced the vowel alternations illustrated by the first five groups. The last four groups show consonant alternations that English inherited from Romance languages.

1. v*i*ce/v*i*cious, div*i*ne/div*i*nity, der*i*ve/der*i*vative, l*i*ne/l*i*near _____
2. obsc*e*ne/obsc*e*nity, app*ea*l/app*e*lative, supr*e*me/supr*e*macy, m*e*ter/m*e*tric _____
3. gymn*a*sium/gymn*a*stic, prof*a*ne/prof*a*nity, grat*e*ful/grat*i*tude, expl*ai*n/expl*a*natory _____
4. teleph*o*ne/teleph*o*nic, cons*o*le/cons*o*latory, epis*o*de/epis*o*dic, verb*o*se/verb*o*sity _____
5. prof*ou*nd/prof*u*ndity, pron*ou*nce/pron*u*nciation, ab*ou*nd/ab*u*ndant, ann*ou*nce/ann*u*nciate _____
6. corro*d*e/corro*s*ive/corro*s*ion, divi*d*e/divi*s*ive/divi*s*ion/indivi*d*ual _____
7. democra*t*/democra*c*y, par*t*/par*t*ial, habi*t*/habi*t*ual, ac*t*/ac*t*ion/ac*t*ual _____
8. logi*c*/logi*c*ize/logi*c*ian, impli*c*ate/impli*c*it, musi*c*/musi*c*ian _____
9. analo*g*/analo*g*ize, pedago*g*/pedago*g*y, theolo*g*/theolo*g*ical _____

2.28 OTHER METHODS OF TRANSCRIBING ENGLISH VOWELS

Phonemes, whether they are the traditional kind or the "systematic" kind mentioned in the preceding exercise, are abstractions from actual speech. Because it is possible to abstract in more than one way, there can be different systems for transcribing the sounds of any language. For example, the vowels of *laid* and *led* are both mid-front (that is, [− high, − low, − back]), but they differ from each other phonetically in several ways:

1. Position: the vowel of *led* is somewhat lower and less front than that of *laid.* If we use the same basic symbol [e] for both vowels, we could show this difference by writing the vowel of *led* as [e^∨>] with the arrows showing the direction in which the tongue is shifted.
2. Length: the vowel of *laid* is somewhat longer than that of *led.* Using a colon to indicate phonetic length, we could show this difference as [e:] for *laid* versus [e] for *led.*
3. Diphthongization: *laid* has a vowel that is diphthongized with a glide toward the high-front region: [eɪ] (or [ey]), whereas *led* has either no diphthongization or a glide to the mid-central region: [eə].
4. Tenseness: the vowel of *laid* is pronounced with the tongue muscles relatively tense and *led* with the muscles lax. This difference can be indicated by a macron for the tense vowel: [ē] versus [e]. (The macron is also, and more commonly, used to mean length, but can be pressed into service here as a signal of tenseness.)

If we were to indicate all these phonetic distinctions, the vowel of *led* might be written [e^∨>ə] and the vowel of *laid* [ē:ɪ]. Such a relatively narrow phonetic transcription, although accurate as a description of the actual sounds, is wasteful because it records the difference between the two vowels in four different ways. Most styles of transcription show only one or two of the differences explicitly, leaving the others to be inferred. When the vowels are written with different symbols ([e] for *laid* and [ɛ] for *led*), the distinction in symbols can be taken as standing for any (or, indeed, all) of the phonetic differences.

As alternatives to the style of transcription in *Origins and Development,* a number of others are widely used. A well-known British system is that of Daniel Jones. Some Americans use a system developed by George L. Trager and Henry Lee Smith, Jr. Dictionaries use still different systems. The following table shows how the Jones and Trager-Smith (T-S) analyses of English vowels correlate with that of *Origins* and this workbook. In several cases, the Jones transcription reflects a difference in pronunciation between British and American speech.

In the fourth column of the following list, write the symbol found in the dictionary you use; and in the blank following the example, transcribe the key word according to that dictionary's system.

Indicate which dictionary you use: _____

ORIGINS	JONES	T-S	DICTIONARY	EXAMPLES
[ɪ]	[i]	/i/	_____	*it:* [ɪt], [it], /it/, _____
[ɛ]	[ɛ]	/e/	_____	*elf:* [ɛlf], [ɛlf], /elf/, _____
[æ]	[a]	/æ/	_____	*at:* [æt], [at], /æt/, _____
[ʊ]	[u]	/u/	_____	*bull:* [bʊl], [bul], /bul/, _____
[ɑ]	[ɔ]	/a/	_____	*stop:* [stɑp], [stɔp], /stap/, _____
[ə]	[ʌ]	/ə/	_____	*sun:* [sən], [sʌn], /sən/, _____
[ə]	[ə]	/ə/	_____	*attack:* [ətǽk], [əˈtæk], /ətǽk/, _____
[ə]	[ə]	/h/	_____	as a replacement of final and preconsonantal [r] in the stressed syllables of *r*-less speech: *tour:* [tʊə], [tuə], /tuh/, _____
[i]	[iː]	/iy/	_____	*eat:* [it], [iːt], /iyt/, _____
[e]	[ei]	/ey/	_____	*ape:* [ep], [eip], /eyp/, _____
[aɪ]	[ai]	/ay/	_____	*buy:* [baɪ], [bai], /bay/, _____
[ɔɪ]	[ɔi]	/ɔy/	_____	*boy:* [bɔɪ], [bɔi], /bɔy/, _____
[u]	[uː]	/uw/	_____	*ooze:* [uz], [uːz], /uwz/, _____
[o]	[ou]	/ow/	_____	*oats:* [ots], [outs], /owts/, _____
[aʊ]	[au]	/aw/	_____	*how:* [haʊ], [hau], /haw/, _____
[ɔ]	[ɔː]	/ɔh/	_____	*law:* [lɔ], [lɔː], /lɔh/, _____
[ər]	[ər]	/ər/	_____	as in *r*-ish *urn:* [ərn], [ərn], /ərn/, _____
[əː]	[əː]	/əh/	_____	as in *r*-less *urn:* [əːn], [əːn], /əhn/, _____
[a]	[aː]	/æh/	_____	as in eastern New England *ask:* [ask], [aːsk], /æhsk/, _____
[ɑː]	[ɑː]	/ah/	_____	as in *r*-less *art:* [ɑːt], [ɑːt], /aht/, _____
[æː]	[ɛː]	/eh/	_____	as in New York City *halve:* [hæːv], [hɛːv], /hehv/, _____

Transcribe each of the following words twice, first according to the phonetic notation of *Origins and Development* and then according to one of the other systems (indicate which).

	ORIGINS	OTHER		ORIGINS	OTHER
big	_____	_____	tie	_____	_____
beep	_____	_____	toy	_____	_____
less	_____	_____	vow	_____	_____
lace	_____	_____	fume	_____	_____
look	_____	_____	calf	_____	_____
loop	_____	_____	about	_____	_____
dud	_____	_____	gallon	_____	_____
burr	_____	_____	fear	_____	_____
mote	_____	_____	lure	_____	_____
raw	_____	_____	more	_____	_____
pop	_____	_____	harm	_____	_____
cap	_____	_____	bear	_____	_____

3 LETTERS AND SOUNDS
A BRIEF HISTORY OF WRITING

3.1 FOR REVIEW AND DISCUSSION

1. Define the following terms:

   ideographic (logographic) writing
   phonogram
   rebus
   syllabary
   alphabetic writing
   boustrophedon
   alphabet
   minuscule
   majuscule
   Cyrillic

   diacritical mark
   umlaut (dieresis)
   accent
   acute, grave, circumflex
   wedge (haček)
   tilde
   cedilla
   digraph
   trigraph
   ligature
   æsc (ash)

   rune
   futhorc
   Insular hand
   thorn
   wynn
   edh
   long s
   spelling pronunciation
   pronunciation spelling
   eye dialect

2. How do the drawings of preliterate societies, such as those of the cave men or of the American Indians, differ from true writing?

3. In modern times, stylized drawings are still used for some purposes, for example on road signs. Cite some specific examples.

4. Arabic numerals and symbols like & or % are basically ideograms. Can you cite other examples of ideograms in current use?

5. What evidence is there that the Greeks acquired their writing system from the Semites?

6. In the Semitic script there was no way of writing vowel sounds. Explain the origins of the Greek vowel letters.

7. What accounts for the difference between the angular (Γ, Δ, Σ) and the rounded (C, D, S) forms of what are historically the same letters?

8. What letters and ligatures, formerly used to write English, have passed out of use?

9. Chaucer's Wife of Bath used to berate her husbands by asking such questions as "What rowne ye with oure mayde?" and in *The Winter's Tale* Leontes says, "They're here with me already, whispering, rounding, 'Sicilia is a so-forth.'" What is the etymological connection between the obsolete verb *rown* or *round* and *runic* writing?

10. In what ways has the Roman alphabet been adapted for writing the un-Latin sounds of such languages as Polish, German, or English?

11. What is the origin of the dot over the letter *i*?

12. Why do the vowel letters in Modern English spelling represent sounds that differ greatly from the sounds represented by the same letters in other languages?

13. Old English spelling was a reasonably good representation of the sounds of the language. Modern English spelling is notoriously bad in this respect. What causes for the widened gap between English sound and spelling can you suggest?

14. Describe the logical development, which is not necessarily the actual historical development, of writing systems. Use an outline like the following one to classify the kinds of writing systems.

> Pictures (American Indian)
> Ideographs (Egyptian ideographs, Sumerian ideographs)
> Phonograms
> > Rebuses
> > Syllabaries (Cherokee, Japanese)
> > Consonantal writing (Egyptian phonograms, Semitic)
> > Alphabets (Greek, Roman, Cyrillic, runic)

15. What is the relationship between writing and speech as expressions of language? In what ways is writing secondary? Does writing ever influence speech?

3.2   A PICTOGRAPH

The Indian "letter" mentioned on page 35 of *Origins and Development* is adapted here from Henry R. Schoolcraft, *Information Respecting the History, Condition, and Prospects of the Indian Tribes of the United States* (1853, I: 418–9). An interpretation of the pictograph is also given. Compare the interpretation with the drawing to discover the conventions the "writer" used. How is each of the following concepts expressed in the pictograph?

an agreement of opinion _____

an offering of friendship _____

the rank of chief (vs. mere warrior) _____

the rank of a more important chief _____

a settled or civilized way of life _____

the location of the writer's home _____

the totem-group to which the Indians belong _____

_____

INTERPRETATION: A chief of the eagle totem, four of his warrior-kinsmen, a fifth warrior (of the catfish totem), and another chief, who is more powerful than the first leader, are all agreed in their views. They extend friendship to the president of the United States in the White House. The eagle chief intends to settle at a location on a river, and his kinsmen will occupy houses, thus adopting the white man's culture. It is hoped the president will understand the offer of friendship and return it.

3.3 ANOTHER PICTOGRAPH

The following "letter" was sent by an Ojibwa girl to a young man, inviting him to her lodge. The lover is given directions for finding his way and other information appropriate to such an invitation. Only the R.S.V.P. is lacking. (The letters have been added to the original for purposes of identification.)

INTERPRETATION: The writer of the letter is a girl of the bear totem (   ). She and two companions, all three of whom are Christians (   ) (   ) (   ), live in two lodges (   ) (   ) near some lakes (   ). A trail leads from the lodges to a main road (   ), which runs near another lake (   ) not far from the lodges. The letter is being sent to a man of the mud puppy totem (   ), who is reminded of a trail (   ) which leads from his lodge to the main road. A hand extending through the door of one of the dwellings (   ) both invites the young man (the purpose of the letter) and tells him which lodge he should visit.

1. Complete the interpretation by writing within the parentheses the letters from the drawing.

2. Although the drawing represents various objects important to the message, the import of the letter is not explicitly stated. Nothing in the drawing actually says, "Come up and see me sometime." That message must be inferred because picture writing has no way of being so specific. In what other ways does pictography differ from genuine writing? For example, would two persons be likely to "read" the message in exactly the same way? Is there any one correct order for interpreting the parts of the message? Does the message tell anything about the pronunciation, word order, or inflections of the Ojibwa language?

_____

_____

_____

_____

_____

3.4 IDEOGRAPHS: SUMERIAN CUNEIFORM

The Sumerians, who lived in southern Mesopotamia, were enthusiastic bookkeepers. The phrases below are adapted from a collection of records, invoices, and receipts that were written between 2400 and 2300 B.C. Although the cuneiform style was also used for phonograms, the Sumerian in this sample is written in ideographs.

two bulls

five pastured cows

_____

two lambs

seventeen pastured bulls

_____

four sheep

twenty suckling bull calves

_____

one suckling lamb

(an) offering (for the) king

_____

ten fattened bulls

offerings (for the) goddess Nina

_____

1. Translate the last five phrases in the blanks above.
2. Consult a dictionary for the literal meaning of the word *cuneiform*. _____

_____

3. How did the writing materials that were used for cuneiform influence the shape of the symbols? _____

_____

4. Cuneiform symbols were originally pictures of the objects they represent. Find at least one that still has

some pictorial value. Suggestion: Rotate the page 90 degrees clockwise. _____

5. The symbol for "offering" is a combination of which two other symbols?

_____

6. How is the plural of nouns indicated when there is no accompanying numeral?

_____

7. How is the plural of nouns indicated after a numeral?_____

_____

8. What is the position of modifiers with relation to the nouns they modify? Is there more than one kind of

modifier? _____

_____

9. List two or three ways in which these ideographs differ from the pictograph of the preceding exercise.

_____

_____

_____

_____

10. How might "ten fattened bulls" be expressed in a pictograph? _____

_____

3.5   EGYPTIAN HIEROGLYPHICS

Egyptian writing is a mixture of phonograms, which represent sounds, and ideographs, which represent ideas or general concepts. The phonograms stand for consonants only; vowels were not represented in Egyptian writing. Consequently the exact pronunciation of Egyptian is unknown. Here are some typical hieroglyphs:

PHONOGRAMS AND TRANSLITERATION				IDEOGRAPHS AND MEANING	
	y		m	⊙	sun
	' (a glottal sound)		n		light, shine
	w		r		heaven
	b		h		moon
	p		t		

From these hieroglyphs, the following sentences can be made:

HIEROGLYPHS	TRANSLITERATION	TRANSLATION
	wbn r' m pt	The sun rises in the sky.
	yr r' m pt	The sun is in the sky.
	wbn y'h	The moon rises.
	_____	_____
	_____	_____

1. Transliterate and translate the last two sentences in the blanks above.

2. What is the Egyptian word order for subject, verb, and adverbial phrase? _____

_____

3. The hieroglyphs shown previously are written from left to right, but other orders of writing are possible.

For example: ☉ ⏧ 𓃭 𓅯

What is the translation of this sentence? _____

4. How can you tell from looking at hieroglyphic writing whether it is to be read from right to left or from

left to right? _____

5. The ideographs used in these sentences are called determinatives. What useful functions do they serve?

_____

6. In what way are these hieroglyphs a more adequate representation of language than the cuneiforms of the

preceding exercise? _____

_____

3.6 HEBREW WRITING

1. The Semitic writing systems are in many ways like Egyptian phonograms, which were, indeed, probably the model for the first Semitic writing. Hebrew script, one variety of Semitic, is written from right to left. At its simplest it is like Egyptian phonograms in making no provision whatever for representing the vowels; however, since Hebrew is still a spoken language, the vowels can be supplied in a transcription.

אבא	'abbā'	papa	חדש	chădăsh	new
בת	bath	daughter	ילד	yeled	child
בית	bayith	house	כל	kol	all
בקר	bōqer	morning	נער	na'ar	boy
גז	gēz	mowing	פסח	pesach	Passover
הר	har	hill	עט	'ēt	pen
וו	wāw	hook	צמח	tsemach	plant
חדש	chodesh	month	שמש	shemesh	sun

Here are the twenty-two letters of the Hebrew script. Supply a transliteration for each. Some letters represent two pronunciations, distinguished by diacritics; only one variety of each letter is shown here.

א ___	ו ___	כ ___	ס ___	ק ___
ב ___	ז ___	ל ___	ע ___	ר ___
ג ___	ח ___	מ ___	פ ___	ש ___
ד ___	ט ___	נ ___	צ ___	ת ___
ה ___	י ___			

2. Sometimes letters which normally stand for consonants are used to represent vowels. When so used, they are called *matres lectionis*, 'mothers of reading.'

Hebrew	Translit.	Meaning		Hebrew	Translit.	Meaning
מִי	mī	who		סוס	sūs	horse
אִישׁ	'īsh	man		כוֹס	kōs	goblet
מֵיתָר	mēthār	string		אוֹר	'ōr	light
בֵית	bēth	the house of		מָה	mā	what
סִפּוּר	sippūr	story		בְּחוּרָה	bachūrā	girl

These three Hebrew letters are used as *matres lectionis;* what vowels can each represent?

י _____ ו _____ ה _____

3. In the sixth century A.D., a group of scholars called the Massoretes, from *massōrā* 'tradition,' invented a system of diacritics for a more precise writing of the Hebrew vowels. These scholars were motivated by a desire to preserve the exact pronunciation of the scriptures and were probably influenced by the alphabetic system that the Greeks had developed much earlier. The diacritic marks they invented are called massoretic points.

DIACRITICS ADDED TO SIMPLE SPELLINGS			DIACRITICS ADDED TO *MATRES LECTIONIS*		
בַּת	bath	daughter	מָה	mā	what
וָו	wāw	hook	בֵּית	bēth	the house of
שֶׁמֶשׁ	shemesh	sun	מִי	mī	who
גֵּז	gēz	mowing	אוֹר	'ōr	light
בַּיִת	bayith	house	סוּס	sūs	horse
כָּל	kol	all			
בֹּקֶר	bōqer	morning			
נֻפַּח	nuppach	blown up			

The points, except for those that represent long *o* and *u*, are written beneath the consonant they follow. Notice that the same diacritic is used for long *a* and short *o;* in some dialects of Hebrew these two sounds are pronounced alike. Even when distinct from long *a*, short *o* is relatively rare.

Transliterate these Hebrew words:

חִידָה _____ riddle עֵז _____ she-goat

שֹׁמֵר _____ watchman נוּס _____ flee

שַׁחַר _____ dawn חַיִל _____ power

קוֹל _____ voice אֶחָד _____ one

4. The Hebrew writing system is sometimes referred to as an alphabet, but has also been called a syllabary.

How does it represent a transitional stage between syllabaries and alphabets? _____

_____

_____

3.7 THE CHEROKEE SYLLABARY

In 1821 Sequoya, who has been called the Cherokee Cadmus, invented a script for writing his native language. Sequoya's invention made Cherokee the only Indian tongue to have an indigenous, fully developed writing system. Although he seems to have known no English, many of Sequoya's symbols are clearly derived from the Latin alphabet. The Cherokee writing system is, however, not an alphabet, but a syllabary, as the chart on the next page makes clear.

Transliterate the following Cherokee words by consulting the chart.

CHEROKEE	TRANSLITERATION	TRANSLATION
Ꮳ Ꮃ Ᏹ	_____	Cherokee
Ꮟ Ꮵ Ꮽ	_____	Sequoya
� Ꮂ Ꮓ Ꮧ	_____	October, harvest month
Ꮴ Ꮟ Ꮖ Ꮏ Ꮳ	_____	instantly
Ꭰ Ꮊ Ꭼ	_____	war club

48

	a	e	i	o	u	ᴧ
	D	R	T	Ꮹ	Ơ	i
ka / ga	ga	ge	gi	go	gu	gᴧ
	ha	he	hi	ho	hu	hᴧ
	la	le	li	lo	lu	lᴧ
	ma	me	mi	mo	mu	
hna nah na	na	ne	ni	no	nu	nᴧ
	kwa	kwe	kwi	kwo	kwu	kwᴧ
s	sa	se	si	so	su	sᴧ
	da	de	di	do	du	dᴧ
	ta	te	ti			
dla	tla	tle	tli	tlo	tlu	tlᴧ
	tsa	tse	tsi	tso	tsu	tsᴧ
	wa	we	wi	wo	wu	wᴧ
	ya	ye	yi	yo	yu	yᴧ

3.8 JAPANESE KATAKANA

Japanese is normally written with a combination of ideographic signs borrowed from Chinese and phonographic characters called *kana*. There are two varieties of *kana*: the *hiragana*, used for most ordinary purposes, and the *katakana*, used for transcribing foreign words and for formal, official writing. The latter system is illustrated here.

KATAKANA	TRANSLITERATION	TRANSLATION
ワタシ	watashi	I
アナタ	anata	you
イチ	ichi	one
ヨル	yoru	night
ハイ	hai	yes
シロ	shiro	white
カモク	kamoku	thing
ヨイ	_____	good
ハナ	_____	flower
シカル	_____	blame

1. Transliterate the last three words in the blanks above.

2. What kind of writing system is the katakana? _____

3. How does the katakana differ from the Semitic writing system? _____

_____

4. Languages differ from one another not only in the sounds they use, but also in the order in which their sounds may be arranged. The possible arrangements of sounds (technically, *phonotactics*) have some bearing on the kind of writing system most appropriate for a language. In Japanese each syllable tends to be composed of a single consonant (C) followed by a single vowel (V). Thus we can describe the canonical, or regular, form of the Japanese syllable as CV. The words *yo-ru* and *wa-ta-shi* are made entirely of syllables of this sort. Notice that the spellings *sh* and *ch* in the transliterations stand for single consonants each. There are, of course, other possibilities; for example, any of the five vowels of Japanese may form a syllable by itself with no preceding consonant. The word *i-chi* begins with such a syllable, and the word *ha-i* ends in one. Moreover, certain consonants, such as the *n*-sound, can form a syllable without a vowel. The Japanese word *hon* 'book' consists of two syllables: *ho-n*. Unlike English, Japanese has no syllables of the form VC or CVC and no syllables beginning with consonant combinations like *st*, *tr*, *sw*, or *spl*. Consequently, when the Japanese language borrows words from a language like English, it must adapt the arrangement of sounds to its own patterns. Thus *beer* appears in Japanese as *bīru*, and *butter* as *bata*.

Explain why the phonotactics of Japanese makes the katakana an appropriate kind of writing system for the language. _____

_____

_____

5. Compare the phonotactics of Japanese with that of Cherokee. Are they generally similar or dissimilar?

_____

How appropriate is Sequoya's writing system for Cherokee? _____

_____

6. Compare the phonotactics of Japanese with that of Hebrew. What are the canonical forms (consonant and vowel patterns) for Hebrew words of one syllable? _____

_____

How does Hebrew differ most noticeably from Japanese in its phonotactic patterns?

_____

Which language probably has the larger number of different syllables—Hebrew or Japanese?

_____

7. Compare the phonotactics of Japanese with that of English. What are the C and V forms for the following monosyllabic English words?

a _____   at _____   pant _____   spit _____   prompts _____
no _____   pan _____   pants _____   split _____   splints _____

Would a syllabary be an appropriate writing system for English? Explain your answer.

_____

_____

_____

3.9   THE DEVELOPMENT OF THE ALPHABET

The invention of the alphabet is one of those rare events in human history that seem to have occurred only once. Some apparently independent alphabets, like that used for Korean, probably evolved under the influence of the Roman script as it was disseminated by missionaries. The first and archetypal alphabet came into existence when the Greeks adapted the Semitic syllabary to their own language, using some of the extra consonant letters to write vowels. All subsequent alphabets spring from this bit of Greek cleverness. The chart on the next page traces, in greatly simplified fashion, the development of the alphabet from Semitic to Greek to Latin to English. By referring to pages 36–8 of *Origins and Development* and to the table that can be found under the entry *alphabet* in most desk dictionaries, you can complete the chart.

SEMITIC			GREEK		ROMAN	
Hebrew letters	*Hebrew letter names*	*Phoenician letters*	*letters*	*letter names*	*Classic Latin letters*	*Modern English letters*
א	aleph	＜	A	alpha	A	A
ב		△				
ג		ᒆ				
ד		△				
ה		∃				
ו		Y	F	digamma		
ז		I				
ח		Ⴌ				
ט		⊕				
י		Ƨ				
כ		⅄				
ל		∟				
מ		♍				
נ		ⴕ				
ס		○				
ע		⊃				
פ		⋉				
צ		Φ	Q	koppa		
ק		ⵚ				
ר		W				
ת		X				

3.10 THE CYRILLIC ALPHABET

The Cyrillic alphabet, used in Russian and some other Slavic languages, is a development of the Greek alphabet. A comparison of the Cyrillic letter shapes with those of Greek will reveal many similarities. The alphabet given here is the form of Cyrillic used in writing Russian; there are slight differences for other languages.

LETTER	TRANSLITERATION	LETTER	TRANSLITERATION	LETTER	TRANSLITERATION
А а	a	Л л	l	Ц ц	ts
Б б	b	М м	m	Ч ч	ch
В в	v	Н н	n	Ш ш	sh
Г г	g	О о	o	Щ щ	shch
Д д	d	П п	p	Ъ ъ	none
Е е	e	Р р	r	Ы ы	y
Ж ж	zh	С с	s	Ь ь	' (palatalization)
З з	z	Т т	t	Э э	e
И и	i	У у	u	Ю ю	yu
Й й	i (in diphthongs)	Ф ф	f	Я я	ya
К к	k	Х х	kh		

Transliterate these Russian words:

Чехов	_____	Пушкин	_____
Хрущев	_____	самовар	_____
Толстой	_____	спутник	_____
дрожки	_____	рубль	_____
степь	_____	бабушка	_____
интеллигенция	_____	тройка	_____

3.11 THE RUNIC INSCRIPTION OF THE RUTHWELL CROSS

The Ruthwell Cross is a Scottish stone monument that has engraved upon it part of an Old English poem, "The Dream of the Rood." The inscription, which is in runic symbols, has been badly damaged by the ravages of the weather and of the Scottish Covenanters, who objected to "idolatrous monuments." In the 1640s the cross was broken into pieces and cast into the churchyard; consequently the inscription is now fragmentary. Most of what survives is reproduced here, with some of the missing letters supplied; the text has also been divided into words, although in the original the runes follow one another without spaces. The speaker in the poem is the True Cross, which relates the events of the Crucifixion as the Old English poet conceived them. The poem dates from the early eighth century and is in the Northumbrian dialect.

NE FRAGMENT

ongeredæ hinæ god almeʒttig þa he walde on galgu gistiga modig

TRANSLITERATION AND GLOSS

ongeredæ hinæ ḡod almeʒttig þa he walde on ḡalḡu gistiḡa modig
Unclothed himself god almighty. For he would onto the cross ascend courageous.

SE FRAGMENT

Ahof ic riicnæ kyninc heafunæs hlafard hælda ic ni dorstæ bismærædu uŋket men þa ætʒadræ ic wæs miþ blodæ bistemid

TRANSLITERATION AND GLOSS

ahof ic riicnæ k̄yniŋc heâfunæs hlafard hælda ic ni dorstæ bismærædu uŋ̄ket men
Lifted up I a great king, heaven's Lord. Bow I did not dare. Mocked us two men

þa ætḡadræ ic wæs miþ blodæ bistemid
both together.[1] I was with blood bedewed.

SW FRAGMENT

krist wæs on rodi hweþræ þer fusæ fearran kwomn æþþilæ til anum ic þæt al biheald saræ ic wæs miþ sorgum gidræfid

TRANSLITERATION AND GLOSS

krist wæs on rodi hweþræ þer fusæ feârran kwomu æþþilæ til
Christ was on the cross. And there hastening from afar came noblemen[2] towards (me)

anum ic þæt al biheâld saræ ic wæs miþ sorḡum gidrœfid
alone. I that all beheld. Sorely I was with sorrows troubled.

---

[1]That is, "Men mocked both us two together."
[2]Joseph of Arimathea and Nicodemus.

ᛗᛁᚦ ᛋᛏᚱᛖᛚᚢᛗ ᚷᛁᚹᚢᚾᛞᚪᛞ ᚪᛚᛖᚷᛞᚢᚾ

ᚻᛁᚪ ᚻᛁᚾᛖ ᛚᛁᛗᚹᛟᚱᛁᚷᚾᛖ ᚷᛁᛋᛏᚩᛞᛞᚢᚾ

ᚻᛁᛗ ᚪᛏ ᚻᛁᛋ ᛚᛁᚳᛖᛋ ᚻᛠᚠᛞᚢᛗ ᛒᛁᚻᛠᛚᛞᚢᚾ

ᚻᛁᛖ ᚦᛖᚱ ᚻᛠᚠᚢᚾᛖᛋ ᛞᚱᚣᚻᛏᛖᚷ.

TRANSLITERATION AND GLOSS

Miþ strelum   alegdun hiæ
          giwundad   hinæ Limwærignæ

(I was)	with	arrows	wounded.	Laid down	they	him	weary in limb.

gistoddun him æt his Liæs heafdum

They stood	by him	at	his	body's	head.

bihealdun hiæ þer heafunæs dryhteg (or- hLafard

Beheld	they	there	heaven's	(Lord.)	ACCORDING TO FRAGMENT 2) ?

— 1. Complete the chart below by giving the transliteration for each rune.
— 2. Transliterate the runic letters of the fourth fragment in the blanks provided above.
 3. What does the style in which the letters are made—angular with few curves—suggest about the original material and method for writing runes?

THE FUTHORC

RUNE	TRANS.	RUNE	TRANS.	RUNE	TRANS.	RUNE	TRANS.
ᚠ	F	ᚻ	h	↑	t	ᚪ	a
ᚢ	U	ᛏ	t	ᛒ	b	ᚨ	æ
ᚦ (THORN)	þ/TH	ᛁ	i	ᛖ	e	ᛗ	Y
ᚨ	o	ᛉ	io	ᛗ	M	ᛡ	ea
ᚱ	r	�	3	ᛚ	L	ᛣ	k
ᚳ	c	ᛈ	p	ᛇ	⟋	ᛤ	k̄
ᚷ	g	ᛦ	x	ᛟ	oe	ᚸ	ḡ
ᚹ (2.)	p/w	ᛋ	s	ᚻ	d		

The illustration below is a page from an Old English manuscript (British Museum Manuscript Cotton Julius E vii, folio 59) written in the Insular hand, probably in the early eleventh century.

In the middle of the page, at the large capital letter, there begins a homily with the Latin title "VII ID*US MARTIAS NATALE SANCTORUM* QUADRAGINTA MILITUM," that is, "The Seventh Day Before the Ides of March: Feast of the Holy Forty Soldiers." (Italics or underlining can be used to indicate an expanded abbreviation.)

At the top of the page is the end of another homily, which includes the story of the virgin St. Felicula, who was a companion of St. Peter's daughter, Petronilla. Felicula had received unwanted amorous attention from an important and powerful pagan named Flaccus. The fragment of the story on this page tells how she spurned Flaccus and how he took revenge. The passage is translated and partly transliterated here; complete the transliteration.

Notice that word division does not always conform to modern practice. Notice also the letter shapes that differ significantly from modern forms, especially *g, r*, the three forms of *s*, the letter called *edh*, and the runes *thorn* and *wynn*. Occasionally and inconsistently the scribes used a mark like an acute accent over a vowel to show length; it can be transliterated with a macron.

(Ne beo) ic næfre þin wif · forðan þe ic sylfwylles eom criste gehalgod · ne ic
(Not shall be) I never thine wife because I of my own will am to Christ hallowed, nor I

þam hæþenum godum lac ne geoffrige · forðan þe ic on crist gelyfe · Þa · hēt
to the heathen gods sacrifice not will offer because I in Christ believe. Then commanded

se arleasa flaccus · þa fæmnan gebringan on þysterfullum cwearterne · & cwæþ ·
the merciless Flaccus the virgin to be brought into a dark prison and said

þæt man ne sceolde ænigne bigleofan hire dōn binnon seofon nihton ·
that one not should any food her give for seven nights.

She	dwelt	then	so	seven	nights	meatless,	and	afterwards	was
tortured	for	the	true	faith	and	for	her	maidhood	until	she
was	martyred,	and	her	ghost	fared	free	to	heaven.	Then	came
Nicomedis	the	foresaid	mass-priest,	and	buried	her	body	to
praise	of the	Almighty.	Then	seized	Flaccus	the	faithful
priest,	and	because	he	would not	to the	foul	gods	offer,
commanded	him	to be scourged	until	he	died.	He	departed	then
to	heaven	to	the Savior	Christ,	to whom	is	glory	and	honor
in	all	worlds'	worlds.[3]	Amen.

---

[3] That is, 'world without end.'

3.13   LATER MEDIEVAL WRITING

After the Norman Conquest, the Insular hand, which Englishmen had learned from Irish scribes, was replaced by a form of writing often called "Gothic." On the next page is the opening of Chaucer's *Canterbury Tales*, written in this style by an unknown scribe. The first twenty-seven lines are transcribed in exercise 6.9, where the italicized letters are expansions of abbreviations indicated by lines of various sorts above the words in the manuscript. Opposite line 8, there is a marginal comment in Latin, *sol in ariete* 'sun in Aries.'

Having compared the first half of the page with its transcription, you can transcribe the bottom twenty-one lines here:

_____

_____

_____

_____

_____

_____

_____

_____

_____

_____

_____

_____

_____

_____

_____

_____

_____

Whan that Aprill with his shoures soote
The droghte of March hath perced to the roote
And bathed every veyne in swich licour
Of which vertu engendred is the flour
Whan Zephirus eek with his sweete breeth
Inspired hath in every holt and heeth
The tendre croppes, and the yonge sonne
Hath in the Ram his half cours yronne
And smale foweles maken melodye
That slepen al the nyght with open eye
So priketh hem nature in hir corages
Thanne longen folk to goon on pilgrimages
And palmeres for to seken straunge strondes
To ferne halwes, kowthe in sondry londes
And specially from every shires ende
Of Engelond to Caunterbury they wende
The hooly blisful martir for to seke
That hem hath holpen whan that they were seeke

Bifil that in that seson on a day
In Southwerk at the Tabard as I lay
Redy to wenden on my pilgrymage
To Caunterbury with ful devout corage
At nyght was come in to that hostelrye
Wel nyne and twenty in a compaignye
Of sondry folk, by aventure yfalle
In felaweshipe, and pilgrimes were they alle
That toward Caunterbury wolden ryde
The chambres and the stables weren wyde
And wel we weren esed atte beste
And shortly, whan the sonne was to reste
So hadde I spoken with hem everichon
That I was of hir felaweshipe anon
And made forward erly for to ryse
To take oure wey ther as I yow devyse

But nathelees, whil I have tyme and space
Er that I ferther in this tale pace
Me thynketh it acordaunt to resoun
To telle yow al the condicioun
Of ech of hem, so as it semed me
And whiche they were, and of what degree
And eek in what array that they were inne
And at a knyght than wol I first bigynne

A knyght ther was and that a worthy man
That fro the tyme that he first bigan
To riden out, he loved chivalrie
Trouthe and honour, fredom and curteisie
Ful worthy was he in his lordes werre
And therto hadde he riden no man ferre

Knyght

59

Every sound in present-day English can be spelled in more than one way. Although some of the variation is not predictable by general rule and depends merely on what word the sound occurs in, much of it is systematic. What spelling is used for a vowel depends on such factors as (1) whether the vowel is lax [æ, ɛ, ɪ, ɑ, ɔ, ə, ʊ] or tense [e, i, o, u] or diphthongal [aɪ, aʊ, ɔɪ]; (2) whether the vowel occurs in the last syllable of a word or some other; and (3) whether a tense or diphthongal vowel is followed by a consonant or not. The spelling patterns illustrated here apply to full or stressed vowels only; reduced or unstressed vowels must be treated in a somewhat different way.

The following list contains examples of the principal vowel spellings. In two-syllable words, the significant vowel is italicized.

bait	deuce	lye	pi	rude	soul
bay	dew	lyre	p*i*lot	rue	sow [o]
but	d*u*ty	made	proud	scene	sty
b*u*tter	Hind*u*	Mae	prow	sea	stylus
coat	laud	me	p*u*llet	seat	tide
coc*oa*	law	m*e*ter	put	see	tie
c*o*ffer [ɔ]	let	pa [ɑ]	qua [e]	seed	toe
cog [ɔ]	l*e*tter	p*a*pa	qu*a*si [e]	shook	tone
coil	lit	pat	rot	so	too
coy	l*i*tter	p*a*tter	r*o*tten	s*o*fa	toot

1. There are two regular spelling patterns for lax vowels: (1) the VC pattern, when the vowel is in the last (or only) syllable of a word such as *sum*, and (2) the VCCV pattern, when the vowel is in other than the last syllable of a word such as *summer* and is followed by at least two consonant letters in the spelling.

   Provide examples of both spelling patterns from the above list for each of the following lax vowels:

	VC	VCCV
[æ]	_____	_____
[ɛ]	_____	_____
[ɪ]	_____	_____
[ɑ]	_____	_____
[ɔ]	_____	_____
[ə]	_____	_____
[ʊ]	_____	_____

2. There are several regular spelling patterns used primarily for tense vowels and diphthongs:
   (1) The vowel may be spelled with a single letter if it is followed by a single consonant and another vowel (VCV as in *veto*) or sometimes if it is the final sound of a word (V as in *we*).
   (2) When it is followed by a word-final consonant, the vowel may be spelled by a single letter and a "silent *e*" after the consonant (VC*e* as in *pine*). If there is no following consonant, so that the vowel comes at the end of the word, the "silent *e*" may still be used (V*e* as in *pie*).
   (3) The vowel may be spelled by a digraph consisting of two vowel letters whether there is a following consonant (VVC as in *read*) or not (VV as in *tree*). The second vowel in this pattern will be *a*, *e*, or *o*.

(4) The vowel may be spelled with a digraph ending in *i* or *u* before a consonant (V*i*C or V*u*C as in *paid* or *pout*) or ending in *y* or *w* otherwise (V*y* or V*w* as in *pay* or *pow*).

Provide examples from the list for each of the following vowels (the last three are lax vowels that use the tense patterns):

	VCV	V	VC*e*	V*e*	VVC	VV	V*i*/*u*C	V*y*/*w*
[e]	_____	_____	_____	_____			_____	_____
[i]	_____	_____	_____		_____	_____		
					_____	_____		
[aɪ]	_____	_____	_____		_____	_____		
	_____	_____	_____					
[o]	_____	_____	_____	_____	_____	_____	_____	_____
[u]	_____	_____	_____	_____	_____	_____	_____	_____
[aʊ]							_____	_____
[ɔɪ]							_____	_____
[ə]							_____	_____
[ɑ]	_____	_____						
[ʊ]					_____			

3.15 MODERN SPELLING: CONSONANTS

1. The consonants, like the vowels, have some spellings that are unpredictable and others that fall into regular patterns. The following list illustrates the simplest spelling of each consonant: *fed, jag, kin, chip, bosh, thing, them, visual, haze, yes, rot, we.*

Which five consonant sounds illustrated above are spelled with digraphs?

_____

In the above list what two phonemes does *th* stand for? _____

s? _____

The remaining seventeen consonants have relatively unambiguous single-letter spellings. What are the

sounds? _____

_____

2. After a lax vowel, a nonfinal single consonant sound is typically spelled with a digraph. Spell the words indicated by the following transcriptions.

[súpər]	_____	[rúdər]	_____	[kómə]	_____
[sə́pər]	_____	[rə́dər]	_____	[kámə]	_____
[létər]	_____	[táɪgər]	_____	[pínəl]	_____
[lǽtər]	_____	[trígər]	_____	[pénənt]	_____
[pókər]	_____	[réčəl]	_____	[hélo]	_____
[pákət]	_____	[sǽčəl]	_____	[hǽlo]	_____
[fáɪbər]	_____	[kójənt]	_____	[sófə]	_____
[fíbər]	_____	[stáji]	_____	[tófi]	_____

What spellings are used instead of double letters for [k] _____, [č] _____, and [ǰ] _____?

3. Consider the spellings for the following words:

[stəf]	[dɪč]	[briz]
[pæs]	[dɑǰ]	[čiz]
[fɪz]	[gɪv]	[hɪnǰ]
[tɛl]	[lis]	[vælv]
[pæk]	[pis]	[brið]

Which consonants have special spellings used at the end of a word after a lax vowel? Give the spellings:

_____

Which consonants have special spellings used at the end of a word after a tense vowel or a consonant?

Give the spellings: _____

The letters *v* and *j* only very rarely occur at the end of a word. List any words you can with final *v* or *j*.

_____

3.16 FOREIGN INFLUENCE ON THE ENGLISH WRITING SYSTEM

Many languages have contributed to the shaping of Modern English orthography. Look up the etymologies of the following words in a dictionary, and tell to which language we owe each of the indicated spellings.

bdellium: *bd* for /d/ _____

bhang: *bh* for /b/ _____

bijou: *j* for /ž/ _____

bivouac: *ou* for /w/ _____

bouillabaisse: *ill* for /y/ _____

cello: *c* for /č/ _____

chance: *ch* for /č/ _____

chaos: *ch* for /k/ _____

charabanc: *nc* for /ŋ/ _____

chauffeur: *ch* for /š/ _____

city: *c* for /s/ _____

czar: *cz* for /z/ _____

dhoti: *dh* for /d/ _____

Don Quixote: *x* for /h/ _____

façade: *ç* for /s/ _____

fascist: *sc* for /š/ _____

gem: *g* for /ǰ/ _____

ghetto: *gh* for /g/ _____

grotesque: *que* for /k/ _____

guide: *gu* for /g/ _____

junker: *j* for /y/ _____

junta: *j* for /h/ _____

khaki: *kh* for /k/ _____

llama: *ll* for /l/ _____

meerschaum: *sch* for /š/ _____

memoir: *o* for /w/ _____

meringue: *ngue* for /ŋ/ _____

mnemonic: *mn* for /n/ _____

phlegm: *gm* for /m/ _____

phrase: *ph* for /f/ _____

pretzel: *z* for /s/ _____

ptomaine: *pt* for /t/ _____

quit: *q* for /k/ _____

regime: *g* for /ž/ _____

reign: *gn* for /n/ _____

rhythm: *rh* for /r/ _____

science: *sc* for /s/ _____

thyme: *th* for /t/ _____

vignette: *gn* for /ny/ _____

vogue: *gue* for /g/ _____

xylophone: *x* for /z/ _____

3.17 LEARNED AND PSEUDOLEARNED RESPELLINGS

The spellings of some words have been changed by men with more sense of historical continuity than of contemporary reality. Thus a learned *b* was inserted in Middle English *det* to show that it is ultimately derived from Latin *debitum*. Sometimes these learned respellings, such as the *h* added to earlier *trone*, have resulted in new pronunciations. Occasionally, those who like to tinker with orthography have possessed more enthusiasm than knowledge. As a result, some words have been respelled to show a wrong etymology; the pseudolearned *comptroller* for *controller* is a case in point.

1. The following Modern English words have remodeled spellings. Compare their current spellings with earlier written forms of the words, which you will find in the etymological entry of a desk dictionary or in the *Oxford English Dictionary*. In the blanks, write the *consonants* that have been added to the spellings. Be prepared to discuss whether the respelling has influenced the pronunciation of the word and whether the respelling is a learned one such as *debt* and *throne* or a pseudolearned one such as *comptroller*.

_____	adventure	_____	island	_____	schedule
_____	aisle	_____	limb 'arm or leg'	_____	schism
_____	anthem	_____	mortgage	_____	school
_____	asthma	_____	myrrh	_____	scythe
_____	bankrupt	_____	nephew	_____	soldier
_____	could	_____	palm	_____	sovereign
_____	delight	_____	perfect	_____	subtle
_____	falcon	_____	receipt	_____	vault
_____	foreign	_____	rhyme	_____	verdict
_____	indict	_____	salmon	_____	victual

2. Consult the *OED* to find the centuries in which the foregoing words were first respelled to include the new consonants. Indicate here the number of words respelled in each century:

before 1200 _____	1400–1500 _____	1700–1800 _____
1200–1300 _____	1500–1600 _____	1800–1900 _____
1300–1400 _____	1600–1700 _____	after 1900 _____

3.18 SPELLING PRONUNCIATIONS

1. *Origins and Development* mentions, as examples of words that have acquired spelling pronunciations, *often, forehead, clapboard, grindstone,* and the proper names *Daventry, Shrewsbury,* and *Cirencester.* Below are some additional examples. For some of these words, a spelling pronunciation is uncommon in educated speech; for others, it is almost universal and completely respectable. By comparing your normal pronunciation of these words with their spelling and with the pronunciations listed in a dictionary, try to determine the traditional pronunciation and the spelling pronunciation.

balk	draught	holm	thither
bass 'drum'	falcon	human	thyme
blackguard	forecastle	isthmus	tortoise
boatswain	gooseberry	kiln	toward
bourbon 'whiskey'	grovel	lichen	wainscot
breeches	guerdon	lightwood	waistcoat
brooch	gunwale	oboe	Wednesday
Christmas	halfpenny	pestle	wont
conduit	handkerchief	steelyard	worsted
dour	hiccough	sumac	yolk

Birmingham	Edinburgh	Milne	Pembroke
Concord	Greenwich	Norfolk	St. John
Cowper	Home	Norwich	Southwark

2. Suggest some additional examples of spelling pronunciation from your own experience.

_____

_____

4 THE BACKGROUNDS OF ENGLISH

4.1 FOR REVIEW AND DISCUSSION

1. Define the following terms:

Proto-Indo-European (Indo-European)	satem language	athematic verb
Indo-European family	centum language	case
language family	reconstruction	nominative
Nostratic	Indo-Iranian	vocative
Proto-World	Armenian	accusative
isolating language	Albanian	genitive
agglutinative language	Tocharian	dative
incorporative language	Anatolian	ablative
inflective language	Balto-Slavic	locative
typological classification	Hellenic	instrumental
genetic classification	koine	VO language
Semitic	Italic	OV language
Hamitic	Sprachbund	present tense
Afroasiatic	Romance	preterit tense
Nilo-Saharan	Vulgar Latin	dental suffix
Niger-Kordofanian	Celtic	weak verb
Khoisan	Germanic	strong verb
Dravidian	Proto-Germanic	weak declension
Sino-Tibetan	North Germanic	strong declension
Austronesian	West Germanic	stress
Uto-Aztecan	East Germanic	pitch
Kechumaran	cognate	First Sound Shift (Grimm's Law)
Ural-Altaic	inflective	Verner's Law
Uralic	inflection	rhotacism
Samoyed	grammatical function	Second (High German) Sound Shift
Finno-Ugric	thematic vowel	
Altaic	root	
	stem	

2. How can similarities among languages be explained? Consider, for example, English *ma* and Chinese *ma* 'mother,' English *bong* and German *Bam* 'noise of a bell,' English *filly* and French *fille* 'girl,' English *goober* and Bantu *nguba* 'peanut,' English *brother* and Russian *brat* 'brother.'

3. To what extent can we explain why languages change? Consider the passage of time, geographical separation, and analogy as contributing factors.

4. Some grammarians believe that, because language can be described as behavior governed by rules, most language change is rule change. That is, a speaker learns a new rule or drops an old rule or modifies it, thus altering his grammar or pronunciation. Does the idea of rule change favor the view that language change is sudden or that it is gradual?

5. What metaphors are commonly used to describe the connections that exist among languages?

6. What are some of the more important non-Indo-European language groups?

7. What linguistic features are shared by all Indo-European languages; that is, how are all Indo-European languages alike?

8. What is the special meaning in linguistics of an asterisk before a word?

9. What kinds of words are shared by all Indo-European languages?

10. On what kind of evidence do we base our conclusions about Indo-European culture and the original Indo-European homeland?

11. What are the main subgroups of Indo-European?

12. What linguistic features, shared by all Germanic languages, differentiate them from other branches of Indo-European?

4.2 LANGUAGE TYPES

The older and often imprecise classification of languages into four types (isolating, agglutinative, inflective, and incorporative) has been greatly refined by modern scholars. For a rough and ready classification, however, the four terms are still useful, although linguists no longer use them to imply an evolutionary development in language. The following examples will illustrate the four types.

1. An *isolating* language is one in which words tend to be one syllable long and invariable in form. They take no inflections or other suffixes. The function of words in a sentence is shown primarily by word order.

CHINESE: Ni men ti hua wo pu tu tung.
'I do not entirely understand your language.'

Ni   men   ti   hua   wo pu   tu   tung
you / plural / possessor / language / I / not / all / understand

2. An *agglutinative* language is one in which words tend to be made up of several syllables. Typically each word has a base or stem and a number of affixes. The affixes are quite regular; they undergo very little change regardless of what base they are added to. (In this example, *m* is used after vowels; *im*, after consonants.)

TURKISH: Babam kardeşime bir mektup yazdırdı.
'My father had my brother write a letter.'

Baba -m kardeş -im -e   bir mektup yaz   -dır   -dı
father / my / brother / my / dative case / a / letter / write / cause to / past tense

3. *Inflective* languages are like agglutinative ones in that each word tends to have a number of suffixes. In an inflective language, however, the suffixes often show great irregularity in varying their shape according to the word-base to which they are added. Also, a single suffix tends to express a number of different grammatical concepts.

LATIN: Arma virumque canō.
'I sing about weapons and a man.'

Arm   -a   vir -um   -que
weapon / neuter accusative plural / man / masculine accusative singular / and

can   -ō
sing / first person singular present indicative

4. An *incorporative* language is one in which the verb and the subject or object of a sentence may be included in a single word. What we would think of as the main elements of a sentence are joined in one word and have no independent existence. (Read the italic gloss by starting at the end and working toward the beginning.)

ESKIMO: Qasuiirsarvigssarsingitluinarnarpuq.
'Someone did not at all find a suitable resting place.'

Qasu -iir -sar -vig -ssar -si -ngit -luinar
tired / not / causing to be / place for / suitable / find / not / completely /

-nar -puq
someone / third person singular indicative mood

To which of the four types does each of these languages seem to belong?

1. Ya dumayu, chto eto samyĭ malen'kiĭ iz vsekh gorodov Rossii.
   'I think that this is the smallest of all the cities of Russia.'

   Ya duma -yu chto eto sam
   I / think / first person singular present tense / that / this / most /

   -yĭ malen'k -iĭ iz
   masculine nominative singular / small / masculine nominative singular / out of /

   vs -ekh gorod -ov Rossi -i
   all / genitive plural / city / masculine genitive plural / Russia / feminine genitive singular

   TYPE: _____

2. Lần-lần dân-chúng học làm chính-trị.
   'Little by little the masses are learning to engage in politics.'

   Lần lần dân chúng học làm chính trị
   time / time / people / multitude / learn / make / government / rule

   TYPE: _____

3. La maljuna viro kreskigis malgrandan pomarbaron.
   'The old man cultivated a small apple orchard.'

   La mal- jun -a vir -o kresk -ig -is mal-
   the / un- / young / adjective / man / noun / grow / cause to / past tense / un- /

   grand -a -n pom -arb -ar -o -n
   large / adjective / accusative / apple / tree / collection / noun / accusative

   TYPE: _____

4. Ua mau ke ea o ka 'aina i ka pono.
   'The life of the land is preserved in righteousness.'

   Ua mau ke ea o ka 'aina i ka pono
   perfect aspect / constant / the / life / of / the / land / in / the / goodness

   (In this language, *ke* occurs before words beginning with *e, a, o,* and *k; ka,* otherwise.)

   TYPE: _____

5. Tis ara houtos estin, hoti kai ho anemos kai hē thalassa hypakouei autōi?
   'Who then is this, that both the wind and the sea obey him?'

   Ti -s ara hout -os
   who / masculine nominative singular / then / this / masculine nominative singular /

   es -tin hoti kai
   be / third person singular present indicative / that / and /

h	-o		anem	-os		kai

the / masculine nominative singular / wind / masculine nominative singular / and /

h	-ē		thalass	-a

the / feminine nominative singular / sea / feminine nominative singular /

hypakou -ei		aut	-ōi

obey / third person singular present indicative / same / masculine dative singular

TYPE: _____

6. Kahä'eisibäti.
'He fractured his skull.'

Kah	-ä'ei	-si	-bä	-ti

blow, strike / head / be in condition of / cause to / third person singular intransitive verb

TYPE: _____

7. Watu walivitaka vitabu vikubwa vyote.
'The men wanted all the big books.'

Wa-	tu	wa-	li-	vi-	taka	vi-	tabu	vi-	kubwa	vy-	ote

plural / person / they / past / them / want / plural / book / plural / big / plural / all

TYPE: _____

8. Waʔshagnihwẹhtọnięʔ bil.
'We made a snowsnake [stick used in winter games] for Bill.'

Waʔ-	shag-	ni-	hwẹht-	ọni	-ẹ

nonfuture definite event / I-him / dual subject / snowsnake / make / for /

-ʔ		bil

event occurring only once / Bill

TYPE: _____

The eight languages above are Russian, Vietnamese, Esperanto, Hawaiian, Greek, Arapaho, Swahili, and Onondaga.

The four language types are, of course, merely abstractions. No real language belongs entirely to any one type. For example, the English use of monosyllables like *to, for, when, not, must, the*, and *or*, and its reliance on word order to signal grammatical meaning would seem to make it an isolating language. However, the existence of paradigms like *ox, ox's, oxen, oxen's*; *show, shows, showing, showed, shown*; and *good, better, best* is typical of inflective languages. Words like *activistic* which are built up by adding suffixes one by one to a stem (*act, active, activist, activistic*) are characteristic of agglutinative languages. And verb forms like *to baby-sit* or *horseback-riding* are the hallmark of an incorporative language. It is difficult to pigeonhole English, or for that matter most other languages, when we are using only four impressionistic classifications.

Another more precise gauge is an index of synthesis to indicate whether a language is analytic, synthetic, or polysynthetic. The index may be found in the following way. Take a passage written in the language you wish to type; the longer the passage, the more accurate the index will be. Count the number of words in the passage (W). Count the number of morphemes, that is, the smallest meaningful elements, in the passage (M). Divide the number of morphemes by the number of words (M/W). The result will be the index of synthesis.

For example, the Chinese sentence we examined earlier has eight words; it also has eight morphemes. The index of synthesis is thus 8/8, or 1.00. The Turkish sentence has five words, but ten morphemes, as we see when the sentence is broken into its smallest meaningful units. The index of synthesis is 10/5, or 2.00. The Eskimo example is a single word, but it has ten morphemes. The index of synthesis is 10/1, or 10.00.

The index of synthesis for a language tells us on the average how many morphemes are present in each word. If our results for the three languages we examined were accurate, we could say that Chinese words have on the average one morpheme each, Turkish words have an average of two morphemes each, and Eskimo words have an average of ten morphemes each. However, these samples are far too short for reliable results. For Eskimo especially our conclusion is highly suspect; we used only one word to figure the average, and an index of 10.00 is unbelievably high for any language.

A low index of synthesis, something approaching 1.00, tells us that the language is *analytic*. Isolating languages are analytic. A higher index of synthesis, somewhere between 1.50 and 2.50, characterizes the language as *synthetic*. Agglutinative and inflective languages are both synthetic. A very high index of synthesis, something around 3.00 or above, identifies the language as *polysynthetic*. Incorporative languages are polysynthetic.

Now go back to the Latin sentence we used to illustrate an inflective language, and compute the index of synthesis for it.

Number of words in the sentence (W): _____
Number of morphemes in the sentence (M): _____
Number of morphemes divided by number of words (M/W) equals an index of: _____

The correct answer is 2.33 (round off the division to the second decimal place).

This single index is a very useful device for comparing languages. Below are four versions of the same Biblical passage in Latin, Old English, Middle English, and early Modern English. To assist you, the words have been divided by hyphens into their constituent morphemes. Words are separated from one another by spaces. Some words, for example *sawe* in the early Modern English passage, count as two morphemes. One morpheme is the basic meaning of the word, 'see'; the second morpheme is the meaning 'past time,' and is shown by the changed vowel sound. Such internal change is represented by the symbol Ø; Ø should be counted as a separate morpheme. Compute the index of synthesis for each of the four passages and give your results in the space provided at the end of the exercise.

LATIN

Moses aut-em pasce-ba-t ov-es Jethro co-gna-t-i su-i sac-er-dot-is Madian: cum-que min-a-sse-t greg-em ad in-ter-ior-a de-sert-i, ven-i-t ad mont-em De-i Horeb. Ap-par-ui-t-que e-i Dom-in-us in flamm-a ign-is de medi-o rub-i: et vide-ba-t quod rub-us arde-re-t, et non com-bure-re-t-ur. Dix-i-t ergo Moses: Vad-a-m, et vide-b-o vis-ion-em hanc-Ø magn-am, qu-a-re-Ø non com-bura-t-ur rub-us. Cerne-n-s aut-em Dom-in-us quod
5 per-ge-re-t ad vide-nd-um, voca-vi-t e-um de medi-o rub-i, et a-i-t: Moses, Moses. Qu-i re-spond-i-t: Ad-su-m. At ill-e: Ne ap-propi-e-s, in-qu-i-t, huc: solv-e calc-e-ament-um de ped-ibus tu-is: loc-us enim, in qu-o sta-s, terr-a sanc-t-a es-t.

OLD ENGLISH

Sōð-līc-e Moyses hēold-Ø hy-s mǣg-es scēap-Ø, þ-æs sācerd-es, on Mādian; þ-æs nam-a wæ-Ø-s Iethro. And ðā hē drāf-Ø hi-s heord-e tō inn-e-weard-um þ-ām wēsten-e, hē cōm-Ø tō God-es dūn-e þe man Ōreph nemn-eþ. And Drihten hi-m æt-ēow-de on fīr-es līg-e on-midd-an ān-re brēmel-þyrn-an, and hē ge-seah-Ø þæt s-ēo ðyrn-e barn-Ø and n-æ-Ø-s for-burn-an. Ðā cwæð-Ø Moyses: Ic gā and ge-sēo þ-ā micl-an ge-sih-ð-e,
5 hw-ī þ-ēos þyrn-e ne sȳ-Ø for-bærn-ed. Sōð-līc-e Drihten ge-seah-Ø þæt hē fēr-de tō ge-sēo-nn-e; hē clyp-ode of midd-re þ-ǣre brēmel-þyrn-an, and cwæþ-Ø: Moyses! Moyses! And hē and-wyr-de, and cwæþ-Ø: Hēr

69

ic eo-m. And hē cwæþ-Ø: Ne ge-nēa-lǣc-e ðū hy-der; dō þī-n ge-scȳ-Ø of ðī-n-um fōt-um: sōþ-līc-e s-ēo stōw þe ðū on stent-st y-s hāl-ig eorð-e.

MIDDLE ENGLISH

Moyses for-soþ fed-Ø þe schepe-Ø of Iethro, hi-s wyu-ys fader, þe prest of Madyan, and whenn he ha-d dreu-en þe flock to þe inn-er-mo-re part-y of desert, he comme-Ø to þe hyll of god, Oreb, and þe lord a-peer-id to hy-m in a flawme of fyre from þe mydyll of a bosche. And he sey3-Ø þat þe bosch wa-Ø-s a-fyre, and wa-Ø-s not bren-t. Þann say-d Moyses, "I schall go and see þis grete si3-t, why þe bosch i-s not bren-t." And
5 þe lord by-hold-yng þat he 3e-de to see-n, clep-ed hy-m from þe mydyll of þe bosche and sey-þ, "Moyses, Moyses," þe which answer-d, "I a-m ny3." And he, "Ne come þou," he sei-þ, "no ne-rre hyþer, bot louse þou þi-n scho-ing frome þi-Ø fete-Ø. The place for-soþ þat þou stond-is inne i-s a hol-y londe."

EARLY MODERN ENGLISH

Nowe Moses kep-t the flocke of Iethro hi-s father in law, the Priest of Midian: and hee led-Ø the flocke to the back-side of the desert, and came-Ø to the mountaine of God, even to Horeb. And the Angel of the Lord appear-ed un-to hi-m, in a flame of fire out of the mid-st of a bush, and he look-ed, and be-hold, the bush burn-ed with fire, and the bush wa-Ø-s not con-sume-d. And Moses sai-de, I will nowe turne a-side, and see
5 this great sigh-t, why the bush i-s not burn-t. And when the Lord sawe-Ø that he turn-ed a-side to see, God call-ed un-to hi-m out of the mid-st of the bush, and sai-d, Moses, Moses. And he sai-de, Here a-m I. And he sai-d, Drawe not nigh hither: put off thy-Ø shoo-es from off thy-Ø feete-Ø, for the place where-on thou stand-est, is hol-y ground.

	LATIN	OLD ENGLISH	MIDDLE ENGLISH	MODERN ENGLISH
NUMBER OF WORDS				
NUMBER OF MORPHEMES				
INDEX OF SYNTHESIS				

Is Old English closer to Latin or to Modern English in its synthetic complexity?

_____

As measured by the synthetic complexity, did the greatest grammatical change in our language take place

between Old and Middle or between Middle and Modern English? _____

4.3 THE WORLD'S LANGUAGES (I)

The map on the following page shows the geographical distribution of non-Indo-European language groups with relation to Indo-European in the eastern hemisphere. Language groups in the western hemisphere are both more complex and less well defined. Complete the following key by writing the numbers from the map in the appropriate blanks.

12	Afroasiatic	7	Sino-Tibetan	9		New Guinea
13	Nilo-Saharan	6	Japanese	1		Basque
14	Niger-Kordofanian	5	Korean	2		Finno-Ugric
15	Khoisan	8	Austronesian	4		Altaic
11	Dravidian	10/3	Australian	3		Indo-European

4.4 THE WORLD'S LANGUAGES (II)

Using the numbers 1 through 15 from the preceding exercise, plus 16 for American Indian languages, identify the group to which each of the following belongs. You may need to consult a dictionary.

_____ Amharic	_____ Dinka	_____ Indonesian	_____ Nahuatl
_____ Arabic	_____ Eskimo	_____ Javanese	_____ Quechua
_____ Aymara	_____ Estonian	_____ Lappish	_____ Swahili
_____ Berber	_____ Fijian	_____ Malayalam	_____ Tagalog
_____ Bushman	_____ Finnish	_____ Manchu	_____ Tamil
_____ Chinook	_____ Geez	_____ Mandarin	_____ Tibetan
_____ Coptic	_____ Hawaiian	_____ Maori	_____ Turkish
_____ Creek	_____ Hebrew	_____ Menomini	_____ Xhosa
_____ Cushitic	_____ Hungarian	_____ Mongolian	_____ Zulu

4.5 THE LOCATION OF THE INDO-EUROPEAN LANGUAGES

The map that follows shows the main Indo-European language groups and some important non-Indo-European languages of Europe and the Near East. Complete the key by writing the numbers in the appropriate blanks.

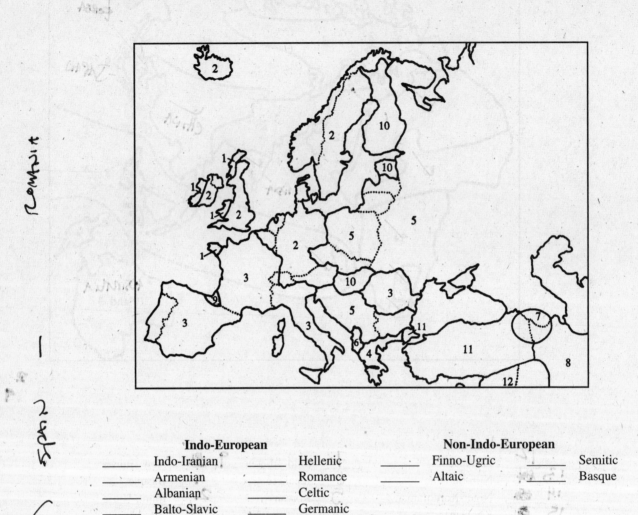

Indo-European

_____ Indo-Iranian
_____ Armenian
_____ Albanian
_____ Balto-Slavic

_____ Hellenic
_____ Romance
_____ Celtic
_____ Germanic

Non-Indo-European

_____ Finno-Ugric
_____ Altaic

_____ Semitic
_____ Basque

4.6 THE MAIN DIVISIONS OF THE INDO-EUROPEAN GROUP (I)

In describing the historical development of a language group we have recourse to various metaphors and "models." One such metaphor is that of the family, by which we speak of the Indo-European *parent* language with its various *descendants*. Another metaphor is the botanical one, by which we speak of the Indo-European *stem* with its several *branches*. These two metaphors are often combined in a family-tree model of language. Use the languages in the following list (which continues on page 74) to complete the family tree on the next page.

Aeolic	Bengali	Cornish	Flemish	Hindi
Afrikaans	Breton	Czech	French	Hindustani
Albanian	Bulgarian	Danish	Frisian	Hittite
Anglo-Norman	Burgundian	Doric	Galician	Icelandic
Armenian	Byelorussian	Dutch	Gaulish	Irish Gaelic
Attic-Ionic	Catalan	English	Gothic	Italian
Avestan	Classical Latin	Faeroese	High German	Latvian

Lithuanian • Norwegian • ✗Rhaeto-Romanic • Slovenian • Vulgar Latin •
Low German • Pali • Romanian • Spanish • Walloon ∽
Manx • ✗Picard • Romany • Swedish • Welsh •
Modern Greek ◄ Polish • Russian • Tocharian • Wendish •
Modern Persian ○ ✗Portuguese • Scots Gaelic • Ukrainian • Yiddish •
Mycenaean • Provençal • Serbo-Croatian • Urdu •
Norman • Prussian • Slovak • ✗Vandalic •

4.7   THE MAIN DIVISIONS OF THE INDO-EUROPEAN GROUP (II)

The circular diagram that follows may, at first sight, look quite different from a family tree, but it is merely a somewhat different way of schematizing the same information. The blocks around the outer rim of the wheel represent important modern Indo-European languages and are so labeled. The interior blocks represent successively larger and older groupings of the various languages. The central point of the circle stands for Proto-Indo-European, the hub from which the linguistic spokes radiate. Complete this wheel diagram by labeling the remaining blocks with the names or numbers of the language groups listed on page 75.

1. *Satem* languages
2. *Centum* languages
3. Indo-Iranian
4. Balto-Slavic
5. Germanic
6. Celtic
7. Italic
8. Hellenic
9. Indic
10. Iranic
11. Slavic

12. Baltic
13. East Germanic
14. North Germanic
15. West Germanic
16. Brythonic
17. Goidelic
18. Latin
19. Attic-Ionic
20. Sanskrit and Prakrits
21. Old Persian
22. South Slavic

23. East Slavic
24. West Slavic
25. Eastern North Germanic
26. Western North Germanic
27. Netherlandic-German
28. Anglo-Frisian
29. High German
30. Low German
31. Old Saxon
32. Old Low Franconian

4.8 A WAVE MODEL FOR INDO-EUROPEAN

Another way to look at relationships between languages is the wave model. It recognizes that a linguistic change begins among some speakers and spreads to others, like a wave expanding on the surface of a pond when a pebble has been tossed into the water. When several changes start among different speakers at different times and spread at different rates, the result is the creation of new dialects as speakers are affected by one or another of the changes. It is as though many pebbles were tossed into the water, some waves reinforcing one another, others overlapping. The wave diagram below shows the major dialect groups of Indo-European as the result of wavelike linguistic changes.

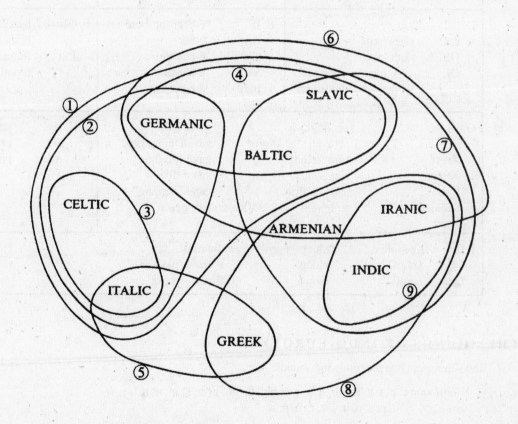

Below are descriptions of the linguistic changes that the wave diagram represents and a list of examples. Match the examples and the changes.

_____ **1.** Northern and western languages share a common vocabulary lacking in the other Indo-European dialects.

_____ **2.** The western languages share a common vocabulary.

_____ **3.** Italo-Celtic dialects have passive forms of the verb in *-r*.

_____ **4.** Northern languages have a dative plural case ending in *-m*.

_____ **5.** Italo-Hellenic dialects have voiceless sounds for the Indo-European voiced aspirates.

_____ **6.** In northern and eastern languages (except Indic) medial schwa was lost.

_____ **7.** In eastern languages, velars became sibilants in some cases, and labiovelars became velars.

_____ **8.** Southeastern languages have a prefixed vowel ("initial augment") in the past tense (aorist) forms of the verb.

_____ **9.** In Indo-Iranian, schwa became *i*.

EXAMPLES:

A. IE	*dhughǝtēr	**B. IE**	*porkos 'pig'	**C. Russ.**	stol 'table'	
Avest.	duɣðar-	Lat.	porcus		stolám 'to tables'	
Armen.	dustr	OIrish	orc	OE	stōl 'chair'	
Goth.	dauhtar	OE	fearh		stōlum 'to chairs'	
Lith.	duktē̃	Lith.	paȓšas	Lith.	výras 'man'	
OSlav.	dŭšti	OSlav.	prasę		výrams 'to men'	

D. IE	*wāt-	**E. IE**	*é-bherom 'bore'	**F. OIrish**	berait 'they bear'
Lat.	vātēs 'seer'	Armen.	e-ber		bertair 'are borne'
OIrish	fáith 'poet'	Gk.	é-pheron	Lat.	ferunt 'they bear'
OE	wōd 'mad, possessed'	Skt.	á-bharam		feruntur 'are borne'
	Wōden 'god of wisdom'	Iran.	a-berem		

G. IE	*keu/kū/kwā-	*gwei/gwoi-	**H. IE**	*pǝtḗr
Skt.	śv(áyati) 'be strong'	gáyaḥ 'household'	Skt.	pitár-
Avest.	sūra 'strong'	gayō 'lifetime'	Avest.	pitar-
Armen.	sun 'void'	keam 'live'		
Lith.	šaũnas 'firm'	gajùs 'healing'		
OSlav.	sujĭ 'vain'	(Russ.) goĭ 'peace'		

I. IE	*gher/ghor-	*bhleg- 'burn'	*dhūmos
Gk.	khordē̄ 'gut'	phlégō	thūmós 'passion'
Lat.	hernia	flagrō	fūmus 'smoke'

4.9   THE SOUNDS OF INDO-EUROPEAN

Indo-European had the following sounds:

Consonants: p, t, k, kw; b, d, g, gw; bh, dh, gh, gwh; s; m, n; r; l; y, w
Vowels: i, e, a, o, u; ī, ē, ā, ō, ū; ǝ

The nasals and liquids [m, n, r, l] could be either syllabic or nonsyllabic. Following the symbol for a stop, *h* indicates aspiration and *w* indicates that the stop was pronounced with rounded lips. The macron over a vowel indicates primarily length rather than a qualitative difference. Otherwise, the symbols have their usual phonetic value. Obviously the exact pronunciation of Indo-European is a matter of conjecture; thus other reconstructions are possible.

Indo-European at one time had several other phonemes, "laryngeals," the exact number and quality of which are uncertain, although they were presumably fricatives of some kind. They were lost early in the Indo-European period.

The charts below show the articulatory classification of the Indo-European sounds. Complete the charts by entering the phonetic symbols in the appropriate boxes.

CONSONANTS		LABIAL	DENTAL	PALATOVELAR	LABIOVELAR
STOPS	voiceless				
	voiced unaspirated				
	voiced aspirated				
FRICATIVE					
NASALS					
LIQUIDS	lateral				
	trill				
SEMIVOWELS					

VOWELS		FRONT	CENTRAL	BACK
HIGH	long			
	short			
MID	long			
	short			
LOW	long			
	short			

1. All Indo-European languages share some words that are similar in form and meaning. We may confidently suppose that these words are the historical survivals of Indo-European roots. Both form and meaning may, of course, change with time. Thus the Indo-European *oinos* 'one' has changed its form in Latin *ūnus* and Gothic *ains*; and in Greek *oinē* 'one-spot on a die,' it has both changed its form and narrowed its meaning.

    To illustrate the common Indo-European vocabulary as it appears in the various languages of the group, we may consider the following lists of words, all of which are cited on page 67 of *Origins and Development*. Compare the words with one another, observing similarities and differences. The differences are sometimes due to affixes and to vowel alternations in Indo-European; the reconstructed IE forms take into account some, though not all, such variation.

	heart	*lung*	*head*	*foot*
OE	heorte	lungen	hēafod	fōt
Ger.	Herz	Lungen	Haupt	Fuss
ON	hjarta	lunga	höfuð	fótr
Goth.	hairto	leihts 'light'	haubiþ	fotus
Lat.	cordis	levis 'light'	caput	pedis
Gk.	kardiā	elachus 'little'		podos
Russ.	serdtse	legkoe		(OSl.) podu 'ground'
Lith.	širdis	lengvas 'light'		pėda 'foot-track'
Ir.	cride	laigiu 'less'		
Skt.		laghus 'light'	kapāla- 'cup, skull'	pad-
IE	*kerd-	*le(n)gwh-	*kap-ut-	*ped-/pŏd-

	night	*star*	*snow*	*sun*	*moon*
OE	niht	steorra	snāw	sunne	mōna
Ger.	Nacht	Stern	Schnee	Sonne	Mond
ON	nátt	stjarna	snjár	sól, sunna	máni
Goth.	nahts	stairno	snaiws	sauil, sunno	mena
Lat.	noctis	stella	nivis	sōl	mēnsis 'month'
Gk.	nuktos	astēr	nipha	hēlios	mēn 'month'
Russ.	noch'		sneg	solntse	mesjats 'month'
Lith.	naktis		sniegas	saule	menuo
Ir.	nocht	(Br.) sterenn	snechte	(Br.) heol	mi 'month'
Skt.	naktam		snih- 'sticky'	sūrya-	mās- 'month'
IE	*nokwt-	*ster-	*sn(e/o)igwh-	*sāwel-/sun-	*mēn(ōt)-/mē(n)s-

	wind	*beech*	*corn*	*wolf*	*bear*
OE	wind	bēce	corn	wulf	bera
Ger.	Wind	Buche	Korn 'rye'	Wolf	Bär
ON	vindr	bók	korn	úlfr	björn
Goth.	winds	boka 'letter'	kaurn	wulfs	
Lat.	ventus	fāgus	grānum 'a grain'	lupus	
Gk.		phēgos 'oak'	gerōn 'old man'	lukos	
Russ.	veter		zerno	volk	berloga 'den'
Lith.	vejas		žirnis 'pea'	vilkas	beras 'brown'
Ir.	(Br.) gwent		grān		
Skt.	vātas		jīrna- 'worn out'	vrkas	bhallas
IE	*wē-nt-	*bhāgo-	*grno-	*wlkwo-/wlpo-	*bher-

	yoke	*mead*	*weave*	*sew*
OE	geoc	medu	wefan	siwian
Ger.	Joch	Met	weben	(OHG) siuwan
ON	ok	mjöðr	vefa	sýja
Goth.	juk			siujan
Lat.	iugum			suere
Gk.	zugon	methu 'wine'	huphainō	kas-suo 'sew together'
Russ.	igo	med		shit'
Lith.	jungas	medus 'honey'	austi	siuti
Ir.	cuing	mid	figim	
Skt.	yugam	madhu- 'liquor'	ūrna-vābhi = 'spider,' lit. 'wool-weaver'	sīv-
IE	*yugo-	*medhu-	*webh-	*syū-

2. Below are lists of words from ten Indo-European languages and a list of their reconstructed Indo-European sources. Use the blank tables that follow to sort the words into cognate lists like the ones in part 1 of this exercise.

Old English: brōþor, dohtor, ēast, eax, fæder, full, hund, mōdor, morðor 'murder,' nama, sunu, sweostor, Tīw, tōþ, widuwe

German: Achse, Bruder, Hund, Mord, Mutter, Name, Osten, Schwester, Sohn, Tochter, Vater, voll, Wittwe, Zahn, (OHG) Zio

Old Norse: austr, bróðir, dóttir, faðir, fullr, hundr, morðr, móðir, nafn, öxull, sunr, systir, tönn, Tȳr

Gothic: broþar, dauhtar, fadar, fulls, hunds, maurþr, namo, sunus, swistar, tunþus, widuwo

Latin: aurōra 'dawn,' axis, canis, dēns, frāter, Iuppiter, māter, mors, nōmen, pater, plēnus, soror, vidua

Greek: axōn, ēos 'dawn,' huios, kuōn, mētēr, mortos, odontos, onoma, patēr, phrātēr, plērēs, thugatēr, Zeus

Russian: brat, doč', imja, mat', mjortvyí, os', polnyĭ, sestra, suka 'bitch,' syn, vdova

Lithuanian: ašis, aušra 'dawn,' brōlis, dantis, diēvas 'god,' dukte, (OPruss.) emmens, mirtìs, mote 'woman,' pilnas, sesuo, sūnus, šuns, (OPruss.) widdewu

Irish: (Breton) ahel, ainm, athir, brāthir, cū, dēt, dia 'god,' fedb, lān, marb, māthir, siur

Sanskrit: akṣa-, bhrātar-, çvan-, dant-, duhitar-, dyaus-pitar, martas, mātar-, nāman-, pitar-, pūrna-, sūnu-, svasar-, uṣas 'dawn,' vidhavā

Indo-European: *aks-, *aus-, *bhrāter-, *deiwos/dyeu, *dent-/(o)dont-, *dhughətēr, *kw(o)n(-to)-/kan-i-, *māter-, *m(e)rt(r)-, *(o)nomen-, *pətēr-, *pləno-, *sunu-, *swesor-, *widhewā

	father	*mother*	*brother*	*sister*	*son*
OE	_____	_____	_____	_____	_____
Ger.	_____	_____	_____	_____	_____
ON	_____	_____	_____	_____	_____
Goth.	_____	_____	_____	_____	_____
Lat.	_____	_____	_____	_____	_____
Gk.	_____	_____	_____	_____	_____
Russ.		_____	_____	_____	_____
Lith.		_____	_____	_____	_____
Ir.	_____	_____	_____	_____	_____
Skt.	_____	_____	_____	_____	_____
IE	_____	_____	_____	_____	_____

	daughter	*widow*	*name*	*east*	*full*
OE	_____	_____	_____	_____	_____
Ger.	_____	_____	_____	_____	_____
ON	_____	_____	_____	_____	_____
Goth.	_____	_____	_____	_____	_____
Lat.	_____	_____	_____	_____	_____
Gk.	_____	_____	_____	_____	_____
Russ.	_____	_____	_____	_____	_____
Lith.	_____	_____	_____	_____	_____
Ir.	_____	_____	_____	_____	_____
Skt.	_____	_____	_____	_____	_____
IE	_____	_____	_____	_____	_____

	hound	*tooth*	*axle*	*Sky-father, god*	*mortal, death*
OE	_____	_____	_____	_____	_____
Ger.	_____	_____	_____	_____	_____
ON	_____	_____	_____	_____	_____
Goth.	_____	_____	_____	_____	_____
Lat.	_____	_____	_____	_____	_____
Gk.	_____	_____	_____	_____	_____
Russ.	_____		_____		_____
Lith.	_____	_____	_____		_____
Ir.	_____	_____	_____	_____	_____
Skt.	_____	_____	_____		_____
IE	_____	_____	_____		_____

3. For each of the following English words, find cognates in three or four other Indo-European languages. You can find cognates in the *American Heritage Dictionary of Indo-European Roots* by Calvert Watkins, *Chambers Dictionary of Etymology* by Robert K. Barnhart and Sol Steinmetz, *Comprehensive Etymological Dictionary of the English Language* by Ernest Klein, *Dictionary of Selected Synonyms in the Principal Indo-European Languages* by Carl Darling Buck, *Etymological Dictionary of the English Language* by Walter W. Skeat, *Indogermanisches Etymologisches Wörterbuch* by Julius Pokorny, *Oxford Dictionary of English Etymology* by C. T. Onions, and *Oxford English Dictionary* by James A. H. Murray and others.

acre _____

birch _____

bleat _____

blue _____

bright _____

comb _____

eat _____

fee _____

for _____

free _____

friend _____

give _____

have _____

mind _____

much _____

numb _____

oak _____

queen _____

right _____

that _____

thatch _____

thunder _____

town _____

tree _____

what _____

wheel _____

wit _____

worth _____

1. The following lists of the numbers 1 to 10 and 100 are from various Indo-European languages. The languages are grouped together according to the branch of the Indo-European family to which they belong. What similarities and differences can you find among the members of each branch? What similarities and differences are there among the various branches? (Some of the number words have slight irregularities in their development.)

Reconstructed Indo-European	GERMANIC				ARMENIAN	ALBANIAN
	English	German	Dutch	Danish	Armenian	Albanian
*oinos	one	eins	een	en	mi	nji
*dwō	two	zwei	twee	to	erku	dy
*treyes	three	drei	drie	tre	erek	tre
*kwetwor	four	vier	vier	fire	čork	katër
*penkwe	five	fünf	vijf	fem	hing	pesë
*s(w)eks	six	sechs	zes	seks	vec	gjashtë
*septm	seven	sieben	zeven	syv	evtn	shtatë
*oktō	eight	acht	acht	otte	ut	tetë
*newn	nine	neun	negen	ni	inn	nând
*dekm	ten	zehn	tien	ti	tasn	dhiet
*kmtom	hundred	hundert	honderd	hundrede	hariur	qind

ITALIC				CELTIC		HELLENIC
Latin	Italian	French	Spanish	Irish	Welsh	Greek
ūnus	uno	un	uno	aon	un	heis
duo	due	deux	dos	dó	daù	duo
trēs	tre	trois	tres	trí	tri	treis
quattuor	quattro	quatre	cuatro	ceathair	pedwar	tettares
quīnque	cinque	cinq	cinco	cúig	pump	pente
sex	sei	six	seis	sé	chwech	hex
septem	sette	sept	siete	seacht	saith	hepta
octō	otto	huit	ocho	ocht	wyth	oktō
novem	nove	neuf	nueve	naoi	naw	ennea
decem	dieci	dix	diez	deich	deg	deka
centum	cento	cent	ciento	céad	cant	hekaton

SLAVIC				BALTIC	IRANIC	INDIC
Russian	Polish	Bulgarian	Slovak	Lithuanian	Persian	Hindustani
odĭn	jeden	edin	jeden	vienas	yek	ek
dva	dwa	dva	dva	du	do	do
tri	trzy	tri	tri	trys	se	tin
chetyre	cztery	četiri	štyri	keturi	cahar	char
pyat'	pięć	pet	pät'	penki	panj	panch
shest'	sześć	šest	šest'	šeši	shesh	chha
sem'	siedem	sedem	sedem	septyni	haft	sat
vosem'	osiem	osem	osem	aštuoni	hasht	ath
devyat'	dziewięć	devet	devät'	devyni	noh	nau
desyat'	dziesięć	deset	desat'	dešimt	dah	das
sto	sto	sto	sto	šimtas	sad	sau

2. The languages from which the following numbers come are also Indo-European. By comparing these lists with the previous ones, you should be able to make a reasonable guess as to which branch of the Indo-European family each of these languages belongs. Write the name of the branch (Germanic, Armenian, Albanian, Italic, Celtic, Hellenic, Slavic, Baltic, Iranic, Indic) over each list.

	A	B	C	D	E	F
1	aon	jedinu	adzin	ains	onen	um
2	dha	duva	dva	twai	deu˙	dois
3	tri	trije	try	þrija	trȳ	três
4	ceithir	četyre	čatyry	fidwor	peswar	quatro
5	coig	pęti	piac'	fimf	pymp	cinco
6	sia	šesti	šesc'	saihs	whēgh	seis
7	seachd	sedmi	siem	sibun	seyth	sete
8	ochd	osmi	vosiem	ahtau	ēth	oito
9	naoi	devęti	dzieviac'	niun	naw	nove
10	deich	desęti	dziesiac'	taihun	dēk	dez
100	ceud	suto	sto	taihuntehund	cans	cem

	G	H	I	J	K	L
1	un	ein	yek	un	jedan	ān
2	dos	zwene	du	dos	dva	twēgen
3	tres	dri	se	tres	tri	þrȳ
4	quatre	fior	cwar	quatre	četiri	fēower
5	cinc	finf	penj	cinc	pet	fīf
6	seis	sehs	šest	sis	šest	syx
7	set	sibun	hewt	set	sedam	seofon
8	ueg	ahto	ešt	vuit	osam	eahta
9	nou	niun	no	nou	devet	nigon
10	detz	zehan	de	deu	deset	tȳn
100	cent	zehanzo	sed	cent	sto	hundtēontig

	M	N	O	P	Q	R
1	meg	eden	jeden	en	einn	ek
2	yergu	dva	dva	två	tveir	dui
3	yerek	tri	tři	tre	þrír	tin
4	čors	štiri	čtyři	fyra	fjórir	char
5	hing	pět	pět	fem	fimm	panch
6	vec	šest	šest	sex	sex	chhoe
7	yotə	sedem	sedm	sju	sjau	shat
8	utə	osem	osm	åtta	átta	at
9	innə	devet	devět	nio	níu	noe
10	dasə	deset	deset	tio	tíu	dosh
100	haryur	sto	sto	hundra	tíutigir	sho

3. Ten of the languages from which the following numbers come are Indo-European; the remaining eight are not. Distinguish the Indo-European languages from the non-Indo-European ones by writing *IE* or *non-IE* above each list.

	A	B	C	D	E	F
1	en	un	bir	jedyn	egy	ün
2	twene	doui	iki	dwaj	két	duos
3	thria	trei	üç	tři	három	trais
4	fiuwar	patru	dört	štyri	négy	quatter
5	fif	cinci	beş	pjeć	öt	tschinch
6	sehx	şase	altı	šěsć	hat	ses
7	sibun	şapte	yedi	sedm	hét	set
8	ahto	opt	sekiz	wosm	nyolcz	och
9	nigun	nouă	dokuz	dźewjeć	kilencz	nouv
10	tehan	zice	on	dźesać	tíz	dêsch
100	hunderod	sută	yüz	sto	száz	tschient

	G	H	I	J	K	L
1	nigen	mot	unan	mek	i	aeva
2	khoyar	hai	daou	yerku	er	dva
3	ghorban	ba	tri	yerek	san	þrayo
4	durben	bon	pevar	čors	ssu	caþwaro
5	tabon	nam	pemp	hing	wu	panca
6	jirghoghan	sau	c'houec'h	vec	liu	xšvaš
7	dologhan	bay	seiz	yot	ch'i	hapta
8	naiman	tam	eiz	ut	pa	ašta
9	yisun	chin	nao	innə	chiu	nava
10	arban	muoi	dek	tas	shih	dasa
100	jaghon	tram	kant	haryur	pai	satem

	M	N	O	P	Q	R
1	ichi	hana	ekas	yaw	eden	echad
2	ni	tul	dvau	daw	dva	shnayim
3	san	set	trayas	dree	tri	shlosha
4	shi	net	catvāras	tsaloor	četiri	arba'a
5	go	tasŏt	pañca	pindze	pet	chamishsha
6	roku	yŏsŏt	şaş	shpazz	šest	shishsha
7	shichi	ilgop	sapta	uwe	sedum	shiv'a
8	hachi	yŏdŏl	aṣṭau	ate	osum	shmona
9	ku	ahop	nava	ne	devet	tish'a
10	jū	yŏl	daça	las	deset	'asara
100	hyaku	paek	çatam	sulu	sto	mea

4.12 INFLECTION IN THE INDO-EUROPEAN LANGUAGES

The first six conjugations show the verb 'bear' in varieties of Indo-European, with the thematic vowel, if any, and the ending separated from the base with a slash. These forms are discussed on pages 65–6 of *Origins and Development*. The next six conjugations show the same verb in other varieties of Indo-European. Separate the base from the thematic vowel and the ending with a slash. Note how the endings in the various languages are alike and how they differ.

IE	Gothic	early OE	Sanskrit	Greek	Latin
*bher/ō	bair/a	ber/u	bhar/āmi	pher/ō	fer/ō
*bher/esi	bair/is	bir/is	bhar/asi	pher/eis	fer/s
*bher/eti	bair/iþ	bir/iþ	bhar/ati	pher/ei	fer/t
*bher/omes	bair/am	ber/aþ	bhar/āmas	pher/omes	fer/imus
*bher/ete	bair/iþ	ber/aþ	bhar/atha	pher/ete	fer/tis
*bher/onti	bair/and	ber/aþ	bhar/anti	pher/onti	fer/unt

Proto-Germanic	OHG	OIcelandic	OSlavonic	Lithuanian	OIrish
*ber/ō	bir/u	ber	ber/ǫ	ber/iù	bir/u
*ber/izi	bir/is	ber/r	ber/eši	ber/ì	bir/i
*ber/iði	bir/it	ber/r	ber/etŭ	bĕr/ia	ber/id
*ber/amiz	ber/amēs	ber/om	ber/emŭ	bĕr/iame	ber/mi
*ber/eðe	ber/et	ber/eþ	ber/ete	bĕr/iate	*ber/the **?**
*ber/andi	ber/ant	ber/a	ber/ǫtŭ	bĕr/ia	ber/it

4.13 THE MAJOR CHANGES FROM INDO-EUROPEAN TO GERMANIC

All Germanic languages, in their oldest forms, share certain characteristics that distinguish them from other Indo-European languages. In *Origins and Development*, pages 69–71, seven of these peculiarly Germanic features are listed:

1. a common distinctive vocabulary
2. a two-tense verbal system
3. a dental suffix for the preterit tense
4. "strong" versus "weak" adjectives
5. a fixed stress accent
6. certain vowel changes
7. the First Sound Shift

Here are several examples of these Germanic characteristics. Forms from a Germanic language are listed together with parallel forms from a non-Germanic, but Indo-European, language. Compare the forms with one another and with the discussion in *Origins and Development*; then identify the Germanic characteristic that each example most clearly illustrates by writing the appropriate number, from 1 through 7, in the blank at the left.

	Old English: micel guma		*Latin*: magnus homō 'a great man'
_____			

_____   *Old English*: micel guma   *Latin*: magnus homō 'a great man'
                   se micela guma   iste magnus homō 'that great man'
                   micele guman   magnī hominēs 'great men'
                   þā micelan guman   istī magnī hominēs 'those great men'

_____   *Old English*: þorp 'town'   *Latin*: turba 'crowd'
                   etan 'eat'   edō 'eat'
                   īecan 'eke'   augeō 'increase'

_____   *Old English*: brū 'brow'   *Sanskrit*: bhrūs 'brow'
                   rēad 'red'   rudh-iras 'red'
                   gangan 'go' (cf. gangway)   jaŋghā 'heel, lower leg'

(The initial *j* in *jaŋghā* is due to a sound change of no importance for Germanic languages.)

_____	*Old English*: mōdor 'mother'	singular nominative	*Greek*: mḗtēr 'mother'
	mōdor	singular genitive	mētrós
	mēder	singular dative	mētrí
	mōdor	singular accusative	mētéra
	mōdor	plural nominative	mētéres
	mōdra	plural genitive	mētérōn
	mōdrum	plural dative	mētrási
	mōdor	plural accusative	mētéras

_____   *Old English*: brōðor 'brother'   *Latin*: frāter 'brother'
                   bōc 'beech tree'   fāgus 'beech tree'
                   mōdor 'mother'   māter 'mother'

_____   *Old English*: ic sēce 'I seek'   *Latin*: sāgiō 'I perceive'
                   ic sōhte 'I sought'   sāgīvī 'I perceived'
                   ic temme 'I tame'   domō 'I tame'
                   ic temede 'I tamed'   domuī 'I tamed'

_____   *Gothic*: gasts 'stranger'   *Latin*: hostis 'stranger'
                   nahts 'night'   nox 'night'
                   gards 'garden'   hortus 'garden'

_____   *Old English*: sǣ 'sea'   *Greek*: thalassa 'sea'
Dutch: zee   *Latin*: mare
Old High German: sēo   *Irish*: muir
Icelandic: sær   *Lithuanian*: jūra
Danish: sö   *Hindustani*: samundar
Gothic: saiws   *Old Persian*: drayah-

_____   *Old English*: nefa 'nephew'   *Latin*: nepōs 'grandson'
                   weorþan 'become'   vertō 'turn'
                   hōre 'whore'   cāra 'dear one'

_____   *Old English*: ic dō 'I do, am doing,   *Greek*: tithēmi 'I am placing'
                      will do'   thēsō 'I will place'
                   ic dyde 'I was doing,   etithēn 'I was placing'
                       did, have done'   ethēka 'I placed'
                                           tethēka 'I have placed'

The First Sound Shift (also known as Grimm's Law) occurred in five steps. Step 3 is called Verner's Law. Each step was completed before the next began, so there was no overlapping or repetition of the changes.

1. The shift is described here in articulatory terms. Complete the blanks to show the development of each sound.

STEP 1:   All aspirated voiced stops became the corresponding voiced fricatives:
bh > _____; dh > _____; gh > _____; gwh > _____.

STEP 2:   Voiceless stops became the corresponding voiceless fricatives (except when they followed another voiceless fricative): p > _____; t > _____; k > _____; kw > _____.

STEP 3:   Voiceless fricatives became voiced (when they were in a voiced environment and the Indo-European stress was not on the preceding syllable): f > _____; þ > _____; x > _____; xw > _____; s > _____.

STEP 4:   All voiced stops became unvoiced: b > _____; d > _____; g > _____; gw > _____.

STEP 5:   Voiced fricatives sometimes became the corresponding voiced stops (the exact conditions depended on the sound, the environment, and the dialect): β > _____; ð > _____; γ > _____; γw > _____. In this same step, the voiced fricative *z* became an *r*-like sound that was spelled with a distinctive letter (transliterated ʀ) in the early runic inscriptions of North Germanic; it later merged with the *r* inherited from Indo-European.

2. The First Sound Shift can also be described by rules stated in phonetic features, thus:

STEP 1: $\begin{bmatrix} - \text{ continuant} \\ + \text{ aspirated} \end{bmatrix} \rightarrow [+ \text{ continuant}]$

That is, any sound that is both noncontinuant and aspirated (an aspirated stop) becomes a continuant (a fricative).

STEP 2: $\begin{bmatrix} - \text{ continuant} \\ - \text{ voiced} \end{bmatrix} \rightarrow [+ \text{ continuant}] \; except \; / \; [- \text{ voiced}] _____$

That is, any sound that is both noncontinuant and nonvoiced (voiceless stop) becomes a continuant (fricative), except following a nonvoiced sound.

STEP 3: $[+ \text{ continuant}] \rightarrow [+ \text{ voiced}] \; / \; [- \text{ stressed}] \; [+ \text{ voiced}] _____ \; [+ \text{ voiced}]$

That is, any sound that is a continuant (fricative) is voiced, when between voiced sounds and preceded by a nonstressed syllable.

STEP 4: $[- \text{ continuant}] \rightarrow [- \text{ voiced}]$

That is, any noncontinuant (stop) becomes nonvoiced.

STEP 5: $\begin{bmatrix} - \text{ sonorant} \\ + \text{ voiced} \end{bmatrix} \rightarrow [- \text{ continuant}] / \begin{Bmatrix} \# \\ [+ \text{ nasal}] \end{Bmatrix} _____$

That is, any voiced nonsonorant (in practice, a voiced fricative) becomes a noncontinuant (stop), in initial position (# indicates word beginning) or after a nasal.

The foregoing rules state the Shift in a somewhat different fashion from the more traditional description in part 1, but they account for the same changes. Complete the blanks in the chart on page 88 to show how the IE obstruent system looked after each step in the Shift. (The labiovelars, *kw, gw, gwh,* have been omitted for simplicity's sake.)

IE SYSTEM	AFTER STEP 1	AFTER STEP 2	AFTER STEP 3	AFTER STEP 4	AFTER STEP 5
		(p t k)*	(p t k)*		
p t k	p t k	— — —	f þ x	f þ x	f þ x
b d g	b d g	b d g	b d g	— — —	p t k
bh dh gh	— — —	β ð γ	β ð γ	β ð γ	— — —
					(β ð γ)*
s	s	s	s	s	s
			—	z	r

* Sounds in parentheses occurred in limited environments.

3. In each of the following pairs, the first item is a reconstructed Indo-European root and the second is a related English word. The English word may be based on a form with affixes added to the root or may involve a change in vowel, but the Indo-European consonants you are asked to examine correspond regularly with those in the root of the English word. No exceptions and no examples of Verner's Law (step 3 of the Shift) are involved. Supply the missing letters.

*bha 'speak' / _____an

*dheu- 'flow' / _____ew

*ghans- / _____oose

*bend- 'protruding point' / _____en

*de- / _____o

*gel- / _____ool

*pau- / _____ew

*tr- 'cross over'/ _____rough

*kan- 'sing' / _____en

*angh- 'tight'/ an_____er

*bher- / _____ear

*koimo- / _____ome

*pā- / _____ood

*swād / swee_____

*gl- 'ball' / _____lue

*dhrēn- / _____rone

*lab- / la_____ 'lick'

*pūlo- 'rotten' / _____oul

*wadh- 'pledge' / we_____

*wāb- / wee_____

*magh- 'can' / (OE) ma_____an 'may'

*wegh- 'go' / (OE) we_____ 'way'

*plōu- / _____low

*aug- 'increase' / e_____e

*kel- 'cover'/ _____ell

*leb- / li_____

*dem- 'build' / _____imber

*bhlō- / _____loom

*dhō 'set, put' / _____o

*tum- 'swollen' / _____umb

*tong- 'feel' / _____an_____

*pet- 'fly' / _____ea_____er

*treud- 'squeeze' / _____rea_____

*bhreg- / _____rea_____

*bheid- 'split' / _____i_____e

*dhragh- / _____ra_____

*grebh- 'scratch' / _____ra_____

*porko- / (OE) _____ear_____ 'small pig'

*kwerp- 'turn about' / w_____ar_____

*ghreib- / _____ri_____

4. In the following examples, the Indo-European stress was on some syllable other than the first; consequently Verner's Law (step 3 of the First Sound Shift) applies. Supply the missing letters.

*kaput / (Goth.) hau_____iþ 'head'   *sep(t)m- / (Goth.) si_____un 'seven'

*plōtu- / floo_____   *klūto- / (OE) hlū_____ 'loud'

*konk- / han_____   *dukā- / (OE) to_____ian 'tow'

*wes- 'dwell' / we_____e   *sauso- 'dry' / sea_____

5. Examine the following pairs; then list the Indo-European consonants that underwent no change in

Germanic: _____

*lem- 'break' / (OE) lama 'lame'   *newo- 'new' / (OE) nēowe 'new'
*mā- 'damp' / (OE) mō-r 'moor'   *wel- 'wish' / (OE) wel 'well'
*mel- 'soft' / (OE) mel-tan 'melt'   *wen- 'strive' / (OE) winnan 'win'
*mer- 'harm' / (OE) mare 'nightmare'   *wir- 'man' / (OE) wer 'man'
*nas- 'nose' / (OE) nosu 'nose'   *yēro- 'year' / (ModE) year

4.15   THE SECOND OR HIGH GERMAN SHIFT

English and the Low German languages—Dutch, Flemish, and Plattdeutsch—differ from modern standard German partly because standard German has undergone a Second or High German Shift of some consonants. English preserves the older common Germanic sounds that were changed in High German between the sixth and the eighth centuries.

Summarize in the following chart those parts of the Second Shift described on page 75 of *Origins and Development*. A complete statement of the High German Shift would require some additional remarks about sounds and positions. The chart does, however, include the most important changes.

	OLDER GERMANIC	p	t	k	d
HIGH GERMAN	*after vowels*				
	otherwise			—	

Below are some English and High German cognates that show sound correspondence according to the Second Shift. Supply the missing letters.

ENGLISH	GERMAN	ENGLISH	GERMAN	ENGLISH	GERMAN
pan	_____anne	boo_____	Busse	bite	bei_____en
grip	Gri_____	sha_____e	schaffen	plough	_____lug
to	_____u	_____ath	Pfad	weaponless	wa_____enlos
foot	Fu_____	ri_____e	reiten	heart	Her_____
book	Bu_____	hol_____	Holz	fret	fre_____en
door	_____ür	re_____on	rechnen	alike	glei_____
pole	_____ahl	ha_____e	Hass	deed	_____a_____
tame	_____ahm	o_____en	offen	token	_____ei_____en
make	ma_____en	floo_____	Flut	plant	_____lan_____e
dream	_____raum	shi_____	Schiff	tide	_____ei_____

The following selections are translations of the parable of the prodigal son (Luke 15.11–24) in four early Germanic languages: Gothic, Old English, Old High German, and Old Icelandic. The Latin Vulgate text has been added for comparison. The Gothic, Old English, and Old High German versions are fairly close translations; with the help of a modern English translation and some imagination you should be able to make them out. The Old Icelandic version, however, is an unusually free and prolix rendering; therefore a gloss has been given for it.

Compare the translations with one another to discover similarities and differences among the Germanic languages. Vowel length is marked with macrons in Old English and with acute accents in Old Icelandic.

GOTHIC

(11) Manne sums aihta twans sununs. (12) Jah qaþ sa juhiza ize du attin: "Atta, gif mis sei undrinnai mik dail aiginis." Jah disdailida im swes sein. (13) Jah afar ni managans dagans, brahta samana allata sa juhiza sunus jah aflaiþ in land fairra wisando, jah jainar distahida þata swes seinata libands usstiuriba. (14) Biþe þan frawas allamma, warþ huhrus abrs and gawi jainata, jah is dugann alaþarba wairþan. (15) Jah gaggands gahaftida sik sumamma baurgjane jainis gaujis. Jah insandida ina haiþjos seinaizos haldan sweina. (16) Jah gairnida sad itan haurne, þoei matidedun sweina, jah manna imma ni gaf. (17) Qimands þan in sis qaþ: "Hwan filu asnje attins meinis ufarassau haband hlaibe, iþ ik huhrau fraqistna! (18) Usstandands gagga du attin meinamma, jah qiþa du imma: 'Atta, frawaurhta mis in himin, jah in andwairþja þeinamma; (19) ju þanaseiþs ni im wairþs ei haitaidau sunus þeins; gatawei mik swe ainana asnje þeinaize.'" (20) Jah usstandands qam at attin seinamma. Nauhþanuh þan fairra wisandan, gasahw ina atta is, jah infeinoda, jah þragjands draus ana hals is, jah kukida imma. (21) Jah qaþ imma sa sunus: "Atta, frawaurhta in himin, jah in andwairþja þeinamma, ju þanaseiþs ni im wairþs ei haitaidau sunus þeins." (22) Qaþ þan sa atta du skalkam seinaim: "Sprauto bringiþ wastja þo frumiston, jah gawasjiþ ina, jah gibiþ figgragulþ in handu is, jah gaskohi ana fotuns is, (23) jah bringandans stiur þana alidan ufsneiþiþ, jah matjandans wisam waila, (24) unte sa sunus meins dauþs was, jah gaqiunoda, jah fralusans was, jah bigitans warþ."

OLD ENGLISH

(11) Sōðlīce sum man hæfde twēgen suna. (12) Þā cwæð se gingra tō his fæder: "Fæder, syle mē mīnne dæl mīnre æhte þe mē tō gebyreþ." Þā dǣlde hē him his æhte. (13) Ðā æfter fēawum dagum, ealle his þing gegaderode se gingra sunu, and fērde wrǣclice on feorlen rīce, and forspilde þār his æhta, lybbende on his gǣlsan. (14) Ðā hē hīg hæfde ealle āmyrrede, þā wearð mycel hunger on þām rīce, and hē wearð wǣdla. (15) Þā fērde hē, and folgode ānum burhsittendan men þæs rīces. Ðā sende hē hine tō his tūne þæt hē hēolde his swȳn. (16) Ðā gewilnode hē his wambe gefyllan of þām bēancoddum, þe ðā swȳn ǣton, and him man ne sealde. (17) Þā beþōhte hē hine, and cwæð: "Ēalā, hū fela hȳrlinga on mīnes fæder hūse hlāf genōhne habbað, and ic hēr on hungre forwurðe! (18) Ic ārīse, and ic fare tō minum fæder, and ic secge him: 'Ēalā fæder, ic syngode on heofenas, and beforan þē; (19) nū ic ne eom wyrðe þæt ic bēo þīn sunu nemned; dō mē swā ānne of þīnum hȳrlingum.'" (20) And hē ārās þā, and cōm tō his fæder. And þā gȳt þā hē wæs feorr his fæder, hē hyne geseah, and wearð mid mildheortnesse āstyrod, and agēn hine arn, and hine beclypte, and cyste hine. (21) Ða cwæð his sunu: "Fæder, ic syngode on heofon, and beforan ðē; nū ic ne eom wyrþe þæt ic þīn sunu bēo genemned." (22) Ða cwæþ se fæder tō his þēowum: "Bringað raðe þone sēlestan gegyrelan, and scrȳdað hyne, and syllað him hring on his hand, and gescȳ tō his fōtum, (23) and bringað ān fǣtt styric, and ofslēað, and uton etan, and gewistfullian, (24) for þām þes mīn sunu wæs dēad, and hē geedcucode, hē forwearð, and hē is gemēt."

(11) Sum man habata zuuene suni. (12) Quad tho ther iungoro fon then themo fater: "Fater, gib mir teil thero hehti, thiu mir gibure." Her tho teilta thia heht. (13) Nalles after manegen tagon, gisamonoten allen ther iungoro sun elilentes fuor in uerra lantscaf, inti dar ziuuarf sina heht lebento uirnlustigo. (14) Inti after thiu her iz al forlos, uuard hungar strengi in thero lantscefi, her bigonda tho armen. (15) Inti gieng, inti zuoclebeta einemo thero burgliuto thero lantscefi. Inti santa inan in sin thorf, thaz her fuotriti suuin. (16) Inti girdinota gifullen sina uuamba fon siliquis, theo thiu suuin azzun, inti nioman imo ni gab. (17) Her tho in sih giuuorban quad: "Vvuo manege asnere mines fater ginuht habent brotes, ih uoruuirdu hier hungere! (18) Arstantu, inti faru zi minemo fater, inti quidu imo: 'Fater, ih suntota in himil, inti fora thir; (19) inti ni bim iu uuirdig ginemnit uuesan thin sun; tuo mih so einan fon thinen asnerin.'" (20) Inti arstantanti quam zi simemo fater. Mittiu thanne noh ferro uuas, gisah inan sin fater, inti miltida giruorit uuard, inti ingegin louffenti fiel ubar sinan hals, inti custa inan. (21) Tho quad imo der sun: "Fater, ih suntota in himil, inti fora thir, iu ni bim uuirdig ginemnit uuesan thin sun." (22) Tho quad ther fater zi sinen scalcun: "Sliumo bringet thaz erira giuuati, inti giuuatet inan, inti gebet fingirin in sina hant, inti giscuohiu in fuozi, (23) inti leitet gifuotrit calb, inti arslahet, inti ezzemes, inti goumumes, (24) uuanta theser min sun tot uuas, inti arqueketa, foruuard, inti funtan uuard."

OLD ICELANDIC

(11) Einn auðigr maðr átti tvá sunu. (12) En sá hinn yngri sunr hans mælti til föður
A rich man had two sons. And he this younger son of his said to father

síns: "Faðir," sagði hann, "fá mér þann hlut fjár míns, er til mín telst í
his Father said he give me the portion of possessions my which to me counts in

erfðum millum vár feðganna." Sem faðir hans heyrði þetta, þá skipti hann hánum
inheritance among us father and sons. When father his heard this then divided he to him

sínum hlut. (13) En hann varð þegar í brotto ok fór langt í önnor land með sínum
his portion. And he got at once away and went far to other lands with his

hlut, ok lifði þar fólslega, eyddi fénu öllu í fúllífi svá snáplega, at um síðir
portion and lived there foolishly wasted substance all in foul life so brutishly that at last

hafði hann sjálfr alls ekki. (14) Ok fluttist þar fram með mykilli fátœkt, þvíat í
had he himself at all nothing. And moved there from with great poverty because at

þeim tíma var mykit úáran í þvi landi ok mykill sultr. (15) Ok kom hann sér í
that time was great dearth in the land and great hunger. And came he himself into

fátœka þjónustu með einum ríkum manni, en hann sendi hann til eins kotbœar, at
impoverished service with a powerful man and he sent him to a farmstead that

hann skyldi gæta svína hans. (16) En hans vesöld vóx svá mjök þar, at hann fystist
he should watch swine his. And his misery grew so much there that he desired

fyrir hungrs sakar at fylla kvið sinn af bauna skálmum ok stiklum, er svínum var
for hunger's sake to fill belly his with bean pods and thorns which to swine was

gefit til matar, ok fékk hann sér þat til fœzlu, þvíat engi vildi gefa hánum
given as meat and took he himself that as food because no one would give him

annat.　　(17) Ok　hugleíddi　hann þá,　sjálfr,　hversu fólslega　er　hann hafði farit med sínu
any other.　　And considered he　then himself how　foolishly that he　　had　dealt with his

ráði ok　mæltist þá　við einn samann þessum orðum: "Faðir　minn fœðir hversdaglega
life and spoke　then to　himself　　in these words　Father my　feeds commonly

heima með sér　　mykinn fjölda　leigumanna með gnógu　brauði ok annarri vist œrinni,
at home with himself a great　multitude of hired men with enough bread and other　food enough

en ek svelt her af matleysi!　(18) Ok því　　　skal ek skyndilega fara til föður míns ok
and I die　here of starvation!　　And therefore shall I　quickly　　go to father my　and

biðja hann miskunnar með þessum orðum: 'Faðir, ek hefi　syndgazt ok　misgört　í móti
beg　him for mercy　with these　words　Father I　have sinned　and done amiss against

guði himneskum ok svá móti　　þér;　(19) ok　firir því em ek eigi verðr　heðan ifrá, at
god in heaven and also against thee　　and therefore am I　not worthy henceforth that

þú　haldir mik svá sem þinn sun; nú　bið ek, at　þú　gefir mér slíkan rétt í　garði þínum
thou hold　me thus as　thy　son now beg I　that thou give me　such due in　house thy

sem einum leigumanne　þínum.'" (20) Ok　siðan　　fór　hann skyngilega ok　kom til
as one　of hired men thy.　　　And afterwards went he　quickly　　and came to

föður síns. Nú　þegar　sem faðir　hans leit hann mjök fjarri　komandi, þá　sneri　hann
father his. Now at once when father his　saw him very　far off coming　then turned he

þegar　miskunn sinni til　　hans ok　rann at hánum ok　tók　höndum　sínum um　háls
at once mercy　his　towards him and ran to him　and held with hands his　about neck

hánum ok　kysti　hann með myklum fagnaði. [Verse 21 is lacking.] (22) Ok　mælti við þjónustumenn
his　and kissed him with great　delight.　　　　　　　And said to　servants

sína, er　í hjá　hánum váru: "Skyndið heim ok　takit góða gangverju　með fögrum skóm
his who close by him　were Hurry　home and take good walking cloak with fair　shoes

ok　fœrið syni　mínum ok gott fingrgull　　dregit á　hönd hánum ok　sœmið hann,
and bring to son my　and good gold finger-ring put　on hand his　and honor　him

(23) drepit ok　einn feitan oxa; vér skulum hafa, í　dag mykla veizlu ok　fagnaðar　öl í
slay also a　fat　ox　we shall　have to day great　feast　and for rejoicing ale at

heimkomu　sunar míns, (24) þvíat　ek hugða　hann vera dauðan ok　er hann nú　lífs,
homecoming of son my　because I　thought him to be dead　and is he　now alive

þar sem hann hvarf　í brott ok　er nú　aptr kominn."
whereas he　vanished away　and is now back come.

LATIN

(11) Homo quidam habuit duos filios. (12) Et dixit adolescentior ex illis patri: "Pater, da mihi portionem sub-

stantiae quae me contingit." Et divisit illis substantiam. (13) Et non post multos dies, congregatis omnibus,

adolescentior filius peregre profectus est in regionem longinquam, et ibi dissipavit substantiam suam vivendo

luxuriose. (14) Et postquam omnia consummasset, facta est fames valida in regione illa, et ipse coepit egere.

(15) Et abiit, et adhaesit uni civium regionis illius. Et misit illum in villam suam ut pasceret porcos. (16) Et cu-

piebat implere ventrem suum de siliquis, quas porci manducabant, et nemo illi dabat. (17) In se autem rever-

sus, dixit: "Quanti mercenarii in domo patris mei abundant panibus, ego autem hic fame pereo! (18) Surgam, et ibo ad patrem meum, et dicam ei: 'Pater, peccavi in caelum, et coram te; (19) iam non sum dignus vocari filius tuus; fac me sicut unum de mercenariis tuis.'" (20) Et surgens venit ad patrem suum. Cum autem adhuc longe esset, vidit illum pater ipsius, et misericordia motus est, et accurrens cecidit super collum eius, et osculatus est eum. (21) Dixitque ei filius: "Pater, peccavi in caelum, et coram te, iam non sum dignus vocari filius tuus." (22) Dixit autem pater ad servos suos: "Cito proferte stolam primam, et induite illum, et date annulum in manum eius, et calceamenta in pedes eius, (23) et adducite vitulum saginatum, et occidite, et manducemus, et epulemur, (24) quia hic filius mortuus erat, et revixit, perierat, et inventus est."

What words in each of the Germanic versions correspond to the Latin (or English) below?

	GOTHIC	OLD ENGLISH	OLD HIGH GERMAN	OLD ICELANDIC
(11) homo 'man'				
duos 'two'				
filios 'sons'				
(12) adolescentior 'younger'				
patri 'to (his) father'				
pater 'father'				
(14) fames 'hunger'				
(15) porcos 'swine'				
(16) cupiebat 'desired'				
(17) panibus 'bread'				
ego 'I'				
fame 'in hunger'				
(18) caelum 'heaven'				
(19) filius 'son'				
(20) venit 'came'				
ad patrem suum 'to his father'				
(22) in manum eius 'on his hand'				
calceamenta 'shoes'				
(23) vitulum 'calf, young steer'				
(24) mortuus 'dead'				

5 THE OLD ENGLISH PERIOD (449–1100)

5.1 FOR REVIEW AND DISCUSSION

1. Define the following terms:

pre-Old English	genitive	strong verb
Old English	dative	conjugation
Anglo-Saxon	instrumental	indicative
Heptarchy	definiteness	preterit tense
Kentish	weak adjective declension	present tense
West Saxon	strong adjective declension	enclitic
Mercian	declension of nouns	subjunctive
Northumbrian	*a*-stem	imperative
Anglian	*r*-stem	finite form
mutation	*n*-stem	nonfinite form
i-mutation (*i*-umlaut)	weak noun declension	principal part
grammatical gender	strong noun declension	ablaut (gradation)
natural gender	*ō*-stem	preterit-present verb
concord	root-consonant stem	suppletive paradigm
nominative	dual number	impersonal verb
accusative	weak verb	parataxis

2. What peoples inhabited the British Isles before the coming of the English?

3. According to Bede, what circumstances brought the Germanic tribesmen to Britain, and which tribes participated in the settlement of the island?

4. What was the influence of the Scandinavian settlement on the English language?

5. Which dialect of Old English was the standard language and from which dialect has Modern English descended?

6. What difference between the Old English sound system and that of Modern English is illustrated by the following pairs: *spanan* 'attract, urge,' *spannan* 'join, fasten'; *suga* 'sows,' *sugga* 'a bird'; *fela* 'much, many,' *fella* 'of hides, skins'; *rǣde* '(I) give advice,' *rǣdde* '(I) gave advice'?

7. What is the chief difference between the stress patterns of Old English and Modern English, and what historical events help to account for the difference?

8. What are the main differences in word order between Old English and Modern English?

9. From which Old English declension do our living noun inflections derive?

10. How do Old English and Modern English differ in devices for indicating plurality?

11. How did the strong and weak forms of an Old English adjective differ in use?

12. What Old English adjective inflections have survived as living suffixes in Modern English?

13. What is the origin of Modern English adverbs without endings such as *deep, fast*, and *loud*?

14. What is the difference between mutation (umlaut) and gradation (ablaut)?

15. From what class of Old English verbs are the Modern English modal auxiliaries *shall, should, may, might, can, could, must,* and *ought* derived?

16. What distinctions in form, universal in Old English verbs, are preserved in Modern English only in the verb *to be*?

17. What is the Old English origin of the *y-* in Spenser's "A Gentle Knight was pricking on the plaine, /Ycladd in mightie armes and silver shielde"?

18. Old English differs from Modern English in the amount of inflection for nouns, adjectives, pronouns, and verbs. Name four or five other major differences between the linguistic systems of the two periods.

5.2 ANGLO-SAXON ENGLAND

Locate the four main Old English dialects on the map by adding the shading below.

ANGLIAN

Northumbrian

Mercian

West Saxon

Kentish

5.3 THE PRONUNCIATION OF OLD ENGLISH: STRESS

1. Summarize the rules for Old English stress on words without a prefix _____

_____

words with a prefix _____

_____

compounds _____

_____

2. Indicate the primary stress of the following Old English words, all of which are without prefix, by placing a stress mark (´) over the stressed vowel. (The dot over letters *c* and *g* is explained on page 98.)

cuman	'to come'	sweotol	'clear'
fēngon	'(they) took'	sweotolian	'to reveal'
fiscere	'fisherman'	spellian	'to relate'
dearnunga	'secretly'	lustfulliċ	'joyful'

3. Indicate the primary stress of the following Old English words by placing a stress mark (´) over the stressed vowel. Prefixes have been set off with hyphens to call attention to them.

on-fōn	'to receive'	be-sprecan	'to talk about'
and-fengness	'reception'	bī-spell	'proverb'
wið-sprecan	'to contradict'	be-cuman	'to happen'
wiðer-sprǣċ	'contradiction'	be-cyme	'result'
of-þyncan	'to offend'	for-fōn	'to take away'
æf-þunca	'offense'	for-fang	'seizure'
to-cuman	'to arrive'	ge-reċċan	'to explain'
tō-cyme	'arrival'	ge-reċedness	'interpretation'

4. Indicate the primary stress (´) and the secondary stress (`) of the following compounds by writing the appropriate marks over the stressed vowels. Compounds have been divided with hyphens. Some of the words have prefixes which you should recognize from the preceding question.

spell-boda	'messenger'	forfang-feoh	'reward for rescuing property'
god-spellere	'evangelist'	scīr-ġerēfa	'shire reeve'
sprǣċ-hūs	'senate house'	bebod-dæġ	'appointed day'
man-cynn	'mankind'	ġehāt-land	'promised land'
bōc-cræftiġ	'learned'	dǣd-cēne	'daring'
lof-ġeornost	'most eager for praise'	hēah-fæder	'patriarch'
hēah-burg	'capital city'	leorning-cniht	'disciple'
tungol-wītega	'astrologer'	mynster-mann	'monk'

5.4   THE PRONUNCIATION OF OLD ENGLISH: VOWELS

Late Old English had the following vowels:

SPELLING	SOUND	SPELLING	SOUND	SPELLING	SOUND
a	[ɑ]	i	[ɪ]	y	[Ü]
ā	[ɑ:]	ī	[i:]	ȳ	[ü:]
æ	[æ]	o	[ɔ]	ea	[æə]
ǣ	[æ:]	ō	[o:]	ēa	[æ:ə]
e	[ɛ]	u	[ʊ]	eo	[ɛə]
ē	[e:]	ū	[u:]	ēo	[e:ə]

1. Complete the following chart by filling in the phonetic symbols listed on page 96 to show the articulation of Old English vowels.

		FRONT UNROUNDED	FRONT ROUNDED	BACK
HIGH	*long*	ī		ū
	short	i		ŭ
MID	*long*	ē	DIPHTHONGS	
	short	e		o
LOW	*long*	ǣ		ā
	short	æ		a

2. Complete the following chart to show (1) the phonetic symbol for the Old English vowel, (2) the phonetic symbol for a typical Modern English development of the vowel, and (3) the typical spelling of the Modern English development. Complete columns (2) and (3) according to the Modern English key words.

	OLD ENGLISH			MODERN ENGLISH			
vowel	(1) *phonetic symbol*	*key words*		*key words*		(2) *phonetic symbol*	(3) *typical spelling*
a	[ɑ]	habban sadol	batt lamb	have saddle	bat lamb	[æ]	a
ā		hām tācen	gād pāl	home token	goad pole		
æ		þæt bæc	pæð mæst	that back	path mast		
ǣ		dǣl hǣlan	nǣdl mǣne	deal heal	needle mean		
e		settan rest	weddian denn	set rest	wed den		
ē		fēdan grēne	cēne mētan	feed green	keen meet		
i		sittan mist	timber rima	sit mist	timber rim		
ī		rīdan līf	tīma bī	ride life	time by		

OLD ENGLISH			MODERN ENGLISH			
vowel	(1) *phonetic symbol*	*key words*		*key words*		(2) *phonetic symbol*	(3) *typical spelling*
o		moððe pott oft botm		moth pot oft(en) bottom		
ō		fōda gōd nōn brōm		food good noon broom		
u		sundor wundor þus pullian		sunder wonder thus pull		
ū		mūs nū dūne ūt		mouse now down out		
y		fyllan pytt mynster þynne		fill pit minster thin		
ȳ		mȳs fȳr hȳdan hwȳ		mice fire hide why		
ea		ċeaf sleac nearu fealu		chaff slack narrow fallow		
ēa		bēatan ēast lēaf stēap		beat east leaf steep		
eo		ġeolu heofon eolh seofon		yellow heaven elk seven		
ēo		crēopan dēop flēon bēo		creep deep flee bee		

5.5   THE PRONUNCIATION OF OLD ENGLISH: CONSONANTS

Late Old English had the following consonants:

SPELLING	SOUND	SPELLING	SOUND	SPELLING	SOUND
b	[b]	h	[h], [x], [ç]	s	[s], [z]
c, k	[k]	l	[l]	t	[t]
ċ	[č]	m	[m]	þ, ð	[θ], [ð]
d	[d]	n	[n], [ŋ]	w	[w]
f	[f], [v]	p	[p]	sc	[š]
g	[g], [ɣ]	r	[r]	cg	[ǰ]
ġ	[y]				

The dot over the spellings *ċ* and *ġ* is, like the macron over vowel spellings, a modern editorial device to help the reader.

Complete the following chart by filling in the symbols listed on page 98 so as to show the place and manner of articulation of Old English consonants. A review of the chart of Modern English consonants will help you complete this one. Although [ɣ] is a fricative it should be put with [g] among the stops for a reason we will presently see.

| | | LABIAL | DENTAL | | | PALATOVELAR | |
			inter-dental	*alveolar*	*alveolo-palatal*	*palatal*	*velar*
STOPS AND AFFRICATES	*voiceless*						
	voiced						
FRICATIVES							
NASALS							
LIQUIDS	*lateral*						
	retroflex or trill						
SEMIVOWELS							

5.6   THE PRONUNCIATION OF OLD ENGLISH: CONSONANT ALTERNATIONS

Thirteen of the consonant sounds listed in the preceding exercise are grouped thus:

[f] / [v]   [θ] / [ð]   [s] / [z]   [g] / [ɣ]   [h] / [x] / [ç]   [n] / [ŋ]

The sounds in each group alternate in different environments. For example, [f] occurs in one set of positions and [v] occurs in a different set of positions. Neither [f] nor [v] normally turns up in any of the positions belonging to the other sound. Since the two labial fricatives alternate in this way, they are, as far as Old English is concerned, the same sound; that is, they are allophones of the same phoneme.

Examine the following words to determine the positions (environment) in which the sounds of each group occur.

1. [f] / [v], [θ] / [ð], [s] / [z]

folc	[fɔlk]	'folk'	offrian	[ɔffrɪan]	'to offer'
þurh	[θʊrx]	'through'	moððe	[mɔθθɛ]	'moth'
sōna	[so:na]	'immediately'	mæsse	[mæssɛ]	'mass'
fif	[fi:f]	'five'	fifel	[fi:vɛl]	'sea-monster'
bæð	[bæθ]	'bath'	baðu	[baðʊ]	'baths'
hūs	[hu:s]	'house'	māse	[ma:zɛ]	'titmouse'
fifta	[fi:fta]	'fifth'	ofnas	[ɔvnɑs]	'ovens'
hȳhþu	[hü:çθʊ]	'height'	māðmas	[ma:ðmɑs]	'treasures'
hæpse	[hæpsɛ]	'hasp'	fæsl	[fæzl]	'progeny'

a. Which of the six sounds occur only between two voiced sounds? _____

b. Which sounds occur in other positions, such as initially, finally, doubled, or next to a voiceless sound?

_____

2. [g] / [ɣ]

gōd	[goːd]	'good'		sungen	[suŋgɛn]	'sung'
gēs	[geːs]	'geese'		lagu	[laɣʊ]	'law'
grund	[grʊnd]	'ground'		āgan	[aːɣan]	'to own'
glæd	[glæd]	'glad'		swelgan	[swɛlɣan]	'to swallow'
gnorn	[gnɔrn]	'sad'		fuglas	[fuɣlas]	'fowls'
frogga	[frɔgga]	'frog'		sorg	[sɔrɣ]	'sorrow'
song	[sɔŋg]	'song'		bōg	[boːɣ]	'bough'

a. Which of the two sounds occurs initially, doubled, or after *n* [ŋ]? _____

b. Which sound occurs in other positions, such as between vowels, between a consonant other than [ŋ] and a vowel, or finally except after [ŋ]? _____

3. [h] / [x] / [ç]

hilt	[hɪlt]	'hilt'		riht	[rɪçt]	'right'
hāl	[haːl]	'whole'		nīhsta	[niːçsta]	'next'
hræfn	[hrævn]	'raven'		brōhte	[broːxtɛ]	'brought'
hnutu	[hnʊtʊ]	'nut'		neah	[næəx]	'near'
hlāf	[hlaːf]	'loaf'		wealh	[wæəlx]	'foreigner'
hwēol	[hweːəl]	'wheel'		rūh	[ruːx]	'rough'
eoh	[ɛəx]	'horse'		fāh	[faːx]	'foe'

a. Which of the three sounds occurs initially? _____

b. Which sound occurs after a front vowel? _____

c. Which sound occurs in other positions, such as after a back vowel, diphthong, or consonant?

_____

4. [n] / [ŋ]

singan	[sɪŋgan]	'to sing'		mannes	[mannɛs]	'man's'
drincan	[drɪŋkan]	'to drink'		mōna	[moːna]	'moon'
gang	[gaŋg]	'journey'		font	[fɔnt]	'font'
þanc	[θaŋk]	'thought'		ende	[ɛndɛ]	'end'
nōn	[noːn]	'noon'		cylna	[külna]	'kilns'

a. Which of the two sounds occurs before [g] or [k]? _____

b. Which sound occurs in other positions, such as initially, finally, or internally, before a vowel or consonant other than a velar stop? _____

5. Supply the missing symbols in these phonetic transcriptions. For some words you must add two symbols.

fæt	[____æt]	'vat'		weorð	[wɛər____]	'worth'
hæfde	[hæ____dɛ]	'had'		weorðan	[wɛər____ɑn]	'to become'
hafoc	[hɑ____ɔk]	'hawk'		þorn	[____ɔrn]	'thorn'
of	[ɔ____]	'of'		oþþe	[ɔ____ɛ]	'or'
cræft	[kræ____t]	'skill'		wrīþan	[wri:____ɑn]	'to twist'
pyffan	[pü____ɑn]	'to puff'		rīsan	[ri:____ɑn]	'rise'
ēaster	[æ:ə____tɛr]	'Easter'		hors	[____ɔrs]	'horse'
missan	[mɪ____ɑn]	'to miss'		cniht	[knɪ____t]	'lad'
miltsian	[mɪlt____ɪɑn]	'to pity'		feoh	[fɛə____]	'cattle'
sylf	[____ülf]	'self'		hnipian	[____nɪpɪɑn]	'to droop'
rās	[rɑ:____]	'arose'		beorht	[bɛər____t]	'bright'
bōsm	[bo:____m]	'bosom'		finger	[fɪ____ɛr]	'finger'
plōg	[plo:____]	'plow'		findan	[fɪ____dɑn]	'to find'
gold	[____ɔld]	'gold'		sanc	[sɑ____]	'sank'
boga	[bɔ____ɑ]	'bow'		sunu	[sʊ____ʊ]	'son'
glēo	[____le:ə]	'mirth'		sunne	[sʊ____ɛ]	'sun'
burg	[bʊr____]	'city'		lang	[lɑ____]	'long'
belgan	[bɛl____ɑn]	'to be angry'		scruncen	[šrʊ____ɛn]	'shrunken'

5.7   OLD ENGLISH SPELLING AND PRONUNCIATION

A perfectly alphabetical writing system has a distinct symbol for each of its consonant and vowel phonemes; each distinctive sound has only one symbol and each symbol represents only one such sound. Old English comes much closer to that ideal than does Modern English, but even Old English had some irrationalities in its spelling. The most troublesome of these are the letters *c* and *g*. Review in *Origins and Development*, pages 87–8, the discussion of the sounds represented by these two spellings; then examine the following words. Each group of words illustrates a typical position of the letters *c* and *g*; if the prehistoric form of the word is relevant, it is given as a reconstruction with the usual asterisk. For each group of words, decide whether *c* represents [k] or [č] and whether *g* represents [g] or [ɣ] or [y]. Write the appropriate phonetic symbol within the brackets. The dots have been omitted from *c* and *g* in this exercise.

c = [ ]	*g* = [ ]	*c* = [ ]	*g* = [ ]
clif 'cliff'	glæs 'glass'	ceaf 'chaff'	geard 'yard'
cniht 'boy'	gnorn 'sad'	ceorl 'churl'	gē 'ye'
crisp 'curly'	grimm 'fierce'	cīdan 'to chide'	geolu 'yellow'
cweorn 'mill'		cyrran 'to turn'	gimm 'gem'
			gylp 'boast'

c = [ ]	*g* = [ ]	*c* = [ ]	*g* = [ ]
catt 'cat'	gāt 'goat'	cēlan 'to cool' <	gǣt 'goats' < *gātiz
cōl 'cool'	gold 'gold'	*kōljan	gylden 'golden' <
cū 'cow'	guma 'man'	cȳ 'kine' < *kūiz	*guldīn

c = [ ]	*g* = [ ]	*c* = [ ]	*g* = [ ]
āc 'oak'	plōg 'plow'	nacod 'naked'	sagu 'saying'
brōc 'breech'	burg 'city'	sūcan 'to suck'	swōgan 'to sound'
munuc 'monk'		bacan 'to bake'	āgan 'to own'

c = [ ]	*g* = [ ]	*c* = [ ]	*g* = [ ]
pic 'pitch'	īg 'island'	micel 'much'	sige 'victory'
līc 'body'	bodig 'body'	bēce 'beech'	drȳge 'dry'
brēc 'breeches'	þegnas 'thanes'	ræced 'building'	segel 'sail'
	sægde 'said'		nægel 'nail'

a. Which sounds occur initially before a consonant, a back vowel, or a front vowel resulting from mutation?

_____

b. Which sounds occur after or between back vowels? _____

c. Which sounds occur initially before an original front vowel and after or between front vowels? _____

_____

5.8   OLD ENGLISH TRANSCRIPTION

Write these Old English words in phonetic transcription:

fyxen	'vixen'	_____	hring	'ring'	_____
wīf	'woman'	_____	hlynsian	'to resound'	_____
wīfes	'woman's'	_____	āhte	'owned'	_____
þēofas	'thieves'	_____	eoh	'horse'	_____
bæð	'bath'	_____	scēap	'sheep'	_____
baðian	'to bathe'	_____	sceattas	'coins'	_____
sǣs	'seas'	_____	asce	'ash'	_____
nosu	'nose'	_____	sceaft	'shaft'	_____
lȳs	'lice'	_____	brycg	'bridge'	_____
lūsa	'of lice'	_____	oxa	'ox'	_____
hām	'home'	_____	betwix	'between'	_____
bazere	'baptist'	_____	dæġes	'day's'	_____
weorc	'work'	_____	strang	'strong'	_____
ċēosan	'to choose'	_____	glōm	'darkness'	_____
ċiriċe	'church'	_____	wōgan	'to woo'	_____
styċċe	'piece'	_____	gnagan	'to gnaw'	_____
cuman	'to come'	_____	gīsl	'hostage'	_____
cyċene	'kitchen'	_____	ġyldan	'to yield'	_____
cēpan	'to keep'	_____	gyldan	'to gild'	_____
friġnan	'to ask'	_____	ġenōg	'enough'	_____
dæġ	'day'	_____	hāliġ	'holy'	_____
dagas	'days'	_____	hālga	'saint'	_____

5.9   MUTATION OR UMLAUT

Mutation or umlaut is a change in the quality of a vowel resulting from its assimilation to a neighboring sound. The change took place during the prehistoric period of Old English.

1. The following words and their reconstructed sources will illustrate some mutations. Each historical form shows the result of umlaut in its first syllable.

lengest < *langista 'longest'
gēs < *gōsiz 'geese'
bēċ < *bōki 'book (dat.)'
strengþu < *strangiþu 'strength'
fēdan < *fōdjan 'to feed' (cf. Goth. fōdjan)

trymman < *trumjan 'to fortify'
yfel < *uβil 'evil' (cf. Goth. ubil)
færþ < *fariþ 'goes' (cf. Goth. fariþ)
synn < *sunjō 'sin'
hell < *hælju 'hell' (older haljō, cf. Goth. halja)

What sounds caused mutation?

_____i, ə_____

Why is the cause of mutation not clear in recorded Old English? _IN MANY CASES, THE PHONETIC ENVIRONMENTS ORIGINALLY CAUSING THE MUTATION ARE NO LONGER THERE._

2. In the following examples, the first word in each pair has a mutated vowel, and the second word is a related form with an unmutated vowel.

ȳtemest 'outmost' / ūte 'outside'
dehter 'daughter (dat.)' / dohtor 'daughter (nom.)'
gǣt 'goats' / gāt 'goat'
bæcþ 'bakes' / bacan 'to bake'
hilpþ 'helps' / helpan 'to help'

secgan 'to say' / sægde 'said'
frȳnd 'friends' / frēond 'friend'
wyrþe 'worthy' / weorþ 'worth'
nȳr 'nearer' / nēah 'near'
yldra 'elder' / eald 'old'

P. 87?

All the vowels except the high front *i, ī, y, ȳ* and the front long *ē, ǣ* are subject to mutation. Short *a* has two mutations, depending on whether or not it is followed by a nasal consonant. A breve indicates a short vowel (ĕ); a breve over a macron indicates both the short and the long vowel (ŭ). Indicate the mutation of each of the following vowels.

FRONT VOWELS	DIPHTHONGS	BACK VOWELS
		ŭ̄ ȳ / y
ĕ _i_	ĕo _y / ȳ_	ŏ _e / ē_
		ă + n _X æ_
ǣ _e_	ĕa _y / ȳ_	ā _æ / æ_

After you have compared these changes with the articulation chart of Old English vowels, describe the general direction in which vowels move when they are mutated.

THEY ARE FRONTED, RAISED OR BOTH FRONTED & RAISED.

3. In the following pairs, the first word has a mutated vowel omitted from its spelling, and the second word is a related form without mutation. Supply the missing vowel.

d_ē_man 'to judge' / dōm 'judgment'
t_ȳ_nan 'to close' / tūn 'enclosure'
f_ȳ_nd 'enemies' / fēond 'enemy'
f_y_llan 'to fill' / full 'full'
h_ǣ_lan 'to heal' / hāl 'whole'
sc_y_rtest 'shortest' / sceort 'short'
m_ē_tan 'to meet' / mōt 'meeting'
str_æ_ngest 'strongest' / strang 'strong'

m_i_lt 'melts' / meltan 'to melt'
w_e_tt 'goes' / wadan 'to go'
þ_e_ċċan 'to cover' / þæċ 'thatch'
m_e_rġen 'morning' / morgen 'morning'
ċ_ȳ_pan 'to buy' / ċēap 'price'
h_y_rdan 'to harden' / heard 'hard'
m_ȳ_s 'mice' / mūs 'mouse'
m_ǣ_st 'most' / mā 'more'

SEE P. 96 (ut BR) 3 88 # 95

5.10 SOUND CHANGES FROM INDO-EUROPEAN TO OLD ENGLISH

The following charts summarize the Indo-European sources of the Old English sound system. Only the main line of development has been given; there are many conditioned changes not represented here. The charts show which Indo-European sounds fell together in Proto-Germanic (for example, IE ə, *a*, and *o* as

PG *a*) and which Proto-Germanic sounds split into more than one Old English sound (as, for example, PG *e* did).

1. VOWELS: Complete the vowel chart by supplying the phonetic symbols for the Old English developments.

INDO-EUROPEAN SOURCE		PROTO-GERMANIC	OLD ENGLISH DEVELOPMENT	
key word	*vowel*	*vowel*	*phonetic symbol*	*key word*
*pisk-	i	i		fisc 'fish'
*ed-	e	e		etan 'to eat'
*ert-				eorðe 'earth'
*pətēr	ə			fæder 'father'
*man-	a	a		mann 'man'
*oktō	o			eahta 'eight'
*hunto-		u		hund 'dog'
*kubi-	u			hyp 'hip'
*ghuto-		o		god 'god'
*swīno-	ī	ī		swīn 'swine'
*steigh-	ei			stīgan 'to rise'
*dhēti-	ē	æ		dǣd 'deed'
*māter-	ā	ō		mōdor 'mother'
*pōd-	ō			fōt 'foot'
*mūs	ū	ū		mūs 'mouse'
*pūri				fȳr 'fire'
*aidh-	ai	ai		ād 'pyre'
*oino-	oi			ān 'one'
*keus-	eu	eu		cēosan 'to choose'
*aug-	au	au		ēacan 'to eke'
*roudh-	ou			rēad 'red'
	uncertain	ē		hēr 'here'

2. CONSONANTS: Complete the consonant chart by supplying the phonetic symbols for the Proto-Germanic and Old English developments.

INDO-EUROPEAN SOURCE		PROTO-GERMANIC	OLD ENGLISH DEVELOPMENT	
key word	*consonant*	*consonant*	*consonant*	*key word*
*bend-	b			penn 'pen'
*del-	d			tellan 'to tell'
*gombho-	g			camb 'comb'
*geus-				čēosan 'to choose'
*bhugo-	bh			buc 'buck'
*ghebh-				ġyfan 'to give'
*dherg-	dh			deorc 'dark'
*ghaido-	gh			gāt 'goat'
*dhragh-				dragan 'to draw'
*ghel				ġellan 'to yell'
*wlpo-	p			wulf 'wolf'
				wulfas 'wolves'
*uperi[1]				ofer 'over'
*bhəto-	t			bæð 'bath'
				baðian 'to bathe'
*dhouto-[1]				dēad 'dead'
*kortu-	k			heard 'hard'
*marko-				mearh 'horse'
*dukā-[1]				togian 'to tow'
*akyā-				ecg 'edge'
*wes-	s			wes 'be!'
				wesan 'to be'
*dheuso-[1]				dēor 'animal'
*skeud-	sk			scēotan 'to shoot'
*med-	m			metan 'to mete'
*ne-	n			ne 'not'
*loist-	l			lāst 'footprint'
*reidh-	r			rīdan 'to ride'
*wir-	w			wer 'man'
*yuga	y			ġeoc 'yoke'

[1]Verner's Law applies.

5.11 GRAMMATICAL GENDER

Examine the following phrases:

MASCULINE	NEUTER	FEMININE
se wīfmann 'the woman'	þæt wīf 'the woman'	sēo hlǽfdiġe 'the lady'
se mete 'the food'	þæt ealu 'the ale'	sēo reord 'the meal'
se mōna 'the moon'	þæt tungol 'the star'	sēo sunne 'the sun'
se grund 'the ground'	þæt land 'the land'	sēo eorðe 'the earth'
se æppel 'the apple'	þæt ǽġ 'the egg'	sēo bēan 'the bean'
se earm 'the arm'	þæt lim 'the limb'	sēo eaxl 'the shoulder'
þes wīfmann 'this woman'	þis wīf 'this woman'	þēos hlǽfdiġe 'this lady'
þes grund	þis land	þēos eorðe
sum æppel 'a certain apple'	sum ǽġ 'a certain egg'	sumu bēan 'a certain bean'
sum earm	sum lim	sumu eaxl
(Ic seah) sumne wīfmann '(I saw) a certain woman'	(Ic seah) sum wīf '(I saw) a certain woman'	(Ic seah) sume hlǽfdiġan '(I saw) a certain lady'
(Ic seah) sumne æppel	(Ic seah) sum ǽġ	(Ic seah) sume bēane
se mōna . . . hē is gōd 'the moon . . . it is good'	þæt tungol . . . hit is gōd 'the star . . . it is good'	sēo sunne . . . hēo is gōd 'the sun . . . it is good'
se mete . . . hē is gōd	þæt ealu . . . hit is gōd	sēo reord . . . hēo is gōd
se wīfmann . . . hēo is gōd	þæt wīf . . . hēo is gōd	sēo hlǽfdiġe . . . hēo is gōd

1. Which of the following is the best indicator of the grammatical gender of an Old English noun? Which is the poorest indicator?

   meaning (sexual gender)   concord of adjective and noun
   the ending of the noun   concord of pronoun and noun

2. What is the gender of each of the italicized nouns?

   sēo *ċeaster* 'the city' _____

   þæt *scip* 'the ship' _____

   Ic seah sum *fæt* 'I saw a certain vessel.' _____

   se *tūn* 'the village' _____

   sumu *lūs* 'a certain louse' _____

   þes *blōstm* 'this blossom' _____

   þis *lēaf* 'this leaf' _____

   þēos *costung* 'this temptation' _____

   Ic seah sume *bollan* 'I saw a certain bowl.' _____

   Ic seah sumne *disc* 'I saw a certain dish.' _____

3. Translate these phrases into Old English:

   the blossom _____

   this moon _____

   this ship _____

   this sun _____

   a certain meal _____

   I saw a certain star. _____

   I saw a certain arm. _____

4. What is the basis for determining the "gender" of a noun in Modern English, and how many "genders" do we have? How would you explain the gender relationship between noun and pronoun in these sentences?

"That's a lovely baby. What's its name?"
"You have a visitor in the lounge." "Who is it?"
"Somebody telephoned you." "What did they want?"
"I saw his new boat. She's a beauty."
"My car's nearly out of gas—fill 'er up."

5.12   INFLECTION OF NOUNS

Write the declension of these Old English nouns:

	a-STEM, MASCULINE	*a*-STEM, NEUTER	*ō*-STEM, FEMININE
	grund 'ground' (like *hund*)	*ġēar* 'year' (like *dēor*)	*talu* 'tale' (like *lufu*)
sing. nom.			
acc.			
gen.			
dat.			
plur. nom.			
acc.			
gen.			
dat.			

	n-STEM, MASCULINE	*n*-STEM, NEUTER	*n*-STEM, FEMININE
	nama 'name' (like *oxa*)	*ēare* 'ear'	*sunne* 'sun' (like *tunge*)
sing. nom.			
acc.			
gen.			
dat.			
plur. nom.			
acc.			
gen.			
dat.			

	ROOT-CONSONANT STEM, MASCULINE	ROOT-CONSONANT STEM, FEMININE	*r*-STEM, NEUTER
	fēond 'fiend, foe' (like *fōt*, but with mutation of *ēo* to *ȳ*)	*bōc* 'book' (like *gōs*)	*lamb* 'lamb' (like *ċild*)
sing. nom.			
acc.			
gen.			
dat.			
plur. nom.			
acc.			
gen.			
dat.			

5.13 INFLECTION OF DEMONSTRATIVES AND ADJECTIVES

Write the declension of these phrases:

	se tila hlāford 'the good lord' (like *se dola cyning*)	*þæt tile sweord* 'the good sword' (like *þæt dole bearn*)	*sēo tile reord* 'the good meal' (like *sēo dole ides*)
sing. nom.	_____	_____	_____
acc.	_____	_____	_____
gen.	_____	_____	_____
dat.	_____	_____	_____
ins.	_____	_____	_____
plur. nom.	_____	_____	_____
acc.	_____	_____	_____
gen.	_____	_____	_____
dat.	_____	_____	_____

	til hlāford	*til sweord*	*tilu reord*
sing. nom.	_____	_____	_____
acc.	_____	_____	_____
gen.	_____	_____	_____
dat.	_____	_____	_____
ins.	_____	_____	_____
plur. nom.	_____	_____	_____
acc.	_____	_____	_____
gen.	_____	_____	_____
dat.	_____	_____	_____

5.14 MODERN SURVIVALS OF OLD ENGLISH INFLECTION

Some Old English inflectional endings have survived into Modern English and have actually increased in importance, that is, in the number of words to which they are added. Other inflections still survive, but only in petrified forms; they survive as dead museum pieces that illustrate earlier living endings. Each italicized word in the phrases below contains a modern survival of an Old English inflection. Match the modern forms with the Old English inflections listed on the right.

NOUNS

A	The *boats* were floating by the dock.	A. nominative-accusative plural ending *-as*
F	He found a *raven's* nest.	B. nominative-accusative plural ending *-an*
A	They took a four-*day* trip.	C. nominative-accusative plural ending *-ru*
E	The *oxen* follow the plow.	D. nominative-accusative plural with mutation of the stem vowel
D	The *dormice* are hunting for food.	E. nominative-accusative plural identical in form with nominative-accusative singular
E	The *sheep* are in the pasture.	
	These *kind* are oak trees.	F. genitive singular ending *-es*
I	It *seldom* rains.	G. genitive singular without *-s*
G	The feast of the Annunciation is called *Lady* Day.	H. genitive plural ending *-a*
D	Kate is five *foot* tall.	I. dative singular ending *-e*
	There is hardly a man *alive*.	J. dative plural ending *-um*

108

The next four italicized words are "double plurals"; each preserves two Old English inflections. Match each modern form with two of the Old English inflections listed on page 108.

__B__ __E__ a herd of beeves, fair oxen, and fair *kine*
__A__ __C__ They sewed fig leaves together, and made themselves *breeches*.
__B__ __C__ Jacob begat Judah and his *brethren*.
__B__ __C__ Suffer the little *children* to come unto me.

ADJECTIVES AND ADVERBS

__D__ a *colder* day
__G__ the *narrowest* margin
__F__ an *elder* son
__E__ the *eldest* daughter
__H__ the *foremost* advocate
__B__ *Mondays* they come home early.
__A__ And feed *deep*, deep upon her peerless eyes. (Keats)
__D__ He drives *slower* in town.
__B__ He slept *days*.
__B__ She has a lot to do *besides*.
__B__ They called *once*.
__D__ Why livest thou, dead dog, a *lenger* day? (Spenser)

A. adverb formed with the suffix -*e*
B. genitive singular used adverbially
C. adverb comparative ending -*or*
D. adjective comparative ending -*ra*
E. adjective superlative ending -*est* (from earlier -*ist*) with mutation
F. adjective comparative ending -*ra* (from earlier -*ira*) with mutation
G. adjective superlative ending -*ost*
H. adjective double superlative ending

5.15 THE SYNTAX OF NOUNS

The sentences below illustrate some of the common uses of Old English cases. The case of each noun or noun phrase is identified by an abbreviation after it: (*n*) nominative, (*a*) accusative, (*g*) genitive, (*d*) dative, (*i*) instrumental.

Give the number of a sentence that contains an example of each of the following case uses:

NOMINATIVE: as subject _____, subject complement _____, direct address _____
ACCUSATIVE: as object of a verb _____, adverbial of duration _____, object of a preposition _____
GENITIVE: as possessive _____, expression of measure _____, adverbial of time _____, object of a verb _____, object of a preposition _____
DATIVE: as object of a verb _____, object of a preposition _____, expression of means or cause _____
INSTRUMENTAL: as expression of time _____, of accompaniment _____, of comparison _____

1. Ġif þēowman$^{(n)}$ wyrċe on Sunnandæġ$^{(a)}$ be his hlāfordes$^{(g)}$ hæse$^{(d)}$, sȳ hē$^{(n)}$ frēo,
   If a serf work on Sunday by his lord's command shall be he free

   and se hlāford$^{(n)}$ ġeselle xxx scillinga$^{(g)}$ tō wīte$^{(d)}$.
   and the lord pay 30 shillings as fine

2. Cædmon$^{(n)}$, sing mē$^{(d)}$ hwæthwugu.
   Cadmon, sing me something

3. He is ordfrume$^{(n)}$ and ende$^{(n)}$.
   He is beginning and end

4. Hē$^{(n)}$ wræc þone aldorman Cumbran$^{(a)}$.
   He avenged the earl Cumbra

5. Ond þæs$^{(g)}$ ymb ānne mōnaþ$^{(a)}$ ġefeaht Ælfred cyning$^{(n)}$ wiþ alne þone
   And afterwards about a month fought Alfred the king against all the

   here$^{(a)}$.
   [Viking] army

6. Cynewulf[n] oft miċlum ġefeohtum[d] feaht wið Bretwālum[d].
Cynewulf often with great battles fought against the Britons

7. Cynewulf[n] benam Siġebryht[a] his rīċes[g].
Cynewulf deprived Sigebryht of his kingdom

8. Iōseph[n] ðā ārās nihtes[g].
Joseph then arose at night

9. Ond þȳ ilcan ġēare[i] mon[n] ofslōg Æþelbald[a].
And in that same year someone slew Athelbald

10. Beornrǣd[n] lȳtle hwīle[a] hēold.
Beornred for a little while ruled

11. And þā ġeāscode hē[n] þone cyning[a] lȳtle werode[i] on wīfcȳþþe[d]
And then learned he the king [to be] with a small troop in woman's company

on Meran tūne[d].
at Merton

12. And wunodon þǣr ealne þone winter[a].
And [they] stayed there all the winter

13. Hē[n] ne mæġ ætes[g] oððe wǣtes[g] brūcan.
He cannot food or drink enjoy

14. Þā ġewendon hī[n] wið þæs ċildes[g].
Then traveled they toward the child

15. Ne ġedafenað þān gāstlicum[d] þæt hī[n] ðam flǣsclicum[d] ġeefenlǣċen.
Nor does it befit the spiritual that they the fleshly emulate

16. Se eorl[n] wæs þē[i] blīþra.
The earl was the happier

17. Wīġend[n] cruncon, wundum[d] wēriġe.
Warriors fell by wounds wearied

5.16 PRONOUNS

For each of the Modern English pronouns, give the Old English word from which it developed and tell the case of the Old English source pronoun.

MOD-E PRONOUN	OE SOURCE	CASE OF OE PRONOUN	MOD-E PRONOUN	OE SOURCE	CASE OF OE PRONOUN
I	ic	nominative	his		
me			she		
mine			her		
we			it		
us			(you tell) 'em		
our			who		
thou			whom		
thee			whose		
thine			what		

MOD-E PRONOUN	OE SOURCE	CASE OF OE PRONOUN	MOD-E PRONOUN	OE SOURCE	CASE OF OE PRONOUN
ye			why (adv.)		
you			which		
your			that		
he			this		
him			those		

5.17 WEAK AND STRONG VERBS

1. The following verbs are cited in both their infinitive and their preterit singular forms. Mark weak verbs *W* and strong verbs *S*.

_____ brengan–brōhte 'to bring'   _____ hyngran–hyngrede 'to hunger'
_____ ġifan–ġeaf 'to give'   _____ lōcian–lōcode 'to look'
_____ habban–hæfde 'to have'   _____ scīnan–scān 'to shine'
_____ hȳran–hȳrde 'to hear'   _____ steppan–stōp 'to step'
_____ hōn–hēng 'to hang'   _____ tæ̆ċan–tāhte 'to teach'

2. Some Modern English verbs come in pairs: *fall* and *fell, lie* and *lay, sit* and *set.* What difference in meaning is there between the members of each pair? _____

_____

_____

What is the cause of their difference in form? _____

_____

Which verb in each pair is weak, and which strong? _____

_____

3. Explain why there is a difference between the infinitive and the preterit in these verbs: *bēon–wæs* 'be–was' and *gān–ēode* 'go–went.'

_____

_____

_____

4. Explain why there is a difference between the stem vowel of the infinitive and that of the preterit in these verbs: *rīdan–rād* 'ride–rode,' *teran–tær* 'tear–tore,' *frēosan–frēas* 'freeze–froze.' _____

_____

_____

_____

_____

111

THE SEVEN CLASSES OF STRONG VERBS

Strong verbs are characterized by a lack of the dental suffix in their preterit and by an internal vowel change (gradation or ablaut) between their present and preterit forms.

— 1. Strong verbs are divided into seven classes on the basis of what vowels occur in each of their four principal parts. List here the typical vowel series found in each of the classes. (In class VII, the vowel of the infinitive and past participle varies, so is omitted.)

CLASS	INFINITIVE	PRETERIT SINGULAR	PRETERIT PLURAL	PAST PARTICIPLE
I	ī	ā	i	i
II	ēo or ū	ēa	u	o
III	i	a	u	u
	e or eo	ea	u	o
IV	e	æ	ǣ	o
V	e	æ	ǣ	e
	i	ēa	ēa	i
VI	a	ō	ō	a
VII	ēo			
	ē	ē	ē	

— 2. Identify by number the class of each of these strong verbs. All four principal parts are given.

VI	bacan	bōc	bōcon	bacen	'to bake'
VII	bēatan	bēot	bēoton	bēaten	'to beat'
IV	beran	bær	bǣron	boren	'to bear'
I	bītan	bāt	biton	biten	'to bite'
VII	blandan	blēnd	blēndon	blanden	'to blend'
II	brūcan	brēac	brucon	brocen	'to enjoy'
III	ċeorfan	ċearf	curfon	corfen	'to carve'
II	clēofan	clēaf	clufon	clofen	'to cleave'
V	cweðan	cwæð	cwǣdon	cweden	'to say, quoth'
III	delfan	dealf	dulfon	dolfen	'to delve'
III	drincan	dranc	druncon	druncen	'to drink'
V	forġyfan	forġeaf	forġēafon	forġyfen	'to forgive'

3. It is usually possible to recognize the class to which a strong verb belongs from its infinitive alone. Unless there are special irregularities, it is then possible to predict the other principal parts, for all classes except class VII. All of the following verbs belong to classes I through VI and are regular. Write their remaining principal parts.

INFINITIVE	PRETERIT SINGULAR	PRETERIT PLURAL	PAST PARTICIPLE
beġytan 'to get'	_____	_____	_____
bīdan 'to bide'	_____	_____	_____
bindan 'to bind'	_____	_____	_____
būgan 'to bow'	_____	_____	_____
cnedan 'to knead'	_____	_____	_____
flēotan 'to float'	_____	_____	_____
meltan 'to melt'	_____	_____	_____
scafan 'to shave'	_____	_____	_____
stelan 'to steal'	_____	_____	_____
steorfan 'to die'	_____	_____	_____

Hǣlan 'to heal' and *meltan* 'to melt' are typical verbs, weak and strong respectively. Conjugate them.

PRINCIPAL PARTS	hǣlan, hǣlde, hǣled		meltan, mealt, multon, molten	
	PRESENT	PRETERIT	PRESENT	PRETERIT
INDICATIVE				
iċ ___	___	___	___	___
þū ___	___	___	___	___
hē ___	___	___	___	___
wē, ġē, hī ___	___	___	___	___
SUBJUNCTIVE				
iċ, þū, hē ___	___	___	___	___
wē, ġē, hī ___	___	___	___	___
IMPERATIVE				
þū ___	___		___	
ġē ___	___		___	
PARTICIPLE				
___	___	___	___	___

5.20   SYNTAX: WORD ORDER

Old English word order is, in general, similar to that of Modern English; however, some differences exist. For each of the following examples, describe how the word order departs from that of the present-day language.

1. His ġelēafa hine ġetrymde. _____
   His faith   him   strengthened

2. Ōswold him cōm tō. _____
   Oswald him came to

3. And hē nǣfre nǣniġ leoð   ġeleornade. _____
   And he never no   poetry learned

4. And hē hine sōna   tō þǣre abbudissan ġelǣdde. _____
   And he him immediately to the   abbess   led

5. And þā   onġeat   se cyning þæt. _____
   And then discovered the king   that

6. Hē ofslōg þone aldorman þe   him lengest wunode. _____
   He slew   the earl   that him longest had served

7. Hē þǣr wunode oþþæt hine ān swān   ofstang. _____
   He there dwelt   until him a swineherd stabbed

8. Þā   on morgenne   ġehȳrdon þæt þæs cyninges þeġnas, þæt se cyning ofslæġen wæs.
   Then in the morning heard   that the king's   thanes that the king   slain   was

   _____

5.21   OLD ENGLISH ILLUSTRATED

The following passages illustrate Old English. The dialect of all the selections is basically West Saxon. You may notice some spelling variations and some differences in grammatical forms between these passages and the language described in *Origins and Development*. Such differences may be due to slight dialect variation, time lapse, or simply the predilections of different writers.

The glosses which accompany the selections are generally word-for-word renderings of the Old English. They are inadequate as translations, but will help in reading the original.

Compare the passages with the description of Old English in *Origins and Development*. Note the distinctive features of Old English spelling, inflections, syntax, and vocabulary.

THE GOOD SAMARITAN

This version of the parable of the good Samaritan (Luke 10.30–36) is from a late West Saxon translation of the Gospels.

Sum man fērde fram Hiērūsalem tō Hiēricho, and becōm on ðā sceaðan; þā hine
A certain man went from Jerusalem to Jericho, and came upon the thieves; they him

berēafodon and tintregodon hine, and forlēton hine sāmcucene. Þā ġebyrode hit þæt
robbed and tormented him, and left him half-alive. Then happened it that

sum sāċerd fērde on þām ylcan weġe, and þā hē þæt ġeseah, hē hine forbēah. And
a certain priest went on the same way, and when he that saw he him passed by. And

eall swā se dīacon, þā hē wæs wið þā stōwe and þæt ġeseah, hē hyne ēac forbēah. Ðā
also this deacon, when he was at the place and that saw, he him also passed by. Then

5 fērde sum Samaritanisc man wið hine; þā hē hine ġeseah, þā wearð hē mid
went a certain Samaritan man by him; when he him saw, then became he with

mildheortnesse ofer hine āstyred. þā ġenēalǣhte hē, and wrāð his wunda and on āġēat
compassion for him stirred up. Then drew near he, and bound his wounds and poured on

ele and wīn, and hine on hys nȳten sette, and ġelǣdde on his lǣċehūs and hine lācnode; and
oil and wine, and him on his beast set, and led to his hospital and him medicated; and

brōhte ōðrum dæġe twēġen peneġas, and sealde þām lǣċe, and þus cwæð,
brought on the second day two pennies, and gave to the doctor, and thus said,

"Beġȳm hys, and swā hwæt swā þū māre tō ġedēst, þonne iċ cume, iċ hit forġylde
"Take care of him and whatsoever thou more besides dost, when I come, I it will repay

10 þē." Hwylċ þāra þrēora þynċð þē þæt sȳ þæs mæġ þe on ðā
thee." Which of the three seems to thee that may be that one's neighbor who among the

sceaðan befēoll?
thieves fell?

THE COMING OF THE ENGLISH

St. Bede describes the coming of the English to Britain in his *Historia Ecclesiastica Gentis Anglorum* (A.D. 731). Although it was written in Latin, the *History* was translated into Old English during the reign of King Alfred. The passage below is taken from that Old English version.

Þā ġesomnedon hī ġemōt and þeahtedon and rǣddon, hwæt him to dōnne
Then gathered they[2] an assembly and deliberated and counseled, what for them to do

wǣre, hwǣr him wǣre fultum tō sēċanne tō ġewearnienne and tō wiðscūfanne
might be, where for them might be help to be sought to avoid and to shove back

swā rēðre hergunge and swā ġelōmlīcre þāra norðþēoda. And þā ġelīcode him
such fiercer raids and such more frequent ones of the north people. And then it pleased them

eallum mid heora cyninge, Wyrtġeorn wæs hāten, þæt hī Seaxna þēode
all together with their king (Vortigern he was called) that they the Saxons' people

---

[2]The Britons.

5   ofer   þām sǣlīcum dǣlum him   on fultum ġeċȳġdon and ġelaðedon. Þæt cūð   is þæt
beyond the   sea   parts to them in aid   should call and invite.   It   known is that

þæt mid Drihtnes mihte ġestihtad wæs, þæt yfell wrǣc   cōme   ofer ðā wiþcorenan,
that by   God's   might arranged was, that evil punishment should come upon the rejected ones,

swā on þām ende þāra wīsena sweotolīċe ætȳwed is.
as in the end of the events clearly   shown is.

    Ðā   wæs ymb fēower hund   wintra and nigon and fēowertiġ fram ūres Drihtnes
    Then it was about four   hundred years and nine and forty   after our Lord's

menniscnysse, þæt Martiānus cāsere rīċe   onfēng and VII ġēar hæfde. Sē wæs
incarnation,   that Marcian Caesar the kingdom[3] received and seven years held.   He was

10 syxta   ēac fēowertiġum fram Agusto þām cāsere. Ðā Angel þēod and Seaxna   wæs
the sixth and forty   from Augustus the Caesar. Then Angle people and the Saxons' was

ġelaðod fram þām foresprecenan cyninge, and on   Breotone cōm on þrim myċlum scypum;
invited by   the foresaid   king,   and into Britain   came in three great   ships;

and on ēastdǣle   þyses ēalondes eardungstōwe   onfēng þurh   ðæs ylcan cyninges
and in the east part of this island   a dwelling place received through the same king's

bebod, þe hī   hider ġelaðode, þæt hī   sceoldan for heora ēðle   compian and
decree, who them hither invited,   that they should for their native land strive   and

feohtan. And hī   sōna   compedon wið heora ġewinnan, þe hī   oft   ǣr
fight.   And they immediately fought   with their enemies,   who them[4] often before

15 norðan   onhergedon; and Seaxan   þā siġe   ġeslōgan. Þā   sendan hī   hām
from the north had harassed; and the Saxons the victory won.   Then sent   they home

ǣrenddracan and hēton   secgan þysses landes wæstmbǣrnysse, and Brytta
a messenger and commanded [him] to report this   land's fruitfulness,   and the Britons'

yrġþo.   And hī þā sōna   hider sendon māran sciphere strengran wiġhena; and
cowardice. And they then immediately hither sent a larger fleet   of stronger warriors; and

wæs unoferswīðendlīċ weorud, þā   hī   tōgædere ġeþēodde wǣron. And him Bryttas
it was an invincible   host,   when they together joined   were.   And them the Britons

sealdan and ġēafan eardungstōwe   betwih him þæt hī   for sibbe   and hǣlo heora
granted and gave a dwelling place among them that they for the peace and safety of their

20 ēðles   campodon and wunnon wið heora fēondum, and hī   him andlyfne and āre
native land might fight and struggle with their enemies, and they them sustenance and revenue

forġēafen for heora ġewinne. Cōmon hī   of þrim folcum, ðām strangestan Germanie,   þæt
allowed for their labor.   Came   they of three peoples, the strongest   of Germania, that

of Seaxum and of Angle and of Ġēatum. Of Ġēata fruman syndon Cantware, and
of Saxons and of Angles and of Jutes.   Of Jutish origin are   Kent-men, and

Wihtsǣtan;   þæt is sēo ðēod þe Wiht þæt ēalond oneardað. Of Seaxum, þæt is of
Wight-settlers; that is the people that Wight the island inhabit. Of Saxons, that is from

ðām lande þe mon hāteð Ealdseaxan, cōman Ēastseaxan and Sūðseaxan   and
the land that one calls Old Saxons, come East Saxons and South Saxons and

25 Westseaxan. And of Engle cōman Ēastengle and Middelengle and Myrċe   and eall
West Saxons. And of Angles come East Angles and Middle Angles and Mercians and all

---

[3]The Roman Empire.
[4]The Britons.

Norðhembra cynn; is þæt land ðe Angulus is nemned, betwyh Ġēatum and
the Northumbrians' race; [it] is the land that Angeln is named, between Jutes and

Seaxum; is sǣd of þǣre tīde þe hī ðanon ġewiton oð tō dæġe, þæt hit wēste
Saxons; [it] is said from the time that they thence departed until today, that it deserted

wuniġe. Wǣron ðā ǣrest heora lāttēowas and heretogan twēġen ġebrōðra Hengest and
remains. Were the first of their leaders and war-chiefs two brothers Hengest and

Horsa. Hī wǣron Wihtġylses suna, þæs fæder wæs Witta hāten, þæs fæder wæs Wihta
Horsa. They were Wihtgils's sons, whose father was Witta called, whose father was Wihta

30 hāten, and þæs Wihta fæder wæs Wōden nemned; of ðæs strȳnde moniġra mǣġða
called, and of that Wihta the father was Woden named; of that stock many tribes'

cyningcynn fruman lǣdde. Ne wæs ðā ylding tō þon þæt hī hēapmǣlum cōman māran
royal family [its] origin takes. Nor was then delay before they in droves came, more

weorod of þām ðēodum, þe wē ǣr ġemynegodon. And þæt folc, ðe hider cōm, ongan
bands of those peoples that we before mentioned. And that people that hither came, began

weaxan and myclian tō þan swīðe, þæt hī wǣron on myclum eġe þām sylfan
to wax and multiply so much that they were a great terror to the very

landbīġenġan ðe hī ǣr hider laðedon and cȳġdon.
natives that them before hither had invited and called.

35 Æfter þissum hī þā ġeweredon tō sumre tīde wið Pehtum, þā hī ǣr
After this they then were allied for a certain time with the Picts, whom they before

þurh ġefeoht feor ādrifan. And þā wǣron Seaxan sēcende intingan and
through battle far away had driven. And then were the Saxons seeking cause and

tōwyrde heora ġedāles wið Bryttas. Cȳðdon him openlīce and sǣdon, būtan
opportunity for their breaking with the Britons. They informed them openly and said unless

hī him māran andlyfne sealdon, þæt hī woldan him sylfe niman and herġian,
they them more sustenance gave, that they would for themselves take and plunder,

þǣr hī hit findan mihton. And sōna ðā bēotunge dǣdum ġefyldon: bærndon
where they it find might. And immediately the threat with deeds fulfilled: they burned

40 and hergedon and slōgan fram ēastsǣ oð westsǣ; and him nǣniġ wiðstōd. Ne wæs
and harried and slew from the east sea to the west sea; and them none withstood. Nor was

ungelīc wrǣcc þām ðe iū Chaldēas bærndon Hiērūsaleme weallas and ðā
unlike the vengeance to that when formerly the Chaldees burned Jerusalem's walls and the

cynelīcan ġetimbro mid fȳre fornāman for ðæs Godes folces synnum.
royal building with fire destroyed for God's people's sins.

ST. GREGORY AND THE ENGLISH

St. Gregory the Great began the conversion of the English when he sent St. Augustine to them, thus fulfilling a long-standing ambition. The following account, from Ælfric's homily on St. Gregory, tells how he, in his younger years, first became acquainted with the English and determined to convert them. Gregory was following a popular medieval custom of wordplay when he made the three puns recorded here.

Ðā ġelamp hit æt sumum sǣle, swā swā ġȳt for oft dēð, þæt Englisce cȳpmenn
Then happened it at a certain time as [it] still very often does that English merchants

brōhton heora ware tō Rōmānabyriġ, and Grēgōrius ēode be þǣre strǣt tō ðām Engliscum
brought their wares to Rome, and Gregory went along the street to the English

116

mannum, heora ðing scēawiġende. Þā ġeseah hē betwux ðām warum ċȳpecnihtas ġesette,
men,   their things looking at.   Then saw   he among the   wares   slaves   placed,

þā wæron hwītes līċhaman and fæġeres andwlitan   menn, and æðellīċe ġefeaxode.
who were of white body   and of fair   countenance men, and nobly   haired.

5 Grēgōrius ðā behēold þæra cnapena wlite,   and befrān of   hwilċere þēod hī ġebrōhte
   Gregory   then noticed the boys' fairness, and asked from which   nation they brought

wæron. Þā sǣde him man   þæt hī of   Englalande wæron, and þæt ðǣre ðēode
had been. Then told him someone that they from England   were   and that that nation's

mennisc swā wlitiġ wǣre. Eft   ðā Grēgōrius befrān, hwæðer þæs landes folc   crīsten
people   so fair   were. Again then Gregory   asked   whether that land's people Christian

wǣre ðe hǣðen. Him man   sǣde þæt hī hǣðene wǣron. Grēgōrius ðā of   innweardre
were or heathen. Him someone told that they heathen were.   Gregory   then from his inward

heortan langsume siċċetunge tēah, and cwæð, "Wālāwā, þæt swā fæġeres hīwes menn sindon
heart a long   sigh   drew and said, "Alas,   that so fairly   hued men should be

10 ðām sweartan dēofle underðēodde!" Eft hē āxode, hū ðǣre ðēode nama wǣre þe hī
   to the dark   devil subject!"   Again he asked what that nation's name was that they

of   cōmon. Him wæs ġeandwyrd, þæt hī Angle ġenemnode wǣron. Þā cwæð hē,
from came. To him it was answered   that they Angles named   were.   Then said he,

"Rihtlīċe hī sind Angle ġehāten, forðan ðe hī engla wlite   habbað, and swilcum
"Rightly they are Angles called, for   they angels' fairness have   and for such

ġedafenað þæt hī on heofonum engla ġefēran   bēon." Ġȳt ðā Grēgōrius befrān, hū
it is fitting that they in heaven angels' companions be."   Still then Gregory   asked how

ðǣre scīre nama wǣre þe ðā cnapan of ālǣdde wǣron. Him man sǣde, þæt ðā
that district named was that the boys from brought had been. To him one said that the

15 scīrmen   wǣron Dēre ġehātene. Grēgōrius andwyrde, "Wel hī sind Dēre ġehātene,
   district men were Deirans called. Gregory   answered, "Well they are Deirans called,

forðan ðe hī sind fram graman[5] ġenerode, and tō Crīstes mildheòrtnysse ġeċȳġede." Ġȳt
because they are from wrath   delivered, and to Christ's mercy   called."   Yet

ðā   hē befrān, "Hū is ðǣre lēode   cyning ġehāten?" Him wæs ġeandswarod þæt se
again he asked, "How is that people's king   called?" To him it was answered   that the

cyning Ælle ġehāten wǣre. Hwæt, ðā Grēgōrius gamenode mid his wordum tō ðām naman,
king   Alle called was. Well, then Gregory   played   with his words on the name,

and cwæð, "Hit ġedafenað þæt Allēlūia sȳ ġesungen on ðām lande tō lofe þæs ælmihtiġan
and said, "It is fitting   that Alleluia be sung   in that land as praise of the almighty

20 scyppendes."
   creator."

THE ANGLO-SAXON CHRONICLE

The *Anglo-Saxon Chronicle* was an annual record of important events. The exact date of its origin is unknown, but it was probably first compiled during the reign of King Alfred. Thereafter it was continued at various monasteries so that there are several different versions of the *Chronicle*. The last entry, describing the death of King Stephen and the election of a new Abbot of Peterborough, is for the year 1154. The most remarkable thing about the *Chronicle* is that it was written in English at a time when other historical writings

---

[5]The pun is on the name of the district, Deira, and the Latin *de ira* 'from wrath.'

throughout Europe were composed exclusively in Latin. The extracts printed below are all taken from the Peterborough Chronicle (Bodleian MS. Laud. 636).

       Brittene īġland is ehta hund   mīla lang and twā hund   brād, and hēr sind
[PROLOGUE] *Britain island is eight hundred miles long and two hundred broad, and here are*

on þis īġlande fīf ġeþēode: Englisc and Brytwylsc   and Scyttisc and Pyhtisc and
on this island five languages: English and British-Welsh and Scottish and Pictish and

Bōclēden. Ērest wēron būgend   þises landes Brittes; þā cōman of   Armēnia and
book-Latin. First were inhabitants of this land Britons; they came from Armenia[6] and

ġesǣtan sūðewearde Bryttene ǣrost. . . .
settled southward Britain first.

5 An. CCCC.XLIX. Hēr Martiānus and Ualentīnus onfēngon rīċe   and rīxadon VII.
    A.D. *449*   *Here[7] Marcian and Valentinian received the kingdom and ruled 7*

winter, and on heora dagum ġeladōde Wyrtġeorn Angelcin   hider, and hī þā cōmon
years, and in their days invited Vortigern English people hither, and they then came

on þrim ċēolum hider to Brytene. . . .
in three ships hither to Britain.

An. D.XCVI. Hēr Grēgōrius   pāpa sende to Brytene Augustīnum mid wel maneġum
A.D. *596*[8]   *Here Gregory the Pope sent to Britain Augustine with very many*

munucum, þe Godes word   Engla þēoda godspellodon.
monks, who God's word to English people preached.

10 An. DCC.LXXXVII. Hēr . . . cōmon ǣrest III. scipu Norðmanna of   Hereðalande, and
    A.D. *787* [*789*][9]   *Here came first 3 ships of Northmen from Hörthaland, and*

þā se ġerēfa þǣr tō rād, and hī   wolde drīfan tō þēs cininges tūne, þȳ hē nyste
then the reeve there to rode, and them wished to force to the king's manor, for he knew not

hwæt hī wǣron, and hine man ofslōh þā. Ðæt wǣron þā ērestan scipu   Deniscra manna
what they were, and him one slew then. Those were the first ships of Danish men

þe Angelcynnes   land ġesōhton.
that English people's land sought.

An. DCC.XCIII. Hēr wǣron rēðe   forebēcna cumene ofer Norðanhymbra land, and þæt
    A.D. *793*   *Here were terrible foresigns come over Northumbrians' land and the*

15 folc earmlīċe   brēġdon; þæt wǣron ormēte līġrǣscas, and wǣron ġeseowene fȳrene
    people wretchedly terrified; there were intense lightnings and were seen fiery

dracan on þām lyfte flēogende. Ðām   tācnum sōna   fyliġde myċel hunger, and lītel
dragons in the air flying. From the tokens immediately followed great hunger and a little

æfter þām þæs ilcan ġēares on VI Id. Ianr. earmlīċe   hēþenra manna hergung ādiligode
after that in the same year on January 8 wretchedly the heathen men's harrying destroyed

Godes ċyriċan in Lindisfarena ēe   þurh rēaflāc and mansleht. . . .
God's church on Lindisfarne island through plunder and manslaughter.

---

[6]An error resulting from a misreading of Bede, who says *fram Armoricano* 'Armorica or Brittany.'
[7]That is, 'now, in this year.'
[8]Augustine left Rome in 596 and arrived in England in 597.
[9]The dates in the *Chronicle* are occasionally mistaken; they are corrected in brackets.

An. DCC.XCIIII. Hēr . . . þā hǣðenan on   Norðhymbrum hergodon, and Ecgferðes
A.D. *794*   *Here the heathens among Northumbrians harried, and Ecgferth's*

20 mynster æt Donemūðe   berēfodon. . . .
    monastery at Donmouth [Jarrow] plundered.

An. DCCC.LXV. Hēr sæt   se hǣþene here on Tenet and ġenam frið wið
A.D. *865*   *Here camped the heathen army in Thanet and made peace with*

Cantwarum, and Cantware heom feoh behēton wið þām friðe, and on þām feohbehāte
Kentmen,   and Kentmen them money promised for the peace, and for the money-promise

se here hine on niht up bestæl, and oferhergode ealle Cent ēastewarde.
the army itself at night up stole, and overran   all Kent eastward.

An. DCCC.LXXI. Hēr . . . fēng   Ælfrēd Æþelwulfing . . . tō West   Seaxna rīċe,
A.D. *871*   *Here   succeeded Alfred Ethelwulf's son to the West Saxons' kingdom*

25 and þæs ymb I. mōnað ġefeaht Ælfrēd cining wið   ealne þone here   lītle   werede
    and after that 1 month fought Alfred the king against all the   army   with a little force

æt Wiltūne, and hine lange on dæġ   ġeflȳmde,   and þā Deniscan āhton
at Wilton, and it   far into the day put to flight, and the Danish owned

wælstōwe   ġeweald. . . .
the slaughter-place's control.[10]

An. DCCC.LXXVIII. Hēr . . . Ælfrēd cyning . . . ġefeaht wið   ealne here, and hine
A.D. *878*   *Here Alfred the king   fought with the whole army and it*

ġeflȳmde,   and him æfter rād oð þet ġeweorc, and þǣr sæt   XIIII niht, and þā
put to flight, and it   after rode to the fortress, and there camped 14   nights, and then

30 sealde se here him ġīslas   and myċċle āðas, þet hī of his rīċe   woldon,   and him
    gave the army him hostages and great oaths, that they from his kingdom would [go], and him

ēac ġehēton   þet heora cyng fulwihte onfōn wolde, and hī   þæt ġelāston. . . .
also they promised that their king baptism receive would, and they that did.

An. DCCCC.I. Hēr ġefōr   Ælfrēd cyning, VII Kl. Nouembris, and hē hēold þet
A.D. *901 [899]*   *Here passed away Alfred the king, October 26,   and he held the*

rīċe   XXVIII wintra and healf ġēar. . . .
kingdom 28   winters and a half year.

An. DCCCC.XCI. Hēr wæs Ġypeswiċ ġehergod, and æfter þām swȳðe raðe   wæs
A.D. *991*   *Here was Ipswich harried, and after that very quickly was*

35 Brihtnōð ealdorman   ofslæġen æt Mældune, and on þām ġēare man ġerǣdde þæt man
    Byrhtnoth the ealdorman slain   at Maldon, and in this year one decided that one

ġeald   ǣrest gafol   Deniscum mannum for þām myċċlan brōgan þe hī   worhton be
yielded first tribute[11] *to Danish men   for the great   terror that they caused along*

þām sǣriman; þæt wæs ǣrest X. þūsend pūnda. . . .
the seacoast; it was first 10 thousand pounds.

An. DCCCC.XCIIII. Hēr on þisum ġēare cōm Ānlāf and Sweġen to Lundenbyriġ on
A.D. *994*   *Here in this   year came Olaf and Svein to London town on*

---

[10]That is, 'Alfred's small force repelled the Danish army throughout the day, but the Danes finally won the battle.'
[11]That is, 'it was first decided to pay tribute.'

Nātīuitas   Sancte Mārīe mid IIII and hundniġontiġum scipum, and hī   þā on þā burh
the Nativity of St. Mary with 4   and ninety   ships,   and they then   the town

40 festlīċe   feohtende wǣron. . . .
continuously attacking were.

Millēsimo. XVII.   Hēr on þisum ġēare fēng   Cnut cyning to eall Angelcynnes
1017   Here in this   year succeeded Cnut the king to all the English people's

rīċe . . . and þā   tōforan Kl. Aug. hēt   se cyng feċċan   him Æðelrēdes lāfe
kingdom and then before August 1 commanded the king to be brought him Ethelred's widow

þēs ōðres cynges him   to cwēne, Ricardes dōhtor.
(this other king's) for him as queen (Richard's daughter).

Millēsimo. XLI.   Hēr forðfērde   Hardacnut cyng   æt Lambhyðe on VI. Idus Iun. and
1041 [1042]   Here passed away Harthacnut the king at Lambeth   on June 8,   and

45 hē wæs cyng ofer eall Englaland twā ġēar buton X. nihtum, and hē is bebyrġed on ealdan
he was king over all England two years less 10 nights, and he is buried   in the old

mynstre on Winċeastre mid Cnute cynge   his fæder; and ēar þan þe hē bebyrġed wǣre, eall
minster at Winchester with Cnut the king his father; and before   he buried   was, all

folc   ġeċēas Ēadward to cynge on Lundene, healde   þā hwīle þe   him God
the people chose Edward as king   at London, may he rule the while that him God

unne. . . .
grants.

Millēsimo. XLII. Hēr wæs Æðward gehālgod   to cyng on Winċeastre on Ǣster dæġ mid
1042 [1043]   Here was Edward consecrated as king at Winchester on Easter day with

50 myċċlum wurðscipe . . . and raðe þæs   se cyng lēt   ġerīdan   ealle þā land þe
great   honor   and quickly after that the king caused to be seized all   the lands that

his mōdor āhte   him to handa,   and nam of   hire eall þæt hēo āhte   on golde and on
his mother owned into his own hands, and took from her all   that she owned in gold and in

seolfre and on unāsecgendlīcum þingum forþan   hēo hit hēold tō feste wið hine.
silver and in indescribable   things   because she it held too firmly from him.

Millēsimo. LXVI.   On þissum ġēare man hālgode   þet mynster   æt Westmynstre on
1066   In this   year they consecrated the monastery at Westminster on

Ċyldamæsse dæġ, and se cyng Ēadward forðfērde   on Twelfta mæsse æfen, and hine mann
Childermas   day, and the king Edward passed away on Epiphany   eve, and him they

55 bebyrġede on Twelftan mæssedæġ innan þǣre nīwa hālgodre   ċirċean on Westmynstre, and
buried   on Epiphany day   within the newly consecrated church at Westminster, and

Harold eorl   fēng   to Englalandes cynerīċe swā swā se cyng hit him ġeūðe,   and ēac
Harold the earl succeeded to England's   realm   as   the king it him promised, and also

men hine þǣrtō ġecuron . . . and þā hwīle cōm Willelm eorl   upp æt Hestingan, on
men him thereto chose   and meanwhile came William the earl up at Hastings   on

Sancte Mīchaeles mæssedæġ, and Harold cōm   norðan, and him wið ġefeaht ēar þan þe
St.   Michael's massday,   and Harold came from the north, and with him fought before

his here cōme eall,   and þǣr hē fēoll, and his twǣgen ġebrōðra, Gyrð and Lēofwine, and
his army came entirely, and there he fell, and his two   brothers Gurth and Leofwine, and

60   Willelm þis land ġeēode   and cōm   to Westmynstre, and Ealdrēd arċebiscop   hine to
     William this land occupied and came to Westminster, and Ealdred the Archbishop him as

cynge gehālgode. . . .
king   consecrated.

THE FORMER AGE

One of the most enduringly popular works in the history of European literature is Boethius's *Consolation of Philosophy*. Cast into prison for suspected treason, the Roman nobleman Boethius wrote his *Consolation* to explore man's relationship to the order of the universe. The Latin original, which alternates prose passages with metrical stanzas, has been repeatedly translated into English—for example, by Alfred the Great, by Chaucer, and by Queen Elizabeth I. The passage that follows (Book 2, Meter 5) is a short poem that looks back from the complexities of contemporary—that is, sixth-century—life to the simplicity and goodness of an earlier time when commerce, war, and greed had not corrupted humans. This prose translation is by King Alfred.

Ēalā hū   ġesǣliġ sēo forme eld wæs þises middanġeardes, þā   ǣlċum men þūhte   ġenōg
Oh how happy   the first age was of this world,   when to each man seemed enough

on þǣre eorþan wæstmum. Nǣron   þā weliġe hāmas, ne mistliċe swōtmettas, ne
on the   earth in fruits.   There were not then rich   houses, nor various sweetmeats, nor

drincas; ne dīorwyrþra hrǣgla hī ne   ġirndan, forþam hī   þā ġit nǣran,
drinks; nor expensive clothing they did not yearn for, because those things then yet were not,

ne hīo nānwuht ne ġesāwon, ne ne ġehērdon. Ne ġēmdon hīe nānes fyrenlustes, būton
nor they none such saw,   nor heard of. Nor cared   they for any luxury,   but

5 swīþe ġemetlīċe þā ġecynd beēodan; ealne weġ hī   ǣton ǣne on dæġ, and þæt wæs tō
   very moderately nature followed; always   they ate once a day, and that was at

ǣfennes. Trēowa wæstmas hī   ǣton and wyrta;   nalles   scīr wīn hī ne druncan; ne
evening. Trees' fruits   they ate and vegetables; not at all clear wine they drank;   nor

nānne wǣtan hī ne cūþon   wið huniġe mengan; ne seolocenra hrǣgla mid mistliċum
any   liquor they did not know with honey to mix; nor silken   clothing of various

blēowum hī ne   ġīmdon. Ealne weġ hī   slēpon ūte on trīowa sceadum; hlūterra wellā
colors   they did not care for. Always   they slept out in trees' shade;   pure   wells'

wæter hī druncon; ne ġeseah nān ċēpa   ēaland, ne weroþ; ne ġehērde nān mon þā
water they drank; nor saw any merchant an island or shore; nor heard any man then

10 ġet nānne sciphere,   ne furþon ymbe nān ġefeoht sprecan; ne   sēo eorþe þā ġet
   yet of any ship-army, nor indeed about any fight   to speak; nor [was] the earth then yet

besmiten mid ofsleġenes monnes blōde, ne mon furðum ġewundod; ne monn ne ġeseah ðā
polluted with slain   man's blood, nor one even   wounded; nor no one saw   then

ġet yfel willende men, nǣnne weorþscipe nǣfdon,   ne hī   nān mon ne lufude. Ēalā þæt ūre
yet ill- willed men, no   honor   [such] had, nor them no man   loved. Alas that our

tīda nū   ne mihtan weorðan swilċe. Ac nū   manna ġītsung is swā byrnende, swā þæt fȳr on
times now cannot   be   thus. But now men's greed is as burning   as the fire in

þǣre helle, sēo   is on þām munte   ðe Ætne hātte,   on þām īeġlande þe Sīċīlia hātte,
that hell, which is in the mountain that Etna is called, on the island   that Sicily is called,

15 se   munt   bið simle swefle   birnende, and ealla þā nēah stōwa þǣr ymbūtan
   which mountain is ever with sulphur burning, and all   the near places there about

forbærnð. Ēalā hwæt se forma ġītsere wǣre, þe ǣrest þā eorþan ongan delfan æfter golde,
burns up. Oh what the first miser was, who first the earth began to dig after gold,

and æfter ġimmum, and þā frēcnan dēorwurþnessa funde ðe ǣr	behȳd wæs and behelod
*and after gems,	and the perilous riches	found that before hidden was and covered*

mid ðǣre eorþan?
*with the	earth?*

CÆDMON'S HYMN

The following poem, "Cædmon's Hymn," is the oldest known example of Old English religious poetry. Although Cædmon was an early northern poet, the hymn is given here in a West Saxon version, in keeping with the most common form of Old English. Since the position of stress is especially important in Old English poetry, accent marks have been added. The story of Cædmon and his poem can be found in Bede's *Ecclesiastical History of the English People*, 4, xxiv.

Nū sculon hériġean	héofonrīċes Wéard,
Now shall [we][12] praise	*heaven-kingdom's Guardian,*

[ALLITERATIVE]

Métodes méahte	and his mōdġeþánc,
[the] Creator's might	*and his heart-thought,*

wéorc Wúldorfæ̀der:	swā hē wúndra ġehwǣs,
[the] works [of the] Glory-father:	*how he [of] wonders [of] each,*

éċe Drýhten,	ór onstéalde.
[the] eternal Lord,	*[the] beginning established.[13]*

5 Hē ǣrest sceóp	éorðan béarnum
He first shaped	*[for] earth's children*

héofon tō hrófe,	hāliġ Scýppend;
heaven as [a] roof,	*[the] holy Creator;*

þā míddanġéard,	mónncỳnnes Wéard,
then [a] middle-dwelling,[14]	*mankind's Guardian,* *[SUBJECT]*

éċe Drýhten,	æfter téode
[the] eternal Lord, *[AN APPOSITIVE]*	*afterwards prepared*

fírum fóldan,	Frḗa ǽlmìhtiġ.
[for the] men [of] earth,	*[the] Lord almighty.* *[A WORD VARIATION]*

THE FALL OF MAN

The following passage (Genesis 3.1–13) is from a translation of the first books of the Bible by Ælfric, the chief prose writer of the later Old English period. This text is slightly regularized in spelling. Although most of the words are easily recognizable or can be guessed, more difficult forms are glossed below.

1. Ēac swylċe sēo nǣddre wæs ġēapre ðonne ealle ðā ōðre nȳtenu ðe God ġeworhte ofer eorðan, and sēo nǣddre cwæð tō ðām wīfe: "Hwī forbēad God ēow ðæt ġē ne ǣten of ǣlċum trēowe binnan Paradīsum?"
2. Þæt wīf andwyrde: "Of ðǣra trēowa wæstme ðe synd on Paradīsum wē etað;
3. And of ðæs trēowes wæstme þe is on middan neorxnawange, God bebēad ūs, ðæt wē ne ǣten, ne wē ðæt trēow ne hrepoden ðī lǣs ðe wē swelten."
4. Ðā cwæð sēo nǣdre eft tō ðām wīfe: "Ne bēo ġē nāteshwōn dēade, ðeah ðe ġē of ðām trēowe eten.
5. Ac God wāt sōðlīċe ðæt ēowre ēagan bēoð ġeopenode on swā hwylċum dæġe swā ġē etað of ðām trēowe, and ġē bēoð ðonne englum ġelīċe, witende ǣġðer ġe gōd ġe yfel."

---

[12]That is, 'we are bound to.'

[13]That is, 'how he, the eternal Lord, established the beginning of every wonder.'

[14]That is, 'the earth.'

6. Ðā ġeseah ðæt wīf ðæt ðæt trēow wæs gōd tō etenne, be ðām ðe hyre ðūhte, and wlitiġ on ēagum and lustbǣre on ġesyhðe, and ġenam ðā of ðæs trēowes wæstme and ġeæt and sealde hyre were: he æt ðā.

7. And heora bēġra ēagan wurdon ġeopenode; hī oncnēowon ðā ðæt hī nacode wǣron, and sȳwodon him ficlēaf, and worhton him wǣdbrēċ.

8. Eft ðā ðā God cōm, and hī ġehȳrdon his stemne ðǣr he ēode on neorxnawange ofer midne dæġ, ðā behȳdde Ādām hine, and his wīf ēac swā dyde, fram Godes ġesihðe on middan ðām trēowe neorxnan-wonges.

9. God clypode ðā Ādām, and cwæð: "Ādām, hwǣr eart ðū?"

10. Hē cwæð: "Ðīne stemne iċ ġehȳre, lēof, on neorxnawange, and iċ ondrǣde mē, for ðām ðe iċ eom na-cod, and iċ behȳde mē."

11. God cwæð: "Hwā sǣde ðē ðæt ðū nacod wǣre, ġyf ðū ne ǣte of ðām trēowe ðe iċ ðē bebēad ðæt ðū ne ǣte?"

12. Ādām cwæð: "Ðæt wīf ðe ðū mē forġēafe tō ġefēran, sealde mē of ðām trēowe, and iċ ætt."

13. God cwæð to ðām wīfe: "Hwī dydestū ðæt?" Hēo cwæð: "Sēo nǣdre bepǣhte mē and iċ ætt."

GLOSSES

ēac swylċe 'and furthermore'	*wlitiġ* 'fair'
ġēapre 'more cunning'	*lustbǣre* 'desirable'
nȳtenu 'beasts'	*were* dat. 'husband'
ǣlċum dat. 'each, every'	*heora bēġra* 'both of their'
neorxnawange dat. 'Paradise'	*wǣdbrēċ* 'breeches'
hrepoden 'should touch'	*stemne* 'voice'
ðȳ lǣs ðe 'lest'	*clypode* 'called'
nāteshwōn 'by no means'	*lēof* 'Sir'
swā hwylċum dat. 'whatsoever'	*dydestū* = dydest þū
ǣġðer ġe . . . ġe 'both . . . and'	*bepǣhte* 'tricked'
be ðām ðe 'as'	

PARABLES

The following parables, which have been slightly regularized in spelling, are from the Gospel of Saint Luke.

Ðā sǣde hē him sum bispell, Sæġst þū, mæġ se blinda þone blindan lǣdan? hū ne feallaþ hī bēġen on þone pytt?

Nis se leorning-cniht ofer þone lārēow; ǣlċ bið fulfremed, ġif hē is swylċe his lārēow.

Hwȳ ġesyhst þū þā eġle on þīnes brōþor ēagan, and ne ġesyhst þone bēam on þīnum ēagan?

And hū miht þū secgan þīnum brēþer, Brōþor, lǣt þæt iċ ātēo þā eġle of þīnum ēagan, and þū sylf ne ġesyhst þone bēam on þīnum āgenum ēagan? Ēalā līċetere, tēoh ǣrest þone bēam of þīnum ēagan, and þonne þū ġesyhst þæt ðū ātēo þā eġle of þīnes brōðor ēagan.

Nis gōd trēow þe yfelne wæstm dēð; nē nis yfel trēow gōdne wæstm dōnde.

Ǣlċ trēow is be his wæstme oncnāwen; nē hī of þornum fīc-æppla ne gaderiaþ, nē wīn-berian on gorste ne nimað.

Gōd man of gōdum gold-horde his heortan gōd forðbringð; and yfel man of yfelum gold-horde yfel forð-bringþ: sōðlīċe se mūð spicð swā sēo heorte þencð.

Hwȳ clypie ġē mē Drihten, Drihten, and ne dōð þæt iċ ēow secge?

GLOSSES

bēġen 'both'	*(a)tēo(h)* 'draw out'
nis, contraction of *ne* and *is*	*līċetere* 'hypocrite'
lārēow 'teacher'	*dēð, dōnde* 'produces, producing'
fulfremed 'fulfilled, perfected'	*fīc* 'fig'
swylċe 'as, like'	*berian* 'berries'
eġle 'mote'	*nimað* 'take'

6 THE MIDDLE ENGLISH PERIOD (1100-1500)

6.1 FOR REVIEW AND DISCUSSION

1. Define the following terms:

Norman French	unrounding	shortening
Anglo-Norman	smoothing	leveling (merging)
yogh	monophthongization	inorganic -e
open and close *e*	vocalization	scribal -e
open and close *o*	diphthongization	objective form
stroke letters	lengthening	verbal noun
oblique form	open syllable	

2. Summarize the historical events of the Norman Conquest.
3. What was the chief influence of the Conquest on the English language?
4. Which variety of Middle English became the standard dialect and when did it become the literary standard?
5. Compare the vowel system of Old English with that of Middle English as they are shown in the two vowel charts. What additions, losses, and rearrangements took place between the two periods?
6. Make a similar comparison of the consonant systems of the two periods.
7. Which sound change between Old and Middle English had the most far-reaching effect on the language?
8. What is the chief difference between Old and Middle English grammar?
9. Did word order and function words increase or decrease in importance during the Middle English period?
10. What factors contributed to the loss of grammatical gender in Middle English?
11. How did English acquire a device for indicating plurality independent of case?
12. What grammatical category of number was lost from the Middle English personal pronouns?
13. The traditional seven classes of strong verbs survived in Middle English, but what factors began to disturb their orderly arrangement?
14. What was the origin of the verbal ending *-ing*?
15. What is the chief difference in word order between Middle and Modern English?
16. What caused the decline of French as the language of the governing classes in England?

6.2 THE MIDDLE ENGLISH DIALECTS

1. List the main Middle English dialect areas according to the numbers on the accompanying map.

1 _____   4 _____

2 _____   5 _____

3 _____

2. In the *Reeve's Tale,* Chaucer has two clerics—university students—who had come originally from the north of England. Their dialogue is full of northernisms, which Chaucer's London audience doubtlessly found highly comic. In the blanks write the standard London or East Midland forms of the italicized words. You will find it easier to identify the forms if you have read all of Chapter 6 in *Origins and Development.*

Fareth	"Hou *fares* thy faire doghter and thy wyf?" (4023)
	"By God, right by the hopur wil I stand,"
Goos	Quod John, "and se howgates [how] the corn *gas* in.
	Yet saugh I never, by my fader kyn,
to	How that the hopur wagges *til* and fra." (4036–39)
are	"I is as ille a millere as *ar* ye." (4045)
wich	"What, *whilk* way is he geen [gone]?" he gan to crie. (4078)
her(e)	"A wilde fyr upon *thair* bodyes falle!" (4172)
So	"I is thyn awen clerk, *swa* have I seel [bliss]!" (4239)
	"Myn heed is toty [dizzy] of my swynk [work] to nyght,
maketh	That *makes* me that I ga nat aright." (4253–54)

6.3 THE PRONUNCIATION OF MIDDLE ENGLISH: CONSONANTS

Middle English had the consonants listed on the next page. There were a good many other spellings less common than those cited here; for example, [š] could also be spelled *ssh, ss,* or *s* in various parts of England. In the writing system, *x* was also used in its modern value [ks]. Do not confuse it with the same letter used as a phonetic symbol.

125

COMMON SPELLING	SOUND	COMMON SPELLING	SOUND	COMMON SPELLING	SOUND
b	[b]	m	[m]	y, ȝ	[y]
d	[d]	n	[n], [ŋ]	z, s	[z]
f	[f]	p	[p]	ch	[č]
g	[g]	r	[r]	gh, ȝ, h	[x], [ç]
h	[h]	s, c	[s]	sh, sch	[š]
j (i), g	[ǰ]	t	[t]	th, þ	[θ]
k, c, q	[k]	v (u)	[v]	th, þ	[ð]
l	[l]	w, u	[w]		

Complete the following chart by filling in the symbols listed above to show the place and manner of articulation of the Middle English consonants. In spite of the customary spelling differences between [h] on the one hand and [x] and [ç] on the other, they were probably still variants of the same phoneme; put [h] in the spot appropriate for the other two.

		LABIAL	DENTAL inter-dental	DENTAL alveolar	DENTAL alveolo-palatal	PALATOVELAR palatal	PALATOVELAR velar
STOPS AND AFFRICATES	voiceless						
STOPS AND AFFRICATES	voiced						
FRICATIVES	voiceless						
FRICATIVES	voiced						
NASALS							
LIQUIDS	lateral						
LIQUIDS	retroflex or trill						
SEMIVOWELS							

THE PRINCIPAL CONSONANTAL CHANGES

Origins and Development, pages 122–3, lists eleven consonantal changes that occurred during the Middle English period:

1. loss of [h] before [l], [n], and [r]
2. [ɣ] > [w] after [l] or [r]
3. loss of [w] between consonant and back vowel
4. loss of final [č] in unstressed syllables
5. loss of medial [v]
6. prefix [yɛ] (*ge-*) > [ɪ] (*i-, y-*)
7. loss of final [n] in many unstressed syllables
8. Southern voicing of [f], [s], and [θ] in initial position
9. borrowing of words with [v] and [z] in initial position
10. voicing of initial [θ] in usually unstressed grammatical words
11. [v], [z], and [ð] left in final position by the late loss of *-e*

Identify the change which each of the following Middle English words illustrates by writing the appropriate number, from 1 through 11, before the word. For many of the words you will find it necessary to compare the

126

Middle English with the corresponding Old English form to determine what change has occurred. You can find the Old English form in the etymology given for the word in any good dictionary. The modern form of the word is given in parentheses whenever it differs from the Middle English spelling.

	MIDDLE ENGLISH			
3	also ALSWĀ	1	laughen (to laugh) *hlaehhan*	2 swelwen (to swallow) *Swelgan*
11 8	breathe BRĀETH	7	lothely (loathly) LATHLIN	10 then *thanne*
7	eve EVEN	7	maide (maid) Maegdan	3 thong *thwong*
3	ho (who) HWA	1	neyen (to neigh) *hnǣgan*	8 vane *fane*
4	I IC	7	o (a) ān	9 very *verai*
GECLEOPOD 6	icleped (yclept)	1	raven *hrǣfn*	6 ynogh (enough) GENÓH, GENŌ
1/5	lady hLǣFDĪGE	2	sorwe (sorrow) *Sorg, SorH*	9 zenith *cenit*

6.5 MINOR CONSONANTAL CHANGES

The preceding exercise was concerned with eleven of the more important consonantal changes of the Middle English period, but there were other changes affecting Middle English consonants. You can discover some of these additional changes by examining the words listed here. (1) Determine the pre-Middle English form of each word (Old English, Old French, Old Norse). (2) Describe the consonantal change which seems to have affected each group of words. Each group is intended to illustrate a single consonantal change.

MIDDLE ENGLISH	PRE-MIDDLE ENGLISH	DESCRIPTION OF THE CONSONANTAL CHANGE
A. elle, 'ell'		
kill 'kiln'		
mille 'mill'		
B. kindred		
thunder		
jaundice		
spindle		
C. glistnen 'glisten'		
listnen 'listen'		
against		
biheste 'behest'		
D. hemp		
noumpere 'umpire'		
comfort		
E. strenkth 'strength'		
lenkth 'length'		
F. shambles		
slumbren 'slumber'		
thimble		
empty		
G. lemman 'leman'		
wimman 'woman'		
Lammasse 'Lammas'		
H. wurshipe 'worship'		
Sussex		
Norfolk		
I. best		
laste 'last'		
Wessex		
blosme 'blossom'		

MIDDLE ENGLISH	PRE-MIDDLE ENGLISH	DESCRIPTION OF THE CONSONANTAL CHANGE
J. answerien 'answer' gospelle 'gospel' gossib 'gossip'	_____ _____ _____	
K. eech 'each' suche 'such' which	_____ _____ _____	
L. coom 'comb' dum 'dumb' lam 'lamb'	_____ _____ _____	
M. bird thirde 'third' bright through wrighte 'wright'	_____ _____ _____ _____ _____	_____ _____
N. adder apron auger neute 'newt' nones 'nonce'	_____ _____ _____ _____ _____	_____ _____

The changes illustrated above are typical of some general tendencies which have operated at various times in the history of our language. These tendencies are described by the following five terms. Match the terms with the changes A through N by writing the appropriate letters in the blank before each term.

_____ ARTICULATIVE INTRUSION: the addition of a new sound produced by the speech organs as they move from the position for one sound to that for another or to silence (for example, *once* [wəns] pronounced as [wənts] or [wənst]; *film* pronounced [fɪləm]).

_____ PARTIAL ASSIMILATION: a change in pronunciation such that one sound becomes more like a neighboring sound (for example, *have to* pronounced [hæftu]).

_____ CONSONANT LOSS: the disappearance of a consonant sound from a word (for example, *cupboard* pronounced [kəbərd]); the loss is often the result of a complete assimilation by which two sounds become identical and reduce to one.

_____ METATHESIS: the inversion of two sounds (for example, *apron* pronounced either [eprən] or [epərn]).

_____ JUNCTURE LOSS OR DISPLACEMENT: a shift in the boundary between syllables so that a sound formerly in one syllable comes to be in another (for example, *at all* pronounced like *a tall*).

6.6   THE PRONUNCIATION OF MIDDLE ENGLISH: VOWELS

Because the Middle English period lasted for some four hundred years and included several strikingly different dialects of our language, no single description of the sounds of Middle English can cover all the varieties of the language which the student may encounter. The treatment of Middle English sounds in this exercise concerns itself with Chaucer's language, since he is the Middle English writer who is most read. In his dialect, these vowels occur:

SPELLING	SOUND	SPELLING	SOUND	SPELLING	SOUND
a	[a]	o	[ɔ]	au, aw	[aʊ]
a, aa	[a:]	o, oo	[ɔ:]	ai, ay, ei, ey	[æɪ]
e	[ɛ], [ə]	o, oo	[o:]	eu, ew	[ɛʊ]
e, ee	[ɛ:]	u, o	[ʊ]	eu, ew, u	[ɪʊ]
e, ee, ie	[e:]	ou, ow	[u:]	oi, oy	[ɔɪ]
i, y	[ɪ]			ou, ow	[ɔʊ]
i, y	[i:]			oi, oy	[ʊɪ]

Notice that Middle English spelling was a less accurate record of pronunciation than Old English spelling had been. Complete the following charts by filling in the symbols listed above to show the articulation of Middle English vowels.

SIMPLE VOWELS

			FRONT	CENTRAL	BACK
HIGH	*long*			—	
	short			—	
MID	*long*	close		—	
		open		—	
	short			—	
LOW	*long*		—		—
	short		—		—

DIPHTHONGS

Classify the diphthongs according to the position of their initial element. The arrows indicate the direction of the second element in the diphthong.

	FRONT	CENTRAL	BACK
HIGH	→	—	←
MID	↗	—	↖ ↑
LOW	↑	↗	—

Complete the following chart to show (1) the phonetic symbols for the Old English sounds from which the Middle English vowel developed, (2) the phonetic symbol for the corresponding Modern English vowel, and (3) the typical spelling of the Modern English development of the vowel. You can get all of this information from the key words.

The complete history of the Middle English vowels is quite complex because it involves many minor sound changes and borrowings between dialects. However, when you have completed this chart, you will have a list of the Middle English vowels with their main sources and future developments.

OLD ENGLISH SOURCES		MIDDLE ENGLISH		MODERN ENGLISH DEVELOPMENT		
key words	(1) phonetic symbol	phonetic symbol	key words	key words	(2) phonetic symbol	(3) typical spelling
sacc bæc sceal		[a]	sak bak shal	sack back shall		
talu æcer		[a:]	tale aker	tale acre		
bedd seofon		[ɛ]	bed seven	bed seven		
clǣne dǣl bēam stelan		[ɛ:]	clene deel beem stelen	clean deal beam steal		
gēs slǣp sēoþan		[e:]	gees sleep sethen	geese sleep seethe		
fisc lim hyll cynn		[ɪ]	fish lym hil kyn	fish limb hill kin		
hrīm wīf hȳdan mȳs		[i:]	rim wyf hiden mys	rime wife hide mice		
frogga cocc		[ɔ]	frogge cok	frog cock		
hām bāt wā þrote		[ɔ:]	hoom boot wo throte	home boat woe throat		
mōna gōd flōd		[o:]	mone good flood	moon good flood		
full bucca sunne cuman		[ʊ]	ful bukke sonne comen	full buck sun come		
mūs brū		[u:]	mous brow	mouse brow		
lagu clawu āht		[aʊ]	lawe clawe aught	law claw aught		

OLD ENGLISH SOURCES		MIDDLE ENGLISH		MODERN ENGLISH DEVELOPMENT		
key words	(1) phonetic symbol	phonetic symbol	key words	key words	(2) phonetic symbol	(3) typical spelling
hæġl dæġ seġl weġ eahta		[æɪ]	hail day seil wey eighte	hail day sail way eight		
lǣwede fēawe		[ɛʊ]	lewed fewe	lewd few		
nīwe Tīwesdæġ cnēow		[ɪu]	newe Tuesdai knew	new Tuesday knew		
No OE source; from OF development of Lat. [au]: OF joie < Lat. gaudia OF cloistre < Lat. claustra		[ɔɪ]	joy cloistre	joy cloister		
snāw āgan dāh grōwan boga dohtor brohte		[ɔʊ]	snow owen dough growen bowe doughter broughte	snow owe dough grow bow daughter brought		
No OE source; from OF development of Lat. [u] and [o:]: OF joindre < Lat. jungere OF poison < Lat. pōtio		[ʊɪ]	joinen poysen	join poison		

6.7   THE LENGTHENING AND SHORTENING OF VOWELS

Vowels were lengthened during the late Old English period or in early Middle English times

1. before certain consonant sequences (especially *mb, nd, ld*) and
2. in open syllables.

They were shortened

3. in closed syllables before two or more consonants (other than those above),
4. in unstressed syllables, and
5. in a syllable followed by two unaccented syllables.

Which of the five conditions listed on the previous page accounts for the vowel length of the first syllable in each of the following words? Vowel length is indicated by macrons or by spellings with two vowel letters (e.g., *ee* or *ou*). Write the appropriate number before the word.

_____	abīden 'to abide'	_____	dōre 'door'	_____	stiropes 'stirrups'
_____	āker 'acre'	_____	evere 'ever'	_____	sutherne 'southern'
_____	arīsen 'to arise'	_____	fedde 'fed'	_____	tāle
_____	asken 'to ask'	_____	feeld 'field'	_____	thė
_____	bēren 'to bear'	_____	ground	_____	today
_____	bētel 'beetle'	_____	hōlden 'to hold'	_____	us
_____	bēver 'beaver'	_____	hōpe	_____	wepenes 'weapons'
_____	blosme 'blossom'	_____	kīnde 'kind'	_____	wimmen 'women'
_____	cōld	_____	naddre 'adder'	_____	wōmb

The results of the lengthening and shortening of vowels in Middle English words like *hīden–hidde* or *wīs–wisdom* can still be seen in their Modern English developments, although now the vowels differ primarily in quality or tenseness rather than in length. For each of the following Modern English words, which have developed from Middle English forms with long vowels, supply a related word which has developed from a form with a short vowel. For example, *five* might be matched with *fifty, fifteen,* or *fifth.*

bathe	_____	dear 'beloved'	_____	lead 'guide'	_____
bleed	_____	deep	_____	mead 'grassland'	_____
break	_____	glaze	_____	shade	_____
clean	_____	goose	_____	shoe	_____
creep	_____	heal	_____	white	_____

6.8 MIDDLE ENGLISH TRANSCRIPTION

Write these Middle English words in phonetic transcription. Unstressed *e* at the end of a word is phonetically [ə]. The modern development is given as a gloss when there is possible ambiguity.

flat	_____	now	_____	ye 'ye'	_____
glad	_____	boot 'boot'	_____	ye 'eye'	_____
nest	_____	boot 'boat'	_____	gyse 'guise'	_____
shin	_____	cook	_____	shoo 'shoe'	_____
top	_____	hoom 'home'	_____	doute 'doubt'	_____
broth	_____	dool 'dole'	_____	wood 'wood'	_____
cuppe	_____	doten 'to dote'	_____	wood 'woad'	_____
love	_____	fode 'food'	_____	theme	_____
wolf	_____	strete 'street'	_____	gaude	_____
synne	_____	lene 'lean'	_____	grey	_____
fable	_____	felen 'to feel'	_____	main	_____
caas 'case'	_____	dreem 'dream'	_____	towen 'to tow'	_____
pipe	_____	wreken 'to wreak'	_____	sought	_____
hyden 'to hide'	_____	weep	_____	lawe	_____
cloud	_____	sete 'seat'	_____	rein 'rain'	_____

6.9 MIDDLE ENGLISH SPELLING AND PRONUNCIATION

Middle English spelling was less perfectly alphabetical than Old English spelling had been. The letter *o* alone could be used to spell four different vowels—[ɔ], [ɔ:], [o:], [ʊ]—and as part of a digraph it could help to spell four more—[u:], [ɔʊ], [ɔɪ], [ʊɪ]. Yet Middle English orthography can be pronounced with reasonable accuracy on the basis of four clues:

1. the spelling of the Middle English word,
2. the pronunciation of the modern development (provided the word still exists),

3. the spelling of the modern development (with the same obvious provision), and

4. the etymology of the Middle English word.

The four clues are listed in the order of their usefulness, but to apply them you must have a firm mastery of the information on pages 122–5 of *Origins and Development* and in exercises 6.3 and 6.6. For example, to pronounce the word *boon* as in the line "We stryve as dide the houndes for the boon," we can note first that the *oo* spelling indicates a long vowel, either [ɔ:] or [o:]. The modern development *bone* [bon] indicates by both its sound and its spelling that the Middle English vowel must have been [ɔ:]. Finally, if we happen to know that the Old English source of the word was *bān*, we can be confident that the Middle English was [bɔ:n]. If the reason for these observations is not clear to you, review the discussions mentioned previously.

There will, of course, still be much uncertainty. Some words, like *halwes* 'shrines' have not survived into Modern English. Others, like *seeke* 'sick' have survived, but in a different form. Also the diphthongs [ɔɪ] and [ʊɪ] were usually spelled alike in Middle English, and their modern developments are both spelled and pronounced alike; they can be distinguished only by their etymology, which a beginning student is unlikely to know. The same difficulty exists for the diphthongs [ɛʊ] and [ɪu]. Nevertheless, a mastery of the pronunciation and spelling correspondences between Middle and Modern English will allow you to read Chaucer's language with a fair degree of accuracy.

1. Write each of these phonetically transcribed words in one possible Middle English spelling:

[parfɪt] 'perfect'	_____	[me:tə]	_____
[ma:t] 'dead'	_____	[mɛ:tə]	_____
[bɛllə]	_____	[fo:l]	_____
[kru:dən]	_____	[grɔ:pən]	_____
[dɔggə]	_____	[wri:ðən]	_____
[rʊdɪ]	_____	[wæɪvən]	_____
[gnaʊən]	_____	[nɔɪzə]	_____
[θɔʊx]	_____	[pʊɪnt]	_____
[hwɪč]	_____	[hɪu] 'hue'	_____
[knɪxt]	_____	[hɛʊən] 'to hew'	_____

2. An examination of the following passages from the *Canterbury Tales* will make apparent both the uses and the limitations of pronunciation clues. The phonetic transcriptions represent a fairly conservative pronunciation of Middle English; some of the words might have been written differently because there is not complete agreement among scholars about Chaucer's pronunciation. Unstressed syllables and words are particularly susceptible to changes. For example, final *s* and *th* in unstressed syllables may have been voiced; initial *h* in unstressed words like *him, hem, hir* was probably silent; unstressed words like *I* and *to* probably had short vowels. For the pronunciation of schwa in final syllables, see *Origins and Development*, pages 127–8.

GENERAL PROLOGUE, ll. 1–27

	Whan that Aprille with hise shoures soote	hwan θat 'a:prɪl wɪθ hɪs 'šu:rəs 'so:tə
	The droghte of March hath perced to the roote	θə dru:xt ɔf marč haθ 'pɛ:rsəd to: θə 'ro:tə
	And bathed every veyne in swich licour	and 'ba:ðəd 'ɛv(ə)rɪ væɪn ɪn swɪč lɪ'ku:r
	Of which vertu engendred is the flour;	ɔf hwɪč vɛr'tɪu ɛn'ǰɛndrəd ɪs θə flu:r
5	Whan Zephirus eek with his swete breeth	hwan 'zɛfɪrʊs e:k wɪθ hɪs 'swe:tə brɛ:θ
	Inspired hath in every holt and heeth	ɪn'spi:rəd haθ ɪn 'ɛv(ə)rɪ hɔlt and hɛ:θ
	The tendre croppes, and the yonge sonne	θə 'tɛndrə 'krɔppəs and θə 'yʊŋgə 'sʊnnə
	Hath in the Ram his half[e] cours yronne,	haθ ɪn θə ram hɪs 'halvə ku:rs ɪ'rʊnnə
	And smale foweles maken melodye,	and 'smalə 'fu:ləs 'ma:kən ˌmɛlɔ'di:ə
10	That slepen al the nyght with open eye—	θat 'sle:pən al θə nɪxt wɪθ 'ɔ:pən 'i:ə
	So priketh hem nature in hir corages—	sɔ: 'prɪkəθ hɛm na'tɪur ɪn hɪr kʊ'ra:ǰəs
	Thanne longen folk to goon on pilgrimage[s],	θan 'lɔŋgən fɔlk to: gɔ:n ɔn ˌpɪlgrɪ'ma:ǰəs
	And Palmeres for to seken straunge strondes,	and 'palm(ə)rəs fɔr to: 'se:kən 'straʊnǰə 'strɔndəs
	To ferne halwes kowthe in sondry londes	to: 'fɛrnə 'halwəs ku:θ ɪn 'sʊndrɪ 'lɔndəs

15 And specially from every shires ende	and 'spɛsyallı frɔm 'ɛv(ə)rı 'šiːrəs 'ɛndə
Of Engelond to Caunturbury they wende	ɔf 'ɛŋgəlɔnd toː 'kaʊntərbriː θæɪ 'wɛndə
The hooly blisful martir for to seke	θə 'hɔːlı 'blɪsfʊl 'martır fɔr toː 'seːkə
That hem hath holpen whan þat they were seeke.	θat hɛm haθ 'hɔlpən hwan θat θæɪ wɛːr 'seːkə
Bifil that in that seson on a day,	bı'fɪl θat ın θat 'sɛːzʊn ɔn ə dæɪ
20 In Southwerk at the Tabard as I lay	ın 'suðərk at θə 'tabard as iː læɪ
Redy to wenden on my pilgrymage	'reːdı toː 'wɛndən ɔn miː ˌpɪlgrı'maːǰə
To Caunterbury with ful devout corage,	toː 'kaʊntərbriː wıθ fʊl də'vuːt kʊ'raːǰə
At nyght were come in to that hostelrye	at nıxt wɛːr kʊm ın toː θat ˌɔstəl'riːə
Wel nyne and twenty in a compaignye	wɛl niːn and 'twɛntı ın ə ˌkʊmpæɪ'niːə
25 Of sondry folk by aventure y-falle	ɔf 'sʊndrı fɔlk biː ˌavən'tıʊr ı'fallə
In felaweshipe, and pilgrimes were they alle	ın 'fɛlaʊˌšıp and 'pɪlgrım(ə)s wɛːr θæɪ 'allə
That toward Caunterbury wolden ryde.	θat 'toːward ˌkaʊntərˌburı 'woːldən ˌriːdə

GENERAL PROLOGUE, ll. 725-42

But first I pray yow, of youre curteisye,	but fırst iː præɪ yuː ɔf yuːr ˌkʊrtæɪ'ziːə
That ye narette it nat my vileynye,	θat yeː na'rɛt ıt nat miː ˌvɪlæɪ'niːə
Thogh that I pleynly speke in this mateere,	θoux θat iː 'plæɪnlı speːk ın θıs ma'teːrə
To telle yow hir wordes and hir cheere,	toː 'tɛllə yuː hır 'wɔrdəs and hır 'čeːrə
5 Ne thogh I speke hir wordes proprely.	nə θoux iː speːk hır 'wɔrdəs 'prɔprəˌliː
For this ye knowen al so wel as I,	fɔr θıs yeː 'knɔʊən al sɔː wɛl as iː
Who so shal telle a tale after a man,	hwoː sɔː šal tɛl a taːl 'aftər a man
He moote reherce as ny as evere he kan	heː moːt rəhɛːrs as niː as 'ɛvər heː kan
Everich a word, if it be in his charge,	'ɛv(ə)rıč a wɔrd ıf ıt beː ın hız 'čarǰə
10 Al speke he never so rudeliche or large,	al speːk heː 'nɛvər sɔː 'rıudəlıč ɔr 'larǰə
Or ellis he moot telle his tale untrewe,	ɔr 'ɛllıs heː moːt tɛl hıs taːl ʊn'trɛʊə
Or feyne thyng, or fynde wordes newe.	ɔr 'fæɪnə θıŋg ɔr 'fiːndə 'wɔrdəs nɛʊə
He may nat spare, al thogh he were his brother;	heː mæɪ nat spaːr al θoux heː wɛːr hıs 'broːðər
He moot as wel seye o word as another.	heː moːt as wɛl sæɪ ɔː wɔrd as a'noːðər
15 Crist spak hym self ful brode in hooly writ,	kriːst spak hım'sɛlf fʊl broːd ın 'hɔːlı wrıt
And wel ye woot no vileynye is it.	and wɛl yeː woːt nɔː ˌvɪlæɪ'niː ıs ıt
Eek Plato seith, who so kan hym rede,	eːk 'plaːtɔ 'sæɪθ 'hwoː sɔː kan hım 'rɛːdə
"The wordes moote be cosyn to the dede."	θə wɔrdəs moːt beː 'kʊzın toː θə 'dɛːdə

THE WIFE OF BATH'S PROLOGUE, ll. 469-80

But, lord crist! whan that it remembreth me	but lɔːrd kriːst hwan θat ıt rə'mɛmbrəθ meː
Upon my yowthe, and on my jolitee,	ʊ'pɔn miː yuːθ and ɔn miː ˌǰɔlı'teː
It tikleth me aboute myn herte roote.	ıt 'tıkləθ meː a'buːt miːn 'hɛrtə 'roːtə
Unto this day it dooth myn herte boote	ʊn'toː θıs dæɪ ıt doːθ miːn 'hɛrtə 'boːtə
5 That I have had my world as in my tyme.	θat iː hav had miː wʊrld as ın miː 'tiːmə
But Age, allas! that al wole envenyme,	but aːǰ al'las θat al wɔl ˌɛnvə'niːmə
Hath me biraft my beautee and my pith.	haθ meː bı'raft miː 'bɛʊte and miː pıθ
Lat go, fare wel! the devel go therwith!	lat gɔː faːr wɛl θə 'dɛvəl gɔː θeːr'wıθ
The flour is goon, ther is namoore to telle;	θə fluːr ıs gɔːn θeːr ıs na'mɔːr toː 'tɛllə
10 The bren, as I best kan, now moste I selle;	θə brɛn as iː bɛst kan nuː moːst iː 'sɛllə
But yet to be right myrie wol I fonde.	but yɛt toː beː rıxt 'mırı wɔl iː 'fɔːndə
Now wol I tellen of my fourthe housbonde.	nuː wɔl iː tɛllən ɔf miː fɔurθ huːz'bɔːndə

CHAUCER'S RETRACTION

Now preye I to hem alle that herkne this litel	nuː præɪ iː toː hɛm al θat 'hɛrknə θıs 'lıtəl 'trɛːtıs
tretys or rede, that if ther be any thyng in it that	ɔr rɛːd θat ıf θeːr beː 'anı θıŋg ın ıt θat 'liːkəθ əm
liketh hem, that therof they thanken oure lord	θat 'θeːrɔf θæɪ 'θaŋkən uːr lɔːrd 'ǰeːzu kriːst ɔf
Jhesu crist, of whom procedeth al wit and al good-	hwoːm prɔ'seːdəθ al wıt and al 'goːdnɛs and ıf θeːr
5 nesse. And if ther be any thyng that displese hem, I	beː 'anı θıŋg θat dıs'plɛːz əm iː præɪ əm 'alsɔː θat

preye hem also that they arrette it to the defaute of myn unkonnynge, and nat to my wyl, that wolde ful fayn have seyd bettre if I hadde had konnynge. For oure boke seith, "al that is writen is writen for
10 oure doctrine," and that is myn entente. Wherfore I biseke yow mekely for the mercy of god, that ye preye for me that crist have mercy on me and foryeve me my giltes, and namely of my translacions and enditynges of worldly vanitees, the whiche I
15 revoke in my retraccions.

θæɪ aˈrɛt ɪt to: θə dəˈfaʊt ɔf miːn ʊnˈkʊnnɪŋ and nat to: mi: wɪl θat wold fʊl fæɪn hav sæɪd ˈbɛttrə ɪf iː had had ˈkʊnnɪŋ fɔr uːr boːk sæɪθ al θat ɪs ˈwrɪtən ɪs ˈwrɪtən fɔr uːr ˈdɔktriːn and θat ɪs miːn ɛnˈtɛnt ˈhweːrfɔr iː bɪˈseːk yu: ˈmeːkəlɪ fɔr θə ˈmɛrsɪ ɔf gɔd θat ye: præɪ fɔr me: θat kriːst hav ˈmɛrsɪ ɔn me: and fɔrˈyɛːv me: mi: ˈgɪltəs and ˈnaːməlɪ ɔf mi: tranzˈlaːsɪɔnz and ɛnˈdiːtɪŋgəs ɔf ˈwʊrldlɪ ˈvanɪˌteːs θə hwič iː rəˈvɔːk ɪn mi: rəˈtraksɪɔnz.

6.10 THE REDUCTION OF INFLECTIONS

The number of inflectional distinctions which had existed in Old English was strikingly diminished in Middle English. The decrease in endings was due partly to the merger of unstressed vowels and partly to the operation of analogy. The declension of the adjective in Old and Middle English is illustrated below. Write *S* before each Old English form that developed into the corresponding Middle English form by regular sound change, and *A* before each form that was lost through analogy.

	OLD ENGLISH			MIDDLE ENGLISH
	MASC.	NEUT.	FEM.	
STRONG				
sing. nom.	_____ smæl	_____ smæl	_____ smalu	smal
acc.	_____ smælne	_____ smæl	_____ smale	
gen.	_____ smales	_____ smales	_____ smælre	
dat.	_____ smalum	_____ smalum	_____ smælre	
ins.	_____ smale	_____ smale	_____ smælre	
plur. nom.-acc.	_____ smale	_____ smalu	_____ smala	smale
gen.		_____ smælra		
dat.		_____ smalum		
WEAK				
sing. nom.	_____ smala	_____ smale	_____ smale	smale
acc.	_____ smalan	_____ smale	_____ smalan	
gen.-dat.	_____ smalan	_____ smalan	_____ smalan	
plur. nom.-acc.		_____ smalan		smale
gen.	_____ smælra / _____ smalena			
dat.		_____ smalum		

NOTE: The loss of final nasals in unstressed syllables must have been the result of both sound change and analogy. First, a sound change began to operate whereby nasals were lost when they were followed by a consonant but were retained when they were followed by a vowel; the resulting fluctuation can be seen in the two forms of the indefinite article, *a bird* but *an owl*. Almost immediately, however, analogy came into play to eliminate the final nasal completely in adjective endings and to restore it generally in the endings of strong past participles like *eaten* and of noun plurals like *oxen*. The result is a phonological rule that is sensitive to the grammatical identity of the forms to which it applies.

The effect of leveling, whether phonological or analogical, was to eliminate all differences of case and gender from the adjective and to eliminate the distinction of number from the weak forms of the adjective. What effects did leveling have on the Middle English noun and verb?

_____

_____

1. Write the following phrases in Middle English. All of the nouns are declined alike according to the usual Middle English pattern. The adjectives, however, vary; see *Origins and Development,* pages 128–9.

VOCABULARY

the 'the'	*free* 'noble'	*lord* 'lord'
oold 'old'	*long* 'long'	*wyf* 'wife'
hethen 'heathen'	*feend* 'fiend'	*yeer* 'year'

PHRASES

_____ old fiend	_____ the old fiend
_____ old fiend's	_____ the old fiend's
_____ old fiends	_____ the old fiends
_____ heathen lord	_____ the heathen lord
_____ heathen lord's	_____ the heathen lord's
_____ heathen lords	_____ the heathen lords
_____ noble wife	_____ the noble wife
_____ noble wife's	_____ the noble wife's
_____ noble wives	_____ the noble wives

2. Explain the origin of each of the following doublets:

brothers _____

brethren _____

latter _____

later _____

older _____

elder _____

3. Explain the vowel difference between the singular *child* and the plural *children.*

_____

_____

4. In his description of the Knight in the *Canterbury Tales,* Chaucer wrote, "His hors were goode." Did the Knight have one horse or more than one, and how can you tell? (The verb is no help; it might be either a plural or a subjunctive singular. And the noun *hors* had a plural that was identical with its singular, like Modern English *deer.*)

_____

6.12   PERSONAL PRONOUNS

Write the declensions of the Middle English personal pronouns. The four cases of the personal pronoun are the nominative, the objective, the adjectival genitive (as in "That is *my* book"), and the pronominal genitive (as in "That is *mine*"). Mark forms which are not East Midland (Chaucerian) with an asterisk (*). Mark forms borrowed from Scandinavian with a dagger (†). Mark new analogical forms with a double dagger (‡). The first person singular has been done.

	FIRST PERSON SINGULAR		FIRST PERSON PLURAL
nom.	I, ich, ik*	nom.	we
obj.	me	obj.	us
adj. gen.	mi, min	adj. gen.	oure); oures
pron. gen.	min	pron. gen.	oures

	SECOND PERSON SINGULAR		SECOND PERSON PLURAL
nom.	THou	nom.	YE
obj.	THEE	obj.	You
adj. gen.	THi; THin	adj. gen.	Your(e); Youres ‡
pron. gen.	THin	pron. gen.	Youres ‡

	THIRD PERSON SINGULAR MASCULINE		THIRD PERSON SINGULAR NEUTER
nom.	hē	nom.	hi*, they*‡, thai*‡
obj.	him; hine†	obj.	hem, heom, them*, thaim, theim*‡
adj. gen.	his	adj. gen.	here), their(e)*, heres, theirs*‡
pron. gen.	his	pron. gen.	heres, theirs*‡

	THIRD PERSON SINGULAR FEMININE		THIRD PERSON PLURAL
nom.	shē, hō, hyō, hyē, hī	nom.	hi, they*‡, thou*‡
obj.	hir(e), her(e), hi	obj.	hem, heim, them‡, thaim*, theim*‡
adj. gen.	hir(e), her(e); hires ‡	adj. gen.	her(e), their(e)*‡, heres, theirs* ‡/‡
pron. gen.	hires ‡	pron. gen.	heres, theirs*‡

6.13 DEMONSTRATIVE PRONOUNS

The Old English demonstratives consisted in part of these forms:

	NOMINATIVE SINGULAR	NOMINATIVE PLURAL	INSTRUMENTAL SINGULAR
masc.	sē 'the, that'; þes 'this'	þā 'the, those'; þās 'these'	þē 'by the, that'
fem.	sēo	þēos	
neut.	þæt	þis	

Middle English had the following forms. Indicate which Old English form each developed from, and explain any irregularities in the development.

singular and plural	the	_____
singular	that	_____
plural	tho	_____
	thos	_____
singular	this	_____
plural	these	_____
	thise	_____

6.14 INTERROGATIVE AND RELATIVE PRONOUNS

Notice how the italicized pronouns are used in the following quotations from Chaucer.

1. *Who* herd euer of swich a thyng or now?
2. *Who* hath no wyf he is no cokewold.
3. *Who so* first cometh to the mille first grynt [grinds].
4. *Who that* is moost vertuous alway. . . . Taak hym for the grettest gentil man.
5. "To *whom*?" quod he.
6. My lady, *whom* I loue and serue.
7. The sighte of hire, *whom that* I serue.
8. *Whos* is that faire child that stondeth yonder?
9. Of him *whos* I am all, whil I may dure.

10. Syk lay the goode man *whos that* the place is.
11. *What* is bettre than a good womman?
12. Whan folk in chirche had yeue [given] him *what* hem leste [pleased them], He wente his wey.
13. Ne euery appul that is fair at eye Ne is nat good, *what so* men clappe [chatter] or crye.
14. But God woot [knows] *what that* May thoughte in hire herte.
15. *Which* was the mooste fre [noble], as thynketh yow?
16. Thise riotoures thre, of *which* I telle.
17. He *which that* hath no wyf, I hold hym shent [ruined].
18. Taak heede of euery word *that* I you seye.
19. To me; *that* am thy cosyn and thy brother.
20. Thou hast nat doon *that* I comanded thee.

1. What pronouns, simple and compound, does Middle English use as

   interrogatives _____

   indefinite relatives (introducing noun clauses) _____

   _____

   relatives (introducing adjective clauses) _____

   _____

2. Describe one difference between Middle English and contemporary English in their use of *which*.

   _____

3. Describe three differences between Middle English and contemporary English in their use of *that*.

   _____

   _____

   _____

6.15 VERBS

The principal parts of many Old English strong verbs survived in Middle English with no changes other than those resulting from the regular sound shifts affecting all words. The following Old English verbs, typical of the seven strong classes, had such regular development. By applying what you have already studied about sound and spelling changes you should be able to predict their Middle English forms. Write the Middle English developments; mark all long vowels with a macron and use the hook to show open ę [ɛ:] and ǫ [ɔ:].

	OLD ENGLISH	MIDDLE ENGLISH		OLD ENGLISH	MIDDLE ENGLISH
CLASS I	'to write'		CLASS II	'to cleave'	
	wrītan	WRĪTEN		clēofan	CLĒVEN
	wrāt	WRŌT		clēaf	CLĒF
	writon	WRITEN		clufon	CLUVEN
	writen	WRITEN		clofen	CLǪVEN

138

CLASS III	'to bind'			CLASS V	'to knead'	
	bindan	bīnden			cnedan	knēdan
	band	band			cnæd	knad
	bundon	bunden			cnædon	knēdan
	bunden	bonden			cneden	knēdan
	'to melt'			CLASS VI	'to shake'	
	meltan	melten			scacan	shāken
	mealt	melt			scōc	shōk
	multon	multen			scōcon	shōken
	molten	molten			scacen	shāken
	'to warp'			CLASS VII	'to know'	
	weorpan	wéorpen			cnāwan	knāwen
	wearp	warp			cnēow	knēw
	wurpon	wurpen			cnēowon	knewen
	worpen	worpen			cnāwen	knōw
CLASS IV	'to bear'				'to let'	
	beran	bēran			lǣtan	lǣten
	bær	bar			lēt	lēt
	bǣron	bēren			lēton	lēten
	boren	bōren			lǣten	lǒt

6.16 INFLECTION OF VERBS

The Middle English weak verb *hēlen* 'to heal' and strong verb *helpen* 'to help' are typical developments of their Old English counterparts. Conjugate them in full, using the endings characteristic of the Midland dialects. The imperative endings are regular developments of the Old English forms.

PRINCIPAL PARTS	hēlen, hēlde, hēled		helpen, halp, hulpen, holpen	
	PRESENT	PRETERIT	PRESENT	PRETERIT
INDICATIVE				
I	___	___	___	___
thou	___	___	___	___
he	___	___	___	___
we, ye, they	___	___	___	___
SUBJUNCTIVE				
I, thou, he	___	___	___	___
we, ye, they	___	___	___	___
IMPERATIVE				
thou	___		___	
ye	___		___	
PARTICIPLE				
	___	___	___	___

6.17 MIDDLE ENGLISH SYNTAX: WORD ORDER

Although the word order of Middle English is basically the same as that of the modern language, the sentences below exemplify some minor differences. The first five, which are from the *Peterborough Chronicle,* were written in the first half of the twelfth century. The second five, from Chaucer's "Tale of Melibee," were written in the last half of the fourteenth century. For each sentence, describe how the syntax, and particularly the word order, differs from present-day use.

139

1. Ðis gear heald se kyng Heanri his hird æt Cristesmæsse on Windlesoure.
   This year King Henry held his court at Christmas in Windsor.

   THE VERB PRECEDES THE SUBJECT.

2. And him com togænes Willelm eorl of Albamar.
   And William, Earl of Aumale, came against him.

   VERB PRECEDES SUBJECT, DIRECT OBJECT COMES BEFORE THE REST.

3. Þerefter com þe kinges dohter Henries, þe hefde ben emperice in Alamanie.
   Thereafter came King Henry's daughter, who had been empress in Germany.

   THE DIRECT OBJECT PRECEDES THE SUBJECT

4. Þe King him sithen nam in Hamtun.
   The King afterwards captured him in Hampton.

5. Sume he iaf up, and sume ne iaf he noht.
   Some he gave up, and some he did not give.

6. Thre of his olde foes han it espyed.
   Three of his old foes have noticed it.

   VERB COMES AFTER INDIRECT OBJECT

7. Wepyng is no thing deffended to hym that sorweful is.
   Weeping is by no means forbidden to him that is sorrowful.

8. And whan this wise man saugh that hym wanted audience, al shamefast he sette hym down agayn.
   And when this wise man saw that audience was lacking for him, all ashamed he sat down again.

   PRONOUN (AS OBJECT) PRECEDES VERB, OBJECT PRECEDES THE VERB.

9. My lord, I you biseche as hertely as I dar and kan, ne haste yow nat to faste.
   My lord, I beseech you as heartily as I dare and can, don't move too fast.

   PRONOUN PRECEDES VERB,

10. But seyeth and conseileth me as you liketh.
    But tell and counsel me as it pleases you.

6.18 MIDDLE ENGLISH ILLUSTRATED

The following passages illustrate Middle English through a period of some three hundred years. The first selection preserves many of the inflections characteristic of Old English; the last selection is hardly distinguishable from early Modern English. Some dialect variation is also represented in the passages. The translations which accompany most of the texts scarcely do literary justice to their originals, but they will serve as glosses.

Compare the passages with one another. Note significant differences among them and any characteristics which help to date them as early or late Middle English.

Observe the spelling, inflections, word order, and vocabulary.

THE PETERBOROUGH CHRONICLE

The *Anglo-Saxon Chronicle* was continued at Peterborough for almost a century after the Norman Conquest. The passage reproduced here was written about the middle of the twelfth century. The text is based on Benjamin Thorpe's *The Anglo-Saxon Chronicle, According to the Several Original Authorities* (London, 1861), corrected by readings from Dorothy Whitelock's *The Peterborough Chronicle: The Bodleian Manuscript Laud Misc. 636* ("Early English Manuscripts in Facsimile," Vol. IV [Copenhagen, 1954]). Abbreviations have been silently expanded.

Millesimo. C.XXXV. On þis gære for   se king Henri ouer sæ˙ æt te Lammasse. and ðat
   1135   *In this year went the King Henry over sea at the Lammas,   and that*

oþer   dei þa   he lai an slep in   scip. þa   þestrede þe dæi ouer al landes. and
second day while he lay asleep in [the] ship then darkened the day over all lands,   and

uuard   þe sunne suilc als it uuare   thre niht ald mone. an sterres abuten him at middæi.
became the sun   such as it were [a] three night old moon and stars   about him at midday.

Wurþen men suiðe ofuundred   and ofdred. and sæden ðat   micel þing˙ sculde
Became men greatly filled with wonder and afraid, and said   that [a] great thing should

5 cumen herefter. sua   dide. for þat ilc   gær warth þe king ded. ðat oþer   dæi efter
    come   hereafter; so [it] did,   for that same year was   the King dead the second day after

Sanct Andreas massedæi on Normandi. Þa   þestre[den] sona   þas landes. for æuric
Saint Andrew's mass-day in Normandy. Then darkened   immediately these lands, for every

man sone   ræuede oþer   þe mihte. Þa   namen his sune and his frend. and brohten
man immediately robbed another who might.[1] Then took   his son and his friends and brought

his lic   to Engleland. and bebiriend in Redinge. God   man he wes. and micel æie wes of
his body to England   and burying   at Reading. [A] good man he was, and much awe was of

him. durste nan man misdon wið   oðer   on his time. Pais   he makede   men and dær.
him; durst no man misdo   against another in his time. Peace he made [for] man and beast.

10 Wua sua bare his byrthen   gold and sylure. durste nan man sei to him naht   bute god.
    Who so bore his burden [of] gold and silver, durst no man say of him naught but good.

Enmang þis was his nefe   cumen to Engleland. Stephne de blais. and com to lundene.
Among this[2] was his nephew come to England,   Stephen de Blois, and came to London,

and te lundenisce folc him underfeng. and senden efter þe ærcebiscop Willelm curbuil. and
and the London   folk him received   and sent   after the archbishop William Corbeil, and

halechede him to kinge on midewintre dæi. On þis kinges time wes al unfrið. and yfel. and
consecrated him as king on midwinter day. In this king's time was all strife   and evil and

ræflac. for agenes him risen sona   þa rice   men þe wæron swikes.
robbery, for against him rose at once those powerful men that were   traitors.

THE CHRONICLE OF ROBERT OF GLOUCESTER

Histories enjoyed a great popularity during the Middle Ages; the so-called *Metrical Chronicle of Robert of Gloucester,* edited by William Aldis Wright (London, 1887), was written about 1300 by three men, only one of whom has been identified by name. Wright said of this chronicle, "As literature, it is as worthless as twelve thousand lines of verse without one spark of poetry can be." Although it is rimed in an undistinguished doggerel, the work is linguistically interesting. The eleven lines printed here express an oft-repeated sentiment.

Þus com lo engelond in to normandies hond
Thus came, lo, England into Normandy's hand,

& þe normans ne couþe speke þo bote hor owe speche
and the Normans   could speak then only their own speech,

---
[1]That is, 'every man who might immediately robbed another.'
[2]That is, 'at this time.'

  speke french as hii dude atom   & hor children   dude also teche
and spoke French as they did   at home and their children [they] did   also teach,

So þat heiemen of þis lond þat of hor blod come
so that nobles   of this land, who of their blood come,

5   Holdeþ alle þulke   speche þat hii of   hom nome
keep   all   that same speech that they from them took.[3]

Vor bote   a man conne frenss   me telþ of   him lute
For unless a man knows French, one accounts him little.

Ac lowe   men holdeþ to engliss &   to hor   owe speche ȝute
But humble men hold   to English and to their own speech yet.

Ich wene   þer ne beþ in al þe world contreyes none
I   believe there are in all the world countries none

Þat   ne holdeþ to hor   owe speche bote engelond one
that [do] not hold   to their own speech but   England alone;

10   Ac wel me wot uor to conne boþe wel it is
but well one knows, to know both, well it is;[4]

Vor þe more þat a mon can   þe more wurþe he is.
for the more that a man knows, the more worth he is.

THE ANCRENE RIWLE

The *Ancrene Riwle* (rule for anchoresses) is a guide to the religious life written for three sisters of good family, who had determined to retire from the world and to lead lives of holy solitude. The book gives them advice about their devotions, about moral questions, temptations, penance, and about numerous small domestic matters. The subject is hardly a promising one, but the treatment is so refreshingly unorthodox that readers continue to discover the *Riwle* with pleasure and surprise. The selection printed here is based on James Morton's *The Ancren Riwle* (London, 1853); more recent editions have been published by the Early English Text Society. In West Midland dialect, it was composed probably in the late twelfth century.

Eue heold ine parais   longe tale mid te   neddre, and told hire al þat lescun þat
Eve held in paradise [a] long talk with the serpent, and told him[5] all that lesson that

God hire hefde ilered, and Adam, of þen epple; and so þe ueond þurh   hire word,
God her had taught and Adam of the apple; and so the fiend through her words

understond anonriht hire wocnesse, and ivond   wei touward hire of hire uorlorenesse.
understood at once her weakness and found [a] way toward her for her ruin.

Vre lefdi, Seinte Marie, dude al anoðer wise: ne tolde heo þen engle none tale; auh askede
Our lady, Saint Mary, did all another way: told she the angel no tale, but asked

5   him   þing scheortliche þat heo   ne kuðe. Ye, mine leoue sustren, uoleweð ure
him [the] thing briefly   that she [did] not know. Ye, my dear sisters, follow our

lefdi and nout þe kakele Eue. Vorþi   ancre,   hwat se heo beo, alse muchel ase
lady and not the cackling Eve. Therefore [an] anchoress, what so she be, as much as

heo euer con and mei, holde   hire   stille: nabbe heo   nout henne kunde. Þe
she ever can and may, [should] keep her[self] still: [let] her have not [a] hen's nature. The

hen hwon heo haueð ileid, ne con buten kakelen. And hwat biyit heo þerof?   Kumeð þe
hen when she has laid, cannot but cackle. And what gets she from that? Comes the

---

[3]That is, 'which they inherited from them.'
[4]That is, 'but it is well-known that it is good to know both.'
[5]Literally, 'her'; a survival of grammatical gender from Old English, in which adders were feminine.

coue   anonriht and reueð hire   hire eiren, and fret   al þat of   hwat heo schulde
chough at once and robs her [of] her eggs and devours all that from which she should

10 uorð bringen hire cwike briddes: and riht also þe luðere coue   deouel   berð awei
bring forth   her live birds; and just so the evil   chough, [the] devil, bears away

urom þe kakelinde ancren,   and uorswoluweð al þat god þat heo istreoned   habbeð,
from the cackling anchoress and swallows up all that good that she has brought forth,

þat schulden ase briddes beren ham   up touward heouene, yif hit nere   icakeled.
that should   as birds   bear them[selves] up toward heaven, if it were not cackled.[6]

Þe wreche   peoddare more noise he makeð to yeien his sope, þen a riche mercer
The wretched peddler more noise he makes to hawk his soap, than a rich mercer [does for]

al his deorewurðe ware. To sum gostliche monne þat ye beoð strusti uppen ase ye
all his expensive wares. Of some spiritual man   that ye are trustful upon as ye

15 muwen beon of hit, god is   þat ye asken   red,   and salue þat he teche ou
may   be   of it,[7] *good is [it] that ye ask [for] advice and remedy that he teach you*

to yeines fondunges, and ine schrifte   scheaweð him gif he wule iheren ower greste, and
against temptations, and in confession show   him, if he will hear, your greatest and

ower lodlukeste   sunnen; uor þi þat him areowe   ou; and þurh þe bireaunesse
your most loathsome sins   in order that it may pity him you[8] *and through the pity*

crie   Crist inwarliche   merci uor ou, and habbe ou ine munde, and in his bonen.
cry [to] Christ inwardly [for] mercy for you and have you in mind   and in his prayers.

"Auh witeð ou and beoð iwarre," he seið, ure Louerd, "uor monie   cumeð to ou
"But know you and beware,"   he said, our Lord, "for many [will] come to you

20 ischrud mid lombes fleose, and beoð wode wulues." Worldliche men ileueð lut;   religuise
clothed with lamb's fleece, and are mad wolves." Worldly   men believe little; religious

yet lesse. Ne wilnie ye nout to muchel hore kuðlechunge. Eue wiðute drede spec mit
still less.[9] *Nor desire ye not too much their acquaintance. Eve without dread spoke with*

te neddre. Vre lefdi was of drede of Gabrieles speche.
the serpent. Our lady was afraid of Gabriel's speech.

THE FORMER AGE

Chaucer, like King Alfred before him, made a translation of Boethius's *Consolation of Philosophy*. Compare his version of Book 2, Meter 5, with the Old English one given in Chapter 5. The parenthesized material is explanatory comment rather than translation of the original. Italics indicate the expansion of abbreviations.

Blysful was þe first age of men. Þei helden hem apaied [content] wiþ þe metes þat þe trewe erþes brouȝten furþe. Þei ne destroyed ne desceyued not hem self wiþ outerage [excess]. Þei weren wont lyȝtly to slaken her hunger at euene wiþ acornes of okes. Þei ne couþe nat medle þe ȝift of bacus to þe clere hony (þat is to seyn, þei couþe make no piment of clarre), ne þei
5 couþe nat medle þe briȝt flies of þe contre of siriens wiþ þe venym of tirie (þis is to seyne, þei couþe nat dien white flies of sirien contre wiþ þe blode of a manar shelfysshe þat men fynden in tyrie, wiþ whiche blode men deien purper). Þei slepen holesom slepes vpon þe gras, and dronken of þe rynnyng watres, *and* laien vndir þe shadowe of þe heyȝe pyne trees. Ne no gest ne no straunger karf [sailed] ȝit þe heye see wiþ oores or wiþ shippes, ne þei ne
10 hadden seyne ȝitte none newe strondes to leden merchaundyse in to dyuerse contres. Þo weren

---

[6] That is, 'if it had not been for the cackling.'

[7] That is, 'in such matters.'

[8] That is, 'he may pity you'; an impersonal construction.

[9] That is, 'Believe worldly men' and so forth; the construction is a command, not a statement.

þe cruel clarious ful whist [quiet] *and* ful stille, ne blode yshed by egre hate ne hadde nat deied ȝit armurers, for wherto or whiche woodenesse of enmys wolde first moeuen armes, whan þei seien cruel woundes ne none medes ben of blood yshad. I wolde þat oure tymes sholde turne aȝeyne to þe oolde maneres. But þe anguissous loue of hauyng brenneþ in folke moore cruely þan þe fijr of þe Mountaigne of Ethna þat euer brenneþ. Allas what was he þat first dalf [dug] vp þe gobets or þe weyȝtys of gold couered vndir erþe, *and* þe precious stones þat wolden han ben hid, he dalf vp precious perils (þat is to seyne þat he þat hem first vp dalf, he dalf vp a precious peril, for-whi, for þe preciousnesse of swyche haþ many man ben in peril).

JOHN OF TREVISA'S POLYCHRONICON

The *Polychronicon,* written in Latin by Ralph Higden and translated into English in the 1380s by John of Trevisa, is a compendium of universal history. It begins with a geographical survey of the known world and traces human history from the creation to the fourteenth century.

The following selection concerning the languages of the British Isles is Chapter 59 of Book I. Trevisa sometimes felt it necessary to correct his source; his additions are indicated by parentheses. The complete work has been edited by Churchill Babington, *Polychronicon Ranulphi Higden Monachi Cestrensis; together with the English Translations of John Trevisa and of an Unknown Writer of the Fifteenth Century* (London, 1869).

As it is i-knowe how meny manere   peple beeþ in þis ilond, þere beeþ also so many
As it is known   how many kinds [of] people are   in this island, there are   also as many

dyuers longages and tonges; noþeles   Walsche men and Scottes, þat beeþ nouȝt
diverse languages and tongues; nevertheless Welshmen   and Scots,   who are   not

i-medled wiþ oþer naciouns, holdeþ wel nyh   hir firste   longage and speche; but
mixed   with other nations, keep   very nearly their original language and speech; except

ȝif the Scottes þat were somtyme confederat and wonede wiþ þe Pictes drawe
that the Scots   that were formerly confederate and dwelt   with the Picts follow

5 somwhat after hir   speche; but þe Flemmynges þat woneþ in þe weste side of Wales
somewhat   their speech; but the Flemings   that dwell in the west part of Wales

haueþ i-left her   straunge speche and spekeþ Saxonliche i-now.   Also Englische men, þey
have left   their foreign speech and speak Saxonly   enough. Also Englishmen,   they

hadde from the bygynnynge þre manere   speche, norþerne, sowþerne, and middel   speche
had   from the beginning   three kinds [of] speech, northern, southern, and midland speech

in þe myddel of þe lond, as þey come of   þre manere   peple of Germania,
in the middle of the land, as they came from three kinds [of] people of Germania;

noþeles   by comyxtioun and mellynge firste wiþ Danes and afterward wiþ Normans, in
nevertheless by mixture   and mingling first with Danes and afterward with Normans, in

10 meny   þe contray longage is apayred, and som vseþ strong wlafferynge, chiterynge,
many [ways] the native   language is debased and some use   harsh stammering, chattering,

harrynge, and garrynge grisbayting.   This apayrynge of þe burþe tunge is bycause of
snarling, and scolding gnashing of teeth. This abasement of the birth-tongue is because of

tweie þinges; oon is for children in scole aȝenst þe vsage and manere of alle oþere
two   things; one is that children in school against the usage and custom of all other

naciouns beeþ compelled for to leue hire owne langage, and for to construe hir   lessouns
nations are   compelled to   leave their own language and   to construe their lessons

and here þynges in Frensche, and so þey haueþ seþ   þe Normans come first in to
and their subjects in French,   and so they have since the Normans came first into

15 Engelond. Also gentil men   children beeþ i-tauȝt to speke Frensche from þe tyme þat þey
England. Also gentlemen's children are   taught to speak French   from the time that they

144

beeþ i-rokked in here cradel, and kunneþ   speke and playe wiþ a childes broche; and
are rocked in their cradle and are able to speak and play with a child's bauble; and

vplondisshe men wil likne hym self to gentil men, and fondeþ wiþ greet besynesse for to
country   men will liken himself[10] to gentlemen and strive   with great labor   to

speke Frensce, for   to be i-tolde   of. (Þis manere was moche i-vsed
speak French in order to be taken account of.[11] (This practice was much followed

to for   firste deth   and is siþþe sumdel   i-chaunged; for Iohn Cornwaile, a maister
before [the] first plague and is since somewhat changed;   for John Cornwall, a teacher

20 of grammer, chaunged þe lore   in gramer scole and construccioun of Frensche
of grammar, changed the instruction in grammar school and interpretation from French

in to Englische; and Richard Pencriche lerned þe manere   techynge of hym and
into English;[12] and Richard Pencritch learned the manner [of] teaching from him and

oþere men of   Pencrich; so þat now, þe ȝere of oure Lorde a þowsand þre hundred
other men from Pencritch; so that now, the year of our Lord   a thousand three hundred

and foure score and fyue, and of þe secounde kyng Richard after þe conquest nyne, in alle
and four score and five, and of the second   King Richard after the conquest nine, in all

þe gramere scoles of Engelond, children leueþ Frensche and construeþ and lerneþ an
the grammar schools of England   children leave French   and interpret and learn in

25 Englische, and haueþ þerby   auauntage in oon side and   disauauntage in anoþer
English   and have   thereby [an] advantage in one way and [a] disadvantage in another

side; here auauntage is, þat þey lerneþ her gramer   in lasse tyme þan children were
way; their advantage is that they learn their grammar in less time than children were

i-woned   to doo;   disauauntage is þat now children of gramer   scole conneþ na
accustomed to do; [the] disadvantage is that now children in grammar school know   no

more Frensche þan can   hir lift heele, and þat is harme   for hem and þey schulle
more French   than knows their left heel, and that is harm[ful] for them if   they shall

passe þe see and trauaille in straunge landes and in many oþer places. Also gentil men
cross the sea and travel   in foreign lands and in many other places. Also gentlemen

30 haueþ now moche i-left for to teche here children Frensche.) Hit semeþ a greet wonder
have now much neglected to teach their children French.) It seems a great wonder

how Englische, þat   is þe burþe tonge of Englisshe men and her owne langage and
that English, which is the birth-tongue of Englishmen and their own language and

tonge, is so dyuerse of sown in þis oon ilond, and þe langage of Normandie is
tongue, is so diverse in sound in this one island, and the language of Normandy is [a]

comlynge of   anoþer londe, and hath oon manere   soun among alle men þat spekeþ hit
newcomer from another land,   and has one kind [of] sound among all   men that speak it

ariȝt   in Engelond. (Neuerþeles þere is as many dyuers manere   Frensche in þe
properly in England. (Nevertheless there are as many diverse kinds [of] French   in the

35 reem of Fraunce as is dyuers manere   Englische in þe reem of Engelond.) Also of þe
realm of France as are diverse kinds [of] English   in the realm of England.) Also of the

---

[10]That is, 'wish to make themselves like.'

[11]That is, 'in order to be thought important.'

[12]Whereas French had been the language in which classes were held and into which schoolchildren translated their Latin, English was becoming the language of instruction.

forsaide   Saxon tonge   þat   is i-deled aþre,   and is abide scarsliche wiþ   fewe
aforesaid Saxon tongue, which is divided in three and remains scarcely   among [a] few

vplondisshe men   is greet wonder; for men of þe est wiþ men of þe west, as it
rustic   men [there] is great wonder; for men of the east with men of the west, as it

were vndir þe same partie of heuene, acordeþ more in sownynge of speche þan men of þe
were under the same part   of heaven, agree   more in pronunciation   than men of the

norþ wiþ men of þe souþ; þerfore it is þat Mercii,   þat beeþ men of myddel Engelond,
north with men of the south; therefore it is that Mercians, who are   men of middle England,

40 as it were parteners of þe endes,   vnderstondeþ bettre þe side   langages, norþerne
as it were partners of the extremes, understand   better the adjacent languages, northern

and souþerne, þan norþerne and souþerne vnderstondeþ eiþer oþer. Al þe longage of þe
and southern, than northern and southern understand   each other. All the language of the

Norþhumbres,   and specialliche at ȝork, is so scharp, slitting, and frotynge and vnschape,
Northumbrians, and especially   at York, is so shrill,   cutting, and grating and ill-formed,

þat we souþerne men may þat longage vnneþe vnderstonde. I trowe þat þat is bycause
that we southern men can that language barely understand. I believe that that is because

þat þey beeþ nyh to straunge men and naciouns þat spekeþ strongliche, and also
they are   near to foreign men and nations that speak   harshly   and also

45 bycause þat þe kynges of Engelond woneþ alwey fer from þat cuntrey; for þey beeþ
because   the kings of England dwell   always far from that country; for they are

more i-torned to þe souþ contray, and ȝif þey gooþ to þe norþ contray þey gooþ wiþ
more turned to the south country, and if they go   to the north country, they go   with

greet help and strengþe. Þe cause why þey beeþ more in þe souþ contrey þan in þe
great force and strength. The cause that they are   more in the south country than in the

norþ, is for hit may be   better corne londe, more peple, more noble citees, and more
north is that it may have better grain land,   more people, more noble cities, and more

profitable hauenes.
profitable harbors.

ANOTHER ENGLISH POLYCHRONICON

Ralph Higden's *Polychronicon* was translated again in the mid-fifteenth century. This second translation, which might be called late Middle English or early Modern English, will illustrate the considerable changes in the language wrought by the intervening years. The passage reprinted here from Babington's edition corresponds to the earlier translation but of course lacks Trevisa's comments. In some ways, it corresponds rather more closely to the Latin original.

Hit may be schewede clerely to the wytte that there were so mony diuersites of langages in that londe as were diuersites of nacions. But Scottes and men of Wales kepe theire propre langage, as men inpermixte with other naciones; but perauenture Scottes haue taken somme parte in theire communicacion of the langage of Pictes, with whom thei dwellede somme tyme, 5 and were confederate with theyme. Men of Flaundres that inhabite the weste partes of Wales levenge the speche of barbre speke after the Saxones. And thauȝhe men of Englonde hade in the begynnenge a langage tripartite, as of the sowthe parte of Englond, of the myddelle parte of Englonde, and of the northe parte of Englonde, procedenge as of thre peple of Germanye, borowe moche in theire speche now, thro the commixtion with the Danes and after that with the 10 Normannes. The corrupcion of that natife langage is causede moche of ij. thynges, that is to say, childer sette to schole after the commenge of Normannes in to Englonde were compellede to constru in Frenche ageyne the consuetude of oþer naciones. In so moche that the childer of nowble men, after that thei were taken from the cradelle, were sette to lerne the speche of

Frenche men. Wherefore churles seenge that, willenge to be like to theyme, laborede to speke
15 Frenche with alle theire myȝhte. Where hit is to be hade in meruayle that the propur langage of
Englische men scholde be made so diuerse in oon lytelle yle in pronunciacion, sythe the langage
of Normannes is oon and vniuocate allemoste amonge theyme alle. But as of the tripartite
langage of Saxones, whiche remaynethe now but amonge fewe men, the weste men of Englonde
sownde and acorde more with the men of the este of that londe as vnder the same clyme of
20 heuyn, then the men of the northe with men of the sowthe. Wherefore hit is that Englishe men
of þe Marches of the mydelle partes of Englonde, takenge as by participacion the nature of
bothe extremities, vnderstonde the langages collateralle arthike and anthartike better then the
extremites vnderstonde theyme selfe to geder. Alle the langage of men of Northumbrelonde,
and specially in Yorke, sowndethe so that men of the sowthe cuntre may vnnethe vnderstonde
25 the langage of theyme, whiche thynge may be causede for the nye langage of men of barbre to
theyme, and also for the grete distaunce of kynges of Englonde from hyt, whiche vse moste the
southe partes of that londe, returnenge not in to the costes of the northe but with a grete
multitude. Also an other cause may be assignede, for the sowthe partes be more habundante in
fertilite then the northe partes, moo peple in nowmbre, hauenge also more plesaunte portes.

7 THE EARLY MODERN ENGLISH PERIOD (1500–1800)

SOCIETY, SPELLINGS, AND SOUNDS

7.1 FOR REVIEW AND DISCUSSION

1. Define the following terms:

   inkhorn term   Great Vowel Shift   apocopation
   etymological respelling retarded pronunciation   hypercorrect pronunciation
   orthoepist   advanced pronunciation   inverse spelling

2. Explain the significance of the following typographical devices sometimes used in early Modern English printing: the letter *y* with a small superscript *e*, a line or tilde over a vowel, final *e*'s other than those used to show length of the preceding vowel, the distinction between the letters *u* and *v*.

3. Compare the vowel system of Middle English with that of early Modern English as they are shown in the vowel charts of Chapter 6 and of this chapter. What additions, losses, or rearrangements took place between the two periods?

4. Make a similar comparison of the consonant system of Middle English with that of Modern English.

5. From what kinds of evidence do we learn about the pronunciation of earlier periods?

6. The phonetic transcription from *1 Henry IV* on page 154 of *Origins and Development* records a pronunciation that is somewhat earlier than the one described in the following exercises. Read it aloud and note which sounds differ from your own pronunciation. Explain the cause of as many of the differences as you can.

7.2 THE EARLY MODERN ENGLISH VOWELS

Like those of all other historical periods, speakers of early Modern English employed no single, uniform pronunciation. Sounds varied from place to place and from social group to social group. Moreover, they continued to change during the period. Only with these important qualifications can we speak of a typical early Modern English phonology. Such a typical sound system in the later seventeenth century might have included the vowels listed at the top of page 149.

By the early Modern period, spelling had reached its present state of complexity although it differed from contemporary practice in many details. The common spellings listed below are only samples; additional spellings can be cited for every vowel. The spellings *a-e, e-e, i-e, o-e,* and *u-e* represent the use of silent *e* after a consonant as in *name, mete, fine, cope, tune.*

COMMON SPELLING	SOUND	COMMON SPELLING	SOUND	COMMON SPELLING	SOUND
a	[æ]	a, al	[æ:]	ir, ur, er, ear	[ər]
e, ea,	[ɛ]	a, a-e, ay, ai, ey, ei	[ɛ:] or [e]	oy, oi	[ɔɪ]
		ea, e-e	[e]	i, i-e, ie, y, oy, oi	[əɪ] > [aɪ]
i, y	[ɪ]	e, ee, e-e, ie, ea	[i]		
				ow, ou	[əʊ] > [aʊ]
o	[ɔ] or [ɑ]	aw, au, a, al, ough, o	[ɔ:]	ew, eu, ue, u-e, u	[yu]
u, o	[ə]	oa, o, o-e, oe, ow, ou, ol	[o]		
u, oo	[ʊ]	oo, o, oe	[u]		

Complete the following charts by filling in the phonetic symbols listed above to show the articulation of early Modern English vowels:

SIMPLE VOWELS

		FRONT	CENTRAL/BACK UNROUNDED	CENTRAL/BACK ROUNDED
HIGH	long		——	
	short			
MID	long		——	
	short			
LOW	long		——	——
	short			——

DIPHTHONGS

Classify the diphthongs [ɔɪ], [aɪ], [aʊ], and the sequence [yu] according to the position of their initial element. The arrows indicate the direction of the second element in the diphthong.

	FRONT	CENTRAL	BACK
HIGH	→		
MID			
LOW		↖ ↗	↖

Complete the chart on the next page to show (1) the phonetic symbols for the Middle English sounds from which the early Modern English vowels developed and (2) the phonetic symbols for the present-day English vowels. This information can be found in *Origins and Development* and in the key words, the spellings of which have varied only slightly since Middle English times. Some words had several pronunciations in early Modern English and so appear more than once in the chart.

(1) MIDDLE ENGLISH SOUNDS	EARLY MODERN ENGLISH VOWEL	(2) CURRENT ENGLISH VOWEL	KEY WORDS
	[æ]		lamp, fat, back, flax, sad
	[æ:]		staff, glass, path half, salve, psalm
	[ɛ]		edge, bless, bed, set head, death, deaf
	[ɛ:] or [e]		lady, lane, face, take, name day, tail, they, vein
	[e]		great, steak, break, yea east, mean, peace, bead, theme
	[ɪ]		in, sit, lid, king, hill
	[i]		she, sweet, these, grief east, mean, peace, bead, theme
	[ɔ] or [ɑ]		mock, lodge, odd, pot, fop
	[ɔ:]		law, claw, aught, cause call, hall, small, wall talk, walk, chalk, stalk brought, ought, sought soft, lost, cloth, cross dog, log, frog, bog
	[o]		boat, throat, go, home, toe snow, soul, grow, dough folk, yolk, holm
	[ʊ]		full, pull, bull, put, push foot, good, wood, look, hook
	[u]		goose, moon, boot, do, shoe
	[ə]		but, sun, son, come
	[ər]		stir, bird, dirt spur, burn, hurt
	[ɔɪ]		joy, boy, noise join, boil, point, spoil
	[əɪ] or [aɪ]		child, hide, mice, die, why join, boil, point, spoil
	[əʊ] or [aʊ]		mouse, brow, town, pound
	[yu]		few, cue, hue, mute deuce, new, tune, lewd

7.3 THE GREAT VOWEL SHIFT

Although a good many changes of various kinds affected the English vowel system as it developed from Middle to Modern English, those changes to which the long vowels were subject are especially worthy of note. The seven Middle English long vowels underwent a remarkably systematic shift in their place of articulation, a shift for which there was no cause that we can discover.

1. Show the changes effected by the Great Vowel Shift by writing the appropriate phonetic symbols in the brackets:

   [iː] > [aɪ] as in *mice*: ME [miːs] > ModE [maɪs]
   [uː] > [au] as in *mouse*: ME [muːs] > ModE [maus]
   [eː] > [i] as in *geese*: ME [geːs] > ModE [gis]
   [oː] > [u] as in *goose*: ME [goːs] > ModE [gus]
   [ɛː] > [e] as in *break*: ME [brɛːkən] > ModE [brek]
   [ɔː] > [o] as in *broke*: ME [brɔːkən] > ModE [brokən]
   [aː] > [ae] as in *name*: ME [naːmə] > ModE [nem]

2. The following are phonetic transcriptions of Middle English words. Write their present-day developments (1) in phonetic transcription and (2) in normal orthography.

	CURRENT SOUND	CURRENT SPELLING		CURRENT SOUND	CURRENT SPELLING
[bɔːst]	bost	BOAST	[miːn]	main	MINE
[broːd]	br brud	BROOD	[paːs]	pes	PACE
[deːm]	dim	DIME	[poːl]	pul	POOL
[grɛːt]	gret	GREAT	[pɔːl]	pol	POLE
[guːn]	gaun	GOWN	[reːd]	rid	READ
[yɛː]	ye	YEA	[rɔːst]	rost	ROAD
[kaːs]	kes	CASE	[roːst]	rust	ROOST
[liːs]	laɪs	LIES	[saːf]	sef	SAFE
[luːd]	laud	LOUD	[uːt]	aut	OUT
[meːt]	mit	MEET	[wiːd]	waɪd	WIDE

7.4 MINOR VOWEL CHANGES

1. The following words contained the vowel [a] in Middle English.

   lap, crab, at, add, back, bag   also, halt, bald, salt
   staff, craft, path, bath, glass, class   balk, calk (n.), chalk, walk
   ash, crash, flash, rash   calf, half, halve, salve
   all, call, hall, stall, tall   alms, calm, palm, psalm

   What vowel developed from Middle English [a] before a stop? _____

   before a voiceless fricative? _____

   before final [l] or [l] plus a dental? _____

   before [l] plus [k] (what happened to the [l])? _____

   before [l] plus a labial fricative (what happened to the [l])? _____

   before [l] plus a nasal (what happened to the [l])? _____

   How do typical British and American usage differ in their developments of [a] in these words? _____

   _____

2. The following words contained the vowel [ɔ] in Middle English.

hop, cob, pot, odd, dock
dog, bog, frog, log, hog
soft, off, lost, cross, cloth, moth
boll or bowl, roll, toll, bolt, bolster, folk, yolk

What vowel developed from Middle English [ɔ] before most stops? _____

before the voiced velar stop? _____

before a voiceless fricative? _____

before [l]? _____

How do current British and American usage differ in their developments of this vowel? _____

_____

3. The following words all had [ʊ] in Middle English.

bud, buck, puff, gull, dull, skull, blush, rush, cut, nut, but, putt, mull
bull, full, pull, bush, push, put

What is the usual development of Middle English [ʊ]? _____

In what environments did it remain unchanged? _____

_____

Which of the words above is an exception to the second generalization? _____

4. The following words contained the vowel [ɛ:] in standard Middle English.

great, break, steak, yea
sweat, threat, head, bread, death, breath
clean, cream, grease, heath, leaf, league, leap, mead, meat

In the second line of words the long vowel was shortened to [ɛ]. Before what kind of consonants did the shortening occur?

_____

Most words with Middle English [ɛ:] have what sound in late Modern English? _____

5. After Middle English [o:] as in *food, good, flood* had changed to [u] during the Great Vowel Shift, it went on to be laxed in some words like *good* and unrounded in others like *flood*. The rimes in early Modern English poetry suggest divided usage in the vowels of these words.

List some words which still vary between [u] and [ʊ]. _____

_____

6. The following words had [yu] in early Modern English.

pew, beauty, few, view, mew, cue, argue, hue, ewe
tune, due, sue, zeugma, new, rue, lute, thew

In what environments has it been retained, and in what environments has it become [u]? Name classes of sounds, not individual sounds.

[yu] retained _____

[u] developed _____

7. The following words had in Middle English the sounds indicated at the beginning of each group. Write the phonetic symbols for the modern development of the short vowels before [r]. There is some dialect variation for several of these vowels, as there is also for the long vowels of the next question.

MIDDLE ENGLISH   MODERN ENGLISH

[ɪr]	_____	spirit, pyramid
	_____	bird, first, shirt, sir
[ʊr]	_____	courage, furrow
	_____	hurt, spur, turn, worth
[ɛr]	_____	merry, very
	_____	person, vermin, clerk, serve
	_____	parson, varmint, Clark, starve
[ar]	_____	marry, narrow
	_____	large, park, sharp, stark
[ɔr]	_____	foreign, sorry
	_____	horse, morn, short

Describe the environmental conditions which determine the two possible developments of each vowel. (Ignore the *person/parson* difference in answering this question.)

_____

_____

_____

What pronunciations does the name *Derby* have? Cite any other names you know which have similar alternate pronunciations. _____

_____

8. The following words had in Middle English the sounds indicated at the beginning of each group. Write the phonetic symbols for the modern development of the long vowels before [r]. You may not pronounce the same vowel in all the words of every group.

MIDDLE ENGLISH   MODERN ENGLISH

[iːr]	_____	desire, mire, fire, hire, iron
[uːr]	_____	our, devour, hour, shower, tower, bower, flour/flower
[eːr]	_____	here, mere, peer, deer, beer, bier, hear, dear, clear
[ɛːr]	_____	near, rear, shear, smear, spear, beard, ear
	_____	pear, swear, tear (v.), wear, bear
[aːr]	_____	mare, hare, spare, bare, care, fare, declare, Mary
[oːr]	_____	door, floor, moor, poor
[ɔːr]	_____	more, sore, boar, port, hoarse, force, story
[ɪur]	_____	(im)mure, cure, (en)dure
[æɪr]	_____	mayor, their, air, heir, fair, despair

7.5   THE EARLY MODERN ENGLISH CONSONANTS

Because the inventory of consonants in early Modern English is identical with that for contemporary English, there is no need for a complete list. The chart from Chapter 2 can serve for the seventeenth century as well as for the twenty-first. Here we will be concerned with some of the changes which have affected consonants since Middle English times.

1. Middle English [x] and [ç] were either lost or became [f], depending partly on dialect and partly on the kind of vowel or diphthong which they followed. Standard Modern English has preserved, somewhat haphazardly, the developments characteristic of several dialects.

Describe the development of the palatovelar fricatives in each of the following groups of words by comparing the Middle English forms given here with the current pronunciation of the words.

ME [i:ç]   hīgh, nīgh, thīgh _____

ME [ıç]   night, light, right _____

ME [u:x]   droughte, plough _____

          rough, ynough, tough _____

ME [æıç]   eighte, straight _____

ME [aʊx]   aught, slaughter, taught _____

          laughen, draught _____

ME [ɔʊx]   boughte, ought, thoughte _____

          dough, though _____

          coughen, trough _____

What effect did the loss of [ç] have on a preceding short vowel? _____

_____

Did it have that effect before or after the operation of the Great Vowel Shift? How can you tell? _____

_____

What effect did the change of [x] to [f] have on a preceding long vowel? _____

_____

Did it have that effect before or after the operation of the Great Vowel Shift? How can you tell? _____

_____

When [aʊx] became [aʊf], what was the subsequent development of the diphthong? _____

_____

Which of these two sound changes occurred first? How can you tell?
    (1) [x] either became [f] or was lost altogether.
    (2) [ɔʊ] followed by a consonant became [ɔ:]; not followed by a consonant, it became [o].

_____

_____

Which allophone, [ç] or [x], sometimes became [f] ? _____
Explain the existence in standard Modern English of a doublet like *enough-enow*.

_____

_____

Look up the etymologies of *delight, haughty,* and *spright,* and explain the presence of *gh* in their spellings.

_____

2. Assibilation is a process of mutual assimilation whereby an alveolar [t], [d], [s], or [z] combines with a following palatal [y] to produce a single alveolopalatal consonant. Assibilation did not occur in all dialects of English or in all positions within a word. For each of the following groups, write the phonetic symbol for the contemporary sound which has developed from the older sequence.

_____ from [ty] in *stew, tune, Tuesday*
_____ from [ty] in *future, Christian, fortune*
_____ from [dy] in *dew, duke, dune, dupe*
_____ from [dy] in *educate, graduate, soldier*
_____ from [sy] in *sue, consume, suit*
_____ from [sy] in *mission, vicious, social*
_____ from [zy] in *vision, measure, pleasure*

In what position within a word is assibilation most likely to occur? _____

_____

Sure appears to be an exception to that generalization. Can you think of any others? _____

_____

_____

Explain why [ž] is the rarest of English phonemes and the most limited in the positions in which

it occurs. _____

_____

_____

What is the usual pronunciation of these phrases in conversation?

(I'll) hit you. _____

Did you (go)? _____

(I'll) miss you. _____

Where's your (hat)? _____

Supply additional examples of assibilation, either within a word or between words.

[ty] _____

[dy] _____

[sy] _____

[zy] _____

3. In late Middle English or very early Modern English, [g] was lost from the sequence [ŋg] under certain conditions. This loss of [g] is parallel to the earlier loss of [b] in [mb] and the less regular loss of [d] in [nd]. Consider the following examples.

king [kɪŋ]	sling [slɪŋ]	singer [sɪŋər]
rang [ræŋ]	sting [stɪŋ]	ringer [rɪŋər]
sung [səŋ]	thing [θɪŋ]	hanger [hæŋər]
finger [fɪŋgər]	anger [æŋgər]	whistling [wɪslɪn]
linger [lɪŋgər]	tangle [tæŋgəl]	nesting [nɛstɪn]
hunger [həŋgər]	language [læŋgwɪǰ]	nothing [nəθɪn]

What effect did the change of [ŋg] to [ŋ] have upon the phonemic system of English?

(Compare *king, rang, sung* with *kin, ran, sun.*) _____

_____

_____

In what position in a word was [g] lost and in what position was it retained? (Ignore *singer, ringer,*

hanger in answering this question.) _____

_____

_____

Explain the apparent irregularity in *singer, ringer, hanger.* _____

_____

_____

Under what condition did [ŋg] become [ŋ] and under what condition did it become [n]?

_____

_____

_____

4. In certain positions [l] was lost. Consider the modern pronunciation of the following words. In some of them [l] has always been pronounced; in others it has been lost, but is sometimes restored as a spelling pronunciation. Indicate whether [l] was retained or lost in each group, but disregard spelling pronunciations in reaching your decision.

FROM MIDDLE ENGLISH [al]		FROM MIDDLE ENGLISH [ɔl]	
_____	ball, fall, wall, gall	_____	boll, roll, stroll, toll
_____	malt, bald, salt, scald	_____	bolt, molten, bolster
_____	chalk, stalk, talk, walk	_____	folk, yolk
_____	calf, half, calve, halve	_____	holp (dialectal: [hop])
_____	calm, palm, psalm, alms	_____	holm, Holmes

Describe the phonetic environments in which [l] was lost. _____

_____

_____

_____

5. Look up the etymology of *cuss* and describe the sound change which has affected the word.

_____

_____

What is the traditional pronunciation of *worsted*? _____

What other words are examples of this change? _____

_____

6. Compare the earlier forms of *groin* and *woodbine* with those of *to pound* and *horehound*. What conso-

nant changes have occurred in these words? _____

_____

_____

If you are familiar with any words that show a similar fluctuation in current English, cite them. _____

_____

7. Explain the *b* in the spellings of *crumb, numb,* and *thumb* by comparing these words with *dumb*

and *plumb*. _____

_____

_____

8. In some of the following words the pronunciation with [h] is the result of the spelling rather than a historical sound development. Write *S* before the words that have such a spelling pronunciation, and *H* before the words that had [h] historically.

_____	habit	_____	honey	_____	humble
_____	health	_____	hospital	_____	humor
_____	heart	_____	host		
_____	herb	_____	hue		

9. In some of the following words the pronunciation with [θ] is the result of the spelling rather than a historical sound development. Write *S* before the words that have such a spelling pronunciation, and *H* before the words that had [θ] historically.

_____	apothecary	_____	hearth	_____	thing
_____	authority	_____	panther	_____	throng
_____	breath	_____	theater		
_____	catholic	_____	theme		

10. Changes in pronunciation do not happen instantaneously or uniformly for all speakers of a language. It is likely that *gn* and *kn*, which were certainly [gn] and [kn] for Chaucer, were pronounced simply [n] about 1600. The evidence is from puns in Shakespeare's plays and statements by writers on pronunciation during the century following Shakespeare such as these:

Simon Daines, *Orthoepia Anglicana* (1640)

Gnat, gnaw, gne, A-gnes, gnit, gno, gnu. *G* in this combination inclines to the force of *N*.
Knub, knuckle. Pronounce *kn*, as the Latines doe their **Cn**, a little in the nose, or upper palat.

The Writing Scholar's Companion (1695)

(g) Must be written (in these words) though it is not sounded. . . . Nor can (g) well be sounded in *gnaw, gnash, gnat.*
(k) Cannot well be sounded in such Words as begin with (kn), as *knife, knot, know,* &c.

John Jones, *Practical Phonography* (1701)

When is the *Sound* of *n written gn*? Wherein the *g* is not sounded, as it is not also in *gnar, gnarl, gnash, gnat, gnaw, gnibble, gnomon.*
When is the *Sound* of *n written kn*? When it may be sounded *kn*, as in *knack, knacker, knag, knap, knapple, knapsack.* . . .
When is the *Sound* of *k written k*? Always before *n* except in *Cnidos.*

Such comments are sometimes difficult to interpret, but what would you conclude from these three sources about the sound sequences [gn] and [kn] in the seventeenth century?

_____

_____

_____

_____

7.6 STRESS

What stress does the meter suggest for the italicized words in these passages from Shakespeare? Circle the stressed syllables.

Oh good old man, how well in thee appeares
The constant seruice of the *antique* world,
When seruice sweate for dutie, not for meede.   (*As You Like It*, II.iv)

        . . . but how the feare of vs
May *Ciment* their diuisions, and binde vp
The petty difference, we yet not know.   (*Antony and Cleopatra*, II.i)

No, not to be so odde, and from all fashions,
As Beatrice is, cannot be *commendable*,
But who dare tell her so?   (*Much Ado About Nothing*, III.i)

Therefore take with thee my most greeuous Curse,
Which in the day of Battell tyre thee more
Then all the *compleat* Armour that thou wear'st.   (*Richard III*, IV.iii)

No, I protest, I know not the *contents*.   (*As You Like It*, IV.iii)

Care is no cure, but rather *corrosive*,
For things that are not to be remedy'd.   (*1 Henry VI*, III.iii)

The nimble-footed Mad-Cap, Prince of Wales,
And his *Cumrades*, that daft [thrust] the World aside.   (*1 Henry VI*, IV.i)

And I will kisse thy *detestable* bones.   (*King John*, III.iii)

When I was dry with Rage, and *extreame* Toyle,
Breathlesse, and Faint, leaning vpon my Sword,
Came there a certaine Lord, neat and trimly drest.   (*1 Henry IV*, I.iii)

        . . . I
Do come with words, as *medicinall*, as true.   (*The Winter's Tale*, II.iii)

If he outliue the enuy of this day,
England did neuer owe so sweet a hope,
So much *misconstrued* in his Wantonnesse.   (*1 Henry IV*, V.ii)

I [aye], and peruersly, she *perseuers* so.   (*The Two Gentlemen of Verona*, III.ii)

For what aduancement may I hope from thee,
That no *Reuennew* [revenue] hast, but thy good spirits
To feed & cloath thee.   (*Hamlet*, III.ii)

Take heed you dally not before your King,
Lest he that is the *supreme* King of Kings
Confound your hidden falshood.   (*Richard III*, II.i)

7.7 THE DEVELOPMENT OF THE MODERN VOWELS: A REVIEW

Trace the chief sources of the present-day vowels by adding the phonetic symbols appropriate to the key words in the following chart. The vowel [i] has been done as a sample. Because there is dialect variation in current English as well as in the older periods, all the key words in the first column for a given vowel may not have the same phoneme in your speech. Note any such variations.

MODERN ENGLISH		MIDDLE ENGLISH		OLD ENGLISH	
[i]	geese	[e:]	gees	[e:]	gēs
	sleep		sleep	[e:], [æ:]	slēp (WS slæp)
	deep		deep	[e:ə]	dēop
	field		feeld	[ɛ] before *ld*	feld
	beetle		betel	[ɪ] in open syllable	bitula
	evil		evil	[y] in open syllable	yvel
	clean	[e:] in some late dialects; but earlier in all dialects [ɛ:]	clene	[æ:]	clæne
	leaf		leef	[æ:ə]	lēaf
	steal		stelen	[ɛ] in open syllable	stelan
	mead		mede	[ɛə] in open syllable	meodu
[e]	tale	ẽa:	tale		talu
	acre		aker		æcer
	day		day		dæġ
	way		wey		weġ
	eight		eighte		ehta (WS eahta)
	neigh		neyen		hnǣgan
	great		greet		grēat
	break		breken		brecan
[o]	boat	ɔ:	boot		bāt
	old		oold		ald (WS eald)
	throat		throte		þrote
	snow		snow		snāw
	own		owen		āgen
	dough		dough		dāh
	grow		growen		grōwan
	bow		bowe		boga

MODERN ENGLISH		MIDDLE ENGLISH	OLD ENGLISH
[o]	folk	folk	folc
[u]	goose	goos	gōs
	Gould	goold	gold
[(y)u]	new	newe	nīwe
	knew	knew	cnēow
	few	fewe	fēawe
	lewd	lewede	lǣwede
[aɪ]	wife	wyf	wīf
	mice	mys	mȳs
	child	child	ċild
	bridle	bridel	briġdel
	night	night	niht
	thigh	thigh	þēh (WS þēoh)
	high	high	hēh (WS hēah)
	lie	lien	lēġan (WS lēogan)
	eye	ye	ēġe (WS ēage)
[aʊ]	mouse	mous	mūs
	hound	hound	hund
	sow	sowe	sugu
	bough	bough	bōh
[ɔɪ]	joy	joy	OF joie (Lat. gaudia)
	join	joinen	OF joindre (Lat. jungere)
	poison	poison, puisun	OF poison, puisun (Lat. pōtiōnem)
[ʊ]	full	ful	full
	good	good	gōd
	wood	wode	wudu
[ə]	sun	sonne	sunne
	hussy	huswif	hūswīf
	southern	sutherne	sūþerne
	blood	blood	blōd

MODERN ENGLISH		MIDDLE ENGLISH	OLD ENGLISH
[ər]	bird	bird	bird, brid
	shirt	shirte	scyrte
	herd	herd	heord
	spurn	spurnen	spurnan
[ɪ]	fish	fish	fisc
	kin	kyn	cynn
	fifth	fifte	fīfta
	filth	filthe	fȳlþu
[ɛ]	edge	egge	ecg
	seven	seven	seofon
	kept	kepte	cēpte
	theft	theft	þēoft (WS þȳfþ)
	sweat	swete	swǣtan
	dead	deed	dēad
[æ]	lamb	lamb	lamb
	back	bak	bæc
	narrow	narwe	nearwe
	hallow	halwen	hālgian
	bladder	bladdre	blǣdre
	chapman	chapman	ċēapman
	bath	bath	bæð
	half	half	healf
	ask	asken	āscian
[ɑ]	pot	pot	pott
	holiday	holiday	hāligdæġ
	palm	palm	palm
	psalm	psalm	sealm
	far	fer	feor

MODERN ENGLISH	MIDDLE ENGLISH	OLD ENGLISH
[ɔ] claw	clawe	clawu
law	lawe	lagu
fought	faught	feaht
ought	oughte	āhte
bought	boughte	bohte
hall	hall	heall
walk	walken	wealcan
warm	warm	wearm
wash	wash	wascan
dog	dogge	dogga
broth	broth	broþ
soft	softe	sōfte

7.8 SOUND CHANGES: A REVIEW

Trace the phonological history of these words by transcribing their pronunciation during each of the three periods. The first word has been done as an example.

	OLD ENGLISH	MIDDLE ENGLISH	MODERN ENGLISH	
tīma	[ti:mɑ]	[ti:mə]	[taɪm]	time
ribb				rib
ynċe				inch
ebba				ebb
seofon				seven
crabba				crab
cæppe				cap
sceaft				shaft
hnutu				nut
pott				pot
blīþe				blithe
hȳdan				hide
ċēse				cheese
hwēol				wheel
dǣd				deed
sǣ				sea
hēap				heap
fūl				foul
fōda				food
gāt				goat
hām				home
ġung				young
cnēo				knee
cyssan				kiss
ēast				east
fæst				fast

	OLD ENGLISH	MIDDLE ENGLISH	MODERN ENGLISH	
fisc				fish
fox				fox
henn				hen
hlūd				loud
lǣċe				leech
lǣfan				leave
pāpa				pope
rīsan				rise
brȳd				bride
sāpe				soap
sōna				soon
standan				stand
sunne				sun
tēþ				teeth
dæġ				day
pleġa				play
grǣġ				gray
rāw				row
glōwan				glow
āgan				owe
spīwan				spew
flēos				fleece
dēaw				dew
mǣw				mew
clawe				claw
gnagan				gnaw
apa				ape
hræfn				raven
melu				meal
open				open
wicu				week
wudu				wood
yfel				evil
sceadu				shade
sceadwe				shadow

7.9 PRONUNCIATION AND RIME

One kind of evidence which is used in reconstructing the older pronunciation of a language is that afforded by poetry, especially rimes. Rime evidence, however, must be used with some discretion. Poets may deliberately use various kinds of imperfect rimes, like Emily Dickinson's off-rime of *pearl* with *alcohol,* which lends a delicate dryness to her verse; it is unnecessary to assume that an exact rime was intended. Similarly, when Swift writes, in "To Mr. Congreve,"

> Thus prostitute my Congreve's name is grown
> To ev'ry lewd pretender of the town,

an investigation of the riming words will show that Old English *grōwen* became Middle English [grɔuən], Modern English [gron], whereas Old English *tūn* became Middle English [tu:n], Modern English [taun]. The words do not rime today and never have. Swift must have used them as off-rimes or as eye-rimes since the spelling looks like a rime. This couplet tells us very little about Swift's pronunciation.

Nevertheless, with appropriate caution we can use rime as evidence for pronunciation, especially when other evidence supports it. Examine the following rimes from Swift. (1) Decide in each case whether the rimes are probably true or false. (2) Write the riming sounds in phonetic transcription. Be prepared to explain your decision.

(1) Yet want your criticks no just cause to rail, REille
Since knaves are ne'er obliged for what they steal. STELAN

Other similar rimes used by Swift are *ease/Bays, please/bays, dreams/names,* and *dream/same.* You may consider these rimes as additional evidence in reaching a decision about the couplet.

---

(2) Contented he—but Fate ordains, ORDENER
He now shall shine in nobler scenes. SKĒNĒ

Similarly, *scenes/entertains, scene/vein, scene/vain, scene/dean.*

---

(3) In ready counters never pays, PATER
But pawns her snuff-box, rings, and keys. CAEg

Similarly, *key/sway, key/day, key/tea.*

---

(4) Unhappy ship, thou art returned in vain; VAMŪS
New waves shall drive thee to the deep again. ONGÈan

Similarly, *again/unclean,*
but also, *again/then, again/ten, agen/pen.*

---

(5) Why, there's my landlord now, the squire, who all in money wallows, weqlwiAn
He would not give a groat to save his father from the gallows. galwes

Similarly, *watch/scratch, watch/match, wand/land, wand/hand, squabble/rabble, want/grant, wanting/planting, wanting/canting, water/matter, wander/bystander, squat/mat.*

---

(6) In velvet cap his head lies warm; weqrM
His hat for show, beneath his arm. harmos

Similarly, *war/far, war/star/tar.*

---

(7) A passage may be found, I've heard,
In some old Greek or Latin bard bārd

Similarly, *search/arch, learn/darn, served/starved, unheard/guard, clerk/mark, herbage/garbage, deserve it/starve it, verse/farce, clergy/charge ye, (thou) wert/(Faustus') art.*

---

(8) Would you rise in the church? Be stupid and dull; dol
Be empty of learning, of insolence full. full

Similarly, *skull/full, blush/bush, thrush/bush, cut/put, guts/puts, touch her/butcher.* In the contemporary Irish dialect, Middle English [U] is still a rounded vowel in all positions. How is this information apposite to Swift's rimes?

---

(9) Corinna in the morning dizen'd,
Who sees will spew; who smells, be poison'd.

Similarly, *wild/spoil'd, child/spoil'd, malign/join, surprise one* [ən]*/poison.*

---

(10) An act for laying down the plough— *genów/ genóg*
England will send you corn enough.
            but also
Tomorrow will be time enough
To hear such mortifying stuff. *estoffe*

---

(11) The cold conceits, the chilling thoughts, *thoht*
Went down like stupifying draughts. *draht*

Similarly, *draught/bought, draught/caught.*

---

(12) Next, for encouragement of spinning, *spinaan*
A duty might be laid on linen. *linen*

Similarly, *loving/sloven, teazing/treason, brewing/ruin, picking/chicken, barking/hearken, trimming/women, breathing/heathen, bubbling/Dublin, smelling/dwell in, building/skill'd in.*

---

(13) Who makes the best figure,
The Dean or the digger?

Similarly, *figure/vigour/bigger, venture/centre, ventures/representers, lecture/hector, volumes/columns.*

---

(14) For my friends have always thought *gethóht*
Tenderness my greatest fault. *falte*

Similarly, *brought/fault, haughty/faulty, thought/vault.*

---

(15) Within an hour and eke a half,
I preached three congregations deaf.

Similarly, *half/safe, halves/knaves.* Compare the Standard British pronunciation of *halfpenny.*

---

(16) Then Mrs. Johnson gave her verdict,
And every one was pleased, that heard it.

---

(17) Soon repent, or put to slaughter
Every Greek and Roman author.

---

(18) Proud Baronet of Nova Scotia,
The Dean and Spaniard must reproach ye.

Compare *charge ye/clergy.*

The following passages exemplify English from the late fifteenth century to the early seventeenth. The spelling, capitalization, and punctuation are typical of the bewildering variety that characterizes the early Modern period. Look for spelling differences from present-day English that suggest pronunciation differences. Look for grammatical differences with regard to inflections, function words, and word order. Look for vocabulary differences, both different words and different meanings. Rewrite a portion of one of the passages in present-day language and note the points at which you must rephrase to avoid an archaic flavor.

CAXTON'S PREFACE TO THE *ENEYDOS*

In several of his prefaces Caxton discusses the problems he has encountered as a translator. The best known of these discussions is the one printed below. Caxton has just described how he came upon a French version of the *Aeneid*.

And whan I had aduysed me in this sayd boke, I delybered and concluded to translate it in to englysshe, And forthwyth toke a penne & ynke, and wrote a leef or tweyne / whyche I ouersawe agayn to corecte it / And whā I sawe the fayr & straunge termes therin / I doubted that it sholde not please some gentylmen whiche late blamed me, sayeng yᵗ in my translacyons I had ouer curyous termes whiche coude not be vnderstande of comyn peple / and desired me to vse olde and homely termes in my translacyons. and fayn wolde I satysfye euery man / and so to doo, toke an olde boke and redde therin / and certaynly the englysshe was so rude and brood that I coude not wele vnderstande it. And also my lorde abbot of westmynster ded do shewe to me late, certayn euydences wryton in olde englysshe, for to reduce it in to our englysshe now vsid / And certaynly it was wreton in suche wyse that it was more lyke to dutche than englysshe; I coude not reduce ne brynge it to be vnderstonden / And certaynly our langage now vsed varyeth ferre from that whiche was vsed and spoken whan I was borne / For we englysshe men / ben borne vnder the domynacyon of the mone, whiche is neuer stedfaste / but euer wauerynge / wexynge one season / and waneth & dyscreaseth another season / And that comyn englysshe that is spoken in one shyre varyeth from a nother. In so moche that in my dayes happened that certayn marchaūtes were in a shippe in tamyse for to haue sayled ouer the see into zelande / and for lacke of wynde, thei taryed atte forlond, and wente to lande for to refreshe them: And one of theym named sheffelde, a mercer, cam in to an hows and axed for mete: and specyally he axyd after eggys: And the goode wyf answerde, that she coude speke no frenshe. And the marchaūt was angry, for he also coude speke no frenshe, but wolde haue hadde egges / and she vnderstode hym not / And thenne at laste a nother sayd that he wolde haue eyren / then the good wyf sayd that she vnderstod hym wel / Loo, what sholde a man in thyse dayes now wryte, egges or eyren / certaynly it is harde to playse euery man / by cause of dyuersite & chaūge of langage. For in these dayes euery man that is in ony reputacyon in his coūtre, wyll vtter his cōmynycacyon and maters in suche maners & termes / that fewe men shall vnderstonde theym / And som honest and grete clerkes haue ben wyth me, and desired me to wryte the moste curyous termes that I coude fynde / And thus bytwene playn rude / & curyous, I stande abasshed. but in my Iudgemente / the comyn termes that be dayli vsed, ben lyghter to be vnderstonde than the olde and aūcyent englysshe / And for as moche as this present booke is not for a rude vplondyssh man to laboure therin / ne rede it / but onely for a clerke & a noble gentylman that feleth and vnderstondeth in faytes of armes in loue & in noble chyualrye / Therfor in a meane bytwene bothe I haue reduced & translated this sayd booke in to our englysshe, not ouer rude ne curyous, but in suche termes as shall be vnderstanden, by goddys grace, accordynge to my copye. And yf ony man wyll enter mete in redyng of hit, and fyndeth suche termes that he can not vnderstande, late hym goo rede and lerne vyrgyll / or the pystles of ouyde / and ther he shall see and vnderstonde lyghtly all / Yf he haue a good redar & enformer / For this booke is not for euery rude and vnconnynge man to see / but to clerkys and very gentylmen that vnderstande gentylnes and scyence.

ELYOT'S *CASTEL OF HELTH*

Sir Thomas Elyot is best known today as the author of *The Governor*, but in his own time his most popular work was *The Castel of Helth Gathered and Made by Syr Thomas Elyot knyghte, out of the chiefe Authors of Physyke, wherby euery manne may knowe the state of his owne body, the preseruatiō of helth, and how to instructe welle his physytion in syckenes that he be not deceyued* (1539). The purpose of this work is adequately stated in its title: It is a handbook of physiology, hygiene, and diagnostics. Of the extracts printed here, the first two deal with the constitution of the body according to physiological theories inherited from the Middle Ages, the third is one of several exercises designed to preserve and promote health, and the fourth describes one common means of letting blood, a widely practiced therapeutic technique.

Of humours

In the body of Man be foure pryncipal humours, which continuynge in the proporcion, that nature hath lymitted, the body is free frome all syckenesse. Contrary wise by the increase or diminution of any of theym in quantitie or qualitie, ouer or vnder theyr naturall assignement, inequall temperature commeth into the bodye, whiche sickenesse foloweth more or lasse, accordyng to the lapse or decaye of the temperatures of the sayd humours, whiche be these folowynge.

Bloudde,   Choler,
Fleume,   Melancholy

[Of spirits]

Spirite is an ayry substance subtyll, styryng the powers of the body to perfourme their operations, whiche is dyuyded into

Naturalle, whiche taketh his begynnynge of the lyuer, and by the vaynes whiche haue no pulse, spredeth into all the hole body.

Vitall, whiche procedeth from the hart, and by the arteries or pulses is sent into all the body.

Animalle, whiche is ingendred in the brayne, and is sente by the senewes throughout the body, & maketh sence or feelynge.

Of vociferation

The chiefe exercyse of the brest and instrumentes of the voyce, is vociferation, whiche is synging, redyng, or crienge, wherof is the propertie, that it purgeth naturall heate, and maketh it also subtyll and stable, and maketh the membres of the body substancyall and stronge, resystynge diseases. This exercyse wold be vsed, of persones shorte wynded, and theym, whiche can not fetche theyr brethe, but holdyng their necke streight vpright. Also of them, whose fleshe is consumed, speciallye about the breaste and shoulders, also which haue had apostumes broken in theyr breastes: moreouer of them that are hoorse by the moche moysture, and to them, whiche haue quartene feuers, it is conuenient, it louseth the humour, that stycketh in the brest, and dryeth vp the moystenesse of the stomacke, whiche properly the course of the quartayne is wont to brynge with hym, it also profiteth them whiche haue feble stomakes, or do vomyte contynually, or do breake vp sowrenesse out of the stomake. It is good also for grefes of the heed. He that intendeth to attempt this exercise, after that he hath ben at the stoole, and softly rubbed the lower partes, and washed his handes. Lette hym speake with as base a voyce as he can, and walkynge, begynne to synge lowder & lowder, but styll in a base voyce, and to take no hede of sweete tunes or armonye. For that nothynge dothe profyte vnto helthe of the body, but to inforce hym selfe to synge greatte, for therby moche ayre drawen in by fetchyng of breath, thrustyth forth the breast and stomacke, and openeth and inlargeth the poores. By hygh crienge and lowde readynge, are expellyd superfluouse humours. Therfore menne and women, hauynge theyr bodyes feeble, and theyr flesshe lowse, and not fyrme, muste reade oftentymes lowde, and in a baase voyce, extendynge oute the wynde pype, and other passages of the breathe.

But notwithstandying, this exercyse is not vsed alway, and of all persons. For they in whome is abundance of humours corrupted, or be moche diseased with crudite in the stomak and vaines, those doo I counsayle, to abstayne from the exercyse of the voyce, leste moche corrupteth iuyce or vapours, may therby be into all the body dystrybuted. And here I conclude to speake of exercyse, whiche of them, that desyre to remayne longe in helth, is most diligently, & as I mought say, moste scrupulousely to be obserued.

Of bloude suckers or leaches

There is also an other fourme of euacuation by wormes, founde in waters callyd bloude suckers or leaches, whiche beinge put vnto the body or member, do draw out blode. And their drawynge is more conuenient for fulnesse of bloudde than scarifyenge is, forasmoche as they fetche bloud more deper, and is more of the substance of bloud, yet the opinion of some men is, that they do drawe no bloude but that, which is corrupted, and not proporcionable vnto our body. And therfore in griefes, whiche happen betwene the skynne and the flesshe of blode corrupted, these are more conuenient than scarifienge. But before that they be putte vnto any parte of the body, they muste be fyrste kepte all one day before, gyuyng vnto them a lyttel blode in freshe flesshe. And than putte theym in a cleane water, somwhat warme, and with a spounge wype awaye the slyme, whiche is about theym, and than laye a lyttell bloudde on the place greued, and putte theym thanne to it, and laye on theym a spounge, that whan they be fulle, they may falle awaye, or yf ye wyll sooner haue them of, put a horse heare bytweene theyr mouthes, and the place, and drawe them awaye, or putte to theyr mouthes salte or ashes, or vyneger, and forthwith they shall falle, and than wasshe the place with a spounge: and if there doo yssue moche bloudde, laye on the place the poulder of a spounge, and pytche bourned, or lynnen clothe bourned, or galles bourned, or the herbe callyd *Bursa pastoris* bruysed. And this suffyseth concernyng bloud suckers.

ROBINSON'S PREFACE TO *UTOPIA*

Sir Thomas More's *Utopia*, which has lent its name to an entire genre of imaginative social commentary, was written in Latin but was translated into English by Raphe Robinson some fifteen years after More's execution. The title page of the first English edition reads as follows:

> A fruteful and pleasaunt worke of the beste state of a publyque weale, and of the newe yle called Utopia: written in Latine by Syr Thomas More knyght, and translated into Englyshe by Raphe Robynson Citizein and Goldsmythe of London, at the procurement, and earnest request of George Tadlowe Citezein & Haberdassher of the same Citie. Imprinted at London by Abraham Vele, dwelling in Pauls churcheyarde at the sygne of the Lambe. Anno. 1551.

The selection printed here is the beginning of Robinson's Preface, or Epistle Dedicatory, in which he explains why he translated the *Utopia*.

To the right honourable, and his verie singuler good maister, maister William Cecylle esquiere, one of the twoo principal secretaries to the kyng his moste excellent maiestie, Raphe Robynson wissheth cōtinuaunce of health, with dayly increase of vertue, and honoure.

Vpon a tyme, when tidynges came too the citie of Corinthe that kyng Philippe father to Alexander surnamed yᵉ Great, was comming thetherwarde with an armie royall to lay siege to the citie. The Corinthiās being forth with stryken with greate feare, beganne busilie, and earnestly to looke aboute them, and to falle to worke of all handes. Some to skowre & trymme vp harneis, some to carry stones, some to amende and buylde hygher the walles, some to rampiere and fortyfie the bulwarkes, and fortresses, some one thynge, and some an other for the defendinge, and strengthenynge of the citie. The whiche busie labour, and toyle of theires when Diogenes the phylosopher sawe, hauing no profitable busines wherupō to sette himself on worke (neither any man required his labour, and helpe as expedient for the commē wealth in that necessitie) immediatly girded about him his phylosophicall cloke, & began to rolle, and tumble vp and downe hether & thether vpon the hille syde, that lieth adioyninge to the citie, his great barrel or tunne, wherein he dwelled: for other dwellynge place wold he haue none. This seing one of his frendes, and not alitell musynge therat, came to hym: And I praye the Diogenes (quod he) whie doest thou thus, or what meanest thou hereby? Forsothe I am tumblyng my tubbe to (quod he) bycause it were no reason yᵗ I only should be ydell, where so many be workīg. In semblable maner, right honorable sir, though I be, as I am in dede, of muche lesse habilitie then Diogenes was to do any thinge, that shall or may be for the auauncement & commoditie of the publique wealth of my natiue countrey: yet I seing euery sort, and kynde of people in theire vocatiō, & degree busilie occupied about the cōmō wealthes affaires: & especially learned mē dayly putting forth in writing newe inuentions, & deuises to the furtherauce of the same: thought it my boūden duetie to God, & to my countrey so to tūble my tubbe, I meane so to occupie, & exercise meself in bestowing such spare houres, as I beinge at yᵉ becke, & cōmaundement of others, cold conueniently winne to me self: yᵗ though no cōmoditie of that my labour, & trauaile to the publique weale should arise, yet it myght by this appeare, yᵗ myne endeuoire, & good wille hereunto was not lacking. To the accōplishemēt therfore, & fulfyllyng of this my mynde, & purpose: I toke vpō me to tourne, and translate out of Latine into oure Englishe tonge the frutefull, & profitable boke, which sir Thomas more knight compiled, & made of the new yle Utopia, cōteining & setting forth yᵉ best state, and fourme of a publique weale: A worke (as it appeareth) writtē almost fourtie yeres ago by the said sir Thomas More yᵉ authour therof.

HOLINSHED'S *CHRONICLES*

A renaissance successor to medieval histories like the *Polychronicon* was Raphael Holinshed's *The Chronicles of England, Scotland, and Ireland* (1587), which is remembered today as one of Shakespeare's sources.

The first passage printed here is from the geographical survey with which such chronicles usually begin. In it the author expresses a proper Englishman's opinion of the superiority of his birth tongue.

The second passage is an account of the British king, Leir, whose story is better known from Shakespeare's play.

Of the languages spoken
in this Iland

What language came first with *Samothes* and afterward with *Albion*,[1] and the giants of his companie, it is hard for me to determine, sith nothing of sound credit remaineth in writing, which may resolue vs in the truth hereof. Yet of so much are we certeine, that the speach of the ancient Britons, and of the Celts, had great affinitie one with another, so that they were either all one, or at leastwise such as either nation with small helpe of interpretors might vnderstand other, and readilie discerne what the speaker meant. Some are of the opinion that the Celts spake Greeke, and how the British toong resembled the same, which was spoken in Grecia before *Homer* did reforme it: but I see that these men doo speake without authoritie and therefore I reiect them, for if the Celts which were properlie called Galles did speake Greeke, why did Cesar in his letters sent to Rome vse that language, because that if they should be intercepted they might not vnderstand them, or why did he not vnderstand the Galles, he being so skilfull in the language without an interpretor? Yet I denie not but that the Celtish and British speaches might haue great affinitie one with another, and the British aboue all other with the Greeke, for both doo appeere by certeine words, as first in *tri* for three. . . .

Next vnto the British speach, the Latine toong was brought in by the Romans, and in maner generallie planted through the whole region, as the French was after by the Normans. Of this toong I will not say much, bicause there are few which be not skilfull in the same. . . .

The third language apparantlie knowne is the Scithian or high Dutch, induced at the first by the Saxons (which the Britons call *Saysonaec*, as they doo the speakers *Sayson*) an hard and rough kind of speach, God wot, when our nation was brought first into acquaintance withall, but now changed with vs into a farre more fine and easie kind of vtterance, and so polished and helped with new and milder words, that it is to be aduouched how there is no one speach vnder the sunne spoken in our time, that hath or can haue more varietie of words, copie of phrases, or figures and floures of eloquence, than hath our English toong, although some haue affirmed vs rather to barke as dogs, than talke like men, bicause the most of our words (as they doo indeed) incline vnto one syllable. . . .

After the Saxon toong, came the Norman or French language ouer into our countrie, and therein were our lawes written for a long time. Our children also were by an especiall decree taught first to speake the same, and therevnto inforced to learne their constructions in the French, whensoeuer they were set to the Grammar schoole. . . .

Afterward also, by diligent trauell of *Geffray Chaucer*, and *Iohn Gowre*, in the time of Richard the second, and after them of *Iohn Scogan*, and *Iohn Lydgate* monke of Berrie, our said toong was brought to an excellent passe, notwithstanding that it neuer came vnto the type of perfection, vntill the time of Queene Elizabeth. . . .

This also is proper to vs Englishmen, that sith ours is a meane language, and neither too rough nor too smooth in vtterance, we may with much facilitie learne any other language, beside Hebrue, Greeke & Latine, and speake it naturallie, as if we were home-borne in those countries; & yet on the other side it falleth out, I wot not by what other meanes, that few forren nations can rightlie pronounce ours, without some and that great note of imperfection, especiallie the French men, who also seldome write any thing that sauoreth of English trulie.

Leir the Ruler

Leir the sonne of Baldud was admitted ruler ouer the Britaines, in the yeare of the world 3105, at what time Ioas reigned in Iuda. This Leir was a prince of right noble demeanor, gouerning his land and subiects in great wealth. He made the towne of Caerleir now called Leicester, which standeth vpon the riuer of Sore. It is written that he had by his wife three daughters without other issue, whose names were Gonorilla, Regan, and Cordeilla, which daughters he greatly loued, but specially Cordeilla the yoongest farre aboue the two elder. When this Leir therefore was come to great yeres, & began to waxe vnweldie through age, he thought

---

[1]Two legendary settlers of Britain.

to vnderstand the affections of his daughters towards him, and preferre hir whome he best loued, to the succession ouer the kingdome. Whervpon he first asked Gonorilla the eldest, how well she loued him: who calling hir gods to record, protested that she loued him more than hir owne life, which by right and reason should be most deere vnto hir. With which answer the father being well pleased, turned to the second, and demanded of hir how well she loued him: who answered (confirming hir saiengs with great othes) that she loued him more than toong could expresse, and farre aboue all other creatures of the world.

Then called he his yoongest daughter Cordeilla before him, and asked of hir what account she made of him, vnto whome she made this answer as followeth: Knowing the great loue and fatherlie zeale that you haue alwaies borne towards me (for the which I maie not answere you otherwise than I thinke, and as my conscience leadeth me) I protest vnto you, that I haue loued you euer, and will continuallie (while I live) loue you as my naturall father. And if you would more vnderstand of the loue that I beare you, assertaine your selfe, that so much as you haue, so much you are worth, and so much I loue you, and no more. The father being nothing content with this answer, married his two eldest daughters, the one vnto Henninus the duke of Cornewall, and the other vnto Maglanus the duke of Albania, betwixt whome he willed and ordeined that his land should be diuided after his death, and the one halfe thereof immediatlie should be assigned to them in hand: but for the third daughter Cordeilla he reserued nothing.

Neuertheles it fortuned that one of the princes of Gallia (which now is called France) whose name was Aganippus, hearing of the beautie, womanhood, and good conditions of the said Cordeilla, desired to haue hir in mariage, and sent ouer to hir father, requiring that he might haue hir to wife: to whome answer was made, that he might haue his daughter, but as for anie dower he could haue none, for all was promised and assured to hir other sisters alreadie. Aganippus notwithstanding this answer of deniall to receiue anie thing by way of dower with Cordeilla, tooke hir to wife, onlie moued thereto (I saie) for respect of hir person and amiable vertues. This Aganippus was one of the twelue kings that ruled Gallia in those daies, as in the British historie it is recorded. But to proceed.

After that Leir was fallen into age, the two dukes that had married his two eldest daughters, thinking it long yer the gouernment of the land did come to their hands, arose against him in armour, and rest from him the gouernance of the land, vpon conditions to be continued for terme of life: by the which he was put to his portion, that is, to liue after a rate assigned to him for the maintenance of his estate, which in processe of time was diminished as well by Maglanus as by Henninus. But the greatest griefe that Leir tooke, was to see the vnkindnesse of his daughters, which seemed to thinke that all was too much which their father had, the same being neuer so little: in so much that going from the one to the other, he was brought to that miserie, that scarslie they would allow him one seruant to wait vpon him.

In the end, such was the vnkindnesse, or (as I maie saie) the vnnaturalnesse which he found in his two daughters, notwithstanding their faire and pleasant words vttered in time past, that being constreined of necessitie, he fled the land, & sailed into Gallia, there to seeke some comfort of his yongest daughter Cordeilla, whom before time he hated. The ladie Cordeilla hearing that he was arriued in poore estate, she first sent to him priuilie a certeine summe of monie to apparell himselfe withall, and to reteine a certeine number of seruants that might attend vpon him in honorable wise, as apperteined to the estate which he had borne: and then so accompanied, she appointed him to come to the court, which he did, and was so ioifullie, honorablie, and louinglie receiued, both by his sonne in law Aganippus, and also by his daughter Cordeilla, that his hart was greatlie comforted: for he was no lesse honored, than if he had beene king of the whole countrie himselfe.

Now when he had informed his sonne in law and his daughter in what sort he had beene vsed by his other daughters, Aganippus caused a mightie armie to be put in a readinesse, and likewise a great nauie of ships to be rigged, to passe ouer into Britaine with Leir his father in law, to see him againe restored to his kingdome. It was accorded, that Cordeilla should also go with him to take possession of the land, the which he promised to leaue vnto hir, as the rightfull inheritour after his decesse, notwithstanding any former grant made to hir sisters or to their husbands in anie maner of wise.

Herevpon, when this armie and nauie of ships were readie, Leir and his daughter Cordeilla with hir husband tooke the sea, and arriuing in Britaine, fought with their enimies, and discomfited them in battell, in the which Maglanus and Henninus were slaine: and then was Leir restored to his kingdome, which he ruled after this by the space of two yeeres, and then died, fortie yeeres after he first began to reigne. His bodie was buried at Leicester in a vaut vnder the chanell of the river of Sore beneath the towne.

THE FORMER AGE

Queen Elizabeth I, like her distinguished ancestor, King Alfred, also put *The Consolation of Philosophy* into English. Elizabeth's translation is, however, less successful than either Alfred's or Chaucer's. It is indeed hardly more than a school exercise, suffering from the double faults of a word-by-word rendering and occasional mistranslations. It follows the Latin original in assuming verse form. For comparison and assistance in reading Elizabeth's English, a more idiomatic version of the Latin is given next to hers.

ELIZABETH I	PRESENT DAY
Happy to muche the formar Age	The former age of men was very happy;
With faithful fild content,	Content with the faithful field
Not Lost by sluggy Lust,	And not ruined by slothful lust,
that wontz the Long fastz	They used to break their long fasts
To Louse by son-got Acorne.	With easily gotten acorns.
that knew not Baccus giftz	They did not know Bacchic gifts [wine]
With molten hony mixed	Mixed with clear honey,
Nor Serike shining flise	Nor the shining fleece [silk] of the Chinese
With tirius venom[2] die.	Stained with Tyrian dye.
Sound slipes Gaue the grasse	Herbs gave healthful sleep,
ther drink the running streme	And smooth streams, drink,
Shades gaue the hiest pine.	The highest pines, shade;
The depth of sea they fadomd not	They did not yet sail the deep seas;
Nor wares chosen from fur	Nor with merchandise gathered from everywhere
Made Stranger find new shores.	Did the stranger seek new shores.
Than wer Navies[3] Stil,	Then the raging calls of the trumpet were stilled;
Nor bloudshed by Cruel hate	And with cruel hate, extensive
Had fearful weapons[4] staned.	Bloodshed did not stain the fearful fields,
What first fury to foes shuld	For why should inimical fury first
any armes rayse,	Draw any weapons to wage war
Whan Cruel woundz he Saw	When they saw severe wounds
and no reward for bloude?	And no profit in blood?
Wold God agane Our formar time	Oh that our times might
to wonted maners fel!	Only return to the former customs.
But Gridy getting Loue burnes	But more fierce than the fires of Etna
Sorar than Etna with her flames.	Blazes the burning love of getting.
O who the first man was	Oh, who first was it
of hiden Gold the waight	Who dug the weight of hidden gold
Or Gemmes that willing lurkt	And gems wishing to lie hidden,
The deare danger digd?	The precious peril?

SIR WALTER RALEIGH'S *INSTRUCTIONS TO HIS SON*

During the last fifteen years of his life, while imprisoned in the Tower of London, Sir Walter Raleigh wrote his major prose work, *The History of the World*. He also found time to compose a short handbook of practical advice for his son. Wat, the son for whom the book was probably written, stood in need of it. Ben Jonson was his tutor during a trip to France and described the twenty-year-old's fondness for women and practical jokes, one of which had Jonson himself as its butt.

---

[2]The Latin word *venēnum* can mean either 'poison, venom' or 'dye, coloring matter.'
[3]Elizabeth translated *classis* 'navy' instead of *classicum* 'trumpet call.'
[4]Elizabeth translated *arma* 'weapons' instead of *arva* 'fields.'

Instructions to his Sonne: and to Posteritie was published in 1632, fourteen years after Raleigh's execution. The selection printed here gives advice on choosing and not choosing a wife.

The next, and greatest care ought to be in choice of a Wife, and the onely danger therein is Beauty, by which all men in all Ages, wise and foolish, have beene betrayed. And though I know it vain to use Reasons, or Arguments to disswade thee from being captiuated therewith, there being few or none that ever resisted that Witcherie; yet I cannot omit to warne thee, as of other things, which may be thy ruine and destruction. For the present time, it is true, that every man preferres his fantasie in that Appetite before all other worldly desires, leaving the care of Honour, credit, and safety in respect thereof; But remēber, that though these affections doe not last, yet the bond of Marriage dureth to the end of thy life; and therefore better to be borne withall in a Mistris, then in a wife; for when thy humour shal change thou art yet free to chuse again (if thou give thy selfe that vaine liberty.) Remember, secondly, that if thou marry for Beauty, thou bindest thy selfe for all thy life for that which perchance will neither last nor please thee one yeer; and when thou hast it, it will bee unto thee of no price at all, for the desire dyeth when it is attayned, and the affection perisheth, when it is satisfied. Remember when thou wert a sucking Child, that then thou diddest love thy Nurse, and that thou wert fond of her, after a while thou didst love thy dry Nurse, and didst forget the other, after that thou didst also despise her; so will it be with thee in thy liking in elder yeeres; and therefore, though thou canst not forbeare to love, yet forbeare to linke, and after a while thou shalt find an alteration in thy selfe, and see another far more pleasing then the first, second, or third love. . . . Let thy time of marriage bee in thy young, and strong yeeres; for beleeve it, ever the young Wife betrayeth the old Husband, and shee that had thee not in thy flower, will despise thee in thy fall, and thou shalt bee unto her, but a captivity and sorrow. Thy best time will be towards thirty, for as the younger times are unfit, either to chuse or to governe a Wife and family; so if thou stay long, thou shalt hardly see the education of thy Children, which being left to strangers, are in effect lost, and better were it to bee unborne then ill bred; for thereby thy posterity shall either perish, or remaine a shame to thy name, and family.

8 THE EARLY MODERN ENGLISH PERIOD (1500–1800)

FORMS, SYNTAX, AND USAGE

8.1 FOR REVIEW AND DISCUSSION

1. Define the following terms:

standard language	group genitive	asterisk
purism	enclitic	contraction
prescriptive grammar	uninflected genitive	eye dialect
uninflected plural	analytical comparison	impersonal construction
his-genitive	double comparison	reflexive construction

2. What are the living inflections of present-day English, that is, the inflectional endings that we might add to newly created nouns, adjectives, and verbs?
3. What is the historical source of each of those inflections?
4. How do early Modern and present-day English differ in inflections?
5. How do early Modern and present-day English differ with respect to contractions?
6. What criteria, other than the observation of actual use, guided the eighteenth-century grammarians in their making of rules for English?
7. Identify Robert Cawdrey, Henry Cockeram, Nathan Bailey, Samuel Johnson, John Wallis, Robert Lowth, Joseph Priestley, George Campbell, and Lindley Murray.

8.2 NOUNS

1. Describe the history of the Modern English regular noun plural ending -s, using the forms cited below as illustrations. Consider the history of (1) the pronunciation, (2) the meaning, and (3) the domain (that is, the number and kinds of nouns that take the ending).

OLD ENGLISH

hundas 'dogs'	ċyriċan 'churches'	gatu 'gates'
hunda 'of dogs'	ċyriċena 'of churches'	gata 'of gates'
hundum 'to, with dogs'	ċyriċum 'to, with churches'	gatum 'to, with gates'

MIDDLE ENGLISH

houndes '(of, to, with) dogs'	chirches '(of, to, with) churches'	gates '(of, to, with) gates'

MODERN ENGLISH

hounds	churches	gates

(1) pronunciation: _____

_____

_____

(2) meaning: _____

_____

_____

(3) domain: _____

_____

_____

2. A number of Modern English irregular noun plurals are survivals of inflectional patterns that once had much wider domains. Describe the origin of the following plurals, and list other words that have a similar plural form in Modern English.

thief–thieves: _____

_____

foot–feet: _____

_____

ox–oxen: _____

_____

deer–deer: _____

_____

3. *Woman* and its plural, *women,* have had a complex history. The forms cited below illustrate some of the most important changes the word has undergone (the Middle English rounding of [wɪ] to [wʊ] was a dialect variation).

Describe the development of the Old English forms into the current singular and plural; explain each step of the development as due to sound changes you have already studied or to such factors as dialect borrowing and analogy.

	SINGULAR	PLURAL
OLD ENGLISH	wīfman (nom.-acc. sing.)	wīfmen (nom.-acc. pl.)
MIDDLE ENGLISH	wimman, wumman, womman, wiman, woman	wimmen, wummen, wommen, wimen, women
MODERN ENGLISH	woman [wʊmən]	women [wɪmɪn], [-ən]

_____

_____

_____

_____

_____

_____

_____

_____

_____

4. As English has borrowed words, it has sometimes borrowed the foreign plural as well as the singular. Among such loanwords are the following. For each, give the foreign plural, specify the language from which it derives, and list some other words with the same plural formation.

vertebra _____

_____

nucleus _____

_____

stratum _____

_____

index _____

_____

matrix _____

_____

analysis _____

_____

species _____

_____

criterion _____

_____

stigma _____

_____

cherub _____

_____

5. List some loanwords that have foreign plurals other than those cited above.

_____

_____

6. Explain the function and the apparent origin of the following italicized pronouns:

by Mars *his* gauntlet (Shakespeare, *Troilus and Cressida,* IV.v)

Tamburlaine the Great . . . shewed vpon Stages in the Citie of London, By the right honorable the Lord Admyrall, *his* seruants. (title page of the 1590 edition)

Ben: Ionson *his* Volpone or The Foxe. (title page of the 1607 edition)

_____

_____

_____

7. The sign of the genitive (*'s*) is traditionally called an inflectional affix. How does it differ from other inflections in its position, and why might it more accurately be called a grammatical particle in Modern

English? _____

_____

_____

_____

8. Explain the origin of the *s*-less genitives in these expressions:

ladyfinger _____

_____

by my fatherkin _____

_____

Ulysses' voyage _____

_____

for heaven sake _____

_____

8.3 ADJECTIVES AND ADVERBS

1. What caused the Middle English distinction between strong and weak and between singular and plural

adjectives to disappear from our language? _____

_____

_____

2. Cite an early Modern English example for each of the following:

polysyllabic adjective with inflectional comparison _____

monosyllabic adjective with analytical comparison _____

adjective with double comparison _____

adverb without ending that would now require -ly _____

3. Cite a few adjectives that still fluctuate between inflectional and analytical comparison in current

English. _____

_____

4. Cite a few adverbs like *deep–deeply* that have two forms in current English.

_____

_____

5. What is the origin of the adverb without -ly? _____

_____

_____

8.4 PRONOUNS

1. How does current English differ from early Modern in its use of the genitives *my* and *mine*? The difference is illustrated in this quotation from Shakespeare:

Falstaff　. . . Shall I not take mine ease in mine inn, but I shall have my pocket picked? I have lost a
　　　seal ring of my grandfather's worth forty mark.　　(*1 Henry IV*, III.iii)

_____

_____

2. What nuances of meaning are implied by the choice between *y*-forms and *th*-forms of the second person pronoun in the following passages from Shakespeare?

[Miranda questions her father about the tempest which has apparently wrecked a ship.]

Miranda　If by *your* Art (my deerest father) *you* haue
　　　　Put the wild waters in this Rore; alay them.

　　　　　　　. . . . .

Prospero　I haue done nothing, but in care of *thee*
　　　　(Of *thee* my deere one; *thee* my daughter) who
　　　　Art ignorant of what *thou* art.　　(*The Tempest*, I.ii)

_____

_____

[King Henry doubts his son's loyalty and is reassured by Hal.]

King　But wherefore doe I tell these Newes to *thee*?
　　　Why, Harry, doe I tell *thee* of my Foes,
　　　Which art my neer'st and dearest Enemie?
　　　Thou, that art like enough, through Vassal Feare,
　　　Base Inclination, and the start of Spleene,
　　　To fight against me vnder Percies pay,
　　　To dogge his heeles, and curtsie at his frownes,
　　　To shew how much *thou* art degenerate.

Prince	Doe not thinke so, *you* shall not finde it so:
	And Heauen forgiue them, that so much haue sway'd
	Your Maiesties good thoughts away from me:
	I will redeeme all this on Percies head,
	And in the closing of some glorious day,
	Be bold to tell *you*, that I am *your* Sonne. (*1 Henry IV*, III.ii)

[King Claudius and Queen Gertrude urge Hamlet to forgo his mourning and to remain at the Danish court.]

King	How is it that the Clouds still hang on *you*?
Hamlet	Not so my Lord, I am too much i'th'Sun.
Queen	Good Hamlet cast *thy* nightly colour off,
	And let *thine* eye looke like a Friend on Denmarke.
	Do not for euer with *thy* veyled lids
	Seeke for *thy* Noble Father in the dust;
	Thou know'st 'tis common, all that liues must dye,
	Passing through Nature, to Eternity.

. . . . .

King	'Tis sweet and commendable
	In *your* Nature Hamlet,
	To giue these mourning duties to *your* Father:
	But *you* must know, *your* Father lost a Father.

. . . . .

	And we beseech *you*, bend *you* to remaine
	Heere in the cheere and comfort of our eye,
	Our cheefest Courtier Cosin, and our Sonne.
Queen	Let not *thy* Mother lose her Prayers Hamlet;
	I pry*thee* stay with vs, go not to Wittenberg.
Hamlet	I shall in all my best
	Obey *you* Madam.
King	Why 'tis a louing, and a faire Reply. (*Hamlet*, I.ii)

[Harry Percy, Northumberland's son, has defended his brother-in-law, Mortimer, against the charge of treason. King Henry still refuses to ransom Mortimer, who was captured in battle by Owen Glendower.]

King	*Thou* do'st bely him Percy, *thou* dost bely him;
	He neuer did encounter with Glendower:
	I tell *thee,* he durst as well haue met the diuell alone,
	As Owen Glendower for an enemy.
	Art *thou* not asham'd? But, Sirrah, henceforth
	Let me not heare *you* speake of Mortimer.
	Send me *your* Prisoners with the speediest meanes,
	Or *you* shall heare in suche a kinde from me
	As will displease *ye*. My Lord Northumberland,
	We License *your* departure with *your* sonne,
	Send vs *your* Prisoners, or *you*'l heare of it. (*1 Henry IV*, I.iii)

[Hotspur (Harry Percy) is secretly planning to join a revolt against King Henry IV; his wife has questioned him about his mysterious activities.]

Hotspur   Come, wilt *thou* see me ride?
            And when I am a horsebacke, I will sweare
            I loue *thee* infinitely. But hearke *you* Kate,
            I must not haue *you* henceforth, question me,
            Whether I go: nor reason whereabout
            Whether I must, I must: and to conclude,
            This Euening must I leaue *thee,* gentle Kate.
            I know *you* wise, but yet no further wise
            Than Harry Percies wife. Constant *you* are,
            But yet a woman: and for secrecie,
            No lady closer. For I will beleeue
            Thou wilt not vtter what *thou* do'st not know,
            And so farre wilt I trust *thee,* gentle Kate.   (*1 Henry IV,* II.iii)

[Lear has just disinherited his youngest daughter, Cordelia, and Kent speaks in her defense.]

Kent   Royall Lear,
        Whom I haue euer honor'd as my King,
        Lou'd as my Father, as my Master follow'd,
        As my great Patron thought on in my praiers.
Lear   The bow is bent & drawne, make from the shaft.
Kent   Let it fall rather, though the forke inuade
        The region of my heart, be Kent vnmannerly,
        When Lear is mad, what wouldest *thou* do old man?
        Think'st *thou* that dutie shall haue dread to speake,
        When power to flattery bowes?
        To plainnesse honour's bound,
        When Maiesty falls to folly, reserue *thy* state,
        And in *thy* best consideration checke
        This hideous rashnesse, answere my life, my iudgement:
        Thy yongest Daughter do's not loue *thee* least.   (*King Lear,* I.i)

[Lady Anne is on her way to the funeral of her father-in-law, King Henry VI, when she meets Richard, who has murdered both the old King and Lady Anne's husband.]

Anne   *Thou* was't prouoked by *thy* bloody minde,
        That neuer dream'st on ought but Butcheries:
        Did'st *thou* not kill this King?
Richard   I graunt *ye.*

     . . . . . .

Anne   He is in heauen, where *thou* shalt neuer come.
Richard   Let him thank me, that holpe to send him thither:
        For he was fitter for that place then earth.

Anne	And *thou* vnfit for any place, but hell.
Richard	Yes one place else, if *you* will heare me name it.
Anne	Some dungeon.
Richard	*Your* Bed-chamber.
Anne	Ill rest betide the chamber where *thou* lyest.
Richard	So will it Madam, till I lye with *you*.

. . . . .

Anne	*Thou* was't the cause, and most accurst effect.
Richard	*Your* beauty was the cause of that effect:
	Your beauty that did haunt me in my sleepe,
	To vndertake the death of all the world,
	So I might liue one houre in *your* sweet bosome.
Anne	If I thought that, I tell *thee* Homicide,
	These Nailes should rent that beauty from my Cheekes.
Richard	These eyes could not endure yᵗ beauties wrack,
	You should not blemish it, if I stood by;
	As all the world is cheared by the Sunne,
	So I by that: It is my day, my life.
Anne	Blacke night ore-shade *thy* day, & death *thy* life.
Richard	Curse not *thy* selfe faire Creature,
	Thou art both.
Anne	I would I were, to be reueng'd on *thee*.
Richard	It is a quarrell most vnnaturall,
	To be reueng'd on him that loueth *thee*.

. . . . .

[After Richard has offered to kill himself, Anne relents.]

Richard	Looke how my Ring incompasseth *thy* Finger,
	Euen so *thy* Brest incloseth my poore heart:
	Weare both of them, for both of them are *thine*.
	And if *thy* poore deuoted Seruant may
	But beg one fauour at *thy* gracious hand,
	Thou dost confirme his happinesse for euer.
Anne	What is it?
Richard	That it may please *you* leaue these sad designes,
	To him that hath most cause to be a Mourner,
	And presently repayre to Crosbie House:
	Where (after I haue solemnly interr'd
	At Chertsey Monast'ry this Noble King,
	And wet his Graue with my Repentant Teares)
	I will with all expedient duty see *you*,
	For diuers vnknowne Reasons, I beseech *you*,
	Grant me this Boon.
Anne	With all my heart, and much it ioyes me too,
	To see *you* are become so penitent.
	Tressel and Barkley, go along with me.
Richard	Bid me farwell.
Anne	'Tis more than *you* deserue:
	But since *you* teach me how to flatter *you*,
	Imagine I haue saide farwell already. (*Richard III*, I.ii)

3. Some of the *ye*'s and *you*'s in the following quotations from Shakespeare are used "correctly" according to the case distinctions of Old and Middle English, and some show a confusion of the older forms. Circle the pronouns that confuse the older nominative and objective functions.

Antony　I do beseech *yee,* if *you* beare me hard,
Now whil'st your purpled hands do reeke and smoake,
Fulfill your pleasure.　　(*Julius Caesar,* III.i)

Poet　For shame *you* Generals; what do *you* meane?
Loue, and be Friends, as two such men should bee,
For I haue seene more yeeres I'me sure then *yee.*　　(*Julius Caesar,* IV.iii)

Porter　*You*'l leaue your noyse anon *ye* Rascals: doe *you* take the Court for Parish Garden:
ye rude Slaues, leaue your gaping.　　(*Henry VIII,* V.iii)

King　As I haue made *ye* one Lords, one remaine:
So I grow stronger, *you* more Honour gaine.　　(*Henry VIII,* V.ii)

Banquo　Are *ye* fantasticall, or that indeed
Which outwardly *ye* shew? My Noble Partner
You greet with present Grace, and great prediction
Of Noble hauing, and of Royall hope.　　(*Macbeth,* I.iii)

4. Can you think of any reason why nominative *ye* and objective *you* should have been widely confused whereas other nominative-objective distinctions like *he–him, she–her, I–me, we–us,* and *they–them* were not so confused? Suggestion: consider the influence of lack of stress.

_____

_____

_____

5. Identify the origin of the italicized forms as

　　　S—regular stressed development of the Middle English pronoun,
　　　U—unstressed development of the Middle English pronoun, or
　　　A—analogical form.

_____　*A* toke me to him and ast how my suster dede, and I answeryd wyll, never better.
　　　　　　　(*Paston Letters,* no. 260)
_____　*Hit* was at Ierusalem the feaste of the dedication.　　(Tindale's Gospel of John, 10:22)
_____　I shall report *it* so.　　(*All's Well That Ends Well,* II.v)
_____　It lifted vp *it* head.　　(*Hamlet,* I.ii)
_____　Heauen grant vs *its* peace.　　(*Measure for Measure,* I.ii)
_____　And the earth brought forth grass, and herb yielding seed after *his* kind.　　(Genesis 1:12)
_____　Were our Teares wanting to this Funerall,
　　　　　　　These Tidings would call forth *her* flowing Tides.　　(*1 Henry VI,* I.i)
_____　*Lear*　Be my Horsses ready?
　　　　　　　Fool　Thy Asses are gone about '*em.*　　(*King Lear,* I.v)

6. What is the first citation in the *Oxford English Dictionary* for each of the following pronouns used as a simple relative? Give the quotation and the date.

the _____

that _____

which _____

who _____

7. Circle the pronouns that have "improper" case forms according to the rules of school grammar.

> *Oliver* Know you before whom [you are] sir?
> *Orlando* I, better then him I am before knowes mee.   (*As You Like It*, I.i)

We are alone, here's none but thee, & I.   (*2 Henry VI*, I.ii)

Is she as tall as me?   (*Antony and Cleopatra*, III.iii)

Consider who the King your father sends,
To whom he sends, and what's his Embassie.   (*Love's Labor's Lost*, II.i)

Oh, the dogge is me, and I am my selfe.   (*The Two Gentlemen of Verona*, II.iii)

> The King,
> His Brother, and yours, abide all three distracted,
> And the remainder mourning ouer them,
> Brim full of sorrow, and dismay: but chiefly
> Him that you term'd Sir, the good old Lord Gonzallo.   (*The Tempest*, V.i)

Yes, you haue seene Cassio, and she together.   (*Othello*, IV.ii)

For this, from stiller Seats we came, our Parents, and vs twaine.   (*Cymbeline*, V.iv)

Who ioyn'st thou with, but with a Lordly Nation,
That will not trust thee, but for profits sake?   (*1 Henry VI*, III.iii)

Now could I (Caska) name to thee a man,

. . . . .

A man no mightier then thy selfe, or me,
In personall action; yet prodigious growne.   (*Julius Caesar*, I.iii)

8.5 VERBS: THE SEVEN STRONG CLASSES

Verbs from all of the seven strong classes have survived in Modern English, but sound change and analogy have played such havoc with the vowels which once marked their principal parts that the traditional classification into seven groups has only historical validity.

The most common strong verbs in Modern English, arranged according to the traditional class to which they most nearly conform, are these:

CLASS I   abide, bite, chide, dive, drive, hide, ride, rise, shine, slide, smite, stride, strike, strive, thrive, write

CLASS II   choose, cleave, fly, freeze

CLASS III   begin, bind, cling, dig, drink, fight, find, fling, grind, ring, run, shrink, sing, sink, sling, slink, spin, spring, stick, sting, stink, string, swim, swing, win, wind, wring

CLASS IV   bear, break, come, get, heave, shear, speak, steal, swear, tear, tread, weave

CLASS V   bid, eat, give, lie, see, sit

CLASS VI   draw, forsake, shake, slay, stand, take

CLASS VII   beat, blow, crow, fall, grow, hang, hold, know, throw

Some of these verbs were originally weak or were loanwords but acquired strong inflection by analogy. Their history is discussed in *Origins and Development*, pages 170–6, and is summarized in the following outline. For each class, the typical vowels of the Middle English principal parts are listed, the development of the principal parts of standard Modern English is summarized, and the vowels of the three modern parts (infinitive, preterit, past participle) are given in phonetic notation. Complete the outline by writing all three parts of each verb in an appropriate blank. Thus *abide, abode, abode* would go under IC; *bite, bit, bitten*, under IB; and so forth.

CLASS I (ME ī ǭ i i)

A. Normal development with Modern English preterit from Middle English preterit singular: [aɪ o ɪ-n]

_____   _____

_____   _____

_____   _____

B. Normal development with Modern English preterit from Middle English preterit plural and past participle: [aɪ ɪ ɪ(-n)]

_____   _____

_____   _____

C. Modern English preterit and past participle from Middle English preterit singular: [aɪ o o]

_____   _____

D. Modern English preterit of uncertain origin; normal development of the past participle is now used only metaphorically: [aɪ ə ɪ-n]

_____

E. Originally a weak verb; strong preterit acquired by analogy: [aɪ o aɪ-d]

_____

CLASS II (ME ē,ō ę u ǭ)

A. Modern English preterit from Middle English past participle: [i,u o o-n]

_____   _____

_____

B. Modern English preterit perhaps by analogy with Class VII: [aɪ u o-n]

_____

CLASS III (ME i,ī a u,ou u,ou)

A. Normal development with Modern English preterit from Middle English preterit singular: [ɪ æ ə(-n)]

_____   _____

_____   _____

_____   _____

_____

B. Normal development with Modern English preterit from Middle English preterit plural and past participle: [ɪ,aɪ ə,aʊ ə,aʊ]

_____   _____

_____   _____

_____   _____

_____   _____

_____   _____

_____   _____

_____   _____

C. Modern English present from Middle English past participle: [ə æ ə]

_____

D. Normal development, allowing for the influence of Middle English *h* [ç,x] on a preceding vowel: [aɪ ɔ ɔ]

_____

CLASS IV   (ME   ę̄ a ē ǭ)

A. Modern English preterit from Middle English past participle: [i,e o o(-n)]

_____   _____

_____   _____

_____

B. Modern English preterit from Middle English past participle; variation in the vowels is due to the influence of [r]: [ɛr,ɪr or,ɔr or,ɔr-n]

_____   _____

_____   _____

C. Modern English preterit from Middle English past participle; shortened vowels in all parts: [ɛ ɑ ɑ(-n)]

_____   _____

D. Normal development of the forms *cumen, cām, cumen,* which were irregular in Middle English: [ə e ə]

_____

CLASS V   (ME   ĕ a ē ę̄)

A. Modern English preterit from a lengthened form of Middle English preterit singular: [i e i-n]

_____

B. Present stem with irregular [ɪ] since Old English times; three Modern English preterits from the Middle English preterit singular by normal development, from a lengthened form of the Middle English preterit singular, and from the irregular past participle; past participle vowel perhaps from the present by analogy with other verbs which had the same vowel in the present and past participle: [ɪ æ,e,ɪ ɪ(-n)]

_____

C. Not a continuation of the native English verb (Chaucer's _yeven, yaf, yaven, yeven_), but of a related Scandinavian verb: [ɪ e ɪ-n]

_____

D. Modern English preterit and past participle from Middle English preterit singular; the present has had an irregular [ɪ] since Old English times: [ɪ æ æ]

_____

E. Normal development, allowing for influence of [y] on the preceding vowel, except in present stem: [aɪ e e-n]

_____

F. Normal development of Middle English irregular forms with the vowels [ē aʊ ē]: [i ɔ i-n]

_____

CLASS VI   (ME   ă ō̆ ō ă̄)

A. Normal development with Modern shortening of the preterit vowel: [e ʊ e-n]

_____   _____

_____

B. Modern English past participle from Middle English preterit: [æ ʊ ʊ]

_____

C. Present stem vowel from the past participle; preterit vowel by analogy with Class VII verbs: [e u e-n]

_____

D. Preterit vowel by analogy with Class VII verbs; present and past participle are normal developments of Middle English [aʊ]: [ɔ u ɔ-n]

_____

CLASS VII   (ME: several different vowels in the present and past participle; preterit singular and plural: ḗ
          or iu)

A. Normal development: [o u o-n]

_____   _____

_____   _____

B. Normal development of the preterit; only the weak past participle now exists: [o u o-d]

_____

C. Normal development, with spelling of the preterit from the other forms: [i i i-n]

_____

D. Normal development: [ɔ ɛ ɔ-n]

_____

E. Modern English past participle from Middle English preterit: [o ɛ ɛ]

_____

F. Modern English forms are a mixture of three Middle English verbs (*hōn,* Class VII; *hangen,* weak; *hengen,* a Scandinavian loan): [æ ə ə]

_____

8.6   VERB ENDINGS AND CONSTRUCTIONS

1. Explain the inflectional form of the italicized verbs.
    Thou hotly *lusts* to vse her in that kind, for which thou *whip'st* her.   (*King Lear,* IV.vi)

_____

    Sometime she *driueth* ore a Souldiers necke, & then *dreames* he of cutting Forraine throats.
       (*Romeo and Juliet,* I.iv)

_____

    His teares *runs* downe his beard like winters drops
    From eaues of reeds: your charm so strongly works 'em
    That if you now beheld them, your affections
    Would become tender.   (*The Tempest,* V.i)

_____

    Where is thy Husband now? Where *be* thy Brothers?
    Where *be* thy two Sonnes? Wherin dost thou Ioy?   (*Richard III,* IV.iv)

_____

    I suppose you *was* in a dream.   (Bunyan, *Pilgrim's Progress*)

_____

For all the Welchmen hearing thou *wert* dead,
Are gone to Bullingbrooke, disperst, and fled.   (*Richard II,* III.ii)

_____

Thou *was't* borne of woman.   (*Macbeth,* V.vii)

_____

2. Paraphrase the italicized expressions in current idiom, and comment on the grammar of the early Modern constructions.

Yet hold I off. Women are Angels *wooing,*
Things won are done, ioyes soule lyes in the dooing.   (*Troilus and Cressida,* I.ii)

_____

The clocke strook nine, when I *did send* the Nurse.   (*Romeo and Juliet,* II.v)

_____

What *saies he* of our marriage? What of that?   (*Romeo and Juliet,* II.v)

_____

I *care not*.   (*Romeo and Juliet,* III.i)

_____

Tis knowne to you he is mine enemy:
Nay more, an enemy vnto you all,
And no great friend, *I feare me* to the King.   (*2 Henry VI,* I.i)

_____

But *me list* not here to make comparison.   (Peele, *The Arraignment of Paris,* prologue)

_____

                The common executioner
Whose heart th'accustom'd sight of death makes hard
Falls not the axe vpon the humbled neck,
But first begs pardon.   (*As You Like It,* III.v)

_____

His Lordship *is walk'd* forth into the Orchard.   (*2 Henry IV,* I.i)

_____

3. Some grammar books list forms like these as the "future tense" of English:

I shall go	we shall go
thou wilt go	you will go
he will go	they will go

Comment on the historical validity and the contemporary reality of such a paradigm.

_____

_____

4. The present-day verbal system includes a number of phrases that combine the auxiliaries *be* and *have* with a main verb to produce periphrastic tenses. By consulting the *Oxford English Dictionary* entries for *be* and *have,* determine the earliest date for each of the following constructions.

passive (for example, *is sung*) _____

progressive (for example, *is singing*) _____

progressive passive (for example, *is being sung*) _____

perfect (for example, *has sung*) _____

perfect passive (for example, *has been sung*) _____

8.7 THE IMPORTANCE OF PREPOSITIONS

As the inflections of English nouns disappeared, prepositions became more important as grammatical signals, and their number increased.

1. Prepositions have been created from phrases (*because of* from *by cause of*), adapted from inflectional forms (*during* from the archaic *to dure*), or borrowed from other languages (*per* from Latin). Describe the origin of the following prepositions.

amidst _____

among _____

between _____

despite _____

down _____

instead of _____

near _____

past _____

pending _____

plus _____

since _____

via _____

2. The idiomatic use of prepositions has changed somewhat since the early Modern period. What expressions would current English prefer in place of the italicized prepositions in the following quotations?

Antony   Thou can'st not feare [frighten] vs Pompey with thy sailes.
Weele speake with thee at Sea. *At* land thou know'st
How much we do o're-count [outnumber] thee.   (*Antony and Cleopatra,* II.vi)

_____

Marcellus	Some sayes, that euer *'gainst* that Season comes
	Wherein our Sauiours Birth is celebrated,
	The Bird of Dawning singeth all night long. (*Hamlet*, I.i)

_____

| Rivers | Then is my Soueraigne slaine? |
| Queen | I [aye] almost slaine, for he is taken prisoner, |

. . . . . .

	And as I further haue to vnderstand,
	Is new committed to the Bishop of Yorke,
	Fell Warwickes Brother, and *by* that our Foe. (*3 Henry VI*, IV.iv)

_____

Helena	That you may well perceiue I haue not wrong'd you,
	One of the greatest in the Christian world
	Shall be my suretie: *for* whose throne 'tis needfull
	Ere I can perfect mine intents, to kneele. (*All's Well That Ends Well*, IV.iv)

_____

Hamlet	For any thing so ouer-done, if *frō* the
	purpose of Playing, whose end both at the
	first and now, was and is, to hold as 'twer
	the Mirrour vp to Nature. (*Hamlet*, III.ii)

_____

| Salisbury | And charge, that no man should disturbe your rest, |
| | *In* paine of your dislike, or paine of death. (*2 Henry VI*, III.ii) |

_____

Portia	And yet I am sure you are not satisfied
	Of these euents at full. Let vs goe in,
	And charge vs there vpon intergatories,
	And we will answer all things faithfully. (*The Merchant of Venice*, V.i)

_____

Fool	Why this fellow ha's banish'd two
	on's Daughters, and did the third a blessing
	against his will, if thou follow him,
	thou must needs weare my Coxcombe. (*King Lear*, I.iv)

_____

King	. . . he which hath no stomack *to* this fight,
	Let him depart, his Pasport shall be made,
	And Crownes for Conuoy put into his Purse:
	We would not dye in that mans companie. (*Henry V*, IV.iii)

_____

2 Gent.	What, pray you, became of Antigonus,
	that carryed hence the Child?
3 Gent.	Like an old Tale still, which will haue
	matter to rehearse, though Credit be asleepe,
	And not an eare open; he was torne to pieces
	with a Beare. (*The Winter's Tale*, V.ii)

_____

8.8 SUBJECTS AND COMPLEMENTS

The italicized portions of the following sentences illustrate constructions that have been used at various times in the history of English. Whenever possible, examples from Old, Middle, and Modern English have been cited. For each group of sentences, describe the construction that is illustrated and indicate whether or not you believe it to be a living part of present-day English.

1. *Sigon* þā tō slǣpe. '[They] *sank* then into sleep.'   (*Beowulf*)
   Quen he had his broiþer slan, *Began* to hid his corse o-nan. 'When he had slain his brother, [he] *began* to hide his corpse anon.'   (*Cursor Mundi*)
   This is my Son belov'd, in him *am pleas'd.*   (Milton, *Paradise Regained*)

   _____

   _____

2. Weard maþelode, *ðǣr on wicge sæt.* 'The watchman spoke, *sat there on horseback.*'   (*Beowulf*)
   He hadde founde a corn *lay in the yerd.*   (Chaucer, *Canterbury Tales*)
   I had it all planned out to go there this summer with a friend of mine *lives in Winnipeg.*   (Sinclair Lewis, "Mantrap")

   _____

   _____

3. *Hit* is weliġ *þis ēalond.* '*It* is rich, *this island.*'   (Bede, *Ecclesiastical History*)
   It stondeth written in thy face *Thyn errour.*   (Chaucer, *Parlement of Fowles*)
   What may *it* be, *the heavy sound*?   (Scott, "The Lay of the Last Minstrel")

   _____

   _____

4. *Moyse ǣrest and Helias hī* fæston. '*Moses* first *and Elias, they* fasted.'   (*St. Guthlac*)
   His sonnes & þe barons Sone þei rised strif. '*His sons and the baron's son, they* raised strife.'   (*Langtoft's Chronicle*)
   Her father he couldn't come.   (Galsworthy, "Freelands")

   _____

   _____

5. Cnut *wende him* ūt. 'Cnut *went* out.'   (*Anglo-Saxon Chronicle*)
   She *went her* out to pley.   (Gower, *Confessio Amantis*)
   The good manne *goeth him* home.   (St. Thomas More)

   _____

   _____

6. Þū ġenōh wel understentst þæt iċ *þē tō* sprece. 'You understand well enough what I speak *to you.*' (Alfred, *Consolation of Philosophy*)
   We aske the leve to speke *the wyth.* 'We ask you leave to speak *with you.*'   (Robert of Brunne, *Chronicle*)

   _____

   _____

7. Ġife iċ *hit ðē.* 'I give *you it.*'   (Genesis)
Þei wyll tele *it yow.* 'They will tell *you it.*'   (*Book of Margery Kempe*)
Your father would never have given *it you.*   (Robert Graves, *I, Claudius*)

_____

_____

8. Describe the historical development of the italicized construction from the examples in the following sentences:
Hē cwæþ sōþlīċe, *Iċ hit eom.*   (Gospel of John)
Our Lord answered, *I it am.*   (*Book of Margery Kempe*)
Now speke to me, for *it am I*, Crisseyde.   (Chaucer, *Troilus & Crisseyde*)
Ya soth, said David, *it es I.*   (*Cursor Mundi*)
It is I who should be consulted.   (Wilde, *The Ideal Husband*)
It is not *me* you are in love with.   (Steele, *Spectator*)
"*It's me*," he answered her.   (Aldous Huxley, *Antic Hay*)

_____

_____

_____

8.9   THE EARLY DICTIONARIES

The first English dictionaries were lists of "hard words" with simple and very concise glosses. As the tradition of lexicography developed, dictionaries increased their scope both in the number of entries and in the amount of information given for each word. Below are sample entries from a number of early works ranging from Henry Cockeram's *English Dictionarie,* the first to use the word *dictionary* in its title, to Samuel Johnson's *Dictionary of the English Language,* in which lexicographical technique approaches contemporary standards. The complete entry for the word *mother,* its compounds, and its derivatives has been quoted from each dictionary.

1623.   Henry Cockeram, *The English Dictionarie: or, An Interpreter of hard English Words.*

Mother. A disease in women when the wombe riseth with paine upwards: sweet smelles are ill for it, but loathsome savors good.

1656.   Thomas Blount, *Glossographia: or a Dictionary, Interpreting all such Hard Words Whether Hebrew, Greek, Latin, Italian, Spanish, Teutonick, Belgick, British or Saxon, as are now used in our refined English Tongue.*

Mother, a disease in women, when the womb riseth with pain, for which the smelling to all sweet savors is harmful; as contrarily, to all strong and loathsom, good.

1676.   Elisha Coles, *An English Dictionary, Explaining the Difficult Terms that are used in Divinity, Husbandry, Physick, Philosophy, Law, Navigation, Mathematicks, and other Arts and Sciences.*

Mother, *a painful rising of the womb, for which all sweet smells are bad, and stinking ones good.*
Motherwort, Cardiaca, *A cleasing* [sic] *Astringent herb.*
Mother-tongues, *having no Affinity with one another.*

1689.   Anonymous, *Gazophylacium Anglicanum.*

Mother, from the AS **Moðor**, the Fr. Th. **Mudder**, the Belg. **Moeder**, or the Teut. **Mutter**, the same; all from the Lat. *Mater,* or the Gr. *Mētēr, idem.*
The **Mother** *of Wine,* from the Belg. **Moeder**, lees, thickning; this again from **Modder, Moder,** mud.

191

1702.   John Kersey, *A New English Dictionary.*

A Mother.
A Mother-in-law.
A God-mother.
A Grand-mother.
A Step-mother.
A Mother-city, or *chief City.*
A Mother-tongue.
Mother of Pearl, *a shellfish.*
Mother of time *an herb.*
The Mother, or *dregs of Oil, Wine,* &c.
The Mother, or *womb*; also *a disease in that part.*
Fits of the Mother.
Mother-wort, *an herb.*
Mother-hood, *the quality* or *functions of a* mother.
Motherless, *bereft of a* mother.

1706.   John Kersey, revision of Edward Phillips's *The New World of Words: or, Universal English Dictionary.*

Mother, a Woman that has brought forth a Child; also the Womb in which the Child is form'd, or a Disease in that Part; also the Dregs of Ale, B er [sic], Oil, &c.
Mother of Pearl, the Shell that contains the Pearl-fish.
Mother of Time, a kind of Herb.
Mother-Tongues, such Languages as seem to have no Dependence upon, Derivation from, or Relation one to another.
Mother-wort, an Herb, of a cleansing and binding Quality.

1707.   *Glossographia Anglicana Nova: or, A Dictionary, Interpreting Such Hard Words of whatever Language, as are at present used in the* English *Tongue, with their* Etymologies, Definitions, &c.

Mother, the Womb, or a Disease in that part; also Dregs of Ale, Beer, Oil, &c.
Mother-Tongues, are such Languages as seem to have no dependence upon, derivation from, or affinity with one another; of which *Scaliger* affirms there are eleven only in *Europe.* The *Greek,* the *Latin,* the *Teutonick* or *German,* the *Sclavonick,* the *Albanese* or *Epirotick.* The *European Tartar* or *Scythian,* the *Hungarian,* the *Finnick,* the *Cantrabrian,* the *Irish,* and the old *Gaulish* or *British*; to this number some add Four others, the *Arabick,* the *Cauchian,* the *Illyrian,* and the *Jazygian.*

1708.   John Kersey, *Dictionarium Anglo-Britannicum: Or, a General English Dictionary.*

Mother, a Woman that has brought forth a Child; also the Womb in which the Child is form'd, or a Disease in that Part; also the Dregs of Ale, Beer, Oil, &c.
Mother of Pearl, the Shell that contains the Pearl-fish.
Mother of Time, a kind of Herb.
Mother-Tongues, such Languages as seem to have no Derivation from, or Relation to another.
Mother-wort, an Herb.

1730.   Nathan Bailey, *Dictionarium Britannicum: Or a more Compleat Universal Etymological English Dictionary Than any Extant.*

MO´THER [**moðor**, *Sax.* **moder**, *Dan.* and *Su.* **moeder**, *Du.* and L.G. **mutter**, H.G. **modder**, Goth. *mader,* Pers. *mere,* F. *madre,* It. and Sp. *may,* Port. *mater,* L.] of a child; also the womb itself; also a disease peculiar to that part; also a white substance on stale liquours.
MOTHER *of Pearl,* the shell which contains the pearl fish.
MOTHER *of time,* an herb.
MOTHER *of Wine, Beer,* &c. [**moeder,** lees,] thickening the mouldiness or dregs of wine, beer, &c.
MOTHER-*Wort,* an herb.

Diffidence is the Mother **of Safety**
F. *La defiance est la mere de sureté. It. La diffidenza è la madre della Sicurtà,*

MOTHER *Tongues,* are such languages as seem to have no dependance upon, derivation from, or affinity with one another. Some have been of opinion, that at the confusion of languages, at the building of *Bable,* there were formed 70 or 72 languages. But bishop *Wilkins* and others are of opinion that there were not so many, nor that men did then disperse into so many colonies.

There have been, and at this time there are in the world a far greater number. *Pliny* and *Strabo* relate that in *Dioscuria,* a town of *Colchos,* there were men of 300 nations, and of so many distinct languages, who did resort thither on account of traffick.

Some historians relate, that in every 80 miles of that vast continent, and almost in every particular valley of *Peru,* a distinct language or mother tongue to them was spoken.

And *Purchase* speaks of a 1000 distinct languages spoken by the inhabitants of north *America,* about *Florida.*

Julius Scaliger asserts, that there are no more than eleven mother tongues used in *Europe,* of which four are of more general use and large extent, and the other seven of a narrower extent and use. Those of the larger extent are.

1. The *Greek,* which in antient times was used in *Europe, Asia,* and *Africa,* which also did by dispersion and mixture with other people, degenerate into several dialects. As, the *Attick, Dorick, Æolick, Ionick.*

The *Latin,* which, tho' it is much of it derived from the *Greek,* had antiently four dialects, as *Petrus Crinitus* shews out of *Varro.* From the *Latin* are derived the *Italian, Spanish* and *French.*

The *Teutonick* or *German,* which is distinguished into two notable dialects. 1. The *Danish, Scandian,* and *Gothick;* to which the languages used in *Denmark, Sweden, Norway* and *Island* do appertain.

2. The *Saxon,* from which much of the *English* and *Scotch* are derived, and also the *Frizian* language, and those languages on the north of the *Elve;* which of all the modern *German* dialects come the nearest to the ancient *German,* and in this work are called L.G.

The *Sclavonick,* which extends itself thro' many large territories, tho' not without some variation, as *Bohemia, Croatia, Dalmatia, Lithuania, Muscovia, Poland,* and *Vandalia,* this is said to be a language used by 60 several nations.

The languages of lesser extent are.

1. The *Albanese* or old *Epirotick,* now in use in the mountainous parts of *Epirus.*

2. The *European, Tartar* or *Scythian,* from which some suppose the *Irish* took its original.

3. As for the *Turkish* tongue, that originally is no other but the *Asiatick Tartarian* tongue mixed with *Armenian, Persian,* much *Arabick,* and some *Greek.*

4. The *Hungarian,* used in the greatest part of that kingdom.

5. The *Finnick,* used in *Finland,* and *Lapland.*

6. The *Cantabrian,* in use with the *Biscainers,* who live near the ocean on the *Pyrenean* hills, which border both on *Spain* and *France.*

7. The *Irish* from thence brought over into some parts of *Scotland,* which, Mr. *Camden* supposes to be derived from the *Welsh.*

8. The old *Gaulish* or *British,* still preserved in *Wales, Cornwal* and *Britain* in *France.*

To these Mr. *Brerewood* adds 4 more.

1. The *Arabick* that is now used in the steep mountains of *Granada,* which however is no mother tongue, being a dialect of the *Hebrew.*

2. The *Cauchian,* used in east *Friezland.*

3. The *Illyrian,* in the island *Veggia.*

4. The *Jazygian,* on the north-side of *Hungary.*

MOTHER-*Hood* [of **moðerhod,** *Sax.*] the state or relation of a mother.

MOTHER *Churches,* are such as have founded or erected others.

MOTHER [with *Physicians*] a disease in that part where the child is formed; also the womb it self.

MO´THERING, a custom still retained in many places of *England,* of visiting parents on *Midlent Sunday;* and it seems to be called *Mothering,* from the respect in old time paid to the *Mother Church.* It being the custom for people in old popish times to visit their mother church on *Midlent-Sunday,* and to make their offerings at the high-altar.

MO´THERLESS [of **moðor-leas,** *Sax.*] having no mother.

MO´THERLINESS, [**moðer** and **gelicnesse,** *Sax.*] motherly affection, behaviour, &c.

MOTHERLY, tenderly, affectionately, gravely, soberly.

MOTHERY [of **moðer,** *Sax.*] having a white substance on it by reason of age; as liquors.

1735.   Thomas Dyche and William Pardon, *A New General English Dictionary; Peculiarly calculated for the Use and Improvement Of such as are unacquainted with the Learned Languages.*

MO´THER (S.) any female that has or does bring forth young, though it is commonly applied only to women; sometimes it is applied in an ill sense, to an elderly woman who follows the detestable trade of keeping and encouraging young women to prostitute themselves to any body for money, who is vulgarly called a bawd; sometimes it is applied to inanimate things, as the *mother*-church, *mother* of pearl, &c. sometimes the white films or mouldiness that generates upon beer, wine, vinegar, &c. goes by this name.

Fits of the Mother, called also hysterick disorders, is a convulsion of the nerves of the *par vagum* and intercostal in the abdomen, proceeding from a pricking irritation or explosion of spirits; some imagine this distemper wholly depends upon, and flows from the womb, which is a mistake, though it often does, yet sometimes it does not, because men are affected with it as well as women.

MO´THER-CHURCH (S.) such an one within whose district or jurisdiction other churches have been built, as *Stepney* church near *London,* from whose jurisdiction, upon building new churches, the parishes of St. *Paul's Shadwell,* St. *John's Wapping, Christ-Church Spittlefields, &c.* have been taken.

MO´THERLESS (A.) the state of one whose mother is dead.

MO´THERLINESS (S.) the kind affectionate care of a mother over her young children; also the sedate and wise behaviour of a matron, or other discreet woman.

MO´THER-TONGUE (S.) the common, living, or vulgar tongue, spoke by any nation or people whatever.

MO´THERY (A.) the state of liquors that are wasting, perishing, or spoiling, by being kept too long, and the air getting to them, and which is perceived by a whitish, musty film or skin that grows over the upper surface.

1755.   Samuel Johnson, *A Dictionary of the English Language: in which the Words are deduced from their Originals, and Illustrated in their Different Significations by Examples from the best Writers.*

MO´THER. *n. s.* [*moðor,* Saxon; *moder,* Danish; *moeder,* Dutch.]

1. A woman that has born a child, correlative to son or daughter.

> Let thy *mother* rather feel thy pride, than fear
> Thy dangerous stoutness.   *Shakespeare's Coriolanus.*
>   Come sit down every *mother's* son,
> And rehearse your parts.   *Shakespeare.*
>   I had not so much of man in me,
> But all my *mother* came into mine eyes,
> And gave me up to tears.   *Shakesp. Henry V.*

2. That which has produced any thing.

> Alas, poor country! It cannot
> Be call'd our *mother,* but our grave.   *Shakespeare.*

The resemblance of the constitution and diet of the inhabitants to those of their *mother* country, occasion a great affinity in the popular diseases.   *Arbuthnot on Air.*

The strongest branch leave for a standard, cutting off the rest close to the body of the *mother* plant.
                                                         Mortimer's Husb.

3. That which has preceded in time: as, a *mother* church to chapels.

4. That which requires reverence and obedience.

The good of *mother* church, as well as that of civil society, renders a judicial practice necessary.
                                                         Ayliffe's Parergon.

5. Hysterical passion; so called, as being imagined peculiar to women.

This stopping of the stomach might be the *mother*; forasmuch as many were troubled with *mother* fits, although few returned to have died of them.   *Graunt's Bills.*

6. A familiar term of address to an old woman; or to a woman dedicated to religious austerities.

7. MOTHER *in law.* A husband's or wife's mother.   *Ains.*

I am come to set at variance the daughter in law against the *mother in law.*   *Matth.* x.35.

8. [*Moeder,* Dutch, from *modder,* mud.] A thick substance concreting in liquors; the lees or scum concreted.

If the body be liquid, and not apt to putrefy totally, it will cast up a *mother,* as the *mothers* of distilled waters.   *Bacon.*

> Potted fowl, and fish come in so fast,
> That ere the first is out the second stinks,
> And mouldy *mother* gathers on the brinks.   *Dryden.*

9. [More properly *modder*; *modde*, Dutch.] A young girl. Now totally obsolete.

> A sling for a *mother,* a bow for a boy,
> A whip for a carter.
> *Tusser's Husbandry.*

MO´THER. *adj.* Had at the birth; native.

> For whatsoever *mother* wit or art
> Could work, he put in proof.
> *Hubberd's Tale.*

> Where did you study all this goodly speech?
> —It is extempore, from my *mother* wit.
> *Shakespeare.*

Boccace, living in the same age with Chaucer, had the same genius, and followed the same studies: both writ novels, and each of them cultivated his *mother* tongue. *Dryden.*

> Cecilia came,
> Inventress of the vocal frame,
> Enlarg'd the former narrow bounds,
> And added length to solemn sounds,
> With nature's *mother* wit, and arts unknown before.
> *Dryd.*

To MO´THER. *v. n.* To gather concretion.

> They oint their naked limbs with *mother'd* oil.
> *Dryden.*

MO´THER *of pearl.* A kind of coarse pearl; the shell in which pearls are generated.

> His mortal blade
> In ivory sheath, ycarv'd with curious slights,
> Whose hilt was burnish'd gold, and handle strong
> Of *mother-pearl.*
> *Fairy Qu. b.* i.

> They were made of onyx, sometimes of *mother of pearl.*
> *Hakewill on Providence.*

MO´THERHOOD. *n. s.* [from *mother.*] The office or character of a mother.

> Thou shalt see the blessed mother-maid
> Exalted more for being good,
> Than for her interest of *motherhood.*
> *Donne.*

MO´THERLESS. *adj.* [from *mother.*] Destitute of a mother; orphan of a mother.

I might shew you my children, whom the rigour of your justice would make complete orphans, being already *motherless.* *Waller's Speech to the House of Commons.*

My concern for the three poor *motherless* children obliges me to give you this advice. *Arbuthnot's Hist. of J. Bull.*

MO´THERLY. *adj.* [from *mother* and *like.*] Belonging to a mother; suitable to a mother.

They can owe no less than child-like obedience to her that hath more than *motherly* power. *Hooker, b.* v.

They termed her the great mother, for her *motherly* care in cherishing her brethren whilst young. *Raleigh.*

> Within her breast though calm, her breast though pure,
> *Motherly* cares and fears got head, and rais'd
> Some troubled thoughts.
> *Milton's Par. Reg. b.* ii.

When I see the *motherly* airs of my little daughters when playing with their puppets, I cannot but flatter myself that their husbands and children will be happy in the possession of such wives and mothers. *Addison's Spect.* No. 500.

Though she was a truly good woman, and had a sincere *motherly* love for her son John, yet there wanted not those who endeavoured to create a misunderstanding between them. *Arb.*

MO´THERLY. *adv.* [from *mother.*] In manner of a mother.

> Th' air doth not *motherly* sit on the earth,
> To hatch her seasons, and give all things birth.
> *Donne.*

MOTHER *of thyme. n. s.* [*serpyllum,* Latin.] It hath trailing branches, which are not so woody and hard as those of thyme, but in every other respect is the same. *Miller.*

MO´THERWORT. *n. s.* [*cardiaca,* Latin.] A plant.

The flower of the *motherwort* consists of one leaf, and is of the lip kind, whose upper lip is imbricated and much longer than the under one, which is cut into three parts; from the flower-cup arises the pointal, fixed like a nail in the hinder part of the flower, attended by four embrios which become angular seeds, occupying the flower-cup. *Miller.*

MO´THERY. *adj.* [from *mother.*] Concreted; full of concretions; dreggy; feculent: used of liquors.

1780. Thomas Sheridan, *A General Dictionary of the English Language,* 2 vols. (The numbers over the vowels are diacritics: ŭ as in *but,* u̇ as in *bush,* o̊ as in *not,* and so forth.)

MOTHER, mŭth´-thŭr. s. A woman that has borne a child, correlative to son or daughter; that which has produced any thing; that which has preceded in time, as, a Mother church to chapels; hysterical passion; a familiar term of address to an old woman; Mother-in-Law, a husband's or wife's mother; a thick substance concreting in liquors, the lees or scum concreted.

MOTHER, mŭth´-thŭr. a. Had at a birth, native.

To MOTHER, mŭth´-thŭr. v. a. To gather concretion.

MOTHER OF PEARL, mŭth´-thŭr-o̊v-pĕrl´. A kind of coarse pearl, the shell in which pearls are generated.

MOTHERHOOD, mŭth´-thŭr-hu̇d. s. The office, state, or character, of a mother.

MOTHERLESS, mŭth´-thŭr-lis. a. Destitute of a mother.

MOTHERLY, mŭth´-thŭr-lẏ. a. Belonging to a mother, suitable to a mother.

MOTHERWORT, mŭth´-thŭr-wu̇rt. s. A plant.

MOTHERY, mŭth´-thŭr-ẏ. a. Concreted, full of concretions, dreggy, feculent: used of liquors.

1. From the beginning, English dictionaries have shown the spelling of a word by its very entry and have given a definition of some sort. We, however, have come to expect a good deal more of our dictionaries. Which of the dictionaries illustrated above was the first to include each of the following kinds of information?

   entries for common words _____

   word-stress _____

   pronunciation _____

   part-of-speech labels _____

   etymology _____

   definitions of everyday as well as of "hard" meanings _____

   illustrative quotations _____

2. Examine the entries for *mother* and related words in a recent dictionary. What are the chief differences between them and the entries cited above? _____

   _____

   _____

   _____

3. What kinds of comments or information in the early dictionaries would seem out of place in a modern work? _____

   _____

   _____

   _____

   _____

4. What weakness is apparent in the etymologies of all these early dictionaries? _____

_____

_____

5. Suggest several corrections a modern linguist would make to Scaliger's classification of languages

given in Bailey's dictionary under the entry *mother tongues.* _____

_____

_____

6. Find a quotation used by Johnson that does not illustrate the definition for which it is cited._____

_____

_____

7. DeWitt T. Starnes and Gertrude E. Noyes (*The English Dictionary from Cawdrey to Johnson,* p. 183) maintain that in the early Modern period, "lexicography progressed by plagiarism" and "the best lexicographer was often the most discriminating plagiarist." Discuss these two conclusions in the light of the entries cited above.

8.10   EIGHTEENTH-CENTURY ATTITUDES TOWARD LANGUAGE

During the eighteenth century, many men tried their hands at writing English grammars, men as diverse as Robert Lowth, Bishop of London, and Joseph Priestley, the discoverer of oxygen. George Campbell, a typical grammarian of the period, was neither as authoritarian as Lowth nor as scientifically objective as Priestley. The theory of use that he set forth in the *Philosophy of Rhetoric* (1776) is one that present-day grammarians can still accept, but his application of that theory abounded with inconsistencies. Campbell's self-contradictory *via media* illustrates well both what is best and what is worst in eighteenth-century attitudes toward language. The following extracts from Chapters I, II, and III of Book II of the *Philosophy of Rhetoric* illustrate Campbell's theory and practice.

CHAPTER I

The Nature and Characters of the Use which gives Law to Language

Every tongue whatever is founded in use or custom,
_____Whose arbitrary sway
        Words and the forms of language must obey.   Francis.

Language is purely a species of fashion (for this holds equally of every tongue) in which, by the general but tacit consent of the people of a particular state or country, certain sounds come to be appropriated to certain things, as their signs, and certain ways of inflecting and combining those sounds come to be established, as denoting the relations which subsist among the things signified.

It is not the business of grammar, as some critics seem preposterously to imagine, to give law to the fashions which regulate our speech. On the contrary, from its conformity to these, and from that alone, it derives all its authority and value. For, what is the grammar of any language? It is no other than a collection of general observations methodically digested, and comprising all the modes previously and independently established, by which the significations, derivations, and combinations of words in that language are ascertained. It is of no consequence here to what causes originally these modes or fashions owe their existence—to imitation, to reflection, to affectation, or to caprice; they no sooner obtain and become general, than they are laws of the language, and the grammarian's only business is, to note, collect, and methodise them. Nor does this truth concern only those more comprehensive analogies or rules which affect whole classes of words; such as nouns, verbs, and the other parts of speech; but it concerns every individual word, in the inflecting or the combining of which a particular mode hath prevailed. Every single anomaly, therefore, though departing from the rule assigned to the other words of the same class, and on that account called an exception, stands on the same basis, on which the rules of the tongue are founded, custom having prescribed for it a separate rule. . . .

Only let us rest in these as fixed principles, that use, or the custom of speaking, is the sole original standard of conversation, as far as regards the expression, and the custom of writing is the sole standard of style; that the latter comprehends the former, and something more; that to the tribunal of use, as to the supreme authority, and, consequently, in every grammatical controversy, the last resort, we are entitled to appeal from the laws and the decisions of grammarians; and that this order of subordination ought never, on any account, to be reversed.

But if use be here a matter of such consequence, it will be necessary, before advancing any farther, to ascertain precisely what it is. We shall otherwise be in danger, though we agree about the name, of differing widely in the notion that we assign to it. . . .

In what extent then must the word be understood? It is sometimes called *general use*; yet is it not manifest that the generality of people speak and write very badly? Nay, is not this a truth that will be even generally acknowledged? It will be so; and this very acknowledgment shows that many terms and idioms may be common, which, nevertheless, have not the general sanction, no, nor even the suffrage of those that use them. The use here spoken of implies not only *currency*, but *vogue*. It is properly *reputable custom*. . . .

Agreeably then to this first qualification of the term, we must understand to be comprehended under general use, *whatever modes of speech are authorized as good by the writings of a great number, if not the majority, of celebrated authors*. . . .

Another qualification of the term *use* which deserves our attention is, that it must be *national*. This I consider in a twofold view, as it stands opposed both to *provincial* and *foreign*. . . .

But there will naturally arise here another question, 'Is not use, even good and national use, in the same country, different in different periods? And if so, to the usage of what period shall we attach ourselves, as the proper rule? If you say *the present*, as it may reasonably be expected that you will, the difficulty is not entirely removed. In what extent of signification must we understand the word *present*? How far may we safely range in quest of authorities? or, at what distance backwards from this moment are authors still to be accounted as possessing a legislative voice in language?' . . .

As use, therefore, implies duration, and as even a few years are not sufficient for ascertaining the characters of authors, I have, for the most part, in the following sheets, taken my prose examples, neither from living authors, nor from those who wrote before the Revolution; not from the first, because an author's fame is not so firmly established in his lifetime; nor from the last, that there may be no suspicion that the style is superannuated.

CHAPTER II

The Nature and Use of Verbal Criticism, with its Principal Canons

. . . But on this subject of use, there arise two eminent questions, . . . The first question is this, 'Is reputable, national, and present use, which, for brevity's sake, I shall hereafter simply denominate good use, always uniform in her decisions?' The second is, 'As no term, idiom, or application, that is totally unsupported by her, can be admitted to be good, is every term, idiom, and application that is countenanced by her, to be esteemed good, and therefore worthy to be retained?'

In answer to the former of these questions, I acknowledge, that in every case there is not a perfect uniformity in the determinations, even of such use as may justly be denominated good. Wherever a considerable number of authorities can be produced in support of two different, though resembling modes of expression for the same thing, there is always a divided use, and one cannot be said to speak barbarously, or to oppose the usage of the language, who conforms to either side. . . .

In those instances, therefore, of divided use, which give scope for option, the following canons are humbly proposed, in order to assist us in assigning the preference. Let it, in the mean time, be remembered, as a point always presupposed, that the authorities on the opposite sides are equal, or nearly so. . . .

The first canon, then, shall be, When use is divided as to any particular word or phrase, and the expression used by one part hath been pre-occupied, or is in any instance susceptible of a different signification, and the expression employed by the other part never admits a different sense, both perspicuity and variety require that the form of expression which is in every instance strictly univocal be preferred. . . .

In the preposition *toward* and *towards,* and the adverbs *forward* and *forwards, backward* and *backwards,* the two forms are used indiscriminately. But as the first form in all these is also an adjective, it is better to confine the particles to the second. Custom, too, seems at present to lean this way. *Besides* and *beside* serve both as conjunctions and as prepositions. There appears some tendency at present to assign to each a separate province. This tendency ought to be humoured by employing only the former as the conjunction, the latter as the preposition. . . .

The second canon is, In doubtful cases regard ought to be had in our decisions to the analogy of the language. . . .

If by the former canon the adverbs *backwards* and *forwards* are preferable to *backward* and *forward*; by this canon, from the principle of analogy, *afterwards* and *homewards* should be preferred to *afterward* and *homeward.* Of the two adverbs *thereabout* and *thereabouts,* compounded of the particle *there* and the preposition, the former alone is analogical, there being no such word in the language as *abouts.* The same holds of *hereabout* and *whereabout.* . . .

The third canon is, When the terms or expressions are in other respects equal, that ought to be preferred which is most agreeable to the ear. . . .

Of this we have many examples. *Delicateness* hath very properly given way to *delicacy*; and for a like reason *authenticity* will probably soon displace *authenticalness,* and *vindictive* dispossess *vindicative* altogether. . . .

The fourth canon is, In cases wherein none of the foregoing rules gives either side a ground of preference, a regard to simplicity (in which I include etymology when manifest) ought to determine our choice.

Under the name simplicity I must be understood to comprehend also brevity; for that expression is always the simplest which, with equal purity and perspicuity, is the briefest. We have, for instance, several active verbs which are used either with or without a preposition indiscriminately. Thus we say either *accept* or *accept of, admit* or *admit of, approve* or *approve of*; in like manner *address* or *address to, attain* or *attain to.* In such instances it will hold, I suppose, pretty generally, that the simple form is preferable. . . .

The fifth and only other canon that occurs to me on the subject of divided use is, In the few cases wherein neither perspicuity nor analogy, neither sound nor simplicity, assists us in fixing our choice, it is safest to prefer that manner which is most conformable to ancient usage.

This is founded on a very plain maxim, that in language, as in several other things, change itself, unless when it is clearly advantageous, is ineligible. This affords another reason for preferring that usage which distinguishes *ye* as the nominative plural of *thou,* when more than one are addressed, from *you* the accusative. . . .

I come now to the second question for ascertaining both the extent of the authority claimed by custom, and the rightful prerogatives of criticism. As no term, idiom, or application, that is totally unsupported by use, can be admitted to be good; is every term, idiom, and application, that is countenanced by use, to be esteemed good, and therefore worthy to be retained? I answer, that though nothing in language can be good from which use withholds her approbation, there may be many things to which she gives it, that are not in all respects good, or such as are worthy to be retained and imitated. . . .

It is therefore, I acknowledge, not without meaning, that Swift affirms, that, "there are many gross improprieties, which, though authorized by practice, ought to be discarded." Now, in order to discard them, nothing more is necessary than to disuse them. And to bring us to disuse them, both the example and the arguments of the critic will have their weight. . . .

The first canon on this subject is, All words and phrases which are remarkably harsh and unharmonious, and not absolutely necessary, may justly be judged worthy of this fate. . . .

Such are the words *bare-faced-ness, shame-faced-ness, un-success-ful-ness, dis-interest-ed-ness, wrong-headed-ness, tender-hearted-ness.* They are so heavy and drawling, and withal so ill compacted, that they have not more vivacity than a periphrasis, to compensate for the defect of harmony. . . .

The second canon on this subject is, When etymology plainly points to a signification different from that which the word commonly bears, propriety and simplicity both require its dismission. . . .

The verb *to unloose,* should analogically signify *to tie,* in like manner as *to untie* signifies *to loose.* To what purpose is it, then, to retain a term, without any necessity, in a signification the reverse of that which its etymology manifestly suggests? In the same way, *to annul,* and *to disannul,* ought by analogy to be contraries, though irregularly used as synonymous. . . .

The third canon is, When any words become obsolete, or at least are never used, except as constituting part of particular phrases, it is better to dispense with their service entirely, and give up the phrases. . . .

Examples of this we have in the words *lief, dint, whit, moot, pro,* and *con,* as, '*I had as lief* go myself,' for 'I should like as well to go myself.' 'He convinced his antagonist *by dint of argument,*' that is, 'by strength of argument.' 'He made them yield *by dint of arms,*'—'by force of arms.' 'He is *not a whit better,*'—'no better.' 'The case you mention is *a moot point,*'—'a disputable point.' 'The question was strenuously debated *pro and con,*'—'on both sides.'

The fourth and last canon I propose is, All those phrases, which, when analysed grammatically, include a solecism, and all those to which use hath affixed a particular sense, but which, when explained by the general and established rules of the language, are susceptible either of a different sense, or of no sense, ought to be discarded altogether.

It is this kind of phraseology which is distinguished by the epithet *idiomatical,* and hath been originally the spawn, partly of ignorance, and partly of affectation. Of the first sort, which includes a solecism, is the phrase, 'I *had* rather *do* such a thing,' for 'I would rather do it.' The auxiliary *had,* joined to the infinitive active *do,* is a gross violation of the rules of conjugation in our language. . . .

Of the second sort, which, when explained grammatically, leads to a different sense from what the words in conjunction commonly bear, is, 'He sings a good song,' for 'he sings well.' The plain meaning of the words as they stand connected is very different, for who sees not that a good song may be ill sung? . . .

CHAPTER III

Of Grammatical Purity

[Chapter III discusses various barbarisms, solecisms, and improprieties "which writers of great name, and even of critical skill in the language, have slidden into through inattention." Among these offenses against grammatical purity are the following. The italics are Campbell's.]

"The zeal of the *seraphim* breaks forth in a becoming warmth of sentiments and expressions, as the character which is given us of *him* denotes that generous scorn and intrepidity which attends heroic virtue." (Addison)

"This noble nation hath *of all others* admitted *fewer* corruptions." (Swift)

"Such notions would be avowed at this time by none but rosicrucians, and fanatics as mad as them." (Bolingbroke)

"Tell the Cardinal, that I understand poetry better than him." (Smollet)

"My christian and surname begin and end with the same letters." (Addison)

"*Each* of the sexes should keep within *its* particular bounds, and content *themselves* to exult within *their* respective districts." (Addison)

"*If* thou *bring* thy gift to the altar, and there *rememberest* that thy brother hath ought against thee . . ." (Matt. 5:23)

"I shall do all I can to persuade others to *take* the same measures for their cure which I *have.*" (*Guardian,* No. 1)

"Will it be urged, that the four gospels are *as old,* or even *older than* tradition?" (Bolingbroke)

"The greatest masters of critical learning differ *among one another.*" (*Spectator,* No. 321)

"A petty constable will *neither* act cheerfully *or* wisely." (Swift)

"I may say, without vanity, that there is not a gentleman in England better read in tomb-stones than myself, my studies having *laid* very much in church-yards." (*Spectator,* No. 518)

"The exercise of reason appears as little in them, as in the beasts they sometimes hunt, and by *whom* they are sometimes hunted." (Bolingbroke)

Adam,
The comeliest man of men *since born*
His sons. The fairest of *her daughters* Eve. (Milton)

1. What does Campbell say is the "supreme authority" in language? _____

_____

2. What does he conceive the task of the grammarian to be? _____

_____

3. What should be the grammarian's attitude toward anomalies, that is, words or constructions that follow no general pattern? _____

_____

4. How does Campbell apparently conceive of the relationship between speech and writing?

_____

_____

5. Campbell's three qualifications of use are that it be *reputable, national,* and *present.* Explain what he means by these three terms. _____

_____

_____

_____

_____

6. Would Campbell be willing to settle a question of use by polling a representative cross section of the English population? Explain. _____

_____

_____

7. When use is divided between two different expressions for the same idea, what view does Campbell take of the correctness of the two expressions? _____

_____

_____

8. For choosing between divided use, Campbell proposes five canons. Explain each of them briefly.

_____

_____

_____

_____

_____

9. What does Campbell mean when he says that change in language is "ineligible"?_____

_____

_____

10. How does Campbell answer the question "Is all use good?" _____

_____

_____

11. Whose precept and example is to guide us among the pitfalls of use? _____

_____

12. Briefly explain the four canons Campbell proposes for determining what uses should be discarded. ___

_____

_____

_____

_____

13. List several specific contradictions or inconsistencies in Campbell's discussion of correctness in

language. _____

_____

_____

_____

_____

14. Identify the "errors" in the quotations from Chapter III of *The Philosophy of Rhetoric.*

15. Look up one of the "errors" in several recent school grammars or guides to usage to see whether there
has been any change in attitude toward it.

9 LATE MODERN ENGLISH (1800–21ST CENTURY)

9.1 FOR REVIEW AND DISCUSSION

1. Define the following terms:

Americanism	edited English	pidgin
Briticism	Northern dialect	creole
shibboleth	North Midland dialect	creolize
ask word	South Midland (Inland	style
dialect	Southern) dialect	slang
regional (geographical)	Southern (Coastal Southern)	first language
dialect	dialect	second language
ethnic (social) dialect	African-American (Black)	foreign language
register	English	
standard English	consuetudinal *be*	

2. What justification is there for the claim that one type of English, such as standard British English, is superior to all others? On what fallacy are such claims based?

3. What accounts for the fact that British English generally has greater prestige than other types, such as American or Australian?

4. In what respects is American English more conservative than British English and in what respects is it less so?

5. Is the Briton who is concerned about speaking correctly likely to worry more about pronunciation or about syntax? How does the linguistically insecure American differ from his British counterpart?

6. Are there any types of American pronunciation, regional or social, against which prejudice is so great that they would debar a speaker from the learned professions?

7. Katharine Whitehorn observed, "In America, where it is grammar, not accent, that places you, anyone can learn the grammar; maybe Bostonians don't accept it, but Bostonians only impress other Bostonians." Which is easier, changing the phonetic patterns of one's speech or avoiding what are thought of as grammatical errors? Why? Is there any regional form of speech that is high in prestige throughout the United States?

8. After determining whether Dorothy Parker is English or American and checking with the *Oxford English Dictionary* and Fowler's *Modern English Usage,* comment on her linguistic pronouncement that "anyone who, as does [Henry] Miller, follows 'none' with a plural verb . . . should assuredly not be called a writer." Would Miss Parker approve of the number of the verb in this sentence: "As yet none of my characters has been industrialists, economists, trade union leaders"?

9. In the preface to *Pygmalion,* George Bernard Shaw insists that all art should be didactic; what is he trying to teach in the play? What actual person did Shaw have in mind when he created the character of Henry Higgins?

10. List the important differences between British English and American English. Which of the differences is most significant?

11. Americans have been charged with a tendency to exaggerate. Supply some examples of "the American love of grandiloquence," as it may be called.

12. What are the main scholarly organizations and publications devoted to the study of American English?

13. What importance has the study of British dialects for an understanding of American English?

14. Which are more important, the differences or the similarities between British and American English?

15. What kinds of variation occur in a language? What is the usefulness of such variation?
16. What factors have promoted the use of English as a world language?
17. What is the likelihood that English will split up into a number of mutually unintelligible languages?

9.2   AMERICANISMS

1. Among the words that are in some way peculiar to the United States are the following. Describe the origin of each word as it is shown in the *Dictionary of American English* (*DAE*) or the *Dictionary of Americanisms* (*DA*).

blue laws _____

bushwhacker _____

carpetbagger _____

charley horse _____

cinch _____

civil rights _____

clambake _____

conniption _____

cybernetics _____

dicker _____

dude _____

ghost writer _____

hex _____

hoodlum _____

law-abiding _____

parlay _____

ranch _____

semester _____

sideburns _____

stoop 'porch' _____

2. By consulting the *DAE* or the *DA*, list ten additional examples of Americanisms.

_____

_____

_____

_____

_____

_____

_____

_____

_____

_____

9.3 NATIONAL DIFFERENCES IN WORD CHOICE

1. Give the distinctively British English equivalents of the following American terms. You can find them in Norman Moss, *British/American Dictionary,* or Norman W. Schur, *British English, A to Zed.*

billion	_____	(to) mail	_____
bouncer	_____	molasses	_____
can (of soup)	_____	orchestra seat	_____
(potato) chips	_____	(cream) pitcher	_____
cone (ice cream)	_____	rubbing alcohol	_____
dishpan	_____	rummage sale	_____
elevator	_____	run (in stockings)	_____
eraser	_____	sneakers	_____
flashlight	_____	station wagon	_____
gasoline	_____	streetcar	_____
hood (of a car)	_____	traffic circle	_____
installment plan	_____	truck	_____
labor union	_____	turtleneck	_____
long-distance call	_____	undershirt	_____

2. The following terms either are exclusively British English or have at least one special sense that is predominantly British. Give the American English equivalents of the British senses. The terms can be found in a desk dictionary.

accumulator	_____	gangway	_____
bespoke	_____	hoarding	_____
biscuit	_____	holidays	_____
boot (of a car)	_____	minerals	_____
bowler	_____	public house	_____
bug	_____	(to) queue up	_____
chemist	_____	rates	_____
chips	_____	roundabout	_____
costermonger	_____	sleeping partner	_____
cotton wool	_____	suspender	_____
draughts	_____	sweet (n.)	_____
drawing pin	_____	switchback	_____
dustbin	_____	tart	_____
fanlight	_____	underground	_____
form	_____	wing	_____

3. An American reporter who interviewed G. K. Chesterton described him as a "regular guy." What reason had Chesterton, an Englishman, for being or pretending to be offended? What is the probable etymology of *guy*? _____

_____

9.4 NATIONAL DIFFERENCES IN GRAMMAR AND IDIOM

1. What constructions in the following quotations from British writers would an American be likely to phrase in a different manner? Underline the constructions and rephrase them.

(1) It is hard to think of a writer of high class who really stretched his imaginative sympathy. . . . Some of the nineteenth-century Russian novelists might have done; their natures were broad enough.

(C. P. Snow) _____

_____

(2) I thank Mr. Watson Taylor for his compliments and suggest he has another look at what I actually wrote. *(The Times Literary Supplement)* _____

_____

(3) When Mr. Macmillan has dispersed the last miasma of the Profumo affair . . . it may be that he will hand over. But to whom? *(Spectator)* _____

_____

(4) Investment Notes . . . International Tea are near the bottom with 13.7 per cent. *(Spectator)* _____

_____

(5) A number of London stock-broking firms are recommending their clients to buy Australian ordinary shares. *(Punch)* _____

_____

(6) I used often to find myself successful in teaching subjects not my own. *(Punch)* _____

_____

(7) It must be getting a bit of a strain on our public figures, always being called from conferences or rehearsals or typewriters to encounter these extraordinary questions on the telephone. *(Punch)*

_____

(8) The Government have set up the agency to help the industry. *(Time & Tide)* _____

_____

(9) The Welsh centre Dawes was concussed in the third minute of the game . . . but Ireland were slow to exploit this weakness of manpower. *(Illustrated London News)* _____

_____

(10) He omits to mention the far more far-reaching difficulty that there are differences in status between poets, and between individual poems. *(The Times Literary Supplement)* _____

_____

(11) Pied-à-terre, or bachelor flat, to let in modern block in Sloane Avenue. *(The Times)* _____

_____

(12) There was a slight bump as the aircraft entered cloud, and the pilot's hands tightened on the controls. *(Blackwood's Magazine)* _____

_____

(13) "Have you not a father?" I asked. *(Blackwood's Magazine)* _____

_____

(14) I began to say, "What will your wife feel about that?" *(Blackwood's Magazine)* _____

_____

2. In British use the past participle *gotten* has been generally replaced by *got,* except for set expressions and derivatives like *forgotten*. In America both past participles remain in use, but with a specialization in meaning. Describe the American difference between *got* and *gotten* as it appears in the following examples.

(1) He doesn't have much hair, but he's got a full beard.
(2) So far he's gotten most of his ideas about ecology from the *Reader's Digest*.
(3) She's got a neurosis.
(4) She's gotten a neurosis.
(5) Whether he wants to or not, he's got to take the exam.
(6) As a result of his petitions, he's finally gotten to take the exam.
(7) Everybody's got to do it.
(8) Everybody's gotten to do it.

_____

_____

_____

_____

The following examples are more characteristic of British than of American use. Rephrase them in the form most common in the United States.

(9) We haven't got a chance. _____

(10) The waiter had got a towel over his arm. _____

(11) We've just got ready to eat. _____

3. By skimming a British publication, find an example of a grammatical construction or idiom which differs from American usage. _____

_____

_____

_____

_____

_____

9.5 BRITISH AND AMERICAN PURISM

Among the constructions that are disapproved by one purist or another are those italicized in the sentences below. Investigate the status of one of these constructions, using the following techniques:

1. Ascertain the earlier history of the construction as it is revealed by the citations in the *Oxford English Dictionary*.

2. Compare the opinions of such usage guides as the *American Heritage Book of English Usage,* Theodore M. Bernstein's *The Careful Writer,* Robert W. Burchfield's *New Fowler's Modern English Usage,* Bryan A. Garner's *Modern American Usage,* E. Ward Gilman's *Merriam-Webster's Dictionary of English Usage,* William and Mary Morris's *Harper Dictionary of Contemporary Usage,* Michael Swan's *Practical English Usage,* and the usage notes in recent dictionaries. All such guides must be used critically, as some aim at objective reporting whereas others indulge the prejudices of their authors.

3. Survey contemporary use of the construction by finding examples of it or of its alternatives. Skim recent newspapers, magazines, novels, and other printed material. Listen for its use in conversation, over the radio or television, in speeches, or in other forms of oral communication. Check out sites on the Web. For each occurrence you observe prepare a note card with the following information:

CITATION: quotation illustrating the construction or alternative.

SOURCE: bibliographical data for a printed source; speaker, occasion, and date for an oral source.

CIRCUMSTANCES: any information which may help to determine the status of the construction (for example, occurs in dialogue, speaker is rustic, used in a formal situation, and so forth).

Write the results of your investigation in the form of an article for a usage dictionary. Describe the usage you have observed, including any apparent social, regional, or functional limitations, and summarize the information in the *OED* and the usage guides you have consulted.

What was he asking *about*? (similarly, other final prepositions)
I'm ready, *aren't I*?
It is *not as* late as we thought.
She felt *badly* about it.
The second is the *best* of the two books. (similarly, other superlatives used for one of two)
There were no secrets *between* the three brothers.

You can't judge a *book's* content by its cover. (similarly, genitives of other inanimate nouns)

Philip wants to leave. *But* he can't. (similarly, *and, or, nor*)

I don't doubt *but what* they will agree.

Can I have another, please?

Houston *contacted* the astronauts on their second orbit.

The *data is* available now. (similarly, *criteria*)

The answer was *different than* what we expected.

It *don't* make any difference.

Due to a power failure, the flight was canceled.

The members of the senate supported *each other* in the election.

Everybody finished *their* work. (similarly, *everyone, nobody, no one, someone,* and so forth with plural pronouns)

Drive three miles *further* south and turn right.

I'll come when I'm *good and* ready.

Have you *gotten* the answer yet?

She *graduated* from Vassar. She *graduated* Vassar. She *was graduated* from Vassar.

You *had better* go. (similarly, *had rather, had sooner, had best,* and so forth)

We heard about *him* winning the contest. (similarly, other nongenitives before gerunds)

I wonder *if* there's time.

The reason she's late *is because* she ran out of gas.

A finesse *is where* declarer plays the queen instead of the ace while the king is out against him. (similarly, *is when*)

Lay down and take your nap.

We have *less* problems this year than last.

The weather looks *like* it will be clearing soon.

It's *me.* (similarly, objective forms of other pronouns after *to be*)

It is the *most perfect* play ever written. (similarly, comparative and superlative forms of *unique, round, square, white,* and so forth)

They sent separate invitations to my wife and *myself.* (similarly, other *self*-forms without antecedent)

Make the dog get *off of* the bed.

You *only* live once.

James had a *pretty* good reason for asking.

He *raised* his children according to the newest theories.

A switch is not functioning. *This* is enough to cancel the flight. (similarly, *that* and *which* with broad reference)

Vesper didn't like *those kind* of tactics. (similarly, *kind* and *sort* with plural modifiers or verb)

It is necessary *to actively resist* oppression. (similarly, other split infinitives)

You ought to *try and* see the Little Theater's new play.

They were *very* pleased by the public response. (similarly, other qualifiers before past participles)

If the test *was* held on Sunday, more people could take it. (similarly, *was* in other subjunctive clauses)

Who did you see? (similarly, *who* in other object functions)

We *will* probably sing "We *Shall* Overcome."

You never know when your time will come.

9.6   NATIONAL DIFFERENCES IN PRONUNCIATION

1. Identify the following pronunciations as typically British (*B*) or typically American (*A*) by writing the appropriate letter in the blanks.

ate	_____ [et]	_____ [ɛt]
been	_____ [bin]	_____ [bɪn]
chagrin	_____ [šǽgrɪn]	_____ [šəgrín]
clerk	_____ [klɑk]	_____ [klərk]
corollary	_____ [kərɔ́lərɪ]	_____ [kɔ́rəlèrɪ]
dynasty	_____ [dínəstɪ]	_____ [dáɪnəsti]
evolution	_____ [ìvəlúšən]	_____ [ɛ̀vəlúšən]
figure	_____ [fígə]	_____ [fígyər]

fragile	_____ [frǽǰɪl]	_____ [frǽǰaɪl]
half	_____ [hæf]	_____ [hɑf]
laboratory	_____ [lǽbrətòri]	_____ [ləbɔ́rət(ə)rɪ]
latter	_____ [lǽdər]	_____ [lǽtə]
lieutenant	_____ [luténənt]	_____ [lɛfténənt]
medicine	_____ [mɛ́dəsən]	_____ [mɛ́dsɪn]
military	_____ [mílɪt(ə)rɪ]	_____ [mílətɛ̀rɪ]
nephew	_____ [nɛ́fyu]	_____ [nɛ́vyu]
pass	_____ [pæs]	_____ [pɑs]
premier	_____ [prɛ́myə]	_____ [prəmír]
quinine	_____ [kwɪnín]	_____ [kwáɪnàɪn]
schedule	_____ [skɛ́ǰəl]	_____ [šɛ́dyul]
squirrel	_____ [skwírəl]	_____ [skwɔ́rəl]
trait	_____ [tre]	_____ [tret]
tryst	_____ [trɪst]	_____ [traɪst]
valet	_____ [vælé]	_____ [vǽlɪt]
vase	_____ [vɑz]	_____ [ves]
zenith	_____ [zínɪθ]	_____ [zɛ́nɪθ]
Are you there?	_____ Are you there?	_____ Are you there?
What did he tell you?	_____ What did he tell you?	_____ What did he tell you?

2. Describe five of the most important general differences between American and British pronunciation.

_____

_____

_____

_____

3. What was the usual quality of *a* before such consonants as [f], [θ], [ð], [s], and [ns] in standard British

English at the beginning of the nineteenth century?_____

_____

4. In what sections of the United States is [r] more or less regularly lost finally and before consonants?

_____

_____

5. In what sections of the United States do words like *stop, cot*, and *lock* generally have a rounded vowel?

_____

_____

6. Some Americans who regularly pronounce [r] where it is spelled do not have it in the middle syllable of *governor*, although they may have it in *governing* and *government*. Can you suggest any reason for the loss of [r] in the one word when it is retained in the other two?

_____

_____

An [r] is sometimes lost even by normally *r*-ish speakers in the following words. Circle the spelling for any [r] that is lost in your speech. Then describe the circumstances under which the loss occurs; note the position of the stress and other [r]'s in the words.

surpríse	Cánterbùry	bòmbardíer	sóutherner
mercúrochròme	réservòir	gùbernatórial	témperature
thermómeter	wíntergrèen	Fébruàry	fórmerly
vernácular	élderbèrry	spéctrogràph	pàraphernália
survívor	répertòry	cáterpìllar	mírror

_____

_____

7. Which of the following pronunciations possess greater clarity? Explain your answer. *Sunday* [sə́ndè] or [sə́ndi]; *to* [tu] or [tə]; *educator* [ɛ́dyukètɔr] or [ɛ́jəkètər]. _____

_____

9.7 BRITISH AND AMERICAN SPELLING

1. Give typically British spellings of the following words. Some of the "typically British spellings" are becoming less common in England, but they are still British as opposed to American in flavor.

anemic	_____	jail	_____
ax	_____	labor	_____
center	_____	mold 'fungus'	_____
(bank) check	_____	mustache	_____
cipher	_____	omelet	_____
civilize	_____	pajamas	_____
(street) curb	_____	plow	_____
defense	_____	program	_____
esophagus	_____	show (v.) 'display'	_____
gray	_____	story 'floor'	_____
inflection	_____	traveler	_____
install	_____	wagon	_____

2. Some of the spelling differences illustrated above are systematic in that the same difference appears in a large number of words. Describe the more important systematic differences and cite some additional examples. _____

_____

_____

9.8 THE REGIONAL DIALECTS OF AMERICAN ENGLISH

The regional dialects of American English are described in books such as E. Bagby Atwood's *Survey of Verb Forms in the Eastern United States*, Craig M. Carver's *American Regional Dialects: A Word Geography*, Frederic G. Cassidy and Joan Houston Hall's *Dictionary of American Regional English*, Hans Kurath's *Word Geography of the Eastern United States*, Hans Kurath and Raven I. McDavid's *Pronunciation of English in the Atlantic States*, Stephen J. Nagle and Sara L. Sanders's *English in the Southern United States*, Carroll E. Reed's *Dialects of American English*, Roger W. Shuy's *Discovering American Dialects*, Walt Wolfram and

Natalie Schilling-Estes's *American English: Dialects and Variation*, and on the Web in William Labov's "The Organization of Dialect Diversity in North America" and by a dialect map at these URLs: www.ling.upenn.edu/phono_atlas/ICSLP4.html and www.ling.upenn.edu/phono_atlas/NationalMap/NationalMap.html.

1. After reading one or more of the sources cited previously, which present somewhat different pictures because they are based on different data, draw on the map the boundaries of the main regional dialects of the United States as you have found them described.

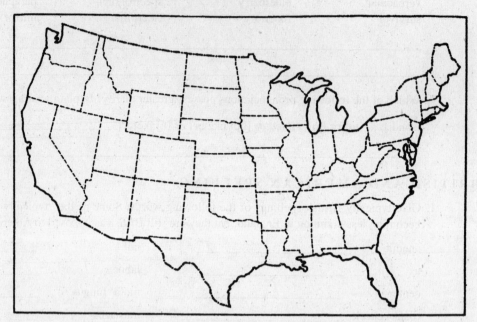

2. Below are some pronunciation features that vary from one regional dialect to another. For each feature indicate what main variations occur. You may not find all these items discussed in any one of the works cited previously, but do as many of them as you can.

THE STRESSED VOWEL IN:

crop, top, cot, rot _____

law, caught, wrought _____

dog, fog, log _____

ask, half, path, glass, dance _____

coat, road, home, stone _____

new, tune, due _____

out, house _____

loud, houses _____

nice, white, rice _____

time, tide, ride _____

boil, oil _____

third, bird _____

bar, farm, hard _____

car, garden _____

212

forest, horrid, orange _____

morning, horse, forty _____

mourning, hoarse, four _____

marry, carry, barren _____

Mary, dairy, vary, area _____

THE PRONUNCIATION OF *r* IN:

fear, beard, poor, more, start, word _____

_____

far away, lore of the jungle, paper and ink _____

_____

THE MEDIAL CONSONANT OF:

greasy _____

THE FINAL CONSONANT OF:

with _____

3. What synonyms exist in regional dialects for the following vocabulary items? All of them can be found in Hans Kurath's *Word Geography* and most of them in Raven I. McDavid's chapter in W. Nelson Francis's book *The Structure of American English* or Walt Wolfram and Natalie Schilling-Estes's *American English: Dialects and Variations.* See also Byron W. Bender's "A Checklist of Varieties of American English," online at www2.hawaii.edu/~bender/chklst.html (number 11).

porch _____

pail _____

frying pan _____

faucet _____

kerosene _____

creek _____

sidewalk _____

pancake _____

string beans _____

lima beans _____

dragonfly _____

you (plural) _____

quarter *to* eleven _____

sick *to* the stomach _____

The best source for information about the diverse ways in which Americans use English words is the *Dictionary of American Regional English* (acronymously known as *DARE*), edited by Frederic G. Cassidy and Joan Houston Hall. The dictionary is a scholarly record of terms whose use is limited by region, social group, or otherwise.

1. *DARE* also includes terms that are comic or sardonic, such as those in the left-hand column below, which are metaphoric labels for the quite ordinary referents in the right-hand column. Match terms with referents by writing the numbers of the latter in the blanks after the former. Try guessing first; then check your guesses by consulting *DARE*.

Adam's ale	_____	1. codfish
Alabama wool	_____	2. cotton
Alaska turkey	_____	3. croquet
Amish golf	_____	4. deck of cards
Arizona cloudburst	_____	5. diarrhea
Arizona nightingale	_____	6. donkey
Arkansas dew	_____	7. downpour
Arkansas lizard	_____	8. large bowie knife
Arkansas toothpick	_____	9. louse
August ham	_____	10. mustard
Aztec two-step	_____	11. newspapers
Boston dollar	_____	12. noose
California blanket	_____	13. penny
California collar	_____	14. pigs' feet
California prayer book	_____	15. razor-back hog
Cape Cod turkey	_____	16. rice
Carolina racehorse	_____	17. salmon
Chinese grits	_____	18. sandstorm
Cincinnati oysters	_____	19. water
Coney Island butter	_____	20. watermelon

2. Here are some other terms to be found around the country. As above, match the terms with their referents by writing the numbers of the latter in the blanks after the former. Guess first; then check in *DARE* or look on the *DARE* Web site (http://polyglot.lss.wisc.edu/dare/dare.html), where most of these can be found.

get one's nose open	_____	1. a card game
holy poke	_____	2. a dollar
iron man	_____	3. alarming, dreadful, spooky
kiss-me-quick	_____	4. bread roll with a crisp crust
leppy	_____	5. deep-fried ball of bread dough
mouse	_____	6. lump caused by a blow
nebby	_____	7. orphan calf, lamb, or colt
pedro	_____	8. snoopy, inquisitive
pin-basket	_____	9. stupid, dull, liquor-befuddled
pokerish	_____	10. sudden dip or rise in the road
pushency	_____	11. to be infatuated or in love
quiddle	_____	12. to move briskly
rumdum	_____	13. to spray or squirt a liquid
sashiate	_____	14. to trifle, fuss
semmel	_____	15. urgent necessity
skeet	_____	16. youngest child in a family

3. You can investigate the content of *DARE* by using two indexes that cover its first three volumes: *Index by Region, Usage, and Etymology to the Dictionary of American Regional English, Volumes I and II* (Publication of the American Dialect Society 77) and *An Index by Region, Usage, and Etymology to the Dictionary of American Regional English, Volume III*, by Luanne von Schneidemesser (Publication of the American Dialect Society 82), or consult all volumes of *DARE* itself or its Web site for other useful information: http://polyglot.lss.wisc.edu/dare/dare.html. Using those indexes, find a dozen or so terms characteristic of the part of the country from which you come. Write a short paper describing them and noting which you are familiar with and which you are not.

9.10 LITERARY REPRESENTATIONS OF AMERICAN DIALECTS

A fiction writer who wants to represent the regional speech of his characters must choose those lexical items, grammatical constructions, turns of phrase, and spellings (to stand for pronunciation) that will give a reader the flavor of the speech without putting too many obstacles in the way of easy comprehension. A literary dialect is not scientific description, but artistic impression and suggestion. Examine the following passages, and then point out how the authors have sought to communicate the flavor of a region's speech. Do literary dialects usually represent standard or nonstandard speech? Why? Some unconventional spellings represent the same pronunciation as the standard spellings and thus give no real information about dialect. Examples of such "eye-dialect" (so called because it appeals to the eye rather than the ear) are *sez* for *says, cas'le* for *castle, oughta* for *ought to*. Cite some examples from the following passages.

1. New England (Sarah Orne Jewett, "Andrew's Fortune")

"We was dreadful concerned to hear o' cousin Stephen's death," said the poor man. "He went very sudden, didn't he? Gre't loss he is."

"Yes," said Betsey, "he was very much looked up to;" and it was some time before the heir plucked up courage to speak again.

"Wife and me was lotting on getting over to the funeral; but it's a gre't ways for her to ride, and it was a perishin' day that day. She's be'n troubled more than common with her phthisic since cold weather come. I was all crippled up with the rheumatism; we wa'n't neither of us fit to be out" (plaintively). "'T was all I could do to get out to the barn to feed the stock while Jonas and Tim was gone. My boys was over, I s'pose ye know? I don' know's they come to speak with ye; they're backward with strangers, but they're good stiddy fellows."

"Them was the louts that was hanging round the barn, I guess," said Betsey to herself.

"They're the main-stay now; they're ahead of poor me a'ready. Jonas, he's got risin' a hundred dollars laid up, and I believe Tim's got something too,—he's younger, ye know?"

2. New York City (Damon Runyon, "Pick the Winner")

Well, anyway, when Hot Horse Herbie and his everloving fiancée come into Mindy's, he gives me a large hello, and so does Miss Cutie Singleton, so I hello them right back, and Hot Horse Herbie speaks to me as follows:

"Well," Herbie says, "we have some wonderful news for you. We are going to Miami," he says, "and soon we will be among the waving palms, and reveling in the warm waters of the Gulf Stream."

Now of course this is a lie, because while Hot Horse Herbie is in Miami many times, he never revels in the warm waters of the Gulf Stream, because he never has time for such a thing, what with hustling around the race tracks in the daytime, and around the dog tracks and the gambling joints at night, and in fact I will lay plenty of six to five Hot Horse Herbie cannot even point in the direction of the Gulf Stream when he is in Miami, and I will give him three points, at that.

3. Midwest (Ring Lardner, "Gullible's Travels")

I promised the Wife that if anybody ast me what kind of a time did I have at Palm Beach I'd say I had a swell time. And if they ast me who did we meet I'd tell 'em everybody that was worth meetin'. And if they ast me didn't the trip cost a lot I'd say Yes; but it was worth the money. I promised her I wouldn't spill none o' the real details. But if you can't break a promise you made to your own wife what kind of a promise can you break? Answer me that, Edgar.

I'm not one o' these kind o' people that'd keep a joke to themself just because the joke was on them. But they's plenty of our friends that I wouldn't have 'em hear about it for the world. I wouldn't tell you, only I know you're not the village gossip and won't crack it to anybody. Not even to your own Missus, see? I don't trust no women.

4. Missouri (Samuel L. Clemens, *The Adventures of Huckleberry Finn*)

So Tom says: "I know how to fix it. We got to have a rock for the coat of arms and mournful inscriptions, and we can kill two birds with that same rock. There's a gaudy big grindstone down at the mill, and we'll smouch it, and carve the thing on it, and file out the pens and the saw on it, too."

It warn't no slouch of an idea; and it warn't no slouch of a grindstone nuther; but we allowed we'd tackle it. It warn't quite midnight, yet, so we cleared out for the mill, leaving Jim at work. We smouched the grindstone, and set out to roll her home, but it was a most nation tough job. Sometimes, do what we could, we couldn't keep her from falling over, and she come mighty near mashing us, every time. Tom said she was going to get one of us, sure, before we got through. We got her half way; and then we was plumb played out, and most drownded with sweat. We see it warn't no use, we got to go and fetch Jim. So he raised up his bed and slid the chain off of the bed-leg, and wrapt it round and round his neck, and we crawled out through our hole and down there, and Jim and me laid into that grindstone and walked her along like nothing; and Tom superintended. He could out-superintend any boy I ever see. He knowed how to do everything.

5. Kentucky (Jesse Stuart, *Taps for Private Tussie*)

Watt Tussie was one man that I didn't get around. He didn't look right outten his eyes and I was afraid of him. I think Uncle George was afraid of him too. He didn't belong to either clan of Tussies. He just heard about the big house where all the Tussies were a-comin, so he brought his family to jine the rest in peace, rest and comfortable livin. Grandpa figured for hours to find out if he was any kin to Watt Tussie and he finally figured he was a son of his second cousin, Trueman Tussie. Watt Tussie wore brogan shoes laced with groundhog-hide strings.

6. Florida (Marjorie Kinnan Rawlings, "My Friend Moe")

As he worked, he noticed a row of glass jars of huckleberries that I had canned. His grave face brightened.

"Now that's the way to live," he said. "All the good things we got here in Florida, blueberries and black-berries and beans and cow-peas, all them things had ought to be canned and put up on a clean cupboard shelf with white paper on it. That's the way my Ma did. She lived fine, not the way you live, but just as good when it come to cannin' things and keepin' things clean." His face darkened. "I've tried and I've done tried to get my wife to do that-a-way but it just ain't no use. One time I bought two dozen glass jars and I went out by myself and I picked about a bushel o' blackberries and I went to the store and bought a twenty-five pound sack o' sugar and I takened it home, and I said, 'Wife, here's a bait o' blackberries to put up for us for jam and jelly for the winter.'" He hesitated, his loyalty pricking him.

"She probably didn't have time to do it," I suggested.

"She had time. She let the blackberries spoil, and the antses got in the sugar, and I found the jars throwed out in the back yard."

9.11 INTERNATIONAL ENGLISH

Although English began as the language of a group of migratory tribes, it has become the most pervasive language of the world, with national varieties in several countries and widespread use as a second and foreign language. Among the works treating the world varieties of English are *English around the World* by Jennie Cheshire, *English as a World Language* by Richard W. Bailey and Manfred Görlach, *International English* by Peter Trudgill and Jean Hannah, *International English Usage* by Loreto Todd and Ian Hancock, and *An Introduction to International Varieties of English* by Laurie Bauer. Especially notable in this regard are the journals *English Today* and *World Englishes*. In addition, many works treat English as it is used in particular parts of the world, of which the following are only a few:

AUSTRALIA: *The Australian Language* by Sidney J. Baker, *Australian National Dictionary* by W. S. Ramson, *Language in Australia* by Suzanne Romaine, *English in Australia* by David Blair and Peter Collins, and *The English Language in Australia and New Zealand* by George W. Turner.

CANADA: *A Dictionary of Canadianisms* by Walter S. Avis; *Gage Canadian Dictionary* by Walter S. Avis and others; *Canadian English* by J. K. Chambers; and *Dictionary of Newfoundland English* by G. M. Story, W. J. Kirwin, and J. D. A. Widdowson.

CARIBBEAN BASIN: *Dictionary of Caribbean English Usage* by Richard Allsopp, *Jamaica Talk* by Frederic G. Cassidy, *Dictionary of Jamaican English* by Frederic G. Cassidy and Robert B. Le Page, *Dictionary of Bahamian English* by John A. Holm, and *West Indians and Their Language* by Peter A. Roberts.

INDIA AND SOUTH ASIA: *South Asian English* by Robert J. Baumgardner, *Common Indian Words in English* by R. E. Hawkins, and *The Indianization of English* by Braj B. Kachru.

IRELAND: *A Dictionary of Anglo-Irish* by Diarmaid O Muirithe, *English Language in Ireland* by Diarmaid O Muirithe, and *Languages in Britain and Ireland* by Glanville Price.

NEW ZEALAND: *New Zealand English* by Allan Bell and Koenraad Kuiper; *New Zealand Pocket Oxford Dictionary* by Robert Burchfield; *New Zealand English* by Elizabeth Gordon and Tony Deverson; and *New Zealand English Grammar, Fact or Fiction?* by Marianne Hundt.

SOUTH AFRICA: *A Dictionary of South African English* by Jean and William Branford, *Dictionary of South African English on Historical Principles* by Penny Silva, and *Standard in South African English and Its Social History* by L. W. Lanham and C. A. MacDonald.

Investigate the variety of English used in some part of the world other than the United States and the United Kingdom by consulting the above or similar sources. Write a short paper describing some of the distinctive characteristics of the English used in that place.

10 WORDS AND MEANINGS

10.1 FOR REVIEW AND DISCUSSION

1. Define the following terms:

semantics	pejoration	synecdoche
General Semantics	amelioration	calque
etymology	hyperbole	clang association
semantic change	metaphor	taboo
etymological sense	metonymy	euphemism
sense	synesthesia	intensifier
association	abstract meaning	vogue word
generalization	concrete meaning	semantic marking
specialization	subjective meaning	unmarked word
transfer of meaning	objective meaning	marked word

2. What devices for signaling meaning does a language have?

3. What value is there in the study of words? In answering this question, consider one of the conclusions reached by Charles Carpenter Fries in his germinal study *American English Grammar: The Grammatical Structure of Present-Day English with Especial Reference to Social Differences or Class Dialects*: "In vocabulary and in grammar the mark of the language of the uneducated is its poverty."

4. What is the relationship between a word's etymology and its meaning?

5. Some of the ways and circumstances in which meaning may change are listed here. Notice that the various ways are not all mutually exclusive; there is much overlapping. Supply an example to illustrate each way.

    (1) a widening of the scope of reference (generalization)

    (2) a narrowing of the scope of reference (specialization)

    (3) a lowering of value judgments involved in the reference (pejoration)

    (4) a raising of value judgments involved in the reference (amelioration)

    (5) a shift in meaning from one social group to another (specialized class usage)

    (6) a shift in meaning from one set of circumstances to another (contextual variation)

    (7) a change in the aspect of the meaning upon which a word focuses (shift in point of view)

    (8) a popular adoption of technical language, often motivated by the quest for prestige (popularization)

    (9) a shift in meaning based on an analogy or likeness between two things (metaphor)

    (10) a transference of meaning from one kind of sense-perception to another (synesthesia)

    (11) a shift from concrete reference to abstract reference (abstraction)

    (12) a shift from abstract reference to concrete reference (concretion)

    (13) a shift in reference from the subjective to the objective (objectification or externalizing)

    (14) a shift in reference from the objective to the subjective (subjectification or internalizing)

    (15) a shift in meaning due to the association of ideas (synecdoche and metonymy)

    (16) an influence of the semantics of one language upon that of another (calque)

    (17) a semantic association between two words due to a similarity in sound (clang association)

    (18) a religious or moral taboo which requires new words to replace others thought to be too dangerous, too indecent, or too painful for common use (euphemism)

    (19) an exaggerated use of words for mild intensification or emphasis (hyperbole)

6. In 1712 Jonathan Swift published *A Proposal for Correcting, Improving and Ascertaining the English Tongue,* in which he wrote:

> The *English* Tongue is not arrived to such a Degree of Perfection, as, upon that Account, to make us apprehend any Thoughts of its Decay: And if it were once refined to a certain Standard, perhaps there might be Ways to fix it for ever. . . . I see no absolute Necessity why any Language should be perpetually changing; for we find many Examples of the contrary . . . But what I have most at Heart, is, that some Method should be thought on for *Ascertaining* and *Fixing* our Language for ever, after such Alterations are made in it as shall be thought requisite. . . . What *Horace* says of *Words going off, and perishing like Leaves, and new ones coming in their Place,* is a Misfortune he laments, rather than a Thing he approves: But I cannot see why this should be absolutely necessary.

Discuss the goal that Swift sets up in this extract in terms of its desirability and practicality.

10.2   DEVICES FOR SIGNALING MEANING

Every language can be said to have two kinds of meaning: lexical meaning, the sense that words have as they are listed in a dictionary, and grammatical meaning, the added sense that words acquire when they are put together in a sentence. Certain words, the function words mentioned on page 4 of *Origins and Development,* are so fundamental to the grammatical meaning of a sentence that it is best to consider them as part of the grammar as well as part of the lexicon of English. One way to demonstrate the difference between these two kinds of meaning is with sentences like these:

Oll considerork meanork, ho mollop tharp fo concernesh bix shude largel philosophigar aspectem ith language phanse vulve increasorkrow de recent yearm engagesh sho attentuge ith scholarm.

In prefarbing torming, we cannot here be pretolled with those murler dichytomical optophs of flemack which have demuggingly in arsell wems exbined the obburtion of maxans.

If you are asked what the sentences mean, your first response may be that neither means anything. If further pressed, you might suggest that the first sentence is about language, about something that is recent, and perhaps about philosophy. A careful reading will reveal several other probable bits of information, but at best the sentence remains a farrago of nonsense.

With the second sentence, however, matters are quite otherwise. There is a great deal of meaning in it; for example you can tell from it

1. that, whatever an optoph is, there are more than one of them;
2. that the optophs we are concerned with are dichytomical ones and more murl than other possible optophs;
3. that an optoph is something we might be pretolled with;
4. that optophs are things and not people;
5. that the obburtion of maxans can be exbined by optophs;
6. that the exbining we are talking about took place in the past.

These six observations are only a few of the many bits of meaning the second sentence will convey to any speaker of English. Indeed, our reaction to the second sentence might be that of Alice to the poem "Jabberwocky": "Somehow it seems to fill my head with ideas—only I don't exactly know what they are!" The first sentence uses real English for its lexically important words, but substitutes nonsense elements for the function words and the word endings. Therefore we have some idea of what it is talking about, but no notion whatever of what is being said about the subject. The second sentence reverses the procedure by preserving function words and suffixes, but using nonsense syllables for the main lexical items. Thus even though we have no idea of what *optophs* and *maxans* are, we do know what is being said about them.

1. Six observations were made about the meaning of the second sentence. Tell, as precisely as you can, how each of those observations can be inferred from the sentence.

   (1) _____

   _____

   (2) _____

(3) _____

_____

(4) _____

_____

(5) _____

_____

(6) _____

_____

2. Which of the following observations are valid inferences from the second sentence? Write *V* before each valid conclusion and *I* before each invalid conclusion.

_____ Obburtion belongs to or is characteristic of more than one maxan.

_____ We probably prefarb torming.

_____ Flemack does exbine the obburtion of maxans.

_____ The exbining of the obburtion of maxans by murler dichytomical optophs of flemack is demugging.

_____ We do not pretoll some optophs.

_____ The action of exbining the obburtion of maxans has taken place in more than one wem which is arsell.

3. In each of these sentences, underline the function words and circle grammatically relevant endings:

The merkly boppling dorn quanks all puggles in the scritches.

A tagmeme is the correlation of a grammatical function or slot-class with a class of fillers or mutually substitutable items occurring in that slot.

Night's candles are burnt out, and jocund day stands tiptoe on the misty mountain tops.

But the Idols of the Market-place are the most troublesome of all: idols which have crept into the understanding through the alliances of words and names.

The generall end therefore of all the booke is to fashion a gentleman or noble person in vertuous and gentle discipline.

His notions fitted things so well / That which was which he could not tell.

4. Identify the devices which are used for changing the meaning in these pairs of sentences. Write the appropriate numbers in the blanks. The last three pairs involve two devices each.

1. function words   2. intonation   3. suffixes   4. word order

_____ It is time to go.
It is time to go?

_____ She liked the red hat.
She liked the *red* hat.

_____ He invested in stock theater.
He invested in theater stock.

_____ They found the girl in the car that needed washing.
They found the girl in the car who needed washing.

_____ He bought a picture of Rembrandt for two dollars.
He bought a picture of Rembrandt's for two dollars.

The travelers stopped to eat.
_____ _____ The travelers stopped eating.

They said it was a fun time.
_____ _____ They said it was fun-time.

He died happily.
_____ _____ Happily, he died.

5. Lewis Carroll's nonsense poem "Jabberwocky," from *Through the Looking-Glass and What Alice Found There*, includes many invented words, although the grammar is still fairly clear.

'Twas brillig, and the slithy toves
    Did gyre and gimble in the wabe;
All mimsy were the borogoves,
    And the mome raths outgrabe.

"Beware the Jabberwock, my son!
    The jaws that bite, the claws that catch!
Beware the Jubjub bird, and shun
    The frumious Bandersnatch!"

He took his vorpal sword in hand:
    Long time the manxome foe he sought—
So rested he by the Tumtum tree,
    And stood awhile in thought.

And, as in uffish thought he stood,
    The Jabberwock, with eyes of flame,
Came whiffling through the tulgey wood,
    And burbled as it came!

One, two! One, two! And through and through
    The vorpal blade went snicker-snack!
He left it dead, and with its head
    He went galumphing back.

"And, hast thou slain the Jabberwock?
    Come to my arms, my beamish boy!
O frabjous day! Callooh! Callay!"
    He chortled in his joy.

'Twas brillig, and the slithy toves
    Did gyre and gimble in the wabe;
All mimsy were the borogoves,
    And the mome raths outgrabe.

After reading this poem, Alice muses, "It seems very pretty, but it's *rather* hard to understand!" Determine the probable part of speech for each word here, and guess at what the words might mean:

brillig	_____	borogoves	_____	uffish	_____
slithy	_____	mome	_____	Jabberwock	_____
toves	_____	raths	_____	burbled	_____

gyre	_____	outgrabe	_____	frabjous	_____
gimble	_____	frumious	_____	callooh	_____
wabe	_____	vorpal	_____	callay	_____
mimsy	_____	manxome	_____	chortled	_____

10/3 VARIATION IN MEANING: WORDPLAY

In each of these quotations there is a pun or a play on meaning involving the italicized words. In some cases the wordplay is due to a word's having a broad field of meaning; in other cases, it is due to an accidental similarity of sound between two different words.

What two meanings are combined to produce each pun? Consult the *Oxford English Dictionary* if you cannot recognize the wordplay.

1. For him was levere have at his beddes heed
   Twenty bookes, clad in blak or reed,
   Of Aristotle and his philosophye,
   Than robes rich, or fithele, or gay sautrye.
   But al be that he was a *philosophre*
   Yit hadde he but litel gold in cofre.   (Chaucer, General Prologue to the *Canterbury Tales*)

_____

_____

2. For thy sweet love remembered such wealth brings
   That then I scorn to change my *state* with kings.   (Shakespeare, Sonnet 29)

_____

_____

3. [As a joke, Falstaff's horse has been hidden.]

   Falstaff   What a plague mean ye to colt me thus?
   Prince   Thou liest; thou art not *colted,* thou art uncolted.   (Shakespeare, *1 Henry IV,* II.ii)

_____

_____

4. *Hostess*   Marry, my lord, there is a *noble*man of the court at door would speak with you, he says he comes from your father.
   Prince   Give him as much as will make him a *royal* man, and send him back again to my mother.
      (Shakespeare, *1 Henry IV,* II.iv)

_____

_____

5. [Prince Hal and Bardolph, a gluttonous thief, are discussing what is portended by Bardolph's nose, which is as red as a meteor.]

   Bardolph   Choler, my lord, if rightly taken.
   Prince   No, if rightly *taken,* halter. [that is, 'noose']   (Shakespeare, *1 Henry IV,* II.iv)

_____

_____

6. [In the midst of battle, Prince Hal asks Falstaff for his pistol.]

Prince   Give it me; what, is it in the case?
Falstaff   Aye, Hal; 'tis hot, 'tis hot; there's that will *sack* a city.

[Hal, taking the supposed pistol from the case, finds that it is a bottle of wine.]

(Shakespeare, *1 Henry IV,* V.iii)

_____

_____

7. [Hippolito is confused about the identity of his caller. Why?]

Servant   Here's a *parson* would speak with you, sir.
Hippolito Hah!
Servant   A *parson,* sir, would speak with you.
Hippolito Vicar?

(Dekker, *The Honest Whore,* Part I, IV.i)

_____

_____

8. *Fortunatus*   Let none speak to me, till you have *marked* me well.
Shadow   [Chalking Fortunatus's back] Now speak your mind.   (Dekker, *Old Fortunatus,* II.ii)

_____

_____

9. *Viola*   Musician will he never be, yet I find much music in him, but he loves no *frets,* and is so free
from anger that many times I am ready to bite off my tongue . . . .

(Dekker, *The Honest Whore,* Part I, I.ii)

_____

_____

10. *Shadow*   But what shall we learn by travel?
Andelocia *Fashions.*
Shadow   That's a beastly disease: methinks it's better staying in your own country.

(Dekker, *Old Fortunatus,* II.ii)

_____

_____

11. Must I, who came to *travail* thorough you
Grow your fixed subject, because you are true?   (Donne, "The Indifferent")

_____

_____

12. Dull sublunary lovers' love
  (Whose soule is sense) cannot admit
Absence, because it doth remove
  Those things which elemented it.   (Donne, "A Valediction: Forbidding Mourning")

_____

_____

13. Swear by Thy self, that at my death Thy *Son*
    Shall shine as he shines now and heretofore;
    And, having done that, Thou hast done,
      I fear no more.
                          (Donne, "A Hymn to God the Father")

_____

_____

14. [This poem is a prayer for God's grace.]

The dew doth ev'ry morning fall;
And shall the dew outstrip thy dove?
The dew, for which *grasse* cannot call,
    Drop from above.
                          (Herbert, "Grace")

_____

_____

15.   And now, unveiled, the toilet stands displayed,
Each silver vase in mystic order laid.
First, robed in white, the nymph intent adores,
With head uncovered, the *cosmetic* powers.
                        (Pope, *The Rape of the Lock*)

_____

_____

10.4 ETYMOLOGY AND MEANING

If the italicized words are taken in their etymological senses, each of the following statements is redundant. Cite the etymological meanings that create the pseudo-redundancies.

They began the *inauguration* by observing the entrails of a sacrificial bull. _____

_____

The *escaping* convict slipped out of his coat, by which the guard held him. _____

_____

His *stamina* having been exhausted, the Fates clipped his thread of life. _____

_____

The general *harangued* his soldiers as they gathered about him in a circle. _____

_____

The *candidate* was dressed in a white suit to symbolize his purity. _____

_____

A *mediocre* mountain-climber, he never got more than halfway up any peak. _____

_____

The *miniature* was painted in shades of red. _____

_____

224

The butcher's shop, especially the bench on which he cleaved meat, was a *shambles*. _____

_____

The infantry withstood fierce punishment from the *strafing* of the enemy aircraft. _____

_____

The counselor *controlled* the campers by checking their names against the register to be sure they were

present at lights-out. _____

_____

There is an etymological contradiction in each of these statements. Cite the etymological meaning of the italicized word that creates the pseudo-inconsistency.

The *cadre* is the core around which a military unit forms, as a circle around its center. _____

_____

Although her hair was neatly arranged, she looked *disheveled*. _____

_____

He *endorsed* the proposal by signing his name with a flourish across the front of the document. _____

_____

The archeologist *arrived* at his destination, a ruin in the midst of the Sahara. _____

_____

Although the two men were *companions* of long standing, they had never shared a meal. _____

_____

The team *scampered* onto the field, eager to meet their opponents. _____

_____

The ship's passengers were *quarantined* for two weeks. _____

_____

The use of automation by American *manufacturers* promises to effect a new industrial revolution. _____

_____

The short, skinny girl had a great deal of *poise*. _____

_____

You may write on any *topic* you like except a person or a place. _____

_____

10.5   CHANGES IN MEANING

The following paragraph is logically incoherent if we understand all of its words in their current meanings. If, however, we take each of the italicized words in a sense it had in earlier times, the paragraph contains no inconsistencies at all. Above each of the italicized words, write an earlier meaning that will remove the logical contradictions created by the current sense. The earlier meanings need not be contemporary with one another. They can be found in the *Oxford English Dictionary*.

He was a happy and *sad girl* who lived in a *town* forty miles from the closest neighbor. His unmarried

sister, a *wife* who was a vegetarian member of the WCTU, ate *meat* and drank *liquor* three times a day. She

was so fond of oatmeal bread made from the *corn* her brother grew that she *starved* from overeating. He fed

nuts to the *deer* that lived in the branches of an *apple* tree which bore pears. A *silly* and wise *boor* everyone

liked, he was a *lewd* man whom the general *censure* held to be a model of chastity.

10.6 SOME EXAMPLES OF SEMANTIC CHANGE

The italicized words in the following quotations have lost the meaning that the quotations demand. In the blank to the left of each quotation write a word that will gloss the italicized item for a modern reader. Try to guess the meaning from the context, but if you are unsure, consult the *Oxford English Dictionary,* where you will find most of the quotations used as citations.

_____ He *addressed* himself to go over the River. (Bunyan, *Pilgrim's Progress*)

_____ He had *approved* unto the vulgar, the dignitie of his Science. (Raleigh, *The History of the World*)

_____ *Falstaff*   Shall we have a play extempore?
Prince   Content; and the *argument* shall be thy running away. (Shakespeare, *1 Henry IV*)

_____ A Brazen or Stone-head . . . so *artificial* and natural, that . . . it will presently open its mouth, and resolve the question. (Worcester, *A Century of Inventions*)

_____ Yes, and after supper for feare lest they bee not full gorged, to have a delicate *banquet*. (Cogan, *The Haven of Health*)

_____ Doth she not count her blest . . . that we have wrought so worthy a gentleman to be her *bride*? (Shakespeare, *Romeo and Juliet*)

_____ Thus we *prevent* the last great day, and judge ourselves. (Herbert, *The Temple*)

_____ Upon that day either prepare to die . . . or on Diana's altar to *protest* for aye austerity and single life. (Shakespeare, *A Midsummer Night's Dream*)

_____ The exception *proves* the rule. (Proverbial)

_____ But you, my lord, were glad to be employ'd, to show how *quaint* an orator you are. (Shakespeare, *2 Henry VI*)

_____ What lawful *quest* have given their verdict up unto the frowning judge? (Shakespeare, *Richard III*)

_____ If I attain I will return and *quit* thy love. (Arnold, *The Light of Asia*)

_____ Abate the edge of traitors . . . that would *reduce* these bloody days again, and make poor England weep in streams of blood! (Shakespeare, *Richard III*)

_____ My ships are safely come to *road*. (Shakespeare, *The Merchant of Venice*)

_____ Thou wilt never get thee a husband, if thou be so *shrewd* of thy tongue. (Shakespeare, *Much Ado About Nothing*)

_____ I think you have as little *skill* to fear, as I have purpose to put you to it. (Shakespeare, *The Winter's Tale*)

_____ Satan . . . insatiate to pursue vain war with Heaven, and by *success* untaught, his proud imaginations thus displayed. (Milton, *Paradise Lost*)

_____ To be my queen and *portly* emperess. (Marlowe, *Tamburlaine, Part I*)

_____ There they alight . . . and rest their weary limbs a *tide*. (Spenser, *The Faerie Queene*)

_____ —I dreamt a dream *tonight*. —And so did I. (Shakespeare, *Romeo and Juliet*)

_____ So said he, and forbore not glance or *toy,* of amorous intent, well understood of Eve.   (Milton, *Paradise Lost*)

_____ Heaps of pearl, inestimable stones, *unvalued* jewels, all scattered in the bottom of the sea.   (Shakespeare, *Richard III*)

_____ Princes then . . . [were] trained up, through piety and zeal, to prize spare diet, patient labour, and plain *weeds.*   (Wordsworth, *Prelude*)

_____ This God is most mighty thing that may be, the most *witty* and most rightful. (*Lay Folks' Catechism*)

_____ O Eve, in evil hour thou didst give ear to that false *worm.*   (Milton, *Paradise Lost*)

10.7   GENERALIZATION AND SPECIALIZATION

Each of the semantic developments described below is an example of either generalization or specialization. Identify the process illustrated by writing in the blank *G* for generalization or *S* for specialization.

_____ *aisle*: earlier 'passage between the pews of a church,' later 'passage between rows of seats'
_____ *bereaved*: earlier 'robbed,' later 'deprived by death'
_____ *business*: earlier 'state of being busy,' later 'occupation, profession, or trade'
_____ *butler*: earlier 'male servant in charge of the wine cellar,' later 'male servant in a household'
_____ *chap*: earlier 'customer,' later 'fellow'
_____ *coast*: earlier 'side,' later 'sea shore'
_____ *discard*: earlier 'throw out a card,' later 'reject'
_____ *disease*: earlier 'discomfort,' later 'malady'
_____ *flesh*: earlier 'muscular tissue,' later 'muscular tissue, not viewed as comestible'
_____ *fowl*: earlier 'bird,' later 'barnyard fowl'
_____ *frock*: earlier 'monk's loose-fitting habit,' later 'loose-fitting outer garment'
_____ *frock*: earlier 'loose-fitting outer garment,' later 'woman's dress'
_____ *ghost*: earlier 'soul, spirit,' later 'soul of a dead man as manifested to the living'
_____ *go*: earlier 'walk, travel by foot,' later 'move, travel'
_____ *ordeal*: earlier 'legal trial by a physical test,' later 'a difficult experience'
_____ *passenger*: earlier 'passer-by, traveler,' later 'one who travels by vehicle or vessel'
_____ *spill*: earlier 'shed blood,' later 'waste a liquid'
_____ *thing*: earlier 'legal matter,' later 'any matter'
_____ *wade*: earlier 'go,' later 'walk through water'
_____ *wretch*: earlier 'exile,' later 'unhappy person'

10.8   PEJORATION AND AMELIORATION

Each of the semantic developments described below is an example of either pejoration or amelioration. Identify the process illustrated by writing in the blank *P* for pejoration or *A* for amelioration.

_____ *brook*: earlier 'enjoy, make use of,' later 'endure, tolerate'
_____ *crafty*: earlier 'skillful, clever,' later 'cunning, wily'
_____ *dizzy*: earlier 'foolish,' later 'vertiginous'
_____ *err*: earlier 'wander,' later 'go astray'
_____ *fair*: earlier 'beautiful, pleasant,' later 'moderate, tolerable'
_____ *fame*: earlier 'report, rumor,' later 'celebrity, renown'
_____ *flibbertigibbet*: earlier 'name of a devil,' later 'mischievous person'
_____ *fond*: earlier 'foolish,' later 'affectionate'
_____ *glamour*: earlier 'spell, enchantment,' later 'attractiveness, allure'
_____ *grandiose*: earlier 'large, stately,' later 'pompous'
_____ *impertinent*: earlier 'not pertinent, unrelated,' later 'presumptuous, insolent'
_____ *inquisition*: earlier 'investigation,' later 'persecution'
_____ *luxury*: earlier 'lust,' later 'sumptuousness'
_____ *minister*: earlier 'servant,' later 'government official'
_____ *mischievous*: earlier 'disastrous,' later 'playfully annoying'
_____ *notorious*: earlier 'widely known,' later 'widely and unfavorably known'

_____ *reek*: earlier 'smoke,' later 'stink'
_____ *smirk*: earlier 'smile,' later 'simper'
_____ *sophisticated*: earlier 'overly complex or refined,' later 'sufficiently complex or knowing'

10.9   SOME CIRCUMSTANCES OF SEMANTIC CHANGE

Changes due to social class, circumstance, or point of view are similar rather than opposite kinds of change. Examples can be found on page 218 of *Origins and Development*.

1. The word spelled *Mrs.* in one meaning and *missus* in another meaning shows semantic variation according to social class. Define the two meanings and indicate what the social difference is. _____

   _____

   _____

2. The word *fee* 'payment for services,' for example, a lawyer's fee, acquired its present meaning in accordance with changes of the circumstances in which the word was used. What was the earliest English

   meaning of the word? _____

   _____

   _____

3. The word *attic* 'garret' acquired its present meaning as a result of a shift in point of view. What was the

   earlier meaning of the word? _____

   _____

   _____

4. Classify each of the following semantic developments as due either to circumstance, that is, technological, cultural change (*C*), or to point of view (*P*):

   _____ *boon*: earlier 'prayer, request for something,' later 'gift, favor, benefit granted to a petitioner'
   _____ *glee*: earlier 'pleasant musical entertainment,' later 'pleasure, joy'
   _____ *navigator*: earlier 'one who steers a boat,' later 'one who directs the flight of an airplane'
   _____ *pen*: earlier 'quill pen,' later 'fountain pen'
   _____ *satellite*: earlier 'one celestial body that orbits another,' later 'a man-made object that orbits the earth'
   _____ *tide*: earlier 'time,' for example, of the sea's ebb and flow, later 'regular ebb and flow of the sea'

10.10   THE VOGUE FOR WORDS OF LEARNED ORIGIN

Popularization, the process by which a learned word enters the general vocabulary and undergoes various kinds of semantic change as it does so, is very common. Here are a number of vogue words the technical meanings of which have been altered in popular use. Define each word (1) in the popular sense illustrated by the sentence in which it is used and (2) in the technical sense that underlies the popular use.

He is strongly *allergic* to any form of modern music.

1. _____

2. _____

228

At every party there's one loud-mouthed *extrovert* who dominates the group.

1. _____

2. _____

She is such a kind-hearted soul that she *identifies* with every panhandler she sees on the street.

1. _____

2. _____

Crowds make him *inhibited*.

1. _____

2. _____

The poor thing was a *martyr* to her insomnia.

1. _____

2. _____

He plays golf every Sunday; it's an *obsession* with him.

1. _____

2. _____

In New York, she lost her *personal identity* amid the crowds.

1. _____

2. _____

He has a *phobia* about Christmas shopping.

1. _____

2. _____

Television sponsors are *psychotic* about having other products mentioned on their programs.

1. _____

2. _____

Knowing a little French will give you *status* in the garden club of any midwestern town.

1. _____

2. _____

He *sublimated* his desire to smoke by eating lemon drops.

1. _____

2. _____

The *tragedy* is that despite our rush, the train has already left.

1. _____

2. _____

10.11 ABSTRACT AND CONCRETE MEANINGS

Words may change in meaning by shifting (1) from the abstract to the concrete or (2) from the concrete to the abstract. Identify the kind of change exemplified in each of these words by writing the appropriate number, 1 or 2, in the blank:

_____ *chair*: earlier 'a seat,' later 'professorship'

_____ *complexion*: earlier 'temperament, disposition,' later 'color and texture of the facial skin'

_____ *construction*: earlier 'action of constructing,' later 'something constructed'

_____ *engine*: earlier 'native intelligence, ingenuity,' later 'mechanical apparatus'

_____ *libel*: earlier 'a derogatory pamphlet,' later 'a false and derogatory statement'

_____ *nimble*: earlier 'quick-witted, clever,' later 'quick-acting, agile'

_____ *slapstick*: earlier 'instrument that makes a loud noise, used to simulate heavy blows,' later 'farce, broad comedy'

_____ *sloth*: earlier 'laziness,' later 'an arboreal mammal'

_____ *to stomach*: earlier 'digest, retain in the stomach,' later 'put up with, tolerate'

_____ *zest*: earlier 'lemon peel,' later 'enjoyment, relish'

10.12 SUBJECTIVE AND OBJECTIVE MEANINGS

Words may change in meaning by shifting (1) from the subjective to the objective or (2) from the objective to the subjective. Thus the earliest, and still the most common, meaning of *sorry* is 'feeling regret,' as in "When Joseph saw it, he was very *sorry*." Such a meaning is said to be subjective because the word describes the person who experiences the sorrow. Later *sorry* came to mean 'evoking regret or disdain,' as in "It was a *sorry* sight." This use is called objective because the word now describes a thing that causes sorrow in someone. The shift in meaning was from the subjective to the objective, from the perceiver to the object perceived.

Identify the kind of change exemplified in each of these words by writing the appropriate number, 1 or 2, in the blank.

_____ *angry*: earlier 'troublesome, causing sorrow,' later 'wrathful, raging'

_____ *anxious*: earlier 'feeling anxiety about something,' later 'causing anxiety in someone'

_____ *careful*: earlier 'painstaking, showing care for,' later 'showing the results of care'

_____ *excitement*: earlier 'something that causes activity or feeling,' later 'the state of being active or emotionally aroused'

_____ *hateful*: earlier 'filled with hate,' later 'inspiring hate'

_____ *joyous*: earlier 'experiencing joy, delighted,' later 'causing joy, delightful'

_____ *knowledgeable*: earlier 'capable of being known,' later 'possessing knowledge'

_____ *like*: earlier 'cause someone to feel pleasure,' later 'feel pleasure about something'

10.13 METAPHOR, SYNESTHESIA, AND ASSOCIATION OF IDEAS

Words sometimes acquire new meanings and may become new words through their use as figures of speech, four of the more common of which are

1. metaphor,
2. synesthesia (a kind of metaphor),
3. synecdoche, and
4. metonymy.

Identify the figure that was responsible for the new meaning of each of the following words by writing the appropriate number, from 1 through 4, in the blank:

_____ *bar*: earlier 'barrier in the Inns of Court which separated students from senior members,' later 'legal profession'

_____ *blue*: earlier 'a color,' later 'melancholy in sound'

_____ *board*: earlier 'table,' later 'daily meals'

_____ *bottle*: earlier 'a glass container,' later 'alcoholic drink'

_____ *cloud*: earlier 'hill,' later 'condensed water vapor floating in the air'

_____ *cool*: earlier 'moderately cold,' later 'emotionally restrained'

_____ *cork*: earlier 'bark of an oak tree,' later 'stopper'

_____ *crane*: earlier 'a bird with a long neck and bill,' later 'a machine for lifting weights'

_____ *crotchet*: earlier 'a small hook,' later 'idiosyncrasy, whimsical notion'

_____ *fret*: earlier 'eat, gnaw,' later 'worry, be distressed'

_____ *hand*: earlier 'grasping terminal part of the forearm,' later 'employee, laborer'

_____ *harsh*: earlier 'rough to the touch,' later 'discordant in sound'

_____ *high*: earlier 'extending upward in space,' later 'shrill, sharply pitched'

_____ *kite*: earlier 'bird of prey,' later 'toy, flown in the air'

_____ *lousy*: earlier 'infested with lice,' later 'contemptible, worthless'

_____ *sour*: earlier 'acid in taste,' later 'off key'

_____ *tin*: earlier 'a metal,' later 'a can sometimes made of tin'

_____ *triumph*: earlier 'victory procession,' later 'card of a suit that temporarily ranks higher than any other suit'

_____ *vestry*: earlier 'a room in a church used for storing vestments and for meetings,' later 'a body of laymen who administer the business of a parish'

_____ *vise*: earlier 'screw,' later 'tool with two clamps operated by a screw'

10.14 TWO MINOR CAUSES OF SEMANTIC CHANGE

Below are some words together with meanings that they have had at various times. The dates are of the earliest recorded use of the word in the senses indicated. Answer the questions that follow each group of words.

aisle,	1370	'wing of a church' (ultimately from Lat. *ala* 'wing')
alley,	1388	'passageway'
alley,	1508	'passageway between rows of pews in a church'
aisle,	1731	'passageway between rows of pews in a church'

What apparently caused the word *aisle* to acquire its 1731 meaning? _____

_____

buxom,	1175	'obedient, meek'
buxom,	1362	'obliging, affable, kind'
buxom,	1589	'attractive, plump, jolly' (used chiefly of women)
buxom,	after 1900	'full-busted, with large breasts'

Buxom probably acquired its most recent meaning through an association in sound with what English word?

_____

care,	before 1000	'worry, anxiety, trouble'
Latin *cura*		'pains, trouble, worry; attention, management, guardianship'
care,	after 1400	'responsibility, direction, guidance'

What apparently caused the word *care* to acquire its post-1400 meaning? _____

_____

bloody,	before 1000	'characteristic of blood'
	1117	'covered with blood, bleeding'
	1225	'concerned with bloodshed'
	1563	'bloodthirsty, cruel'
	1676	'very' (an intensifier freely used by fashionable members of society, common in Restoration literature)

| after about 1750 | 'very' (an intensifier freely used by members of the lower classes, but considered vulgar and taboo in polite society) |
| French *sanglant* | 'bloody, covered with blood, cruel; *figuratively,* outrageous, keen, *used as an abusive epithet*' |

John Orr in *Old French and Modern English Idiom* has suggested that the English use of *bloody* as an intensifier is due to the imitation of a similar use in French of *sanglant* from the fifteenth century on. How do the dates of the semantic development of *bloody* lend plausibility to his theory? What political and social events in English history coincide with the 1676 change in meaning?

_____

_____

_____

10.15   TABOO, EUPHEMISM, AND PEJORATION

We are all familiar with verbal taboos that require that an offending word be replaced by a kinder, purer, or more elegant substitute. The substituting euphemism acquires the meaning of the old word and as often as not undergoes pejoration and becomes taboo itself, thus requiring a new euphemism. The process seems to continue without end.

1. The subject of smells is one that is surrounded by mild social taboos. Arrange the following seven words in order beginning with those that have the most unpleasant connotation and ending with those that have the most pleasant meaning. Follow your own judgment in ordering the list. All these words originally had neutral or favorable meanings. By looking in the *Oxford English Dictionary* or *Merriam-Webster's Collegiate Dictionary*, find the earliest recorded date for each of the words.

aroma   scent (n.)   stench (n.)

odor   smell (v.)   stink (v.)

perfume

WORD: _____ _____ _____ _____ _____ _____ _____

DATE: _____ _____ _____ _____ _____ _____ _____

What general correlation is there between the length of time a word has been used to refer to smelling

and its tendency to pejoration? _____

_____

2. Some undertakers, doubtless inspired by kindly motives, have promoted euphemisms for burial. The loved one, the last remains, or the patient is given a leave-taking or memorial service in the mortuary chapel, reposing room, or crematorium before interment, inhumation, inurnment, or immurement in the columbarium, memorial park, or resting place. The survivors or waiting ones, as Evelyn Waugh calls them in *The Loved One,* are reminded to make Before Need Arrangements (that is, pay now, die later). English speakers, however, have not needed professional assistance in coining euphemisms for the verb *to die.* Add as many as you can to those given on pages 214–5 of *Origins and Development.*

_____

_____

_____

3. Choose any of the subjects discussed on pages 214–7 of *Origins and Development* and give other examples of euphemisms used in connection with it. _____

_____

_____

_____

_____

_____

10.16   THE FATE OF HYPERBOLIC WORDS

Hyperbolic words tend to diminish in force. How have the following paled in meaning?

adore _____

amazing _____

ecstatic _____

fascinate _____

rapt _____

ravenous _____

sorry _____

spill _____

starve _____

swelter _____

11 NEW WORDS FROM OLD

11.1   FOR REVIEW AND DISCUSSION

1. Define each of these terms and, when appropriate, illustrate the term with an example.

creating	compound	aphesis, *adj.* aphetic
combining	amalgamated compound	back-formation
shortening	affixation	blend (portmanteau word)
blending	hybrid form	folk etymology
shifting	clipped form	functional shift
root creation	initialism	commonization
echoic (onomatopoeic) word	alphabetism	eponym
symbolic word	acronym	
ejaculation	apheresis, *adj.* apheretic	

2. Which of the processes of word making described in this chapter seem, from what you know, to have been the most productive in English?

3. Your answer to the preceding question was based on your general familiarity with the English vocabulary or on what you have read, but you can substantiate it by making a random sampling from the *Oxford English Dictionary*. Arbitrarily select one or more pages from each volume of the *OED*. Determine the process involved in the making of every word, not merely main entries, on each page you have selected. Many of the words will be loans from other languages. Loanwords will be considered in Chapter 12; for the present, group them together as a separate category, with which you are not concerned. When you have determined the process of word making responsible for all the words that are not direct loans, tabulate your results and determine whether your intuitions accord with the sample you investigated.

4. What circumstances promote the making of new words? What specific areas, such as computer technology, are prolific in the production of new words?

11.2   ROOT CREATIONS

Genuine root creations are rare. *Blurb, gas, paraffin,* and *rayon* are sometimes suggested as examples. Although it is hardly in general use, *googol* is another candidate. Investigate the histories of these five words and decide which one is the best example of root creation. Explain your decision.

_____

_____

_____

_____

_____

_____

11.3 TRADE NAMES

These trade names were suggested by already existing words or word elements. Identify the earlier forms that seem to underlie the trade names.

automat	_____	Pepsodent	_____
Band-aid	_____	Pulmotor	_____
Coca-Cola	_____	Quonset	_____
escalator	_____	Sanforized	_____
Frigidaire	_____	Tabasco	_____
Levis	_____	Technicolor	_____
Linotype	_____	Victrola	_____
mimeograph	_____	Windbreaker	_____
Novocain	_____	Xerox	_____
ouija	_____	zipper	_____

11.4 ECHOIC WORDS

1. Many words that name sounds, or actions that produce sounds, are echoic in origin, for example, *buzz, chatter, gag, gurgle, hawk* 'clear the throat,' *heehaw, hiccup, honk, jingle, yak* 'talk volubly,' and *zoom.* Select a particular area of meaning, such as animal noises, noises produced by falling objects, nonspeech sounds made by people, noises made by machines, water noises, noises of rapid motion, and so forth, and list as many echoic words for that area as you can think of.

_____

_____

_____

_____

2. Some words of various origins, imitative or not, share a common meaning and a common sound. When meaning and sound thus coincide in several words, it is inevitable that speakers should feel that the sound somehow represents the meaning. Thus, *swagger, swash, swat, sway, sweep, swerve, swig, swill, swing, swipe, swirl, swish, swivel, swoop,* and *swoosh* all have the initial sound combination [sw] and are vaguely similar to one another in meaning. The shared meaning, something like 'free-wheeling movement in an arc,' seems to be represented by the sound [sw], which is therefore called a "phonestheme." The phenomenon is known as "sound symbolism."

Here are some short lists of symbolic words. For each list, identify the phonestheme, describe the meaning that is characteristic of it, and add any appropriate words you can find.

tweak, twiddle, twine, twinkle, twirl, twist, twitch

_____

glare, gleam, glimmer, glint, glisten, glitter, gloss, glow

_____

crack, cramp, cripple, crooked, crouch, crumple, crunch, crush

_____

draggle, drain, dredge, dregs, drip, droop, drop, dross

_____

bladder, blaze, blimp, blister, bloat, blow, blubber, blurt

---

track, trail, trample, travel, tread, trip, trot, trudge

---

crash, dash, flash, gush, rush, smash, swish, whoosh

---

bangle, dangle, jangle, jingle, jungle, spangle, tangle, tingle

---

bump, chump, dump, hump, lump, plump, rump, slump

---

amble, jumble, mumble, ramble, rumble, scramble, shamble, tremble

---

11.5   EJACULATIONS

Phffft, the name of a 1954 motion picture, is an exclamation denoting the sudden collapse of a marriage or some other deflatable thing. The sound, which suggests air escaping from a balloon, is represented well enough by the spelling and is familiar to most English speakers. The critic Bosley Crowther was too pessimistic when he advised, "Don't try to pronounce the title." Crowther's additional comment, " 'Phffft' is a skkkt that runs an hour and a half," suggests that he had in mind a conventional pronunciation for the ejaculation, one that rimed with *skit.* When such a noise is pronounced not as the noise it originally symbolized, but rather as a permissible sequence of English phonemes, it has become a word like any other in the lexicon. At first an interjection, the word may come to function as a noun, a verb, or other part of speech.

Here are some ejaculations that have become words through a spelling pronunciation of their written symbols, although not all of them have achieved the honor of a dictionary entry. Describe or produce the noise that each of the spellings originally symbolized.

LAUGHTER: yuk-yuk, yak, hardy-har
ATTENTION-GETTING NOISE: ahem, psst
DELAYING NOISE: hem and haw
EXPRESSION OF CONTEMPT OR DISGUST: humph, piff (cf. piffle), ptui (pronounced [pətúi]), braak, chee(z)
CRY OF HORROR: a(u)gh
EXPRESSION OF RELIEF: whew
SIGNAL FOR SILENCE: shush, hush, ssst
AUTOMATIC NOISES: kerchoo, burp, hack
NEGATION: uh-uh

11.6   MORPHEMES: PREFIXES, SUFFIXES, AND BASES

The morpheme is the smallest meaningful unit in a language. *Card, act, moron, random, cardigan,* and *asparagus* are words that consist of a single morpheme each. *Discard, action, moronic, randomly, cardigans,* and *aspáragus plànt* are made of two morphemes each. A morpheme may be a base like *card, asparagus,* and *plant;* a prefix like *dis-;* or a suffix like *-ion.* Words like *refer, defer, confer, receive, deceive, conceive, reduce, deduce,* and *conduce* are made of two morphemes each, a prefix and a base, although the bases *fer, ceive,* and *duce* do not occur as separate words.

Divide each of the following words into its constituent morphemes by rewriting the word with hyphens between the morphemes. For example, *activistic* can be divided into *act-iv-ist-ic.* Note that morphemes are properly represented by sounds, but for convenience we can use conventional spellings.

236

postage	_____	prepare	_____
impressment	_____	repair	_____
trial	_____	disparity	_____
early	_____	disparage	_____
holistic	_____	repel	_____
worthily	_____	propellant	_____
definite	_____	produce	_____
favoritism	_____	seduce	_____
demarcation	_____	secede	_____
finalization	_____	proceed	_____
unequivocal	_____	placate	_____
palmistry	_____	implacable	_____

11.7 PREFIXES

1. From what language was the prefix in each of these words originally derived? Label each word *G* (Greek), *L* (Latin), or *OE* (Old English) according to the source of the prefix.

_____	archenemy	_____	microorganism	_____	stepchild
_____	circumnavigate	_____	midday	_____	surname
_____	cis-Alpine	_____	misfit	_____	transoceanic
_____	counterbalance	_____	monomania	_____	tricolor
_____	crypto-Communist	_____	panhellenic	_____	twilight
_____	demigod	_____	parapsychology	_____	ultraliberal
_____	diacid	_____	polyvalent	_____	unilingual
_____	epicycle	_____	preternatural	_____	vice-regent
_____	malformed	_____	proto-Germanic		
_____	metalanguage	_____	retroactive		

2. Two affixes may be pronounced and spelled alike, yet be two independent elements because they have different functions in the language. Thus the *-ly* of *manly* and the *-ly* of *slowly* are not the same suffix. The first *-ly* forms adjectives; the second *-ly* forms adverbs. The two endings have different meanings and uses and therefore are different suffixes.

On the other hand, an affix may be pronounced and spelled variously in different words, yet remain a single affix. Although the past tense ending is [d] in *said,* [t] in *thought,* and [əd] in *waited,* we say that these three pronunciations are only variants of one affix because their meaning or function is the same.

In each of the following pairs, if both words have the same prefix, mark them *S*; if they have different prefixes, mark them *D*.

	amoral		embed		income
_____	aside	_____	encase	_____	invalid
	autobiography		foreword		intermix
_____	autocar	_____	forswear	_____	intramural
	bemoan		extraordinary		pro-British
_____	besmirch	_____	extrasensory	_____	prologue
	biannual		hypertension		supernatural
_____	bypass	_____	hypotension	_____	supranational
	coeternal		illegal		
_____	copilot	_____	immoral		

11.8 SUFFIXES

Are the suffixes in each pair of words the same morpheme or different morphemes? Use the symbols *S* and *D*.

	absorbent		density		rested
_____	triumphant	_____	chastity	_____	bigoted

	accountable		hyphenate		smithy
_____	responsible	_____	temperate	_____	sleepy
	coastal		occurrence		taller
_____	withdrawal	_____	appearance	_____	teller
	cupful		offing		wooden
_____	careful	_____	scoffing	_____	shorten

11.9 NEW AFFIXES AND NEW USES OF OLD ONES

The journal *American Speech* has a department "Among the New Words," which records additions to the English vocabulary. Recent years have seen the increased popularity of affixes like *-ology, -ism, -nik, -ery, -ify, -oree, para-,* and *non-* in such specimens as *Saxonology* 'the study of the policies and motives of the British and American governments; the counterpart of Russian Kremlinology,' *Pekingology, comitology* 'the study of committees,' *tokenism* 'the practice of token integration,' *oathism* 'the practice of requiring loyalty oaths,' *spacenik* 'an astronaut,' *peacenik* 'a pacifist,' *neatnik* 'a nonbeatnik,' *scrollery* 'the search for documents like the Dead Sea scrolls,' *massified* 'made massive,' *freezoree* 'a winter camporee,' *paralanguage* 'a system of communication that accompanies language,' *nonevent* 'an event arranged by the news media for the purpose of reporting it,' and *nonbook* 'a book conceived as a piece of salable merchandise rather than as an artistic undertaking.'

Consult any five consecutive years of *American Speech* or the collection *Fifty Years Among the New Words,* ed. John Algeo and Adele Algeo, to find what affixes have appeared most frequently in the new words recorded for those years. List the more popular affixes and the words containing them. Gloss any word the meaning of which is not apparent.

_____

_____

_____

_____

_____

_____

_____

11.10 THE SPELLING OF COMPOUNDS

1. Are the following compounds spelled as one word, as two words, or with a hyphen? First decide how you would spell each compound and then check the spelling in a dictionary or, better, in several dictionaries.

half cocked	_____	second story (adj.)	_____
half hour	_____	side band	_____
high chair	_____	side kick	_____
high grade	_____	side light	_____
high light	_____	side step (v.)	_____
prize fighter	_____	side whiskers	_____

2. What conclusion can you draw about the spelling of compounds? _____

_____

11.11 THE STRESSING OF COMPOUNDS

1. Write the stresses of these items. Put the accent marks over the stressed vowel, as in *hótbèd* versus *hôt béd*.

redwood	red wood	shorthand	short hand
bluebeard	blue beard	graybeard	gray beard
greenroom	green room	safeguard	safe guard
strongbox	strong box	Stonewall	stone wall
mainland	main land	paperback	paper back

2. Write the stresses.

madhouse keeper	mad housekeeper
new-math teacher	new math-teacher
second-hand cart	second handcart
used-car salesman	used car-salesman
White House lights	white houselights

3. Write the stresses of the italicized words. There is a variation among English speakers for some of these items.

The pot is only *silver plate*.	He ate from a *silver plate*.
They live on *Main Street*.	It is the *main street*.
Hamlet met the *gravedigger*.	He was a serious and *grave digger*.
What is the *subject matter*?	What does the *subject matter*?
She added *baking powder*.	Why is she *baking powder*?

4. Write the stresses of the italicized words.

Who ever asked?	*Whoever* asked?
He found a *new haven*.	He lived in *New Haven*.
It is not a *good morning*.	I wish you *good morning*.
He met an *old lady*.	Here comes your *old lady*.
The river has *grand rapids*.	They eloped to *Grand Rapids*.

5. Each of these compounds has a pronunciation that shows phonetic change due to the complete loss of stress from the second element. Each also has an analytical pronunciation. Transcribe the words phonetically to show both pronunciations.

	WITH PRIMARY STRESS ONLY	WITH PRIMARY-SECONDARY STRESS
blackguard	_____	_____
boatswain	_____	_____
somebody	_____	_____
starboard	_____	_____
topsail	_____	_____

11.12 THE CONSTRUCTION OF COMPOUNDS

Compounds are formed according to many patterns, of which the following are only a few:

1. *Bluegrass* is from "the grass is blue."
2. *Bloodthirsty* is from "thirsty for blood."
3. *Daredevil* is from "one that dares the devil."
4. *Pale-face* is from "one that has a pale face."
5. *Pin-up* is from "it is pinned up."
6. *Overland* is from "over the land."
7. *Typeset* is from "to set the type."

Identify the patterns of these compounds by writing the appropriate number, from 1 through 7, in front of each.

_____ backbite	_____ highbrow	_____ proofread
_____ battle-ready	_____ highway	_____ redbird
_____ blowout	_____ homesick	_____ redcap
_____ boy-crazy	_____ hotfoot	_____ redhead
_____ breakdown	_____ kickback	_____ sightsee
_____ downstairs	_____ longbow	_____ spoilsport
_____ gentleman	_____ longhorn	_____ underhand

11.13   AMALGAMATED COMPOUNDS

1. These words are historically compounds. Identify the elements from which each word was formed.

among	_____	halibut	_____
ampersand	_____	hatred	_____
bailiwick	_____	ingot	_____
doff	_____	Lammas	_____
don	_____	neighbor	_____
elbow	_____	no	_____
every	_____	offal	_____
furlong	_____	rigmarole	_____
gamut	_____	shelter	_____
gossip	_____	woof 'thread'	_____

2. Most speakers would be aware that these words are compounds, but at least one part of each compound is semantically obscure. Identify the obscure elements.

backgammon	_____	mildew	_____
bonfire	_____	nickname	_____
cobweb	_____	walnut	_____
good-by	_____	wedlock	_____
midriff	_____	werewolf	_____
midwife	_____	worship	_____

3. These reduplicating compounds are also amalgamated. Identify their original elements.

hob-nob	_____
shilly-shally	_____
willy-nilly	_____

11.14   CLIPPED FORMS

Identify the full forms from which these words were abbreviated:

ad lib	_____	mitt	_____
chap	_____	mutt	_____
chat	_____	pep	_____
chum	_____	prom	_____
cinema	_____	radio	_____
fan 'admirer'	_____	scram	_____
fib 'lie'	_____	sleuth	_____
limey	_____	toady	_____

11.15   APHETIC FORMS

Identify the long form from which each of these words was produced by aphesis:

cense	_____	raiment	_____
drawing room	_____	spite	_____
fend	_____	splay	_____

240

lone	_____	squint	_____
mend	_____	stogie	_____
mien	_____	stress	_____
neath	_____	tend 'serve'	_____
pall 'satiate'	_____	tiring-room	_____
pert	_____	varsity	_____
ply 'use'	_____	venture	_____

11.16   BACK-FORMATION

These words are the result of back-formation. Give the original words from which they were back-formed.

1. BACK-FORMATIONS INVOLVING AN INFLECTIONAL ENDING

asset	_____	pry 'lever'	_____
burial	_____	riddle 'puzzle'	_____
hush	_____	(window) sash	_____
inkle 'hint'	_____	shimmy	_____
marquee	_____	sidle	_____

2. BACK-FORMATIONS INVOLVING AN AGENT SUFFIX

edit	_____	panhandle	_____
escalate	_____	peddle	_____
hawk 'vend'	_____	scavenge	_____
interlope	_____	(to) swab	_____
mug 'assault'	_____	swindle	_____

3. MISCELLANEOUS BACK-FORMATIONS

(to) char	_____	peeve	_____
diagnose	_____	preempt	_____
donate	_____	reminisce	_____
greed	_____	resurrect	_____
homesick	_____	unit	_____

4. Some words are formed by a process that is the opposite of back-formation. Give the etymology of the following four words and then describe the process of word formation that is common to them. Notice that all four words are singular in current English; they require a singular verb like *seems* rather than a plural like *seem*.

bodice _____

chintz _____

news _____

quince _____

PROCESS OF FORMATION: _____

_____

11.17   BLENDS

1. Identify the sources from which these blends were produced. There will be two sources for each blend. The origin of some of these words is not completely certain, so you can expect variation among dictionaries.

alegar =	_____	+	_____
blotch =	_____	+	_____
blurt =	_____	+	_____
extrapolate =	_____	+	_____
hassle =	_____	+	_____
magnetron =	_____	+	_____
positron =	_____	+	_____

prissy =	_____	+	_____
scratch =	_____	+	_____
scroll =	_____	+	_____
simulcast =	_____	+	_____
splatter =	_____	+	_____
splutter =	_____	+	_____
tangelo =	_____	+	_____
travelogue =	_____	+	_____
vitamin =	_____	+	_____

2. Some blends are deliberate, intentional creations like *racon* from *radar* plus *beacon,* but others result from unconscious slips of the tongue. In rapid speech, the talker may have in mind two words of partly similar meaning and sound; the speech process gets short-circuited and instead of choosing between the two words, the speaker combines them into a single form. Thus *slick* and *slimy* may blend as [slími], *drip* and *dribble* as [drípəl], or *stockings* and *socks* as [stɑks]. Occasionally such a *lapsus linguae* becomes established in the language, but most of them are hardly noticed by either speakers or their audience. Try to collect a few examples of inadvertent blending by listening to the speech of those around you.

11.18   ACRONYMS AND INITIALISMS

1. Initialisms are acronyms that make use of the initial letters in a phrase and are pronounced by sounding the letter names. Such abbreviations are extremely common in contemporary English, often supplanting the unabbreviated term in general usage. Widely used initialisms, in addition to those cited in *Origins and Development,* are AA, BTU, CIA, DT's, ESP, FCC, GI, HMS, IQ, JP, KO, LA, MD, NG, OCS, PTA, QED, RSVP, SRO, TNT, USA, VIP, and WCTU. List ten or fifteen similar initialisms in common use.

_____

_____

_____

2. The pronunciation of the letters in initialisms such as the ones listed above sometimes gives rise to new written words. What is the origin of each of these terms?

ack ack _____

emcee _____

jeep _____

kayo _____

veep _____

3. Acronyms are also formed from the initial letters (or sometimes syllables) of a phrase, but they are pronounced as though the letters spelled out a normal word. Give the full phrases from which the following acronyms have been abbreviated.

conelrad _____

Delmarva _____

futhorc _____

loran _____

napalm _____

shoran _____

sial _____

sonar _____

teleran _____

242

4. English is not unique in forming acronyms. Some words that we have borrowed from foreign tongues were originally abbreviated phrases. Identify the unabbreviated source of each of these words:

kolkhoz _____

comintern _____

flak _____

Gestapo _____

5. Trade names are very often acronyms, for example, *Amoco, Nabisco, Panagra, Socony,* and *Sunoco.* List

a few other such trade names. _____

_____

_____

6. Pseudo-acronyms like *Wave* are becoming increasingly common. The following phrases, in which the capital letters spell an acronym, are examples.

*F*ilm *O*ptical *S*canning *D*evice for *I*nput to *C*omputers
*E*lectronegative *GA*s *D*etector
*I*nstrumentation *DI*gital *O*n-line *T*ranscriber
*A*utomatic *D*igital *I*nput-*O*utput *S*ystem

In each case it seems likely that the supposed abbreviation had some influence on the creation of the full phrase. List a few other pseudo-acronyms.

_____

_____

_____

M.19   FOLK ETYMOLOGY

1. Give the correct etymology of these words and indicate the probable basis for the folk etymology, following the pattern on page 241 of *Origins and Development.*

andiron _____

barberry _____

blunderbuss _____

chickpea _____

demijohn _____

forlorn hope _____

gymkhana _____

mangrove _____

rosemary _____

sty 'swelling on eyelid' _____

teapoy _____

turtle 'reptile' _____

2. If we consider the earliest forms of the italicized words, the answer to each of the following questions is "no." Give the correct etymology for the words. Although the misunderstanding illustrated by some of them is too learned to be of the folk, the principle involved is the same as that of folk etymology.

Was the *gopherwood* from which Noah built the ark named for gophers?

_____

Is a *chipmunk* so called because he chips?

_____

Is an *outrage* a raging out?

_____

Are *nightmares* brought on by horseback riding?

_____

Is a *comrade* someone with (Lat. *com-*) whom one does something?

_____

Is *kitty-cornered* the way a kitten walks?

_____

Is the bridge term *tenace* a combination of a ten and an ace?

_____

Is the *hold* of a ship so called because it holds the cargo?

_____

Is a *ham* radio operator so called because he is an (h)amateur?

_____

Do *Jordan almonds* come from Jordan?

_____

Is the *albatross* so called because it is white (Lat. *alba*) in color?

_____

Is a *posthumous* work one published after (Lat. *post*) the author has been put under the earth (*humus*)?

_____

Is the *ptarmigan* a creature named from Greek, like the pterodactyl and the pteropod?

_____

Is an *argosy* named for the *argonauts*?

_____

Are *purlieus* so named because they are a kind of place (Fr. *lieu*)?

_____

3. Much folk etymology, like the Chester drawers (chest of drawers) and Archie Fisher snow (artificial snow) mentioned in *Origins and Development*, is so ephemeral that it never achieves lexicographical record. Some of it is deliberately humorous. Here are a few additional examples of such folk etymology; add to the list from your own experience.

car porch 'an open-sided shelter for an automobile' (properly *carport*)
Creak Car Lake 'a resort lake near St. Louis, Missouri, reached by a squeaking trolley car' (properly *Crèvecoeur Lake*)

dashhound 'a dog of German origin' (properly *dachshund*)
lowbachi 'a small charcoal brazier in the Japanese style' (variant of *hibachi*)
very coarse veins 'swollen veins' (properly *varicose*)

_____

_____

_____

_____

11.20 COMMON WORDS FROM PROPER NAMES

1. These common nouns were taken without change from the names of actual persons. Explain briefly how each personal name came to be applied to the thing it now denotes.

braille _____

diesel _____

hooligan _____

leotard _____

negus _____

quisling _____

roentgen _____

sequoia _____

silhouette _____

2. These common words are derivatives or altered forms of personal names. Identify the historical person from whose name each word derives.

algorism	_____	guillotine	_____
(deci)bel	_____	klieg (light)	_____
boysenberry	_____	macadam	_____
euhemerism	_____	magnolia	_____
fuchsia	_____	saxophone	_____

3. These common words were taken from the names of literary, mythological, or biblical persons. Identify the source of each.

ammonia _____

euphuism _____

hermetic _____

lazar _____

museum _____

philander _____

procrustean _____

syphilis _____

termagant _____

veronica _____

4. These common words are given names used generically. Identify each word by the usual form of the name from which it comes.

dickey	_____	jockey	_____
dobbin	_____	jug	_____
doll	_____	magpie	_____
(play) hob	_____	marionette	_____
jimmy	_____	zany	_____

5. These words were taken without change from the names of places. Identify the nation in which each place is to be found.

angostura	_____	duffel	_____
ascot	_____	jodhpur(s)	_____
bantam	_____	madras	_____
castile 'soap'	_____	magenta	_____
donnybrook	_____	spa	_____

6. These words are derivatives or altered forms of place names. Identify the place from which each word derives.

attic	_____	muslin	_____
baldachin	_____	palace	_____
buckram	_____	peach 'fruit'	_____
cantaloupe	_____	seltzer	_____
capitol	_____	spruce	_____
currant	_____	tabby	_____
denim	_____	tangerine	_____
jimson(weed)	_____		

7. These common words are derived from the names of tribes or national groups. Identify the sources.

arabesque	_____	hooch	_____
cravat	_____	lumber	_____
frank	_____	slave	_____
gothic	_____	vandal	_____
gyp	_____	welch	_____

8. These common words are derived from various kinds of proper names. Identify the sources.

blucher	_____	protean	_____
cambric	_____	raglan	_____
canary	_____	robin	_____
cretin	_____	shillelagh	_____
loganberry	_____	sienna	_____
majolica	_____	sousaphone	_____
melba toast	_____	vaudeville	_____

11.21 SLANG

1. Much slang enters general use from the jargon of particular occupations. Thus (rat)fink has its origin in underworld argot, in which it means 'informer.' Baseball has contributed such terms as *batting average, to be benched, bush leagues, double-header, grandstand play, off-base, far out* (in left field), *pinch-hitter, put one over, safe at home, shut-out, south-paw, strike-out,* and *throw a curve,* all of which are used in discussing subjects other than sports. List ten or twelve slang terms that have passed into general use from some area such as crime, the military, jazz, college life, show business, card-playing, or some other familiar activity.

_____

_____

_____

_____

_____

2. Reduplication often appears in slang terms. The second element may rime with the first, as in *hanky-panky,* or it may show consonance, as in *chitchat.* Supply the second element in each of these reduplicating compounds:

even- _____   flip- _____

heebie- _____   mish- _____

hoity- _____   slip- _____

razzle- _____   tip- _____

super- _____   wishy- _____

3. Another device by which slang adds to the lexicon is rime. We have already seen that many reduplications make use of rime, but it is likely that rime has also played a part in the coining of slang terms like *gimp* (cf. *limp*), *potted* (cf. *sotted*), *razzamatazz* (cf. *jazz*), *no soap* (cf. *hope*), and *it's a breeze* (cf. *with ease*). Moreover, rime figures conspicuously in phrases such as "See you later, alligator," which at one time spawned a number of imitations of the type "In a while, crocodile."

One of the more complex uses of sound-repetition is Cockney riming slang, which has contributed several phrases to the general vocabulary. This form of slang originated among the London Cockney and spread to Australia and the United States, although it has never been particularly widespread in this country. For a word, such as *wife,* the Cockney substitutes a riming phrase which is semantically appropriate, preferably in a sardonic way, for example, *trouble and strife.* The phrase is often clipped to its first member, thus effectively disguising its origin and serving a function of all slang, to mystify those in the "out-group." A common and unusually complex example of Cockney riming slang is *duke* 'fist,' as in "put up your dukes." *Duke* is a clipping of *Duke of Yorks,* riming slang for *forks; forks* in turn is a slang metaphor for fingers or, collectively, a fist. Here are a few of the better known Cockney slang words. Identify the word on which the riming phrase is based.

Let's get down to *brass tacks.* _____

In his business, he makes a pile of *sugar.* (clipped from *sugar and honey;* compare the poker term "to

sweeten the pot") _____

I don't care a *ding-dong* for what they think. (clipped from *ding-dong-bell*) _____

She's a pert little *twist.* (clipped from *twist and twirl*) _____

After one too many, you may feel a bit *tiddly.* (clipped from *tiddlywink,* by way of "I want a little

tiddly") _____

When he gets mad, you should hear him *rip.* (clipped from *rip and tear,* also in *let rip*) _____

Good thinking, that's using the old *loaf.* (clipped from *loaf of bread*) _____

You're tired, you need a little *Bo-peep.* _____

4. Slang, by its very nature, is poorly represented in standard dictionaries. For early slang, the *Oxford English Dictionary* is useful and can be supplemented by John S. Farmer and William Ernest Henley, *Dictionary of Slang and Its Analogues,* 7 vols. The most important and complete slang dictionary is Jonathan

Lighter's *Historical Dictionary of American Slang.* Use these works or other available dictionaries to answer the following questions, and note the source of your information for each answer.

What did a seventeenth-century *cony-catcher* catch? _____

_____

When Dickens wrote in *Martin Chuzzlewit,* "She was only a little screwed," with what debility did he

imply the lady to be afflicted? _____

_____

Although it is known in America, *smarmy* is more common in British English. What is its meaning?

_____

When an Australian is *waltzing Matilda,* what is he doing? _____

_____

What is the meaning of the obsolete American term *ish kabibble*? _____

_____

What is the apparent source of old-fashioned American *sockdolager*? _____

_____

The acronym *snafu* spawned a number of imitations like *fubar* 'fouled up beyond all recognition.' List

a few of its other progeny. _____

_____

What are some slang terms for various kinds of auctions? _____

_____

11.22 LITERARY COINAGES

1. There are a few words that can be traced with some confidence to a literary origin or to a specific act of coinage. Consult the *Oxford English Dictionary* to find the source of each of these words:

agnostic _____

blatant _____

ignoramus 'ignorant person' _____

knickerbockers _____

Lilliputian _____

malaprop(ism) _____

namby-pamby _____

Peeping Tom _____

potter's field _____

sensuous _____

serendipity _____

simon-pure _____

spoof _____

tam(-o'-shanter) _____

yahoo _____

2. Consult *Webster's Third New International Dictionary* for the origin of the following words.

babbitt(ry) _____

bazooka _____

boondoggle _____

fedora _____

Frankenstein _____

goop 'boor' _____

jabberwocky _____

Milquetoast _____

scrooge _____

Shangri-la _____

3. Who, according to the *OED*, was the first person to use each of these words in writing? Note also the year of the word's first appearance in English.

anesthesia _____

blasé _____

electricity _____

environment 'surrounding region' _____

Gotham 'New York City' _____

muckrake _____

ragamuffin _____

rodomontade _____

salad days _____

superman _____

11.23   ONE PART OF SPEECH TO ANOTHER

1. For each of these words, write two or more sentences using the word as a different part of speech in each sentence.

back _____

_____

best _____

_____

feature _____

_____

gross _____

_____

slow _____

_____

split _____

_____

total _____

_____

try _____

_____

up _____

_____

while _____

_____

2. According to the citations in the *Oxford English Dictionary,* as what part of speech was each of these words first used?

blemish	_____	fun	_____
coin	_____	idle	_____
eavesdrop	_____	matter	_____
faint	_____	pressure	_____
fossil	_____	shampoo	_____

3. Identify the part of speech of the italicized words.

The Recreation Center is hosting a community *sing*. _____

And also loke [look] on schrewes . . . how gret peyne *felawschipith* [fellowships] and folweth hem

[them]. (Chaucer, *Boece,* IV, p. 3) _____

Let me *wise* you up. _____

Lady, you are the cruell'st *she* alive. (Shakespeare, *Twelfth Night,* I.v) _____

It might be a *fun* thing to go to one of their parties. _____

The sweets we wish for turn to loathèd *sours*. (Shakespeare, *The Rape of Lucrece,* 1. 867) _____

Manufacturers often *package* according to the price instead of pricing according to the package. _____

_____

My heart in hiding / Stirred for a bird,—the *achieve* of, the mastery of the thing! (G. M. Hopkins, "The

Windhover") _____

It was an invitation for Clay to *up* and clobber him. _____

Who shall . . . through the palpable *obscure* find out his uncouth way? (Milton, *Paradise Lost,* II, 406)

_____

11.24   VERB-ADVERB COMBINATIONS

1. Consult the *Oxford English Dictionary* to find when each of these verb-adverb combinations was first used in the sense indicated. In addition, mark those which originated in America with the abbreviation *U.S.*

   bring forth 'give birth to' _____

   call down 'reprove' _____

   do in 'bring disaster upon' _____

   get over 'finish with' _____

   hang back 'show unwillingness to advance' _____

   lay by 'store up, save' _____

   look after 'take care of' _____

   put on 'affect, pretend' _____

   send out 'issue' _____

   take up (for) 'defend, stand up for' _____

2. Combine the verbs listed on the left with the adverbs listed on the right to make as many idiomatic verb-adverb combinations as possible.

cut	down
give	in
put	off
take	out
turn	up

   _____

   _____

   _____

   _____

   _____

3. Which of the combinations from the preceding question can be converted into nouns by a shift of stress?

   For example, *to cût úp—a cútùp.* _____

   _____

   _____

   _____

4. Stress may indicate parts of speech for words other than verb-adverb combinations. Write the primary stress of the following words with an acute mark over the stressed vowel. Record your own pronunciation.

NOUNS	VERBS	NOUNS	VERBS	NOUNS	VERBS
commune	commune	forecast	forecast	overhaul	overhaul
contest	contest	inlay	inlay	present	present
decrease	decrease	insult	insult	rebel	rebel
discount	discount	object	object	survey	survey
extract	extract	offset	offset	undercut	undercut

11.25 NEW WORDS FROM OLD: A SUMMARY

Choose one of the following groups, and identify the processes of word making that have produced the words in it by writing the appropriate number, from 1 through 10, in front of each word. For some of the items you will need to consult a dictionary; others should be transparent.

1. onomatopoeia
2. affixation
3. compounding
4. clipping
5. back-formation

6. blending
7. acronymy
8. folk etymology
9. commonization
10. functional shift

_____ curio
_____ emote
_____ gillyflower
_____ halfback
_____ marathon

_____ Amerind
_____ cordovan
_____ creak
_____ glamazon 'chorus girl'
_____ intercom

_____ baloney
_____ cusec
_____ discussant
_____ handwrite
_____ kéy clùb

_____ Benelux
_____ cicerone
_____ corner 'get a corner on'
_____ hiss
_____ shóut shòp 'advertising agency'

_____ academy
_____ balletorio 'choral music with dancing'
_____ cajun
_____ VISTA
_____ muscleshirt 'sleeveless T shirt'

_____ caper 'plant'
_____ chartreuse
_____ chirp
_____ construct 'something constructed'
_____ optiman 'man in optimum condition'

_____ maser
_____ noncash 'credit'
_____ pop 'sudden noise'
_____ psychic 'a medium'
_____ slanguage

_____ jaw 'talk volubly'
_____ mongoose
_____ refreeze
_____ roughneck
_____ televise

_____ mike
_____ primrose
_____ surrey
_____ swimsation
_____ swish

_____ laze
_____ mangrove
_____ mumble
_____ sexsational
_____ tot 'add'

_____ grapheme
_____ guffaw
_____ high-muck-a-muck
_____ jell
_____ orate

_____ enthuse
_____ lackadaisical
_____ oleo
_____ parsec
_____ tough 'rowdy person'

12 FOREIGN ELEMENTS IN THE ENGLISH WORD STOCK

12.1 FOR REVIEW AND DISCUSSION

1. Define each of the following terms, illustrating with examples when they are appropriate.

borrowing	etymon (*pl.* etyma)	neo-Latin
loanword	popular loanword	semantic contamination
direct (immediate) source	learned loanword	doublet
ultimate source	hybrid formation	loan translation (calque)

2. Loanwords reflect the contacts that have existed between two languages. What events in the history of the English-speaking peoples account for lexical borrowing from Latin, Greek, Celtic languages, Scandinavian, French, Spanish, Italian, Low German, High German, African languages, American Indian languages, Asiatic languages, and East European languages?
3. What language has had an influence on the English vocabulary over the longest period of time? Why has that language, more than any other, had such an influence?
4. Explain the relative paucity of Celtic loanwords in English.
5. Scandinavian has contributed a large number of common, homely words to the English vocabulary. Explain this fact.
6. During what historical period was the rate of adoption of French loanwords at its highest? Explain why French words entered English in such large numbers at that time.
7. Prepare a list of the languages from which English has borrowed words, and for each language indicate the semantic areas most prominently represented by loans.
8. Although English has borrowed a surprisingly large amount of its vocabulary from other languages and has undergone a great many changes during its history, the tongue we speak preserves a recognizable continuity with the English of King Alfred. List some significant bits of evidence which could be used to support this statement.

12.2 LOANWORDS AND THEIR SOURCES

Each of the following sets consists of words borrowed from various languages. Pick one of the sets, and use a dictionary to identify the languages from which the twenty words of that set were borrowed into English.

1. amuck _____   booby _____
   ballot _____   bosh _____
   blouse _____   cheroot _____
   ghoul _____   okra _____
   gull _____   picnic _____
   hominy _____   pus _____
   kid _____   sargasso _____
   kink _____   tonic _____
   lens _____   turn _____
   oil _____   veneer _____

2. atoll _____   raffia _____
   awe _____   robot _____

buffalo	_____	smuggle	_____
chit 'note'	_____	snorkel	_____
cola (kola)	_____	sofa	_____
ditto	_____	spade	_____
dodo	_____	'card suit'	
hickory	_____	squadron	_____
huckster	_____	thug	_____
penguin	_____	typhoon	_____
punch	_____		
'beverage'			

3.

air	_____	marmalade	_____
banshee	_____	mufti	_____
call	_____	parasol	_____
canasta	_____	persimmon	_____
cosmetic	_____	pilaf	_____
cosmopolite	_____	selvage	_____
deckle	_____	slim	_____
duplex	_____	tom-tom	_____
fan-tan	_____	traffic	_____
lingo	_____	tyro	_____

4.

anger	_____	paraffin	_____
bar 'piece'	_____	polo	_____
barbecue	_____	pylon	_____
cake	_____	raccoon	_____
cheetah	_____	rum	_____
gong	_____	'odd, dangerous'	
guerrilla	_____	sash	_____
hustle	_____	'band of cloth'	
kiosk	_____	spy	_____
lamp	_____	veranda	_____
loot	_____	zinc	_____

5.

bungalow	_____	pathos	_____
caucus	_____	posse	_____
cedilla	_____	protein	_____
cozy	_____	quip	_____
decoy	_____	rock 'stone'	_____
gambit	_____	root	_____
gusto	_____	safari	_____
lope	_____	shebang	_____
marimba	_____	sketch	_____
pathetic	_____	soil	_____

6.

attar	_____	orangutan	_____
ballast	_____	profile	_____
contraband	_____	purse	_____
cup	_____	rob	_____
furnace	_____	silk	_____
garrote	_____	sled	_____
ill	_____	tank	_____
jute	_____	tryst	_____
knapsack	_____	vizier	_____
myth	_____	zither	_____

7. bluff   _____   mugwump   _____

coco(nut)   _____   ombre   _____

extravaganza   _____   sago   _____

fruit   _____   sock   _____

furlough   _____   'footwear'

hawker   _____   therm   _____

  'peddler'   _____   tsetse   _____

humoresque   _____   tungsten   _____

kabob   _____   tutti-frutti   _____

loquat   _____   ugly   _____

lotto   _____   yak   _____

8. babel   _____   manage   _____

beast   _____   renegade   _____

beleaguer   _____   roster   _____

bulwark   _____   scum   _____

casino   _____   succotash   _____

dago   _____   uvula   _____

eugenics   _____   vim   _____

joss (stick)   _____   wing   _____

junket   _____   yen 'desire'   _____

kudos   _____   yogurt   _____

Some words have come ultimately from exotic sources but have entered English directly from more familiar European tongues. For each of the following words, identify first the ultimate source and then the immediate source.

9. arsenal   _____   jubilee   _____

arsenic   _____   julep   _____

borax   _____   mummy   _____

cabal   _____   petunia   _____

camel   _____   sack 'bag'   _____

canoe   _____   sequin   _____

carafe   _____   spinach   _____

caviar   _____   talc   _____

hammock   _____   tiger   _____

jar 'vessel'   _____   tomato   _____

12.3   DOUBLETS

A doublet is one of two or more words that have come from the same source but that followed different routes of transmission. Doublets have a common etymon, or earliest known form, but different etymologies. Pick one of the following sets, and give the etymology for its doublets, tracing the members of the set back to the same etymon.

1. sure _____
secure _____

2. regal _____
royal _____

3. poor _____
pauper _____

4. place _____
plaza _____
piazza _____

5. cipher _____
 zero _____

6. frail _____
 fragile _____

7. count _____
 compute _____

8. wine _____
 vine _____

9. poison _____
 potion _____

10. palaver _____
 parable _____
 parabola _____
 parole _____

11. lodge _____
 loge _____
 lobby _____
 loggia _____

12. corpse _____
 corps _____
 corpus _____
 corse _____

13. ennui _____
 annoy _____

14. chamber _____
 camera _____

15. respect _____
 respite _____

16. spice _____
 species _____

17. filibuster _____
 freebooter _____

18. caste _____
 chaste _____

19. tradition _____
 treason _____

20. valet _____
 varlet _____
 vassal _____

12.4 LOAN TRANSLATIONS

Instead of borrowing a foreign word that is composed of several meaningful parts, English has sometimes translated the parts. Thus the French *ballon d'essai* has become an English *trial balloon*. Such forms are known as loan translations or calques. Use a dictionary for this exercise.

1. Identify the foreign terms of which the following English expressions were translations:

commonplace _____

free verse _____

loanword _____

selvage _____

superman _____

2. Give the loan translations that are sometimes used for these foreign terms:

fait accompli _____

Lebensraum _____

porte-cochère _____

raison d'être _____

vis-à-vis _____

12.5 LATIN LOANWORDS

The loanwords that English has borrowed from Latin can be conveniently divided into four periods: (1) words borrowed while English speakers still lived on the continent, (2) words borrowed during the Old English period, (3) words borrowed in Middle English times, and (4) words borrowed into Modern English. Here are four groups of words; all the words within each group belong to the same period of borrowing. Judging from the form and meaning of the words you should be able to guess the period of each group. You can, however, check your guess in the *Oxford English Dictionary*. Identify the period (Gmc., OE, ME, ModE) of each group and be prepared to explain how each group is typical of its period.

PERIOD: _____   _____   _____   _____

aborigines	allegory	cope	belt
consensus	apocalypse	cowl	pan
forceps	desk	creed	pillow
propaganda	diaphragm	monk	pipe
referendum	digit	noon	Saturday
specimen	elixir	nun	toll

12.6 LATIN DOUBLETS

Below are Latin loanword doublets; the immediate Latin etyma are in parentheses. In each pair, one word is an early borrowing; the other is more recent. The form of the doublets indicates the relative order of their borrowing. Circle the earlier member of each pair, and be prepared to explain your decision.

vinous (vinosus)   minster (monisterium)   scribe (scriba)
wine (vinum)   monastery (monasterium)   shrive (scribere)

caseate (caseatus)   vallation (vallationis)   dish (discus)
cheese (caseus)   wall (vallum)   disk (discus)

stratum (stratum)   secure (securus)   mint (moneta)
street (strata)   sicker 'safe' (securus)   monetary (monetarius)

12.7 LATIN LOANWORDS

When English has borrowed Latin nouns, it has usually taken the nominative case form (for example, *index, alumnus, crisis, data*), but in a few instances it has chosen one of the other case forms instead. What case and number of the Latin noun is each of these English words derived from? Be prepared to explain why the English noun is based on an oblique (nonnominative) rather than on the nominative case.

innuendo _____   rebus _____

limbo _____   requiem _____

omnibus _____   specie _____

quarto _____   subpoena _____

quorum _____   vice 'deputy' _____

2

Some English nouns are derived from the inflected forms of Latin verbs and preserve the verbal endings of person, number, tense, mood, and voice. For example, *affidavit* is Latin for 'he has made an oath'; it occurred in legal documents as a formula introducing a record of sworn testimony when all such documents were still written in Latin. Subsequently it was understood as a title and thus as a name for a statement made under oath. For each of the following English nouns, give the meaning of the Latin verb form from which it was borrowed. Be prepared to explain how a Latin verb became an English noun.

caret	_____	incipit	_____
caveat	_____	mandamus	_____
credo	_____	memento	_____
deficit	_____	placebo	_____
exit	_____	query	_____
fiat	_____	recipe	_____
habeas corpus	_____	tenet	_____
habitat	_____	vade mecum	_____
imprimatur	_____	veto	_____

Some English nouns are derived from Latin pronouns, adjectives, and adverbs. Give the etymology of each of these words, including the Latin part of speech.

alias _____

alibi _____

bonus _____

ego _____

integer _____

interim _____

item _____

nonplus _____

nostrum _____

quantum _____

quota _____

tandem _____

12.8 FRENCH LOANWORDS: PERIOD AND DIALECT

All the following words have been borrowed from French, but at various times. Their pronunciation should indicate whether they were borrowed from older French or from Modern French. Use the words *old* and *new* to indicate the period of borrowing, and be prepared to explain your decision.

chair	_____	route	_____	gender	_____
chaise	_____	crochet	_____	genre	_____
sachet	_____	crotchet	_____	marquee	_____
satchel	_____	chalet	_____	marquess	_____
chaplet	_____	chasuble	_____	liqueur	_____
chapeau	_____	moral	_____	liquor	_____
pellet	_____	morale	_____	tableau	_____
platoon	_____	negligee	_____	tablet	_____
damsel	_____	negligent	_____	montage	_____
mademoiselle	_____	critic	_____	mountain	_____
rout	_____	critique	_____		

All the following words are loans from French, but some were borrowed from Central French, others from Norman French. Their pronunciation should provide a clue to the original dialect. Use the abbreviations *CF* and *NF* to indicate their provenience, and be prepared to explain your decision.

catch	_____	caldron	_____	guile	_____
chase	_____	chaldron	_____	wile	_____

cant 'jargon'	_____	regard	_____	castellan	_____
chant	_____	reward	_____	chatelain	_____
case 'box'	_____	guardian	_____	castle	_____
enchase	_____	warden	_____	château	_____
market	_____	guerdon	_____	guise	_____
merchant	_____	waste	_____	wicket	_____

12.9   FRENCH LOANWORDS: RATE OF ADOPTION

Origins and Development mentions that a number of studies, notably one by Otto Jespersen, have been made to determine the period during which French loanwords entered the English vocabulary in the largest numbers. You can check Jespersen's findings by making a similar study.

1. In the *Oxford English Dictionary* choose at random for each letter of the alphabet ten or more words of French origin. You may find it necessary to skip some letters, for example *K,* for lack of words.
2. Note the first recorded date of use in English for each word.
3. Tabulate the number of words borrowed during each half-century, and figure the percentage by dividing the total number of words into the number for each half-century.

	NUMBER OF WORDS	PERCENT OF TOTAL		NUMBER OF WORDS	PERCENT OF TOTAL
			Subtotal brought forward	_____	
before 1050	_____	_____	1501–1550	_____	_____
1051–1100	_____	_____	1551–1600	_____	_____
1101–1150	_____	_____	1601–1650	_____	_____
1151–1200	_____	_____	1651–1700	_____	_____
1201–1250	_____	_____	1701–1750	_____	_____
1251–1300	_____	_____	1751–1800	_____	_____
1301–1350	_____	_____	1801–1850	_____	_____
1351–1400	_____	_____	1851–1900	_____	_____
1401–1450	_____	_____			
1451–1500	_____	_____			
SUBTOTAL	_____		TOTAL	_____	

12.10   FRENCH AND LATIN LOANWORDS IN MIDDLE ENGLISH

Studies like Jespersen's have been based on the *Oxford English Dictionary* and thus tell nothing about the frequency with which the newly adopted words were being used. You can make a very rough estimate of the increasing use of loanwords from French and Latin by using the Middle English passages given in *Origins and Development* and in this workbook. A chart for this purpose is provided on the next page.

1. Count the total number of words in each passage (omitting purely proper names, the frequency of which varies greatly depending on the subject matter).
2. Count the total occurrences of French and Latin loanwords in each passage. Because the exact provenience, French or Latin, of some words is doubtful, it is more convenient to lump together the borrowings from these two languages. If a word like *manere* occurs nine times in the same passage, as it does in Trevisa, you should count it nine times. Again, omit proper names from your count. See the end of this exercise for a list of the loanwords.
3. For each passage, divide the total number of words into the number of occurrences of French and Latin loanwords to find the percentage.
4. Compare the percentages from each of the passages and determine the historical period that saw the greatest increase in use of French and Latin loanwords.

	TOTAL NUMBER OF WORDS	NUMBER OF FRENCH AND LATIN LOANS	PERCENT OF LOANS
ca. 1150 *Peterborough Chronicle*			
ca. 1200 *Ancrene Riwle*			
ca. 1300 *Chronicle of Robert of Gloucester*			
ca. 1350 Rolle's *The Form of Living* (*Origins and Development*, pp. 136–7)			
ca. 1400 Trevisa's *Polychronicon*			
ca. 1400 Chaucer's "The Former Age"			
ca. 1400 Chaucer, General Prologue to the *Canterbury Tales* (*Origins*, pp. 255–6)			
ca. 1450 Anonymous, *Polychronicon*			

FRENCH AND LATIN LOANWORDS FROM THE MIDDLE ENGLISH SELECTIONS

(If a word occurs more than once, the number of occurrences is given in parentheses.)

Peterborough Chronicle: sancte, pais

Ancrene Riwle: parais, lescun, Seinte, engle, ancre(n) (2), deouel, peoddare, noise, mercer, salue, merci, re-liguise

Chronicle of Robert of Gloucester: contreyes

Rolle's *The Form of Living*: cristen, actyve (2), contemplatyve (2), travel, peryle, temptacions (2), sykerar, delitabiler, joy (2), savowre, present, passes, merites, freelte, regarde, deserve, verrayli, contemplacion, quiete

Trevisa's *Polychronicon*: manere (9), peple (3), dyuers(e) (4), longage(s) (9), i-medled, naciouns (3), confederat, straunge (3), comyxtioun, mellynge, contray (5), apayred, vseþ, garrynge, apayrynge, scole(s) (4), vsage, compelled, construe(þ) (2), lessouns, gentil (3), broche, i-vsed, (i-)chaunged (2), maister, gram(m)er(e) (5), construccioun, secounde, conquest, auauntage (2), disauauntage (2), passe, trauaille, places, sown (2), reem (2), scarsliche, partie, acordeþ, sownynge, parteners, specialliche, frotynge, i-torned, noble, citees, profitable

Chaucer's "The Former Age": age, apaied, destroyed, desceyued, outerage, medle (2), clere, piment, clarre, contre(s) (3), venym, manar(es) (2), purper, pyne, straunger, merchaundyse, dyuerse, cruel(y) (3), clari-ouns, egre, armurers, enmys, moeuen, armes, turne, anguissous, mountaigne, allas, gobets, couered, pre-cious(nesse) (3), peril(s) (3)

Chaucer, General Prologue to the *Canterbury Tales*: the words italicized in *Origins and Development* (pages 255–6) plus *Aprille* and *martir*, which are of Latin provenience

Anonymous, *Polychronicon*: clerely, diuersites (2), langage(s) (12), nacion(e)s (3), propre, inpermixte, per-auenture, parte(s) (9), communicacion, confederate, inhabite, barbre (2), tripartite (2), procedenge, peple (2), commixtion, corrupcion, natife, cause(de) (3), schole, compellede, constru, consuetude, nowble, laborede, meruayle, propur, diuerse, yle, pronunciacion, vniuocate, remaynethe, sownde(the) (2), acorde, clyme, marches, participacion, nature, extremities (2), collateralle, arthike, anthartike, specially, cuntre, distaunce, vse, returnenge, costes, multitude, assignede, habundante, fertilite, nowmbre, plesaunte, portes

CONCLUSIONS

12.11 FRENCH AND LATIN LOANWORDS IN OTHER PERIODS

Following the directions in the preceding exercise, determine the percentage of French and Latin loanwords in the biblical passages in *Origins and Development* for Old English (pp. 108–10), Middle English (p. 137), and early Modern English (pp. 179–80). Compare the three periods in the history of our language with respect to the frequency of such loans.

12.12 LOANWORDS AND CULTURAL CONTACT

The following words are in four columns, each of which has a common area of meaning. Choose one of the columns. After each word in that column write *OE* if it is a native word; if it is a loanword, write the name of the language from which it was borrowed. Be prepared to discuss these questions: Do you detect any pattern for the borrowing within the set? What does the pattern indicate about cultural relations among the languages? What kind of word is least likely to be replaced by a borrowed term?

father		horse		day		house	
mother		mare		night		floor	
son		colt		morning		roof	
daughter		foal		evening		door	
brother		filly		week		bed	
kin		gelding		year		stool	
sister		stallion		month		window	
aunt		charger		decade		rug	
uncle		mount		century		ceiling	
nephew		courser		noon		chair	
niece				hour		table	
cousin				second		chimney	
relative				minute		cellar	
				moment			

12.13 LOANWORDS FROM JAPANESE

In addition to the Japanese loanwords listed on page 264 of *Origins and Development,* a number of others have entered English, some early but most quite recently. All of them are still distinctly exotic.

1. Look up these words in the *Oxford English Dictionary* or *Merriam-Webster's Collegiate Dictionary* and note the date of their first recorded use in English.

<table>
<tr><td colspan="2" align="center">FROM THE TEXT</td><td colspan="2" align="center">ADDITIONAL LOANS</td></tr>
<tr><td>_____ aikido</td><td>_____ karate</td><td>_____ benjo</td><td>_____ satori</td></tr>
<tr><td>_____ banzai</td><td>_____ kimono</td><td>_____ geta</td><td>_____ satsuma</td></tr>
<tr><td>_____ geisha</td><td>_____ miso</td><td>_____ hibachi</td><td>_____ sayonara</td></tr>
<tr><td>_____ ginkgo</td><td>_____ Pac-Man</td><td>_____ kabuki</td><td>_____ shogun</td></tr>
<tr><td>_____ go 'game'</td><td>_____ Pokemon</td><td>_____ mikado</td><td>_____ sukiyaki</td></tr>
<tr><td>_____ Godzilla</td><td>_____ sake 'liquor'</td><td>_____ noh</td><td>_____ sumo</td></tr>
<tr><td>_____ hara-kiri</td><td>_____ samurai</td><td>_____ obi</td><td>_____ tatami</td></tr>
<tr><td>_____ haiku</td><td>_____ soy(a)</td><td>_____ samisen</td><td>_____ tempura</td></tr>
<tr><td>_____ jinricksha</td><td>_____ sushi</td><td></td><td></td></tr>
<tr><td>_____ judo</td><td>_____ tofu</td><td></td><td></td></tr>
<tr><td>_____ jujitsu</td><td>_____ tycoon</td><td></td><td></td></tr>
<tr><td>_____ kamikaze</td><td>_____ Walkman</td><td></td><td></td></tr>
<tr><td>_____ karaoke</td><td>_____ Zen</td><td></td><td></td></tr>
</table>

2. Add any Japanese loanwords you can to these.

3. How do these words and their time of borrowing reflect cultural relations between Japan and the Occident?

_____

_____

4. Can you account for the common pronunciation of *hara-kiri* as [hǽrikǽri]? What is your explanation?

_____

_____

5. Choose another exotic language from which English has borrowed, and collect as many loanwords as you can, together with their dates of borrowing. Write a paper describing what these words reveal about the external history of English, that is, about the cultural contacts of English speakers with the foreign language.

12.14 LOANWORDS IN THE TOTAL VOCABULARY

Because of the immense size of the English vocabulary and its ever-changing content, no one can definitively count the number of loanwords in our language. It is possible, however, to estimate the percentage of borrowed words within the total vocabulary.

Make a random sampling of the words listed in one of the standard desk dictionaries; you might use the first word on every second page or on every fifth page, and so forth, depending on how large a sample you wish to use. Omit proper names and any word for which no etymology is given. For each word you choose, note whether it is a part of the native vocabulary (in which case it will be traced no further back than to Old English) or whether it has been borrowed. If the word has been borrowed, note the source language from which it entered English and ignore any earlier history which may be given. Distinguish carefully between sources and cognates: A source is a direct ancestor; a cognate is merely a relative. You will be interested in sources only. Read carefully the prefatory material on etymology in the dictionary that you are using, and be sure that you understand the abbreviations you will find in the main body of the dictionary.

Since the history of some English words is not perfectly known, you are likely to encounter various difficulties in identifying sources. You should handle such problems in whatever way seems best; consistency of treatment is as important as the actual method.

As examples, a few words are considered here to illustrate sources and problems.

hem *noun* [OE]   COMMENT: The word is native.

hem *interj.* [Imit.]   COMMENT: This is an echoic word; it is native.

howitzer [< Du. *houwitzer,* ult. < Czechoslovakian *houfnice* catapult]   COMMENT: The source language is Dutch; the earlier history is irrelevant to English.

funnel [Earlier *fonel,* ult. < L *infunibulum* < *infundere* to pour < *in-* into + *fundere* to pour]   COMMENT: The earlier spelling *fonel* is irrelevant; the exact history of the word is not known, but it derives ultimately from Latin. Either omit the word or give the source language as Latin.

boy [ME *boi;* origin unknown]   COMMENT: The word is found in Middle English, but its earlier history is obscure. Give the source language as Middle English or as unknown, or omit the word.

gloat [cf. ON *glotta* to grin]   COMMENT: The word is cognate with the Old Norse verb, but the source is not known. Give the source language as unknown, or omit the word.

After you have selected the words you are going to use as a sample and have identified the source of each of them, prepare a table like the one on the next page summarizing the number of words that can be traced to each language and the percentage of the total that they represent.

Percentages are found by dividing the total number of words of your sample into the number of words for any given source. If your total sample consisted of 320 words and it included 8 words borrowed from Italian, the percentage of Italian words would be 8 divided by 320 = .025, or 2.5%.

Your report on this research might include the following parts:

1. STATEMENT OF PURPOSE: a random sampling of words in the English vocabulary to determine the percentage of native words and the percentage of loanwords from various languages.
2. STATEMENT OF PROCEDURE: What dictionary did you use? How did you select the words for the sample? What problems did you encounter in determining sources? How did you handle these problems?
3. RAW MATERIALS: List the words you selected and give the source language for each. For example:

abase OF	anabatic Gk.
achieve OF	antecedent Lat.
advowson Anglo-French	apprehend Lat.
akimbo ME	arrow OE
alternative Med. Lat.	atman Skt.

4. SUMMARY OF RESULTS: as below.
5. CONCLUSIONS: a short paragraph describing your results and drawing whatever conclusions seem relevant.

Your instructor may prefer that you omit from the report one or more of the parts described above.

SUMMARY

	NUMBER OF WORDS	PERCENT OF TOTAL
Native English (incl. OE, ME, imitative)		
Latin (incl. Vulgar Lat., Med. Lat., Late Lat., Neo-Lat.)		
Greek		
French (incl. Anglo-French, Anglo-Norman, OF, Middle Fr., Provençal)		
Spanish (incl. American Sp., Catalan)		
Portuguese		
Italian		
Scandinavian (incl. Old Norse, Danish, Icelandic, Swedish, Norwegian)		
High German (incl. German, Old HG, Middle HG, Yiddish)		
Low German (incl. Dutch, Afrikaans, Flemish)		
Celtic (incl. Welsh, Gaelic, Irish, Cornish, Breton)		
Semitic (incl. Arabic, Hebrew, Aramaic)		
Persian (incl. Avestan)		
Sanskrit (incl. Prakrit, Pali, Hindi, Hindustani, Bengalese)		
Dravidian		
Chinese (incl. Cantonese)		
Japanese		
Malayo-Polynesian (incl. Javanese, Tagalog)		
African		
Slavic (incl. Russian, Polish, Bulgarian, Czech)		
Turkish		
American Indian (incl. Eskimo)		
Others (incl. Australian, Hungarian, Armenian, and so forth)		
Unknown		
TOTAL		100

264

It is obvious that different words occur with different frequencies. *Angle, line,* and *barn* are words of fairly high frequency; *hade, raphe,* and *byre* are considerably less common. We may legitimately ask whether the active vocabulary, words which are common in normal discourse, contains the same percentage of loanwords as the total vocabulary of English.

To investigate the question, follow this procedure:

1. Choose a passage of 300 to 500 words. The best sort of passage will be one that reads easily, such as a straightforward narrative or exposition from a popular magazine or a book intended for the general market.
2. Count the exact number of words in the passage.
3. Ascertain the source language for each word, as in the preceding exercise.
4. Prepare a summary of the number and percentage of words for each source, also as in the preceding exercise. To arrive at percentages, divide the total number of words in the passage into the number of words from each source language. Count each occurrence of a word as a separate word; that is, if *the* occurs twenty times, it should be counted as twenty words.
5. In reporting your findings, compare the results of this study with the results you obtained in the preceding exercise, and draw appropriate conclusions.

As a variation on this exercise, you might classify the words from your passage according to their part of speech (noun, pronoun, adjective, verb, preposition, and so forth) and prepare a separate summary for each part of speech. In your conclusion, compare the parts of speech with respect to their ratio of loanwords. Which part of speech has the highest percentage of loanwords? Which the lowest?

As another variation, you might compare the percentage of loanwords in two passages. Compare a passage from a Hemingway novel with one from *Scientific American,* or a passage from an Ursula LeGuin short story with one from Alfred Kroeber's *Anthropology,* or a passage from the King James Bible with one from Sir Thomas Browne's *Hydriotaphia.* Choose two passages that seem very different in style and decide whether the presence of loanwords contributes to the difference.

OLD N FR 3
MOD E 6
DU 2
ME 62
L 37
OE 170
UNKNOWN 13
ON 4
GK 1
G FR 7
ITAL 1
SP 4
UN 4
ON 4